ABIGAIL GLENN

FORGED IN CHAOS

DARK REVERIES

BOOK ONE

To all the readers,
Thank you for giving my book a chance.
And thank you for supporting indie authors.
We're so incredibly grateful.

CONTENT WARNING

Violence, gore, murder, death, profanity, sex.
This book also touches on mental health.

Playlist

Headless - Deftones
Swamp Song - Tool
40 Stories - Alluvial
Entombed - Deftones
Pneuma - Tool
Born in Winter - Gojira
The Grudge - Tool
Alkaline - Sleep Token
Heart of Darkness - Grim Salvo, Sect Unit
Beware - Deftones
Right in Two - Tool
You've Seen the Butcher - Deftones
The Summoning - Sleep Token
Sextape - Deftones
Tempest - Deftones
4° - Tool
Moth Grinder - Grim Salvo
CoDA - Dead Poet Society
Black Mambo - Glass Animals
Closure - Chevelle
10,000 Days (Wings Pt 2) - Tool
Saferwaters - Chevelle
Playing God - Polyphia

Daathmore
Jagged Rocks
Sown
Denoden
Hathrowyn
Inner Sanctum
Crosslands
Hwyn
Dwellings Hollow
Nightfall
Quazi Desert
Dusk Hallow
Velemi
Zafai
Adra
Torlean
Rowan's Wake
The Burning Plains
Blazing Woods
Firesteep
Temporra
Brindale
The Boglands
Goldenwood
Befort Pier
Mire
Cragnore
Kilgrif Ocean
Dreaddix
Aranma

ACT I

THE GIFT OF SILENCE

Chapter One

TENAH

Focus.

The word pressed into Tenah Delemor's mind like an icy brand, shooting chills through her nervous system.

Hard to focus with you lurking in my head, she retorted, words dripping with acid.

Mentally, she shoved at her wraith guardian's invasive magic, visualizing shutting him out with an iron door. But it was futile. When Ames infiltrated a mind, it became his to manipulate. He could sift, alter, or melt whatever he discovered inside.

Restless, she shifted her weight on her folded legs, eager to get blood flowing again. Beads of sweat gathered along her hairline, begging to be itched. The late summer sun blazed mercilessly through the window, saturating the musty study with thick heat and illuminating the dust stirred up by Ames's hasty shifting of antique furniture. He didn't appreciate when she set things on fire, even if she swore it was an accident.

More frustrating than her uncomfortable position on the floorboards was the lack of sound. No chirping birds or annoying, buzzing insects outside the cracked window. No breeze rustling the leaves, now permanently shocked red by the invisible film of magic toxins that clung to the grim manor.

It was like death had already staked its claim. Everything about this patch of forest screamed *wrong*.

Well, death could take a fucking hike.

Focus, Ames said again in her mind.

With a huff, Tenah severed her connection to her physical body and projected her mind into the Void—the dimension between worlds. Vast, blue, and frigid, it was easy to believe she'd been dragged to the bottom of a lake or strewn out in the night sky. White slashes of magic danced around her, spanning as far as she could see. They glittered like stars, promising immense power for those capable of harnessing it.

She winced as the familiar, creeping fingers of danger tickled down her spine. Her body might not be present here, but she would still feel the sharp inception of dark magic that had long polluted this space.

Striving to achieve a sense of calm, Tenah pushed out a ragged breath.

A flash of movement caught her eye, followed by the stench of putrid breath. Liquid fear slithered through her veins as two ravenous eyes burst into existence, gleaming hotter than the forges in her kingdom's capital.

Immediately, Tenah snapped back into her body. "Feingrot again."

It was disgusting how hard her heart was beating against her ribcage. Her mouth curved down as she rubbed the sweat from her palms onto her pants.

Ames would read into every bit of her fear, and he would let it continue to haunt her until she came to terms with it.

"You know they cannot physically harm you," he scolded.

"Tweak my brain to remember that then," she muttered, rolling onto her back and spreading her limbs out on the fraying rug, a carcass ready for picking from vultures. "Before you even start in, I get it. You don't want to risk messing me up, but your pep talks really need to improve, Ames."

She almost felt a prickle of guilt for her rotten attitude. She knew that venturing into the Void was worth the risk. Or at least it would be when she located the magic required to fix her father's cursed mind.

The clopping of hooves broke their tense silence, and Tenah's gaze darted to Ames. Framed by golden sunlight, he looked like some blessed spirit come to impart unwanted wisdom. Little flecks of glittering white light hovered around his ghostly form like snowflakes. His beautiful, haunting magic.

Mind magic might have been his thing, accessible only by his race of Ashens, but she'd learned how to read the slightest shifts in his features.

His brow twitched over his silver, pupil-less eyes. An uninvited guest then.

Tenah pushed off the creaky floorboards, hissing at the sudden rush of blood through her tingling legs. She hobbled over to the small window. Fingers clumsy from the overuse of magic, she fought to hoist it open enough to stick her head out.

A lone rider on a dappled horse cut through the maze of trees. They wore a charcoal cloak draped over bronze armor. Their hood was drawn, but the blazing phoenix crest of Vozar was distinguishable enough, pinned to the side of their leather boot.

King Sardoth's elite guard.

Tenah's hands curled into fists. What a day this was turning out to be. Like hell their king was going to ship her father off to the eastern isles for another war. She'd stolen whispers of brewing trouble on the evenings she'd snuck away to Firesteep, but she'd figured her father had earned his peace from slaughtering enemies. He'd sacrificed his health to protect strangers once. Wasn't that enough?

She looked back at Ames, eager for his instruction, but he was more concerned with the tiny vial of beguiler essence now clutched in his hand. Tenah's throat tightened as she watched him dip a needle into the swirling iridescent contents before pricking his finger.

Instantly, his silvery, translucent form soaked up a moonlit complexion. His chin-length hair took on a shade of ashy brown. Sea-glass blue washed through his irises, circling the developing pupil. His specks of visible magic blinked out of existence. Hidden but never gone.

Rage tugged against the fragile leash Tenah held on her emotions. She hated that he felt the need to alter his appearance to keep from unsettling shadows like her—inhumans blessed with an affinity for elemental magic. It wasn't as if Ashens weren't common to the Kandar Isles. They'd immigrated here through the Void from a world called Sathus Morr centuries ago when all portals were still in operation.

Other than a ghostly form and their unique mental abilities, they weren't any different from shadowkind. But the last devastating war had been fought against a wrathful Ashen queen. Until those wounds healed, Ames felt the need to conceal his true nature, more concerned with putting others at ease than remaining true to himself.

When his transformation was complete, he nodded to her. "Manners, Tenah."

Teeth clenched, she stormed from the cramped study and down the main corridor of the behemoth, green-wallpapered corridor. Staff was limited in her family's manor, but the shadows that remained loyal knew better than to answer the door.

She opened it just wide enough to fit her body. The king's elite stepped back. His narrowed, dark eyes snapped to her hands. Assured she wasn't holding a weapon, he took in her ragged tunic, baggy pants, and worn leather boots as if her attire was more egregious than if she'd been caught holding a battle axe.

Tenah flicked a tendril of smoke-colored hair over her shoulder. Elementals, capital folk were so dramatic.

Sometimes during her rare evening strolls through Firesteep, she couldn't help but wish suffering upon them, swimming in their crystal pools by the palace and dining on sweet rolls and grilled kabobs from the eclectic, lively markets.

No one talked about the victims of war like her father, decaying in solitude.

No one cared to understand the dark magic infecting him and so many others.

The elite cleared his throat. "Is the lord of the house present?"

"Is it any of your business?" Tenah countered.

He blinked, confused by the steel cut of her tone. After a pause, he retrieved an envelope with a gold wax seal. "I have a message for Lord

Kherathi—"

Tenah snatched the envelope. "I'm his daughter. I'll pass it on."

So polite, Ames said.

Do you ever get tired of being a nuisance? she asked but pushed thanks through bared teeth before slamming the door in the elite's face and sliding the deadbolts home.

Leaned against the door, she clutched the envelope tight against her chest. The urge to tear into it was strong, but such an act could set her father off, spiraling him into another wave of madness.

Instead, she cut for the attic stairs. Muffled shouts from behind the door at the landing halted her ascent. The air took on a heady stench of copper, coating her tongue and the back of her throat. Whispers coiled around her, dragging along her sweaty skin like the invisible claws of demons.

Anyone who believed hell was below them was a fool. Hell was right here, wearing the shell of her father.

Vessel, the magic whispered in her ear.

The lump in her throat grew painfully large. Of all the magic she'd studied, none of them had ever spoken to her. Whatever had sunk its teeth into her father, whatever disease he'd brought back from Adra, it was evil incarnate. It shouldn't exist. The moment their king or the High Court found out about it, her father would be sentenced to death, and everyone else in the manor would stand to be punished for their involvement.

The door to the attic swung open, and Tenah startled in the middle of the staircase. Ames shut the door behind him promptly, sealing away visibility of the silhouette behind the desk, but not before she witnessed the malevolent eddy of black, smoky magic.

Sweep him under the rug, she couldn't help but think as she charged back down the stairs.

Ames followed, the scent of dark magic clinging to the fibers of his gray shirt and straight-legged pants. It was enough to twist her stomach into knots. "Do you expect to manage the Delemor affairs with that attitude?"

"I don't expect to manage anything," she retorted, her brows furrowing as Ames's gaze drifted, his attention caught by a storm of unfavorable thoughts. What had he been discussing with her father? Something he had discerned from the elite's mind?

"We've had a good run, Tenah. You've progressed far but—"

She winced. "But now you doubt me. You don't think I can fix him. Does he think so too?"

Years. They'd sacrificed years chasing Ames's promise that she would find a cure. That she was capable. That she'd inherited her mother's ability to heal, if only she could find a source of that rare magic in the Void. She'd never had to search for her flames, certain she'd been born with fire in her veins.

Infuriating tears stung her eyes as crimson embers licked at her fingers. She snuffed them out but not before they singed the edges of the envelope she held out to him. "Here."

Ames sighed. "It's not that I doubt you, Tenah. It's just that we're running out of time." He handed the envelope back. "Go ahead. Open it."

Frowning, Tenah slipped a finger under the seal. She skimmed over the elegant writing, blood hammering in her veins.

Please be informed that the Kingdom of Vozar shall be hosting a summer's eve gathering at the Delemor manor on the night of the twenty-first. At this time, we shall discuss the questionable state of your affairs...

She crumpled the letter. "Tell him no."

"I wish it worked like that, Tenah."

"Okay. We run then. Find somewhere more remote to settle down until I figure this magic out."

Last resort, there was always restricted magic to be explored...

"Tenah," Ames said sharply, pinching the bridge of his nose. He looked exhausted. Had their time together been so terrible that he'd lost his faith? She supposed he'd sacrificed the most, giving up his life to care for his war friend and his heathen daughter. "We will host this gathering and prove to the king that there is nothing to hide here. Then we shall carry on with your training, if that is what you wish."

But Ames didn't wait for an answer as he walked away, leaving her to the whispers of dark magic coiling around her like venomous snakes.

Chapter Two
RENTON

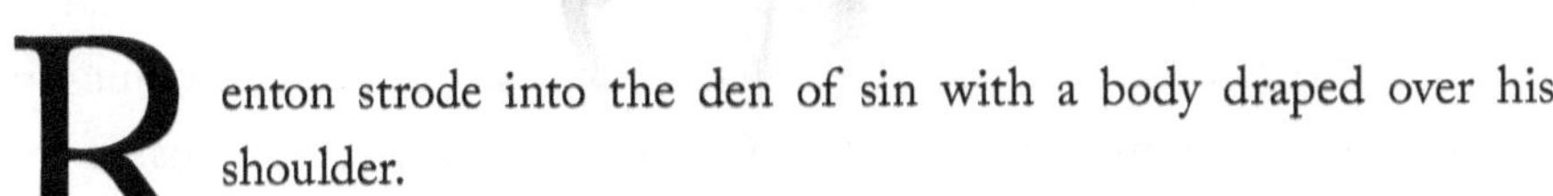

Renton strode into the den of sin with a body draped over his shoulder.

After nearly a month out in the treacherous Boglands, he was near exhaustion. Muscles he didn't know he had ached from overuse. His leather armor was caked in so much sludge and dried blood it was hard to tell what color it had been when he'd purchased it.

He scowled as clouds of amber filled the emerald hall, burning the inside of his nose. Remnants of topaz—a drug from Adra, the easternmost floating isle. It rivaled the metallic stench of the Corrupt he'd been hauling for miles.

Through the haze, hunters positioned around low, dimly lit tables smirked up at him. Some had shed their demon armor and blades to better immerse themselves in vice, gambling away their earnings and splurging on dancers and spirits. Others awaited their next orders, skull helms obscuring their scarred and weathered faces.

Renton's knuckles popped as he tightened his hands into fists. How far the hunting clans had fallen. From protectors of the isles to criminals sworn under the sinister Councilman Boedworth. No matter how he steeled himself against this crushing disappointment, it never made his return to Cragnore any easier.

He delved further into the underground establishment, weaving through mahogany shelves bowed under the mass of rare artifacts he'd helped steal. As he approached his employer's pretentious oak desk, fury bubbled in his gut. His fingers twitched, missing the worn leather hilts of his blades, confiscated the second he'd entered the den. Ignore the fact that he didn't need them to kill.

Councilman Boedworth flashed his characteristic slimy grin. His gray suit was immaculate, polished gold cufflinks reflecting the murky green light from the orbs embedded in the pressed tin ceiling. Renton's gaze flicked to the gaudy rings about to cut off circulation in his employer's plump fingers, paid for by the blood of others. Paid for by his own family. Boedworth rapped them on the desk, aware of his focus on them.

"It's almost as if the hunt has become too easy for you. That makes twelve Corrupt in five weeks, Mr. Murfell," Boedworth said, unwilling to tear his gaze from his meticulous counting of gold and silver krotens.

The Corrupt's ebony scales scraped against Renton's hands as he dumped it on the ground. At the snap of Boedworth's fingers, two armored hunters peeled off the velvety walls to drag the once-shadow's body through a set of fortified black doors behind his desk.

Renton held back a scoff at the talisman embedded in their armor. A tiny bird skull over two semi-circles of jagged bone, inspired by the runes etched into Sakkren's temples, the prime elemental of air. Sakkren would have been ashamed by the shadows bearing her mark. More so by the wasteland her isles had become, torn apart after the war at Roan's Wake and choking on Chaos, the darkest known form of magic.

"I'd deduce the neutralizers are working," Boedworth said.

Renton's frown deepened. "Took two doses before the Corrupt stopped clawing and shrieking. Doesn't seem humane."

Witnessing how the infected shadow had writhed in pain as the injected fluid spread through its body had been a conflicting experience. He despised Corrupt for their choices, but he also wasn't particularly fond of watching a living thing suffer. Not to mention how anticlimactic it was to end a hunt with a simple blow dart. He preferred a fight. It helped justify his purpose.

"Humane?" Boedworth laughed as he slid two stacks of krotens across his desk to join the mountain of others. "Says the machine bred to slaughter them. I hope you don't plan on nurturing those morals, Mr. Murfell."

Renton clamped his jaw tight, refusing to give the councilman more reason to inflict torture. His immediate focus was on shortening this meeting so he could rinse off and fill his stomach with something not charred over a makeshift fire.

Boedworth smirked, eager to prod at old wounds. "Your father often fell onto the wrong side of thinking too. How do you think your old man's enjoying baking in his shallow grave?"

Renton ground his teeth together as he hardened his resolve. No one got to manipulate his emotions. Especially not this demon wearing the flesh of a shadow.

One day, when his younger brother was free from Boedworth's clutches, Renton would sink their father's cherished blade into Boedworth's skull. For every hunter ordered on that suicide mission. For every hunting clan ordered before them, speared on the iron gates and spires of Nightfall like some sort of twisted nightmare.

Until then, he would bury his desire for revenge, right next to his troubling morals.

When Renton didn't take the bait, his employer's smile turned sour. Boedworth yanked open a drawer in his desk and retrieved a black folder. He slapped it down between his blood fortune. "I expect these Corrupt brought to me in a week's time. Alive but incapacitated."

Renton's eyes dropped to the folder. Where would it lead him this time? Across the deserts to Nightfall again? To the outskirts of stormy Adra?

He picked up the file and let it fall open in his dirty palms. Only two targets. His muscles tensed. The first was an ex-assassin to Vozar's king, granted lordship over a small town outside Firesteep's gates. The second was the lord's daughter.

"Vozarian nobility?" Renton questioned.

Hunting beasts in the swamps or deserts was one thing. Crossing into territory ruled by a hate-filled, antagonistic fire king was entirely another. Depending on how far Corrupt these targets were, ripping nobility from their home could result in backlash from a kingdom already pitted against them.

What the hell was Boedworth playing at? What was the angle here? Because when it came to Boedworth, there was always something to be gained.

"Yes, Mr. Murfell. So glad you can read. The lord's highly infected by Chaos. The High Court wants a pulse on him and the child. I want them in chains. Better they rot on the icy plains of Dreaddix than run amok like savages, further infecting the population."

Dreaddix had become the temporary answer to those ruled too dangerous for imprisonment or Ashen mind-melting. Prisoners were dumped onto the uncharted, icy wasteland and left to defend themselves against wrathful nature and its most skilled predators.

Renton's brows furrowed. "Why doesn't the Vozarian king handle them?"

Vozar's king was notorious for snap reactions. Severing alliances at the slightest irritation. Burning trade bridges. Demolishing portals between isles, even though they hadn't churned with a drop of magic since the High Court shut them down during the war to slow the spread of Corruption.

Annoyance flickered across Boedworth's face. "This is why I sit in this seat and you hold the butcher knives. If matters are left to the Vozarian king, the Corrupt will be executed."

"I fail to see how that's a problem. We've been executing them for decades."

Boedworth slammed a fist down on his desk. Krotens sprang out in all directions, cascading to the floor. "I do not employ you to ask questions. Things change. Accept the hunt, or your brother pays. That's always been the deal."

Renton's head tipped slightly. Boedworth typically kept his emotions in check. Why the sudden short fuse? Unless this hunt was important. The glint of feral desperation in his employer's eyes gave Renton hope.

Maybe this was it. The contract he needed to set things right.

He peered down at the file once more, committing coordinates to memory. He'd been instructed to kill hundreds of Corrupt. Why had that changed? It wasn't like they could be controlled. None had ever been healed that he knew of. Neutralizing them only seemed to aid with transporting them, but even that didn't require finesse. Toss them on the back of a winged beast and drop them on a blizzard isle to freeze or tear each other apart.

To hell with it. Renton tossed the file back on the desk, prepared to risk another broken bone for his demand. "My brother walks free at the end of this. I've earned that much."

Boedworth's fingers curled around the edge of his desk, bleached white from his grip. "You're not in a position to barter."

"Then find someone else." Renton crossed his arms over his chest. "But you said it yourself—the hunt is easy for me."

Boedworth pushed out of his chair. "I should punish you for your insolence, boy. Don't forget, I have your precious little ghost brother under my thumb. One wrong move and his bones will be rearranged by the eldest Murfell. And you know just how creative he can be."

Renton didn't budge. Didn't so much as blink as Boedworth stared him down.

After a few huffing breaths, Boedworth reluctantly withdrew a small pouch. He dropped a meager amount of krotens inside and threw it on top of the file. "For transportation," he instructed. "Have my secretary refine the contract and bring it to me for review in the hour. Seven days, Mr. Murfell. Don't assume this one will be a walk in the woods. My last three hunters failed."

The warning echoed in Renton's head as he snatched the coin pouch and stalked from the den, blades soon returned to their rightful place buckled across his spine.

One more hunt. Then his little brother would walk free.

CHAPTER THREE
TENAH

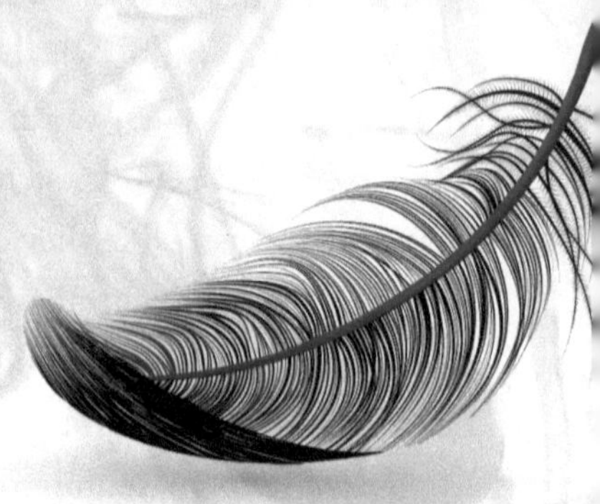

Tenah preferred the rotting gardens over the king's gathering.

Blame the seven years of near solitude. That, or her father's poisonous magic had finally seeped into her mind, twisting and fraying until she'd become something unrecognizable too. Vozar seemed to believe her family was something primal. It was possible they were right.

So yeah, she found comfort in the thorns and overgrowth of the manor courtyard. Wrapped up in nature, she could breathe without choking on a hundred different sources of magic tainting the air. That was the problem with all her training—the heightened senses. She could identify numerous sources of magic birthed from the Void, but she'd failed to find the one source she needed the most.

Tenah poked a droplet of rain balanced on the edge of a leaf from an afternoon flash storm. So delicately balanced, just like her. Clinging on dearly to the present as if it were a tangible, physical thing she could stretch and blanket over her family.

One tremor and everything would fall.

A warm, humid breeze whistled through the trees. Loose waves of hair tickled her bare shoulders and swished the tulle of her champagne-tinted ballgown. She licked her lips, scanning the forest. No sign of movement.

Why was she so keyed up? Her nerves were drawn taut like a fragile string.

She turned to the glass wall of the manor's grand library, her favorite room. Now it was overburdened with shadows clad in fine suits and glistening dresses, conversing and dancing in utter, blissful ignorance of the horrific world they lived in.

You're supposed to be inside. Ames appeared behind her, pumped full of his rare, deceiving essence and dressed in an impeccable, gray three-piece suit. *I'm surprised you're still upright, what with all the wine you've snuck.*

Tenah rolled her eyes, failing to hide her devious grin. Ames was always on the receiving end of her childish behavior because she knew he could handle it. "This gathering is stupid, and so are they for stirring shit up."

He tipped his head up to the starry indigo sky, smooth like velvet this evening. His shoulders drooped. "Neshar and Lorr, be good to me. Please help dear Tenah keep her flames *and* her sharp tongue in check tonight."

"I'm always on my best behavior," she muttered, kicking at a dried weed peeking through the cobblestones with her boot.

Ames shook his head, then leaned in to press an icy kiss to her temple. "That's precisely why I must pray to my gods."

She tried disheveling his hair, but he ducked out of reach.

"Don't mess with perfection." A warm smile transformed his face as he offered his arm. This was why she loved Ames. No matter how mad she drove him, he always stuck around. That was more than she could say about the woman who had given her life.

Tenah looped her arm through his but not before one more peek back at the wall of trees. Just to make sure her instincts were wrong.

Together, they navigated the stream of well-dressed shadows in the manor corridor. She wrinkled her nose, struck with the concoction of sweet, acrid, and herbal magic mingled with thick perfume. It was overwhelming but not so much as the sheer volume of shadows crammed into the library, the only room in the manor large enough to host such an event.

She paused at the double doors. Harrowing notes from a string quartet floated out, thankfully lulling her tumultuous magic back into slumber. Greenery cascaded from the walls of towering bookshelves and half-moon balconies, woven with violets and thorns. The decadent chandeliers brought in by the king's staff to replace the tarnished ones reminded her of constellations, far too blinding for the crowded space.

The lump in her throat grew painfully large. Something about too many bodies in one room made her skin clammy and her pulse quicken.

Just breathe, Ames said. *I'm going to check in on our reclusive host. Go socialize. Be young. Be lively. I'm sure you'll find you're a natural at it.*

Tenah snorted. Left to her own devices, she snatched a glass of champagne—her third one—off a passing serving tray. She planned to drink herself into oblivion tonight. As she pressed her back against the interior wall of bookshelves, she sipped at the bubbly drink and studied the grotesque mural on the ceiling.

Fear has a way of mutating into brutality, her father had explained when she'd questioned his commissioning of the war at Roan's Wake as a child. This library was her sanctuary, and he'd gone and messed it up. The blazing orange eyes of the feingrot—otherworldly monsters that had slipped into their world through the Void—haunted her anywhere she hunkered down for study sessions. No amount of flaky pastries or lemon tea could make her forget them.

She understood her father's lesson though. Vozar's shadows, parading about with lithe movements, feasting and conversing in tight-knit circles, feared her father. And when shadows were afraid of something, they pulverized it.

Lazily, her gaze slid over to the tapestry Ames had hung in the nearest corner. Not because he particularly cared about the Greater Elementals—he worshipped higher gods—but to teach her about the origins of her magic. Stitched into the colorful fabric was a four-pointed star, each arm containing one of the Greater Elementals, beings that had emerged from the Void to imbue knowledge of magic to shadowkind as a means of protection against anything else that managed to leak into the world. Renix, engulfed in flames and magma. Sakkren, the shapeshifting horror that manipulated the air around her. Honestly, *terrifying*. Felnor, with his elegant vines and roots, wrapped in ribbons of healing water.

And then there was Xith, the fallen elemental. His all-black eyes, dark clouds, and lightning didn't exactly prompt the desire to bow down in reverence. He was the first known elemental on Daathmorr to lash out against shadowkind, believed to be sent here by sinister gods.

While Tenah appreciated Ames's efforts, none of that knowledge had done shit to help her access the magic needed to save her father.

Am I not worthy? A question she'd pushed out into the universe almost daily.

She'd considered seeking answers outside of Ames's training and her precious tomes. Far outside Vozar, even. In the hidden vaults of the northern kingdom protected by the Embassy, an infamous organization of assassins, or etched in the rings of Hathrowyn's massive, ancient trees where the High Court imbued sacred knowledge.

Ames swore these quests were futile, but just because he read minds didn't mean he knew everything.

Booming laughter drew her attention to the wall of windows, where King Sardoth sat at a round table with his band of elite. It was hard to understand why Firesteep adored him. Behind his threatening stature and his hawkish eyes, he exuded an air of needing absolute control.

You left me to the wolves, Tenah whined.

No response from Ames. She pursed her lips.

Wine glass empty but mind still not comfortably numb, she dared traverse the hordes in search of food or more alcohol. Anything to ease her discomfort. Anything to drown out their murmurings.

Whispers followed, prodding at her magic.

...her mother...poisoned by her lord father's madness...

How the king still allows them to breathe...

...the offspring of evil. More Corrupt than her father, that one...

She grimaced. *Corrupt*—the scathing term given to those suffering from insidious magic infections. Granted, some shadows had chosen their fate. Then there were those that had been exposed to it against their will, cast out or cut down because of it.

Blizzard-cold magic tore through her mind, wiping it clean of the sudden, violent thoughts. Tenah bit back a frustrated snarl. *You only tune in when you're not wanted, don't you?*

Cool it. The goal is not to draw any negative attention.

Tenah diverted toward a table piled high with delicate puffs of bread dipped in chocolate. Halfway to her destination, she slowed. Prickles crept down her neck, alerting her of someone watching.

Beyond the swaying dancers, she homed in on two electric green eyes. The shadow stood predatory still against the back wall, a head taller than the other guests. His stature was intimidating, broad shoulders and corded thighs clad in dark leather and bone armor. The hilt of two swords poked up over his back as if to confirm that death would be delivered by his hands.

Brows furrowing, Tenah glanced around the library. No one else seemed alarmed by his presence. When her gaze drifted back to the menacing stranger, she no longer saw armor. He wore a tailored black suit that hugged his formidable body. Half of his long, pale wheat hair was tied back and his strong jaw cleanly shaven.

Chugging heartbeats pounded against her ribs as his head tilted sideways, almost as if in taunt, a spider luring prey into his treacherous web.

All right then. If this stranger thought he was summoning some demure, polished noblewoman, he was in for a rude awakening.

Tenah snatched a chocolate dessert off a tray and popped it into her mouth.

She stormed across the library. Forget Ames's warning to behave.

Standing before the stranger, she had to lift her chin high to meet his intense eyes. Her brain fired panic through her nervous system. Regretfully, she inhaled his crisp pine and mountain air scent.

Elementals. Was that what the outside world smelled like?

Odd, there was a note of something bittersweet clinging to him too. A peculiar magic he wore like a second skin, one she did not recognize.

The stranger held out a scarred hand.

"Evening," he said, his voice as deep and smooth as the chocolate still melting on her tongue. "Name's Renton."

Dumbfounded, Tenah stared down at his hand. Somehow, she managed to summon manners from the pit of hell where she kept them hostage and placed her hand in his calloused one. A surge of energy rippled up her arm. Cool shivers danced along her skin as his pupils dilated.

Enemy. An executioner hired by King Sardoth, most likely. Had he been the one lurking in the forest earlier?

Still holding her hand, Renton eased her closer. His next words brushed against the shell of her ear like the wings of a butterfly, doing visceral things to her stomach. "You're awfully tense."

"Annoying of you to notice," she retorted, jerking out of his grip.

His brow arched. "They all watch you. Why is that?"

Heat rose in her cheeks. Was she that much of an anomaly?

Feigning disinterest, she shrugged. "I don't know. None of them should even be here."

"Ah." His expression fell. "You're Kherathi's child."

Tenah frowned. Why else had he been staring at her? She assessed him with a critical look. He had no western accent, and there was a wolfish edge to his posture. "You're not from the Burning Plains."

The corner of his mouth twitched. "Are you asking a question or simply stating a fact?"

She fought the urge to tell him he should try actually smiling but thought better of it when she remembered his hidden blades. This shadow was *dangerous.* Had he used an illusion to hide that fact? That kind of trickery stemmed from the wretched Boglands, a foul eastern isle of treachery.

She narrowed her eyes. "Both."

Mischief twinkled in his rapturing eyes. "Correct on both parts then."

Unable to fight his gravity, she leaned closer and dropped her voice as if they were exchanging secrets instead of threats. "So, tell me then, what exactly are you doing here?"

Her gaze dipped to his mouth as it parted, bracing for his lies. Having spent countless evenings with an ear pressed against keyholes while mature discussions were had, she was confident in her ability to cut through conversational bullshit. Being raised by war strategists helped with that too.

However, Renton's attention had drifted away. Anger flaring, she spun around to see what had caused the distraction and spotted her father standing on the balcony. Long, onyx hair spilled down his signature midnight armor. A haze of black magic surrounded him like a swarm of enticed flies, and his normally ocher irises were stained obsidian, the only physical mark of his madness.

What happened to laying low? she taunted Ames, expectant of his appearance at her father's side. The leash to the monster.

No response came, and dread coiled in Tenah's gut as her thoughts spiraled out of control.

"Excuse me," she said to Renton, cutting for the balcony stairs.

Renton's hand caught her wrist. Another shocking jolt of energy coursed through her.

What was that? She whirled on him, crimson flames awakening with vengeance after having been shoved down all evening. He dropped her wrist as the heat of her magic seeped through her fire-resistant skin.

Still, he took a step forward as if to restrain her, a muscle in his jaw flaring. "It isn't safe."

"Yeah?" she retorted. "Well, he's my father."

Tenah hiked up her cumbersome skirts and rushed for the stairs, hoping the stranger wouldn't take chase. If he tried to stop her, she wouldn't hesitate to light his ass on fire. She probably should have started their conversation with flames.

The lilting music and soft murmur of voices faded away as every fiber of her being tuned in to her father. She leaped up the stairs, hissing at the brush of toxic magic against her bare skin. Hot and metallic, it coated the inside of her nose and mouth. Her limbs slowed, bogged down by an invisible, threatening force.

Black eyes slid to her. She froze on a step, her heart shuddering when her father offered a slow, wicked smile. He lifted a single finger. That was all it took to send a shockwave of black electricity crackling through the library, eliciting a choir of screams.

Tenah slammed into the railing. Tumbling down the stairs, her dress shredded, and her hair tore loose from pins. She hit the floor just as glass shattered and rained down on their guests.

Groaning, she pushed up to her feet, grateful for her choice of boots and not heels. She looked over at the broken wall of windows. Her stomach bottomed out as a sea of monstrous orange eyes stared back.

CHAPTER FOUR
TENAH

Why did the feingrot reek of her father's unholy magic? Could he summon them? Bind them to his will? Had Ames known about this ability?

Tenah's chest throbbed in tune with her injured wrist, used to cushion her fall. Chained in place by shock, she watched shadows race for the nearest doors, launching their bolts of wildfire at the otherworldly beasts.

This had to be a nightmare.

Everything would be set right if she could just wake up. That or the champagne was having a hell of a time with her imagination.

Ames, she tried again desperately. *Where are you?*

She forced her legs to carry her into the smoky corridor. Latching onto the faint vibration of icy magic, she began to track her wraith, not permitting herself to speculate on why his magic felt so weak.

Perspiration slicked her skin as she wound through serpentine halls. So much of this absurd house was small, eclectic spaces built haphazardly. Rounding another curve, she found Ames crumpled at the bottom of the attic staircase. Blood had soaked through his tattered suit from gouges etched into his arms. Black veins pulsed through the light skin along his temples.

Proof of his Corruption.

Sickness hit her like a punch to the gut. Her knees buckled, and she barely caught her weight with her wrist as she dropped to the floor.

Was he breathing?

Was *she* even breathing?

Her limbs stopped responding to her brain's messages. She wanted to crawl to him, but there was a part of her unwilling to confirm the inevitable as blood continued to flow from his wounds.

Frigid magic kissed the edges of her mind, cautious at first, as if Tenah might easily frighten. Then it speared into her, drawing a gasp of pain. Ames burrowed through years of compacted, secondhand toxins in her mind. She wasn't sure what he expected to find, only that he wasn't being gentle anymore.

She struggled against his unrelenting magic as he plunged her into a memory of the Void.

A tall, gaunt boy with silver eyes materialized before her. Something about his untamed auburn hair and deadpan gaze iced her bones. She knew him, didn't she? Something horrible had happened to him, but the memory was so hazy.

Ames stabbed deeper.

Please stop! Please, please, please! she pleaded. Whatever he wanted to recover, it wasn't worth this agony or the strain on his body when he clearly needed help.

In the memory, she reached out a hand to the boy. He drew back as if she was the monster, not the razor-toothed feingrot or sentient magic that thrived in the Void.

You must find the strength to fix this, Tenah, Ames murmured.

She shook her head, tears desperate to spill. *Fix what? I don't understand!*

His magic retracted, and the memory slipped into the foggy recesses of her mind. She was back in the manor, panting as she stared down at her splayed hands on the worn floorboards.

Her head tipped up to Ames, and a ghastly wail tore from her throat.

In the time he'd wasted sifting through her damaged mind, a panther-like feingrot had jabbed its barbed tail into his chest.

She waited for Ames to blink. To move. To crush the mind of the nightmarish fiend with the too-wide jagged smile and twisted horns.

A thunderous boom rattled the foundation of the manor. Dust and debris crumbled from the ceiling. Her father's coppery dark magic pumped through the hall, freed from all restraints. Which could only mean...

Ames was dead.

Tenah's chest hollowed out as if carved by a serrated knife. And the butcher? The parasite rooted in her father, puppeteering these monsters that didn't belong in their world.

Feeling untethered from flesh and bone, she crafted a bolt of crimson flame and hurled it at the feingrot, but the lithe beast dodged it and bolted up the attic stairs. She started after it, prepared to melt it down to nothing more than ash.

Her body locked up when she reached Ames's bloody corpse. She couldn't leave him for another beast to defile. She shouldn't abandon their guests to carnage. After all, this was her fault too. She'd lied to herself and to Ames about her abilities, all because she couldn't fathom the idea of giving up on her family. She'd helped stow away a Corrupt. She'd allowed shadows into his lair, knowing the risk.

And now, who was going to put him down, this monster she'd nurtured? Their dead king? His slaughtered elite? The High Court, who had disowned them thanks to their king's tyranny?

Her father had to be stopped. If that meant relying on the path of destruction, so be it. Let it guide her. Let it burn through the pain and guilt and grief that threatened to lay her out on the floor.

She had nothing left.

Draping Ames's arm over her shoulder, Tenah ignored the flare of pain in her wrist and hefted him upright. Thankfully, the physical aspect of their training had paid off. She hauled his body to the untouched study and rested him on the sofa. She'd bury him later.

Her heart rate spiked as she paused at the study door and leaned her forehead against it. It wasn't that she was afraid of her father. Ames had never allowed it. But without him to take the edge off her fear…

Her hands trembled as she pushed open the door and rushed the burning library, her own flames wrapped around her in defense.

Failure was not an option. No more shadows would die tonight.

But when she reached the library doors, her chest heaved as she glimpsed the fires engulfing her precious books. Decades of history and knowledge vanished in thick plumes of smoke. The ceiling mural had charred to nothing more than an ugly black scar. Beneath it, her father stood in a ring of elite bodies, clutching the King of Vozar by the throat.

She should have struck out, but the memory Ames had tapped into slammed into her once more. One blink, it was the king's life her father held. The next, she stood in her father's place, gripping the neck of the silver-eyed boy.

Tenah winced as his screams echoed through her mind.

The fractured memory retracted, and a flash of movement caught her eye. Renton stood a dozen strides from her father, his blade dripping black blood. It was smeared across his armor and the ends of his light hair as if he'd carved his way through hordes of enemies to get to him. He'd been slaying monsters, and what had she been doing—watching death claim lives unjustly?

In a shocking burst of speed, Renton vanished.

Tenah lunged forward. "No!"

Her father's eyes snapped to her. When Renton reappeared behind him, he'd left a dagger sheathed under her father's raised arm where armor didn't protect.

Tenah felt the sharp pierce of that blade in her soul.

Only, her father smiled. Little rivulets of black magic seeped from his wound, snaking up his arm still holding the king. They crawled into the king's eyes. Burrowed into his ears. His curses stopped. Then his useless flailing.

The King of Vozar became nothing more than black dust, absorbed into her father's body.

The clang of talons against steel jerked her around. Renton stood between her and a feingrot. She'd been too disturbed by the horrific scene playing out in front of her to detect the beast creeping up behind her.

"Get out of here!" Renton ordered.

He didn't understand. She couldn't run. The depth of that guilt would crush her. She needed to fight back. Dredging the bottom of her fire source, she called forth a dragon made from red flames. It spiraled up from her palms, expanding into a massive thing of heat and smoke and fury.

Tenah drew both hands down in command. Her fiery manifestation dove, jaws wide, teeth blazing. She let her eyes drop to her father, bracing for the shattering of her entire world.

His demonic smile was the last thing she saw as a ribbon of his dark magic struck her in the heart. The library exploded into a dizzying array of black and white light.

And then death embraced her.

Chapter Five
RENTON

Heat warped the night. Through the disgusting, undulating waves of it, Renton watched plumes of black smoke climb the sky to blot out the stars.

Blood pumped thick and heavy through his veins. Smoke dried out his throat. His shoulder ached where rubble had collapsed on him when Tenah had brought the library toppling down with a staggering demonstration of fire magic.

Unnatural. That girl… She was nothing more than a ruby-eyed fiend with fire for blood.

Renton swiped a hand across his brow. His skin burned, coated in sweat, ash, and dried feingrot blood. Resting his blade against his shoulder plate, he glanced down from a pile of smoldering debris at the corpses of beasts he'd slain.

Gods, what a hellscape. The night tugged at jagged memories of his first hunt in the Quasi Desert. Though nothing could be worse than that failure.

Sobs drew him toward a splintered column pinning a Vozarian woman. He rushed over, sheathing his blade. He jammed his fingers under the smoldering wood and heaved it up with a grunt. Embers melted the skin on his fingers as muscles in his arms nearly tore from the effort.

As soon as the woman crawled out, he dropped the column, throwing up an arm when hot ash puffed out. The woman remained on the ground. Shoving down his irritation at this entire fucked-up situation, he knelt beside her.

"Can you stand?" he asked roughly.

Her sooty hand wrapped around his forearm, her eyes wide in fright. Jaw clenching, he glared down at where she touched him. She must have mistaken his question as concern. He was only doing his job.

Upon closer examination, the woman bore no signs of Corruption. There were no markings or physical mutations from Lord Kherathi's magical outburst.

Renton exhaled a long breath. He'd cut through too many of them already. Shadows mutated and rendered incapable of rational thought thanks to dark magic called Chaos. Left alive, they would become Corrupt and wreak havoc, just as Kherathi had this evening.

"I'll take that as a no." Renton scooped her up and eased her over his uninjured shoulder. He let out a soft whistle for his winged mount. His eyes never left the ruins, keen senses cast out for threats. His body screamed for relief as it rapidly approached overload.

Just a little bit more.

He needed to track his prey. He'd screwed up everything by letting one of the Delemors go.

He stepped back as his mount—a scaled welkin he'd stolen from a slave trade in Firesteep—smashed down into the ruins. Its pearlescent wings fluttered out wide in show, the membranes glowing red in the firelight.

"A little more finesse would be appreciated." He brushed off embers that landed on his dark leather armor like pesky insects. "Don't forget, I freed you."

The welkin snorted and shook its horned head. Renton tossed it a murderous look before correcting himself. The beast *had* ferried loads of shadows north to safety.

He hoisted the injured Vozarian woman onto the welkin's back. The

but would his brother be spared? That was always the most crucial question.

Beneath that concern, he was surprised by the potency of his disappointment. When she'd walked into that library, he'd found himself jealous of the powerful Ashen on her arm, the thought striking him that he should be the one touching her instead.

After discovering who she was, the idea of throwing her over a shoulder and hauling her to Cragnore had unsettled him. Unless his years of experience and the blasted shard in his chest had failed him, she was not Corrupt. No ache in his chest. No evident signs of Corruption swirling in her lovely, bronze skin. Her mind had been sharp during their brief conversation too.

So why did Boedworth want her? No way the High Court had agreed to systematically eliminate anyone tied to Chaos. That would be barbaric. Was it possible Kherathi had crossed the councilmen and those consequences had branched out to encompass the entire Delemor family?

These thoughts had spiraled Renton into a place of doubt over his contract. He'd made it clear that he would no longer hunt shadows, only Corrupt. And look what that distraction had cost. If only he'd held onto her in the library... Had he truly expected her to persuade her father out of madness?

Scanning the forest one last time, Renton lifted Tenah into his arms. He wouldn't leave her among the broken remains of her life, and she deserved better than eternal rest in his native Boglands. Renton would deliver her body to the High Court, notify the isle leaders of the massacre, and demand reinforcements to hunt down her father and his army of monsters.

Chapter Six
TENAH

Down into a well of satin darkness Tenah fell, tugged by an inescapable force. She flailed against it, seeking purchase in the chilled, viscous air. It stretched and loosened around her, unraveling like fabric, only to reform tighter around her body.

Mine, it seemed to profess.

Enraged, Tenah called upon her flames, but the heat that normally thrived at her core had withered away. It was as if her insides had been scraped clean, her gift of magic revoked.

She bit down on her lip just to see if she could taste blood. Her panic bloomed, constricting around her chest like vines when no blood or pain answered.

Whatever this was, she'd savagely crawl her way out.

Only, there was nothing to thrash against. No walls caging her. No ground beneath her boots. Nothing to cling to or provide leverage out of what she was beginning to believe was madness or the underworld.

Why hadn't anyone helped her? Healed her? She screamed into the abyss until her voice went ragged. Part of her expected Ames's cold magic to wash over her. To hear his voice. But Ames was dead, and her father had proven the depth of his love.

There was no one left to save her. No one else to *care*. A decade of studying and chasing magic in hope of saving her family. All of it a waste.

A small, blue ember carved out the darkness, startling her from a whirlwind of furious thoughts. It dipped and bobbed like the lure of a carnivorous fish, slowly drawing her body down until her boots met blissful, solid ground. The little flame pulsed brighter, almost eager for her presence. Its haunting glow illuminated the shredded remains of her dress and the darkening bruises along her wrist and knees, though they no longer throbbed with a heartbeat of their own.

Limbs heavy, she trailed the flame through the darkness. Two tall, black marble columns materialized. She paused before them, running soft fingers along their ridges, impressed by their seemingly infinite reflection in the polished black floors. The flame glided onward, revealing more evenly spaced columns.

Something lurked in the space with her.

Goosebumps rose along her skin, her heart lurching into her stomach. She kept her gaze on the flame as it stopped above a pool of dark blue fabric. Someone *was* here. Had they been watching her the entire time? Taking pleasure in her terror?

The flame expanded, washing the entire hall in blue light. She took in the male perched on a black throne. A sculptor might have carved him from stone, his features were cut so sharp. His brows were dark slashes angled up into a mess of reddish-brown hair. And his eyes were half-lidded, heavy with menace. One shimmered like liquid mercury, and the other burned a haunting, animal orange that had her pulling her arms in tight against her chest as if to make herself smaller.

"Come here." His voice was a smooth baritone.

Hot energy pumped through her then lurched her forward against her will. Was this some sort of test? Judgment into the underworld? Or was she still ensnared in her father's wicked magic?

"Who are you?" she demanded, her voice wavering.

He stopped drumming his fingers on the stone armrests. The large, blue gem in the ring on his index finger gleamed between tiny silver wings. It looked disturbingly familiar, but when Tenah pushed to remember where she'd seen it, her head lashed out with a sharp whip of pain.

The ebony crown atop his head crackled with ribbons of unholy, black energy. "I'm nothing more than a lost soul like you."

Tenah licked her chapped lips. The terrifying, beautiful king leaned forward on his throne. His honed focus brought alarming heat to her skin.

"I…" She pushed out a jagged breath, infuriated by the tremor in her voice. "I didn't know who I was calling for."

"That's not true." His mismatched eyes turned molten. "Deep down, you knew you needed me, Tenah. Not some god. Not someone of your own blood who betrayed you and leashed your very potential."

Her face scrunched. "Leashed? I have no idea what you're talking about. I don't know you."

The king brushed a finger under his lip. "No? I suppose your father's accomplice robbed you of that too." After all this time apart, you are still so *weak*."

She curled her fingernails into the soft flesh of her palms. Ames had made it clear he would never tamper with her mind. Too often, alterations went wrong, even for a highly skilled master like him.

But then, what had he been doing in her head right before his death?

The king's expression darkened. "The fact that your recollections of me are nonexistent should be proof enough. That Ashen *wrecked* you."

Tenah winced, his words cutting deep. "He wouldn't do that."

The blackholes in her mind were just a side effect of living under the same roof as her father's infection.

The king used his thumb to spin the winged ring around his finger. "Deny it all you wish. Death doesn't care."

Tenah blinked up at him, her heart sinking deeper into her hollowed center. She *was* dead then. Bile rose up in her throat, but she forced it back down, not wanting to embarrass herself further.

Her own father had murdered her.

"What do you want from me?" she asked, dipping into anger.

His inferno eyes glinted. "*Everything.* In exchange, I will grant you a second chance at life."

She bit down on the inside of her lip as her mind whirled to process this horrid situation. Why was it so hard to recall anything beyond the monotony of recent weeks? Her memories lurked in a fog she'd never been able to clear, not that she'd tried very hard in the past. Healing her father had been the most important thing in her life.

"Why?" she asked.

The death king, or whatever he was, rose from his throne and strode to her. The clean, metallic scent of brewing storms clung to his fine robes. His light fingers traced her jaw, driving spikes of unease through her and leaving tingles in their wake. "Because your magic belongs to the world, Void Walker. It was not meant to end, most definitely not by a madman's bloodstained hands."

Tenah wrenched away from him. "How would you know that?'

"What, that you have the power to transcend worlds?"

Her eyes narrowed. This king was *insane.* Did he actually believe she was capable of tearing rifts between worlds? She clenched her teeth around a wild laugh. Like she would be so blessed. Astral projecting into the Void was one thing, but physically entering it? If she had that ability, she would have discovered the magic to heal her father ages ago.

Unless Ames hadn't wanted her to.

Damn it, this was messing with her head. Even if the king spoke truthfully, she couldn't imagine delving into a place that was often the source of her nightmares.

The king folded his arms behind his back and straightened, appearing both militant and bored. "What will it be? Eternity bound to this darkness or a chance to walk worlds again?"

"You will clarify the terms of this agreement," she said, notching her chin higher, though her body quivered.

He made a slow circle around her, eyes perusing freely as if they had the right. "A share in your power to start."

"A binding of sorts?" She mulled this over, sifting through knowledge she'd harvested from tomes. Bonds weren't always permanent. She could accept then find a way to free herself from him.

"You act like that is so horrible." The king's nostrils flared, and Tenah swore she glimpsed the flash of razor-sharp teeth behind his perfectly shaped mouth.

"Yes, because I don't know you."

Black tendrils of magic curled from his body, setting alarms off in her head. She stumbled back a few paces.

What other choice did she have though? If she declined the king's offer, she'd remain here. Submerged in this limbo. Dead, she was no use to anyone. Alive, she could possibly protect those in the path of darkness her father would spread. She could right this wrong.

"I agree and I live?" she asked.

He gave a slight nod. "You live."

Her heart thudded against her ribcage. Voices of reason warned her against this, cultivated by Ames and her father throughout the years. But all of their advice, all of their supposed life lessons, had only served to land her here.

Tenah was surprised by the potency of rage that washed through her. She was pissed that her father had tapped into dark magic, reasoning aside. She was pissed he hadn't fought harder against its hold. Beyond that, she was pissed that he and Ames had been irresponsible with his health. Such carelessness had resulted in the death of so many innocent shadows.

And she was pissed at herself for not doing more to stop it. The souls obliterated by her father's magic and his feingrot—that blood would forever stain her hands too.

"Okay. I accept your deal."

The death king gave a tiny bow. "Go forth and wreak your havoc. But know in time, I will have my payment, Tenah."

She swallowed as the little blue flame plunged into her chest, throwing the hall into darkness once more.

CHAPTER SEVEN
TENAH

Tenah's first new breath crystallized in her lungs as a frigid, cleansing wind howled around her.

Why was her body moving of its own accord?

She pried her frozen eyelids open and instantly regretted it. The sunlight was blinding against a backdrop of snow-dusted landscape and cloudless sky. Her arm shot up to block out the harsh light, but the reflexive motion set her off balance. She teetered, hands snapping out to grasp at the white scales of the welkin beneath her. At the same time, an arm ensnared her waist.

Her body stiffened. She knew no one that owned such a rare beast. Welkins had all but vanished from the Kandar Isles, save for those bound by Ashen magic or a slaver's iron chains.

Who could have possibly swept her from the manor into strange, non-Vozarian lands?

Regardless, she wasn't down to hang around. Tenah smashed an elbow back into her kidnapper's ribs. She yelped as her bone struck unyielding armor.

"I would advise against that," a deep male voice scolded. No trace of the thick, rolling western accent she was accustomed to.

Ordering Tenah to refrain from anything was the equivalent of begging her to do just the opposite. However, the only shadows that knew that were either dead or Corrupt.

Her chest ached at that empty thought, and the world seemed to drop away. How could she be so selfish? She hadn't even thought to ask the death king to revive Ames. Wouldn't he have stood a better chance at defeating her father? That was, if he wasn't in agreement of her father's destruction. Had they misread him? Could he have had ulterior motives when her father brought him home from war?

Panic shot its burning venom into her veins. For the first time since she could recall, she lost all control of her magic. Flames wrapped in black lightning burst from her fingertips. The welkin cut the air with a loud screech and careened sideways. Tenah slid from its back, her hands scrambling to find grip along its front limb.

The beast shrieked, ripping her free with dagger-like claws and tossing her out into the open sky. Tenah's screams were swallowed up by the roar of the wind then silenced by deep, powdery snow as she sank into it. The cold did little to numb the fresh slashes in her thigh and shoulder, burning hotter than the undesirable magic still buzzing in her channels.

Curses spewed from the figure that dropped into the snow next to her. This was headed up by an impressive rant about slaughtering the useless welkin as it glided away, abandoning them in a frozen wasteland.

Seeping blood and dark magic, Tenah rightly freaked. She stumbled to her feet, disoriented and unbearably cold. She made it all of three strides to the tree line before an arm hooked around her middle and pulled her against a solid body.

"Tenah, please!"

She jerked around to face her captor.

Renton.

A mixture of relief and horror flooded through her. In the sunlight, his long hair shone like Vozarian wheat fields, and his eyes glittered bright green with mesmerizing flecks of yellow. He no longer wore his illusion, his bone armor on full display. Her gaze snagged on his weapons as she recalled how he'd stabbed her father for casting the very same magic electrifying her body at the moment.

Releasing a crackle of lightning, she broke free and made another reckless dash for the trees, as if they would protect her. All it would take was a knife to her back, and she'd be downed if he wished it.

No way she'd bargained for another life just to immediately die. What cruel trick was the death king playing?

She squeezed her eyes shut, fighting through the pain. Flashes of the gathering crashed over her. The reverberating clang of weapons. Glass shattering. Rolling flames and splintering wood. A choir of screams and desperate prayers. Blood pooling in the floorboards she'd spent her childhood sprawled across. Her father's black, soulless eyes—dark magic given flesh and blood.

A pit opened inside of her chest, sucking everything in like quicksand. A ruthless, all-encompassing force took and took until she was certain there would be no pieces of her left. It gnawed worse than a ravenous hunger, unable to be satisfied.

Renton caught up to her as her wounded leg gave out. He drew her against his chest, and his back landed in the snow. He rolled them both over, caging her. His harsh expression made her wince, colder than the soaked fabric of her tattered dress.

"I don't know what the fuck is going on, but you need to get control over that magic right now," he said roughly.

Her teeth chattered as she stared up at him with wide eyes and labored breaths. "Frostbite," she whined.

"Magic first or neither of us is getting back up," he emphasized, motioning to the field of black electricity forming around them.

Tenah shook her head. "This isn't mine. I didn't-I didn't summon it. I've never..."

"Hey, it's okay." His voice softened. "Our immediate concern is your injuries."

But whatever this was burning inside of her, it refused to settle. Braced over her with one arm, Renton pulled out a tiny vial churning with pungent charcoal smoke. When he popped the cork, the contents tumbled out. It wrapped around her hands until she no longer felt the searing buzz of toxic magic. The Chaotic storm dissolved above them.

"What did you do to me?" she whispered, examining her hands.

"It's called creeping smoke. Temporarily halts a caster's magic."

Her eyes shot up to him, fear spiking. "You stabbed my father."

"I'm not going to stab you, unless you want to keep it up with that forbidden magic."

"Reassuring," she muttered, throat constricting. Gazing up at the sky, she sucked in a lungful of glacial air. Then she crawled out from under him, ignoring the traitorous part of her brain that wondered what his weight would feel like pressed against her.

Renton didn't hesitate to scoop her up into his arms.

"I'm perfectly capable of walking," she protested. She didn't want his pity. She didn't want to find comfort in him at all.

A muscle in his jaw flexed as his hold tightened. "You demonstrated that quite spectacularly. Tell me, how far do you think you'd make it before you bled out or succumbed to the cold?"

Scowling, Tenah surveyed the snowy field around them, trying to decipher where the welkin had dumped them from her study of maps. "Where are we?"

"At the southern tip of Inner Sanctum."

She muttered a curse that made him chuckle. That put her at least a day's ride from the Burning Plains and miles south of the High Court, where she could have bartered for a mount. Envisioning strolling into her mother's native city had her tensing in Renton's arms. She hadn't sorted through those feelings tied to abandonment, and now didn't seem like a good time to reflect upon them.

Tenah trained her eyes on the pine branches forming a sparse ceiling above their heads. "Why didn't you leave me there?"

Renton halted, his annoyingly handsome face tipping down to look at her. His eyes narrowed. "Your home burned down. There was nothing left."

More sickening thoughts to file away for later processing. Ames had made a habit of calling out her unhealthy suppression tactics, to which she'd always flipped him off.

"Okay." She drew out the word. "I'll ask again. Why not leave me there?"

Why haul her body halfway across the floating isles?

His features shifted between indecipherable emotions as he crafted his answer. "I lost track of Kherathi. While he's alive, your kingdom isn't safe."

Elementals, was he too daft to identify a dead body? She sank her teeth into her bottom lip to hold back a wicked laugh. Then again, she had planned on hauling Ames's body out of the manor too. What if Renton had been taking her somewhere to bury her?

But Ames was family. This hunter…he barely knew her.

"Vozar should be warned," Tenah said.

He picked up his pace. "I already sent word to the High Court."

She glared at him, wishing she could burn through his stupid, collected demeanor. "Who exactly are you?"

"Should I expect a hundred more questions?"

"At least that," she retorted. *Like how did you know my name when I never gave it?*

His raspy laugh vibrated through her, awakening heat low in her core.

"Well?" she pressed.

"I'm a hunter employed by the High Court."

Her mouth turned down. All right, so her initial instincts had been wrong. He wasn't Sardoth's executioner or an enemy from the Boglands. He held a position with the esteemed leaders of the Kandar Isles.

"Why would the High Court send a hunter to Vozar? We're not allied."

Renton's fingers tightened against her. "No, but your father popped up on their radar."

Her stomach twisted. The High Court *had* known about her father. Did that mean they had records on her too? Elementals, that would make this new life a hell of a lot more complicated.

Tenah lost all desire to ask more questions, a sour taste filling her mouth as Renton cut south, the opposite direction of where he claimed to work.

Chapter Eight
TENAH

By the time they reached an inn nestled between thick, snow-dusted trees and dirt crossroads, Tenah was woozy from blood loss.

Her head lolled against Renton's arm as he hauled her into the golden light of The Indigo's rustic lanterns. Inside the lobby, she shuddered in delight at the warmth radiating from a crackling stone fireplace. The airy hall smelled of pine and cinnamon. There were a few long, wooden tables occupied by lone, hardened shadows, mostly in armor.

Somehow, still clutching her as if she weighed nothing, Renton withdrew a bag of krotens and tossed it across the counter at a pretty young woman. Her skin held a slight green tint, contrasted by ringlets of dark brown hair.

High Court shadows were envied for the unique, decadent features, much like their sacred landscapes. Hathrowyn—their capital—was rumored to look and feel like a dream. Shadows born here had deep ties to history and strong connections with restorative magic. Tenah might share their blood, but their talent for healing had thus far evaded her.

"Two rooms for the evening," Renton said, immune to the innkeeper's adoring smile. The woman looked at Tenah, and her expression crumpled.

"Felnor bless you," the woman exclaimed, reciting the name of her elemental. "I'm sorry to say I'm an utter failure when it comes to mending wounds, but I'll check my books to see if we have a healer staying this evening. Though, few travel this close to the Boglands."

The Boglands. Tenah grimaced.

The innkeeper flipped through pages of a leather-bound book splayed on the counter. Discouraged, she hurried over to a shelf to sift through various items Tenah guessed had been left behind.

"I know I have medical supplies around here somewhere. I'll bring them right up to your room as soon as I find them. If only I kept this place organized." The innkeeper gave her rosy cheeks a little slap. "Oh, I almost forgot—I only have one room available this evening."

Groaning, Tenah went limp in Renton's arms. He politely thanked the innkeeper, however, and then carried her up the three flights of stairs to their quaint suite. The two main walls sloped up to a pointed ceiling, and the back wall was made up of glass windows and doors out to a small, snow-dusted balcony. There was a large, quilted bed and enough fluffed pillows to kink up her neck just looking at them.

Renton swept her into a connected bathing room and deposited her in a large, wooden basin. She let her head fall back against the edge as he removed another tiny vial of mysterious substance from his belt.

"Technically, this is kidnapping," she muttered.

When he didn't reply, she turned her head slightly, finding that he'd already unbuckled his bracers, chest piece and blades. Under all that protection, he wore a dark, short-sleeved shirt, taut over defined shoulders. Hundreds of pearly scars decorated his muscular arms.

Hot blood rushed to her cheeks, but she couldn't tear her gaze away from him.

Renton cocked a brow, a hint of a smirk playing at the corner of his mouth. He pressed the small vial into her palm. "Drink."

"What is it?" She eyed the thick liquid suspiciously.

"A very expensive healing tonic."

Uncapping it quickly, she sucked it down. Anything to heal faster so she could plot her escape.

"What do I owe you?" she asked, narrowing her eyes at him.

"Consider it paid for. I probably should have given it to you an hour ago, but I wasn't certain how long it would last. I don't take them often."

A knock on the bedroom door lured him away. Tenah clamped her teeth together as her gaze darted to the window. Too small to fit her body. She snorted at the thought of crawling to the balcony. Then what? Would she simply tumble off the railing? She didn't fancy another drop into the snow.

Renton appeared with a basket of various medical supplies. From his smooth, easy tone, she'd bet krotens he'd made the lovely innkeeper blush again. She had a feeling he could have that effect on most shadows if he desired it.

Tenah frowned, eyes widening as he withdrew a hooked needle and string from the basket. Meticulously, he lined them up next to clean strips of cloth and a bottle of antiseptic.

Her stomach twisted. "Do you even know what you're doing?"

He scooted his wooden stool closer after he threaded the needle. Before she could protest, a cool cloth pressed against her thigh to clean the wound. Then he dumped on antiseptic, making all her muscles seize up.

She hissed. "A warning would have been nice!"

His brows kneaded as he lowered the needle to her skin. "The pain is the same regardless. And yes, I've stitched up enough of my own mistakes to qualify for this job. Now, hold still. Unfortunately, the tonic won't work miracles on these wounds."

Sinking teeth into her bottom lip, she leaned her head back until her eyes settled on the wooden ceiling. "How did someone so young become employed by the High Court?"

"Back to this game, hmm?"

Tenah whimpered, eyes shutting at the tugging sensation of his work. "Talk to me."

"About?"

"Anything. Just distract me from puking."

He gave a low laugh. The sound made her heart skip. Who was this gentle yet murderous male that seemed to care if she lived or died?

"You summon hellfire, but a bit of gore makes you sick?" he asked.

She tightened her fingers on the basin, her knuckles turning bone white.

"I'm not sure I have anything pleasant to talk about."

"Scars." The word slid through her teeth. Damn her curiosity. She glanced down to catch him pausing in contemplation.

"I have thirty tooth marks on my calf."

"Continue."

This earned another soft laugh, then he returned to his work piecing her back together. "I was fishing with my two brothers on the lake outside my family's cottage. I'm not sure why I thought it would be fun. My eldest brother had a way of coercing me into things I didn't want to do. The first time he pressured me into killing, our father ordered us to run thirty laps around the lake for cutting down a harmless Bogland beast protecting its kin. I learned never to strike first. Mias learned to hide his capacity for violence. He preyed on my weakness. He knew wherever my youngest brother went, I went too. So, I found myself on a boat with both of my brothers. When we reached the middle of the lake, Mias pushed me in."

Tenah hissed, and Renton laid a rough hand flat on her thigh to keep it still. The pain had nothing on the jolt of pleasure that shot through her as his concerned eyes found hers.

"Shall I stop?" he asked.

"No. Stitches and talking. Please," she added. His manners with the innkeeper earlier had reminded her a bit of Ames.

"I'm assuming you've never visited the Boglands."

She rolled her eyes. "What gave it away?"

"Several things." He flashed a slow, crooked smile that produced a fluttering in her stomach. "I was born in Mire, a small hunting village in the Boglands. I'm not allied with Adra's rebels, so don't look at me like that."

"What? I wasn't judging," she complained, forcing a neutral expression.

"It's no secret our isles have had their disagreements, but not all eastern islanders fought with Queen Advanth at Roan's Wake. Some of us didn't want war. The aftermath was..." He shook his head, jaw tensing.

"I'm sorry," she whispered.

And she was. That same line of judgment had been cast upon her family countless times. It boiled her blood. Except, after witnessing what her father had been capable of, that judgment didn't seem so unfair now. Her father *was* a monster.

Tenah squirmed. She wasn't ready to dive into the possibility that she might have absorbed a sliver of the infection that had unraveled him.

Renton went back to easing the needle through her skin. "There are many lakes in the Boglands that are unnatural. They're either poisonous or too viscous to swim in. Before my younger brother could pull me out of the thick waters, a creature we call the Lurda had slithered out of its holes along the banks. I wasn't afraid of much at that age. I was first in training camps to volunteer to get the shit kicked out of me and to lead practice hunts. But I was terrified of the Lurda, and Mias knew it."

"Your brother sounds terrible," she said, frowning. Tenah had spent her formative years wishing she'd had a sibling. Maybe those relationships weren't exactly what she'd conjured up in her mind.

Renton's silence rubbed at her wrong, so she did something stupid.

"I was afraid of my father and his magic," she admitted. "When I sensed it in the air, I'd hide for days until Ames convinced me he was well again."

His head tilted, his light hair spilling down one shoulder. "That fear is justified, Tenah. So was my fear of the Lurda when it nearly tore off my leg."

She nodded and tipped her head up to keep the tears stinging in her eyes from falling. Elementals, she was a hot mess. Giving in to emotions right now would only rip open the jagged wound inside of her. That pain would eat her alive. She was certain of it.

"When I found you in the wreckage…" He cut off for several heartbeats. "I was certain you weren't breathing."

His words hovered in the air. She recognized them for what they were. *A test.* Admitting she'd died and had been resurrected by some sort of death king was definitely the wrong answer. He could never know her truth, so she played into ignorance.

"I don't know what happened," she said. "One minute, I was struck down by lightning. The next, I woke up on the back of that hateful welkin."

"Do you know where Kherathi is headed?"

"As if I understand his mind right now." She sniffled. "He belongs in a grave."

Renton eased back on the stool, considering her response. "All right, next wound. Assuming you want to change into clean clothes, it would be easier if we removed this now so you don't tear stitches." He motioned to her tattered gown.

Turning to hide her reddening cheeks, she replied, "I'll need help."

He gripped under her arms and hefted her upright. Efficient fingers worked at the laces along her spine. She sucked in a breath as his calloused hands brushed her calves.

"Is this okay?" he asked, gathering the material of the gown.

A rigid nod was all she could manage.

His knuckles grazed the sides of her legs, her thighs, then her ribs as he removed the gown. Something about those quiet seconds felt too suffocatingly intimate. To her frustration, Renton didn't seem fazed. He tossed the gown onto the floor, never once becoming distracted from his work.

Facing away from him, Tenah hunched down in the basin and covered her chest with her uninjured arm. Thankfully, it didn't take him long to seal up the gash along her shoulder blade, but the moments after, when he'd had to bandage the wound, had her blood pressure rising.

"I'll find you some clothes," he murmured.

Left alone, it was hard not to ruminate on her decision to eliminate her father. Should she dip out now? Pray Renton wasn't as good of a hunter as she expected and race back to the Burning Plains? How many more lives had her father already claimed? Would she be strong enough to defeat him this time? Or should she try to convince Renton to help?

Head throbbing, she smashed her fingertips against her temples. The splitting sensation there didn't mean anything. It could be a culmination of a number of things too. Her death, her tumble from the sky, the tonic she'd consumed…

Renton sauntered back in. He paused, frowning at the obvious pain etched into her face. "I can get you something stronger."

She dropped her hands. "It's fine. I'm just…tired."

He placed a neat stack of clothes and fine leather gloves on the stool. Tenah stared at them, a strange ache in her chest at his thoughtfulness, considering her nails had turned black from the incident in the snowy field.

"Room is yours for the night. Get some sleep," Renton said, not glancing back as he exited the room.

Chapter Nine
RENTON

Night veiled the trees, moonlight glittering like diamonds on patches of snow when Renton stormed from The Indigo.

His mind was in absolute disarray. It was clear Tenah had cast some form of dark magic to shed death. He had to follow through with his contract now. She was a threat to the isles.

So, why was he buying her a room at an inn? And what the hell was with the information shared tonight? A pretty woman gets hurt, and he starts blathering about the past? He might as well march back into that room and tell her what a hypocrite he was. How he struggled to live with himself when he had a damn shard of dark magic embedded in his heart, one that would no doubt Corrupt him too.

Conversations weren't supposed to happen. Empathy for his prey wasn't supposed to happen, no matter the terror in her peculiar eyes when she'd unleashed that forbidden magic.

She hadn't accepted her fate.

Chaos, however, wasn't something you just shook off. It was a living part of her, and she was rightfully afraid of it. Add that in with the fact that she'd just experienced trauma on a level he understood far too well.

Renton paced the tree line, craving the embrace of nature. He wanted to run or fight or wear himself ragged until the world made sense again. Until he could piece it back together in an image of his desire. He leaned back against a tree and ran his hands up and down his face. He was so tired. He hadn't slept in two days. It explained why he wasn't capable of maintaining a rational head. He'd pushed himself beyond his limits to try to earn Aeyis's freedom. To correct his past mistakes.

Maybe he should go back upstairs and find sleep. Address this dilemma in the morning over breakfast. He still had four more days built into his contract for the Delemors.

But if he failed to track Kherathi down in time, he wasn't sure when another contract this important would fall into his hands. Eleven years was far too long to go without seeing his brother.

Renton closed his eyes and drew in the fresh scent of snow and pines. A hint of lavender mingled with the winter air. He whipped his head toward the source, spotting a dark shape limping from the back of the inn.

He growled and stomped after Tenah.

At least she'd dressed in warmer clothing. The dark tunic and pants he'd left on the stool hugged her noticeable curves. Somehow, she'd acquired fur too. A white pelt hung around her neck and shoulders.

And the leather gloves hid the tiny crescents of black that had developed on her nails.

His chest tightened uncomfortably.

"What do you think you're doing?" he called out to her.

Tenah picked up her pitiful speed, and he fought back an exasperated laugh. It didn't feel right to poke fun at her foolishness. Not with her injuries and lack of magic after he'd temporarily robbed her of that with creeping smoke.

She'd hobbled across a road and through an alcove of icy, glistening pine needles before the novelty of her little charade wore off.

"You're going to rip your stitches," he said brusquely.

A few long strides was all it took for him to catch up. He blocked her path, arms crossed over his chest. He'd left his armor and blades in the bathing room. Somehow, it felt like having a limb chopped off.

Tenah glared up at him. "I'm just taking a walk. Clearing my head."

She sidestepped him, and he moved again. "No," he said. "You're trying to shake me."

"No." She mimicked his crossed arms and winced as the motion tugged at her shoulder. "I couldn't sleep."

He raised a brow. Often, silence coaxed out the truth. However, holding her gaze allowed him far too much time to study her features.

Tenah broke as expected, groaning and turning her head away. "Nightmares, okay?"

"So…what? You plan to outrun them all the way home on a bad leg in the freezing cold?"

"I plan to kill my father before he kills anyone else!" she snapped, tossing him a cross look. "If you want to stay here and build snowmen with the innkeeper, so be it."

Excitement sparked in his chest. He appreciated a good challenge, and she presented just that. Something about her rich, sun-warmed skin kissed by freckles and her dark locks settled right with him too. His eyes dipped to her full lips, and he forced away indecent thoughts as blood rushed where it shouldn't.

"No." He drew out the word. "You plan to die face down in the snow before you even make it off this isle. Then again, can you really die, Tenah?"

Her eyes glinted bright red. "I don't know what you mean."

Renton stepped closer, testing his self-control as his mind ran wild, imagining pressing his mouth against hers. She'd probably deliver a fist to his stomach. Oh, but the taste would be worth it.

"Tell me, was it dark magic then?" he prodded. *Convince me otherwise. Convince me I shouldn't turn you in.*

"Why, because you'd have to hunt me then? Do you enjoy it? Slaughtering shadows like animals?"

He invaded her space, causing her to stumble back. "Is that what you believe I do?"

Tenah shrugged, but much of her rage had dissolved as a lovely, rosy tint spread across her cheeks. His nostrils flared. It would be nothing to toss her over a shoulder and carry her back inside the inn.

However, he had respect for boundaries. He'd done enough to maim her today.

What he truly wanted was for Tenah to unleash her rage. His week-long journey home from the desert after the brutal death of his father had been filled with violent outbursts in which he'd expended every bit of his energy more times than he could count.

She'd had one small tantrum. And now, *nothing*. Her vacant expression gnawed at him.

When she tried to step around him again, he almost let her pass. Guilt speared through him as he cuffed her arm. He lowered his head. "I can't let you go."

Furious eyes blazed up at him. Her skin heated slightly under his grip, evidence of strong magic beneath the effect of the creeping smoke. "You came into my home with more than one contract, didn't you?"

He dropped his hand and tucked his fingers loosely into his pockets. There was no point in denying it. He wouldn't insult her with lies. Her hatred would make it easier to finish this contract anyway.

"I should have known," she uttered.

She hobbled back to the inn and slammed the door shut behind her. He lifted his head to the dark sky, releasing a heavy sigh.

Two Chaos casters in exchange for his brother. It was the only way.

Chapter Ten

TENAH

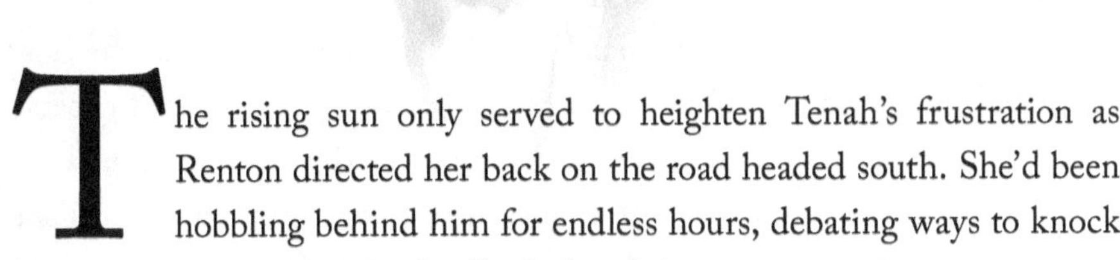

The rising sun only served to heighten Tenah's frustration as Renton directed her back on the road headed south. She'd been hobbling behind him for endless hours, debating ways to knock him unconscious, when he finally declared they were stopping to rest.

"Eat," Renton ordered, handing her a piece of seared meat.

Under different circumstances, she wouldn't have balked at an offering of food. Right now? She refused to accept anything from this hunter, his forced sympathy especially.

"You need to eat to regain your strength," Renton said.

She brushed dirt from her pants. "I'm not hungry."

His eyes darkened, sending a shiver down her body. There was no denying Renton had a presence that couldn't be ignored. His stare had a way of making her feel exposed.

Knees tucked against her chest and arms wrapped around them, she didn't bother looking up from the fire he'd made in the gaping hollow of a giant tree. Nor had she helped him ignite the chunks of wood he'd gathered, though the effects of the tingling creeping smoke had almost faded.

She wasn't sure what she'd done to irk him. One minute, they'd reached a southern road clear of snow, the air warm enough to stop the chattering of her teeth and the trees shooting up to a star-scraping height, and the next, Renton grumbled about taking a rest. He'd been glancing back at her so frequently she wondered if her slow pace was what had caused his foul mood.

Whatever. She was too wrapped up in their surroundings to care. Nature had a way of stealing her breath. It was why she obsessed over maps and all their seemingly impossible features. Now she was catching much-desired glimpses of it, but it was hard to fully savor when she wasn't sure where the hunter was taking her.

Tenah rubbed a fist into her eye, fighting back drowsiness. She *had* tried to sleep at the inn, but the instant she'd drifted off, the silver-eyed boy had made an appearance from wherever Ames had dug him up.

Murderer.

His accusation stuck like a poisonous barb in her skin. Had she hurt him? No, that wasn't possible. She was not her father. She wasn't capable of hurting anyone. The dark magic she'd spilled in the snowy field had her questioning herself though, planting a seed of uncertainty. What *was* she capable of?

Kicking the thought, she peeked out at the massive trees bathed in radiant sunlight.

"Creeping smoke should have worn off by now," Renton said. "How are you feeling?"

"Not quite ready to incinerate you," she admitted. "But close."

He chuckled. "I look forward to it."

A fluttering in her stomach had her scooting until she faced the hollow opening instead of him.

Since her episode in the snowy field, she'd glimpsed anomalies along their trek. Warbles of white light in her peripheral vision. Only, when she turned to examine them, they'd vanished into thin air like teasing mirages. It had to be a side effect of the infuriating throb deep in her skull.

She tensed as Renton sat down in the dirt next to her. One leg bent to support his arm, he rested against the tree trunk.

"Talk to me," he murmured.

Tenah snorted, but it was hard to ignore the maddening warmth spreading in her chest. "About?"

"Anything. Let me know you're here."

Wincing, she gripped her pants tighter, tiny sparks of red snapping from her fingers without command. This sudden issue with control sent ripples of unease through her. When she glanced at Renton, expecting him to launch an attack, he hadn't shifted from his concern for her.

"Let's not pretend you care," she muttered, but as they watched the bonfire dance, his proximity and burdened sigh unraveled her. "My father's a madman, my guardian is dead, and I'm somehow stuck with you as what? A hostage? A prisoner?"

"Tell me about your guardian. Was that the Ashen?"

She caught his eyes shining in reflection as if he was lost in his own troubled memories. She didn't like how that threw her off balance. "He's… he was good. Honest. Kind. Reliable. Everything my family was not. He taught me how to read and write. Taught me how to astral project into the Void." She paused, digging the toe of her boot into the dirt as if applying pressure to a pinch point. "Sometimes it felt like he needed us more than we needed him."

Renton tipped his head back, and she regretted casting another look at him, ensnared by his features. The unholy length of his lashes, shades darker than his pale skin and hair. The strong lines of his nose and jaw. The creases between his brows as if he always wore a scowl. The soft contrast of his mouth…

Her cheeks heated, his sliver of a grin proof he'd caught her staring.

"Take a look at the sky," he said, motioning to the faint scattering of stars about to be bled out by the eager sun.

She obeyed. Clearing her throat, she asked, "What am I looking for exactly?"

His shoulder pressed against hers as his forearm came to rest on her bent knee. Prickles of desire spread through her at the contact, making it difficult to focus.

"There, through the gap in the tallest branches. It's the constellation, Soryn. I seek it out everywhere I go. My home in Hathrowyn has a back porch angled just right so I can spot it through the trees. It's claimed to be a lifeline. A path to hope for those lost."

Tenah was still trying to process the shift in their conversation and the ease he touched her with. "What, did they teach you astronomy in killing camp?"

"I learned it from my father," he said, unfazed. "It guided me out of the darkness when his death threatened to crush me. It took years for me to learn that he could still have a role in my life. Just because your guardian no longer walks this plane doesn't mean he's gone."

And just like that, while her chest tightened with sorrow, Renton shut down. Rising to his towering height, he fetched his blades. "We should keep moving."

She stood, the demons of the last few days settling heavy on her shoulders. At least her stitches held thus far. Her limp was still prevalent, but when she'd rewrapped her wounds with clean strips of cloth as Renton retrieved firewood, she'd marveled at the skin already knitting back together.

Soon she could direct all of her energy on ending her father.

Tenah had been mentally fading in and out while the hunter walked several paces ahead when a flash of silvery white light sprang into her path.

Pulse quickening, she approached it with cautious steps, unnerved by the way it seemed to dance. Her fingers tingled with heat before she even touched the light's vibrating edges. Almost as if she'd been the one to cast this magic.

The hunter turned around. Judging from his kneaded brows, he was just as perplexed by this sudden disturbance.

"Is that..." he trailed off, his mouth opening and closing as his mind still processed.

She dipped a hand into the magic and gasped as it disappeared up to her wrist. Whatever existed on the other side was cold and potent with thrumming magic.

"A rift," she murmured, recalling how the death king had referred to her as a Void Walker. There was *no* possible way.

"Tenah, that's...that's very rare," Renton said, his tone heady with warning.

Did he honestly believe she'd carved it? Then again, did it matter? She could slip through and vanish. Hide out in the Void. Escape the hunter and run home.

She locked eyes with him. He seemed tuned in to her wild thoughts, his entire body going rigid and a hand twitching as if in need of his blade.

Tenah bit down on the inside of her cheek. What if she became trapped inside the Void? What if it spit her out somewhere farther away from Vozar and her father? What if she found herself surrounded by feingrot she'd only ever glimpsed through astral projection? Or worse, sources of dark magic hell-bent on mutating her?

Regretfully, she let her hand fall back to her side. She walked over to the hunter. His tension hadn't uncoiled, and she felt the urge to reach out and comfort him. More than that, she wanted to blast him off the edge of the isle for making her care.

"Answer me," she said. "Why are you escorting me south and not to the High Court? If you suspect me Corrupt, why not cut me down right here?"

Renton's eyes took their time circuiting her face. "High Court policy requires swift execution of Corrupt, but my current contract is with the councilman of the Boglands. He wants you and your father alive."

Tenah held back a shiver of revulsion. Had her father pissed off a councilman or something? She wasn't aware of any business he'd conducted with the Boglands. "Did you happen to ask why?"

Pain flickered across his face.

"You don't care, do you?" she whispered. "You just deliver bodies to him without asking."

His jaw clenched, muscles flexing. "Asking unfavorable questions would result in punishment."

Her eyes dropped to the scar along his neck. Horror gripped her at the thought of an isle leader carving it there. The same leader that wanted her alive.

Renton didn't wait for another question. When he strode away, for some bewildering reason, she silently followed.

Trees thinned, and the sky yawned before them, revealing a massive bridge that spanned the two miles between Inner Sanctum and the Boglands. Her heart soared. How she'd craved this. Open spaces. Bright sky and rippling water and fresh air that made everyday qualms insignificant. There was no reining in her longing for exploration when she'd spent her childhood trapped behind grim walls.

Renton was making a habit of watching her. She sensed his gaze as she placed a hand on the guard rail of the bridge. Crafted from the roots of ancient trees, it hovered thousands of feet above the solemn gray waters of Kilgriff Ocean and Aranma, the mainland.

The isles had once been a part of Aranma centuries ago, before the Greater Elementals had carved them out and cast them into the sky for their bloodlust. Five villainous kingdoms, banished. Shortly after, the Greater Elementals had sacrificed themselves to exile their brethren, Xith, the root of Chaos in the shadow world.

Hathrowyn had become the sixth kingdom, formed by the elders, powerful casters determined to reunite the kingdoms and restore peace.

"You look as though you've never seen the world," Renton said with a solemn expression.

"I can't really argue that studying maps and reading books is equivalent to traveling. I've only really been to Firesteep."

"I must warn you then." His gaze swept out to the lush isle at the end of the bridge. "The Boglands are nothing like Firesteep."

Tenah closed her eyes and soaked in rays of sunlight. She refused to believe it would be her last time. She wouldn't be caged again.

"It's odd to think how cut off all the isles are," she said. "We are gifted with such incredible magic, and we've reverted back to use of motorized carts and winged beasts for transport, if you're lucky enough to convince a welkin not to shred you to pieces. We've taken several steps back, haven't we?"

Her chest tightened. She'd loved talking to Ames about the technology in Nightfall—his native kingdom—though it hadn't compared to how advanced Adra had been centuries ago, what with its snake-like machines that moved on rails.

A zing of nerves rushed through her as Renton sauntered over.

"If you had witnessed the aftermath of Roan's Wake, you would have voted to shut down the portals too," he said solemnly. "When Adra fell into darkness under Advanth's rule, much of its Corrupt spilled into my homelands. I'm not sure I've even made a dent in their numbers."

Tenah's fingernails cut into her palms. Had skilled killers like him not existed, would Corrupt have already overwhelmed the isles?

Eager to finish this confusing trip with him, she stepped onto the bridge. Ahead, the Boglands offered thick curtains of vines and low, dense trees that would aid in her escape.

Renton caught her wrist. "Tenah, I—"

She spun around, teeth bared. "What."

Again, fresh pain scrunched up his features. He took a step closer. His hand tenderly pushed a lock of hair behind her ear, and all rage dissolved from her body. All that mattered was this moment, Renton holding her on the edge of something terrifying, his rough fingers trailing from her jaw down to her chin.

"I can't help but want to save you," he whispered.

Her heart thudded, thick and heavy in her chest, but then Renton was forcing space between them, his eyes refocusing on the Boglands.

"We're going to take a detour," he said.

As he set a new pace, she had to jog to keep up with him.

"Wow. Have you considered becoming a healer instead of a murderer?" she asked. "My leg feels amazing."

She expected an anger-infused response. Instead, he laughed when a swarm of mutant insects peppered her body as soon as her boots touched down on spongy, moss-covered ground. She swatted at them, blood heating. Her boot snagged on a gnarled vine, and Renton gripped her bicep to keep her standing.

"It's called nature," he said.

"I lived in the forest, remember? The big, ugly house that burned down." She slapped an insect into a pool of sludge trapped between a network of tree roots. Its legs twitched as its wings sank into the thick, black substance. "This place isn't natural. I hate it, and I think it hates me back."

Renton shook his head then started hacking through the overgrowth of vegetation blocking the path with a crude dagger. Their pace was slow, and Tenah languished in the humidity, so different from the dry heat back home. Within minutes, she was slick with sweat and panting. She couldn't even appreciate the bittersweet taste of magic that infused the air.

"I've heard terrible things about Bogland shadows," she said, "but how has no one ever brought up the fact that you all live in such insufferable conditions? I think I'm breathing straight water into my lungs."

"Few outsiders survive the Boglands." Renton lifted a hanging vine out of her way before she got caught in it. "Those that do often don't experience the same environment here. The isle plays tricks, weaving illusions. It can affect more than one of your senses."

Her mouth parted in surprise.

"And," he added, his eyes bright with amusement, "Vozarians expend a great amount of energy on teaching hatred of our kind. They don't leave much room to discuss our humidity or sludge problem."

There was truth in his words. Tenah had overheard nobility boast about the evils of beguilers and nothing else. No wonder Ames had been opposed to her attending lectures and casting lessons in the capital. As an eastern islander himself, he wouldn't have wanted her raised among such animosity.

"Humor me." Renton glanced back at her. "What do the fire bloods say about us?"

She frowned. "They say you're all barbaric. That you enslave travelers and sell them to criminals. That you kill for sport. That you drink the blood of your enemies and decorate your swamps with their skulls." Her eyes dipped to his armor. "Though it seems you use them for other purposes. Intimidation maybe?"

Renton invaded her space, and she breathed in his crisp scent, finding herself lost in the flecks of wild yellow and green in his eyes. Was that an illusion too? A tactic to throw her off guard? "Are you intimidated?"

It took a moment to collect her thoughts.

"Not even a little bit," she said, ducking through the vines.

"Shall I share what us swamp heathens say about your kind?" Renton called out.

She rolled her eyes. "Lies, I'm sure."

"Vozarians are hot-blooded, pompous creatures with no regard for the other kingdoms. They grow most of Kandar's food but refuse to share it while others starve. They forge the strongest weapons but refuse to trade with eastern shadows desperate to defend their homes and families from Adra's army of Scourge warriors and Corrupt. They fear anything that appears to be a threat. Anything outside their kingdom with 'tainted blood.' They imprison, torture, and execute what they don't understand."

"Quite the list," Tenah said. "Sadly, you're wrong about a number of things."

But it was hard to sound convincing when her core beliefs were beginning to get muddled, especially when it came to him.

Chapter Eleven
RENTON

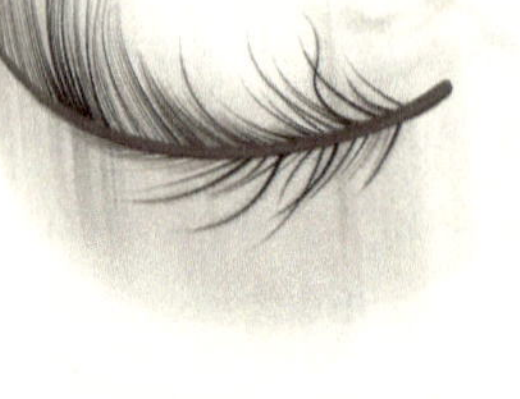

Renton sagged in relief as he glimpsed the misty hills of Mire. It was a sight he never expected to see again.

Home.

He would confirm his brother's safety before he decided what to do with Tenah. Boedworth played too many games to trust his word, contract or not. And after discovering Tenah's ability to locate—if not carve—rifts, he didn't like the idea of his wicked councilman obtaining that kind of raw power.

"What are we doing here?" Tenah asked. She clutched the back of his armor as if she could throttle the answer from him.

"Keep close to me," he instructed.

Draining his feeble reserve of illusion magic, he hid them from view. Against his better judgment, he took her hand, leading her toward a small, white farmhouse on the cusp of the village's gates formed from tree trunks.

It was hard not to give space for all the emotions rising up in his chest like steam. Eleven years he'd been exiled from Mire, tossed out as a child, and now he returned, a soulless hunter, blades stained by blood and body fueled by rage alone. The more Corrupt he slaughtered, the safer the isles would be for his brother.

If anything had happened to Aeyis, Renton would drive a blunt object through Boedworth's head. Screw the consequences.

Footsteps shuffled on dirt nearby, and Renton flattened Tenah against the side of the stables, worried his illusion wouldn't be enough to keep them hidden. Up close, her wide eyes, and parted lips shot blood straight to his cock.

A drop of sweat rolled down the side of his neck. He held a finger up to his mouth as a young boy walked out of the stable doors then disappeared into the farmhouse.

It should have come as a surprise how difficult it was to peel himself away from her as he moved inside the stables, Tenah on his heels. He whispered ancient commands to a roan horse, words bred into all of Mire's horses that belonged to hunters alone. The horse relaxed under this palm. He hoisted a confused but silent Tenah up onto its sleek back. Climbing up behind her, he urged the horse down the hill, full speed through Mire's open gates, clutching onto his illusion like scraps of fabric in the wind.

One glimpse of Aeyis. That was all he needed to confirm that this trade was worth it.

Tenah's fingers gripped the horse's mane next to his hands. "You're scaring me."

"Find trust in me. Please." The words soured on his tongue.

As the horse tore through the gate, Renton's magic sputtered. The shard in his chest gave an awful pulse of molten heat through his body, and he curled slightly into Tenah.

Shit. Had they been detected? Would hunters recognize him, son of honorary Notho, with his strong build and fair hair?

Renton opened the horse up on the cobblestone streets shrouded in milky fog. Streetlamps glowed like the sinister eyes of hungry Bogland creatures. If that wasn't enough to drive away enemies, the legions of hunters Mire produced would. The gates here weren't necessary. Threats that entered were just more practice for hunters. Often, they'd let enemies believe they'd escaped then tracked them down in the swamps for sport.

He uttered the command for the horse to turn down a familiar street, halting only when he spotted a boxy, mint green house settled along the bank of Mire's central lake. He leaped from the horse's back and raced to the door of his childhood home.

Aeyis. He sent the thought out, hoping his brother was already probing the surroundings. Their mother had always kept feelers out.

Renton had to remember how to breathe as he stepped onto the porch. The house seemed small now. Curtains in the front two windows hid the interior. The willful plants in the flower boxes his mother had loved so much had withered away.

Gods, what if his assumption was wrong, and Aeyis wasn't even here, restricted to the one village Renton was never allowed to step foot in again? His mind terrorized him with images of his Ashen brother shackled and malnourished. Locked away in Cragnore's pit or frozen on Dreaddix, believing himself to be alone in this cruel world.

His wild thoughts had him kicking in the door instead of knocking.

Surely, Tenah thought him a maniac at this point as she sat quietly atop the horse. He needed to be quick. Hunters would arrive soon.

As he entered the dark, narrow hallway, the scent of ginger tea hit him. He reached out to touch the wobbly spindles of the stair railing. He didn't allow himself a glance into the adjacent sitting room, where his mother had often lurked. He could smell the thick layer of dust there.

Creeping down the hall, he didn't expect to find a grown male sitting at the dining table. Still far too lean but now considerably tall, Aeyis was hunched over one of their mother's ceramic teacups, laughably small in his massive hand. A mess of white curls hid most of his boyish face.

Silver-ringed white irises flicked up to search Renton in silent assessment.

Renton's chest swelled with a mixture of pride and shame. Pride for the brother who had survived these past eleven years without him. Shame for not having come home sooner, exile be damned.

You're long overdue, Aeyis spoke into his mind.

Renton struggled for the words to span the gap between them when something rested against his back, warm even through his armor. He softened a bit, recognizing Tenah's heat. He liked her touching him. What did that say about him as a hunter?

He didn't have time to delve into that thought as voices flooded in from the open door. Renton cursed, reaching back to grasp his father's blade as Councilman Boedworth stepped out of the connected bedroom, his smile as pristine as his tailored suit. Flanking him were two bulky, stone-faced hunters.

"I had a hunch you'd break the rules, Mr. Murfell. My hunters spotted you on the road near Temporra, turning the wrong direction. And here I'd thought breaking your bones after your last indiscretion would purge you of these sinful ways."

Renton stretched an arm back to push Tenah toward the front door. "Run."

All this did was move her closer to another hunter wearing black-and-gold armor.

"Our contract was for the lord and his offspring. Clearly, your skills are lacking." Boedworth frowned, handing a rolled piece of parchment—their contract—to the hunter on his right. A thin jet of flame shot from the hunter's bracer. Soon, it was nothing more than a pile of ashes on the checkered floor.

"I still have time," Renton argued, to which he felt the singe of two ruby eyes on the back of his head. Her yelp had him spinning around. Fury overtook him as the hunter dragged Tenah outside by her hair. By her fucking *hair.*

Renton squeezed his eyes shut, always one to overthink when he stood on the precipice of a life-changing decision. Should he jump, his actions today might be unforgivable in the eyes of the High Court. Everything he'd worked for these past couple of years would be for naught.

But if he stepped back, he would lose the shadow that had awakened something inside of him beyond rage all these years.

No. She was Corrupt. It was *wrong* to want to save her. It went against everything he'd been taught.

So why did it feel like something was gripping his insides and twisting, eager to break off another piece of his soul when there wasn't much left to give?

"Would it have made a difference, Mr. Murfell?" Boedworth asked. "Some claim you're a Corrupt worshipper. They haven't forgotten the state you were in when you crawled home from the desert that day, covered in the blood of your spineless father and reeking of that dark magic."

The last fiber of Renton's self-control snapped, and adrenaline coursed through him, wicked hot.

Fuck it. He was done.

His blade sang through the air, slashing at Boedworth's neck. One of his hunters parried the attack, throwing Renton back. He used the momentum to bolt for the front door.

It didn't even occur to him until he was out on the street that Aeyis hadn't moved from the dining table. Wrath nearly turned his vision red as he spotted the hunter throwing Tenah, thrashing and spitting, into the back of a windowless prison cart, her wrists bound in shackles. Their eyes met briefly before the doors clanged shut, and in that look, she'd burned every bit of her hatred and pain.

He'd made a horrible mistake bringing her into Mire. He should have left her in the swamps. He should have left her at The Indigo to heal. Stolen a horse for her and sent her off to her kingdom. He never should have pulled her out of the ruins of her home.

His blade arced toward the head of the hunter in black-and-gold armor. The hunter dodged it and slammed a boot into Renton's stomach. Renton grunted but held his ground.

Four more hunters appeared behind him. Fighting one was difficult enough, but five? Why could nothing ever go right for him? He'd fought against all odds. Not once had something turned in his favor. All he'd ever wanted was a better life for Aeyis.

Now, he wanted Tenah's freedom too.

The hunter that had assaulted Tenah struck with a dagger. Renton sidestepped the blade but took a gauntlet to the chin from another hunter. He hit the street hard. Pinned by a knee to the back of his neck, he clenched his throbbing jaw as he heard the jangle of shackles.

"I still had time, damn it," Renton growled, unable to turn his head and glare at the councilman that had leveled his world. "If you imprison me, you're allowing that Chaos lord to carry on killing innocents."

"He's already done that, from what I've heard," Boedworth said. "You've failed, Mr. Murfell. Accept it. There's always another hunter to replace a dead one."

An unnaturally chilling gust of wind tore down the street, raising goosebumps along Renton's skin. The pressure at the base of his skull vanished. Immediately, he pushed up onto his feet in time to watch all five hunters go rigid then walk right into the lake in union. None of them resurfaced.

Renton's shoulders dropped, his blade hanging useless from his hand.

A sound like that of a wounded animal spun him around. He spotted Boedworth on his hands and knees, trapped within a tornado of Ashen magic. Renton couldn't help but relish in it for a moment—the sweet melody of his employer pleading for his life.

That satisfaction rapidly melted as Aeyis emerged from the house. His shoulders were hunched, his hair mussed as if he'd just rolled off the coach, no matter the fact that he'd just killed five hunters as if they were nothing more than stones to throw into the lake.

Vibrating with energy, Renton shook out his sword arm and walked over to the quivering councilman. Ignore the drowning hunters. His employment with Boedworth ended today.

A burst of cold magic smashed through the mental barriers he'd learned to build in camp.

Sorry to interrupt your vengeance, brother, Aeyis said. *Mias is coming.*

"Shit." Facing Mias was worse than anything Renton could imagine. Boedworth enjoyed dishing out punishments, but Mias reveled in torture.

Renton's eyes swept the street for any ripples of magic. He locked on the prison cart rocking up the dirt road, about to be devoured by the dense swamps. He glanced back at Boedworth and Aeyis.

I could melt his mind, but then we face our brother, Aeyis said.

Renton growled, pinching the bridge of his nose. No matter how much he desired Boedworth's death, he also wasn't keen on taking up the title of executioner again.

His stomach twisted at having to give his little brother the order. *No more blood on your hands.*

Aeyis didn't argue. *Escape plan?*

Potentially a very stupid one, Renton answered, breaking for the jutting, moss-covered dungeon on the other side of the lake. He might have been grateful for the seamless communication with his brother, if not for his icy magic sifting through memories better left buried.

Long gone was the frail child immobilized by his overwhelming abilities.

Who the hell trained you? he asked as Aeyis met his pace, crumpling two of the guards at the dungeon's gates. They stormed the dungeon, Renton shoving back guards to give Aeyis a chance to immobilize them temporarily.

"Ren? Is that… Is it really you?" a husky voice called.

Stride faltering, Renton scanned behind them for the source. His body tensed up, his heart picking up speed as he took in the tanned face and chin-length dark hair of the hunter that had appeared in the hall. The hunter looked to Aeyis for confirmation, his features scrunched up in a way Renton had never seen before.

"This isn't a trick?" Gireth asked, words barely above a whisper.

Aeyis shook his head. "No trick."

Without hesitation, Gireth charged Renton, gripping him around the back of the neck and tugging him into a crushing embrace. Renton choked back emotion.

Gireth. His best friend—no, his *brother* who had stood by him during the worst of Mias's cruelty. Had suffered with him in camp, starved and beaten and broken down in the mud and rain and toxins.

Gireth gave him one more solid pat to the back and then pushed him away. "How? Mias told me you were dead. But you're here. Does that mean you're free from Boedworth?"

"Not exactly. I can explain later—"

Horns rang out through Mire, echoing like a pack of wolves at night.

Gireth cracked a wide smile. "Don't tell me those are for you."

Renton couldn't help his own mischievous grin, heart soaring at this surprising reunion. "Would you expect anything less?"

His friend unbuckled his chest plate stamped with the bronze hammer they had balked at as children. Only rejected hunters became guards in Mire's dungeons. What had happened to Gireth to end up here?

"Are you sure this is what you want?" Renton asked. "Understand if you run with me, you face criminal charges, at the very least."

But he already knew the answer. Gireth had no family in Mire. No future beyond violence that he could ever see. His grandfather had shipped him to camp at the age of five, at his wits' end with the boy's inability to do anything well except stir up trouble. Failure to complete camp came with the stipulation that the boy would not be returned but dumped on Dreaddix instead.

"I follow you," Gireth said, rooting his lethal form in their path. "I always have."

Renton nodded, fighting back the tidal wave of what felt like actual happiness. *Years* surviving in hell. He'd dive right back in head first just to experience this moment again. There was no denying it—cracks were forming in the iron he'd cast around his heart.

United, they carved their way through guards to the prison yard. It was where Boedworth kept one of his most valued and dangerous secrets.

Renton had never been so thrilled to see the mammoth, black-scaled welkin. He'd expected Boedworth to slaughter it, fearful of the beast escaping and exacting vengeance after Ashens failed to leash its mind. Hauling it into Mire had proven enough of a hazard that the councilman had decided it belonged in chains, turning instead to more malleable beasts for Dreaddix transportation.

So chained, the welkin had remained here through most of Renton's training.

As the massive welkin lifted its head, it was almost cathartic to stare back into its gleaming red eyes.

It recognizes you, Aeyis said.

For they had all been chained: the welkin to this dungeon, Aeyis to this village, Gireth to the hunting clans, and Renton to a monster parading about as a politician.

Withdrawing a lockpick, Renton freed the welkin from its shackles, aware of its sharp, intelligent gaze. He couldn't help his desire to save things. It was the part of his father that lived on inside of him. The part he couldn't kill off, no matter how hard he'd strived to.

"Please don't eat us. Please don't eat us," Gireth chanted, though he didn't cower away as the beast stretched its head and wings into the fog-smeared sky.

Watching in awe, Renton held back a grin, remembering how he'd scaled these very walls as a child. At first, he'd craved the danger, eager to catch a glimpse of the beast Mias had talked about at dinner the night before. Quickly, though, that curiosity morphed into despair. He didn't fear the beast as it turned its inferno eyes on him. No, he feared how far hunters were being twisted by Boedworth's control.

Somehow, the beast hadn't thought a child a threat. It never so much as blew a lick of flame at him as he'd returned countless times, scaling the outside prison wall and tossing in scraps of meat. He envied the welkin's fortitude, never cowering to its masters, unlike him when Mias flashed that wicked grin that promised pain. Had the welkin known back then that Renton would be its salvation? Or had it just assumed him too weak to bother with?

The prison yard doors slammed open, hunters shouting out orders and hurling sharpened weapons. All were met with a stream of emerald fire from the welkin's maw.

Gireth yelped. "Did you know it could do that?"

Renton scaled the welkin's back, leaping onto the metal platform fused into the bones of its spine, a half-cage meant to ferry prisoners and Corrupt to their fate on Dreaddix. Gireth and Aeyis followed suit.

"I suspected," Renton answered.

The welkin sank its claws into the stone walls. Up it climbed, low growls rumbling from its chest as it fought against the slick, mossy surface and atrophy in its limbs.

That's it. We're almost free.

As the welkin shoved off the prison wall and took uneven flight, Renton peered over the platform railing at the mobs of hunters surrounding the prison.

Oh yes, he should have done this ages ago.

Chapter Twelve

TENAH

Mind frantic with half-feral thoughts, the darkness of the prison cart reminded Tenah too much of death. She scooted to the doors and ran her hands along the surface, searching for hinges or rust spots. Chains dragged at the other end of the cart, and she stilled.

"Don't waste your energy. The doors won't budge, and the shackles are magicked to constrict your abilities." The feminine voice had a thick Vristarian accent like her father. What was a northern fire kingdom native doing in the Boglands?

For show, Tenah ignited a tiny crimson ember in her palm. "Few things are impervious to Delemor flame."

The petite woman's catlike, sky blue eyes widened. She had light brown skin and a sharp bob of black hair. Tenah appreciated the way she wore her leathers and chains with an attitude, arms dangled over her bent knees as if she was used to being labeled dangerous.

"Well." The woman smiled back. "That explains why *you're* here. You wouldn't happen to be related to the murderous Kherathi Delemor? Everyone on the isles heard his declaration of war."

A lump formed in Tenah's throat. "Can it really be considered a declaration of war if he's raving mad with Chaos?"

The woman shrugged, examining her plum-painted nails. Tenah's gaze slid to the gold medallion inlaid on her form-fitted leather armor, an elegant letter E centered between two overlapping diamonds. Her stomach churned. The mark of an Embassy employee—an assassin from Denoden. Her father had the same medallion tucked away in his attic desk. She'd discovered it one morning while left with the manor staff.

"Vesara Sut'hik," the woman said by way of introduction. "So what's our plan, pretty girl?"

Tenah's brows kneaded. "Excuse me?"

"For getting out of here." Vesara rattled her chains. "You're not going to accept this, are you?"

Tenah's mouth parted, but words failed her.

"Listen." The assassin's eyes glittered. "We're not en route to Dreaddix. They transport those prisoners at night. Which means we were packaged up to deliver to Cragnore. It means the crooked councilman of this forsaken isle deemed us worthy of a personal, intimate sentencing. Nothing good will come of this. And judging by your ties to a powerful, renowned criminal, he has plans for you."

The cart lurched to a stop. Tenah went careening into the back wall. Warm hands helped her back onto her feet. "No blood. You'll survive."

A thunderous roar shook the cart. Vesara let out a string of fluent Denesè. "I prayed to Renix to save us. Should salvation come in the form of a Bogland monster, I will question his validity as a benevolent elemental."

Tenah didn't have time to share her own twisted feelings about the Greater Elementals as the lock on the doors screeched. Her pulse hammered. When the doors cracked open, she unleashed her flames, growling when they came out as nothing more than pathetic sparks.

Someone shouted her name. She snuffed her flames, and Renton immediately stepped into the cart, his electric stare intimidating enough to stop the flow of blood in her veins. Stupidly, she didn't bolt when he picked the lock on her shackles and dropped them to the cart floor.

Vesara held out her shackles. "Share the love?"

Awaiting Tenah's nod of approval, Renton freed the assassin. In a flash, Vesara was out of the cart. A tanned male hunter with lean muscle caught her around the waist and swung her around like a child. "Are we sure we want this one running free? Heard rumors about her from other prison guards."

Planting her boots into the ground, Vesara flipped the hunter over her shoulder, dropping him onto his back in a terrifying demonstration of brute strength.

The hunter wheezed. "Yep. She's dangerous."

Tenah's focus slid back to Renton. Her heart was thudding too hard against her ribs at the way he was looking at her. Whatever his intentions, she couldn't want anything from him.

"Stay away from me," she ordered, easing back.

A pained look flashed across his face. "Tenah."

"You took me right to your employer." She blasted a warning shot of fire at his boots. Sparks ricocheted off the floor. "Saving me, stitching me up, taking me away from my home—it was all just to keep me alive long enough to execute some stupid contract. What did you stand to earn? Krotens? Rank?"

"My brother's freedom from eleven years of imprisonment and abuse."

Tenah deflated. He looked so torn up, so defeated, it was messing with her ability to make solid decisions.

"Why are you here?" she asked.

"To set things right," Renton said. "Come with me, and we'll get you off this isle. I promise."

"Consider things righted. I want nothing else to do with you."

She brushed past him, jumping from the cart. Only, the horrible creature that had halted their procession made her want to scramble back inside the iron box, her recently healed wounds pulsing in remembrance.

The welkin stood taller than the trees. Its black, skeletal wings scraped the sky as it fought off a dozen hunters with spears and blades. An Ashen stood atop the platform secured to its back. Snow white dust coalesced around him like a blizzard.

There was *no* way she was flying again. End of story.

A wave of bittersweet magic drew her gaze to the Bogland trees. Two robed figures stepped out of the vines, a towering male wearing a malevolent smile and a curvy woman with a halo of crackling dark magic that made Tenah's body constrict in want of its power.

"Mias," Renton uttered, shielding Tenah.

She frowned, peeking around his broad form. "The brother that pushed you into the lake?"

"Stay alert. He's a dual caster."

Tenah didn't have time to ask what two magics he excelled in when the air around them rippled. The hooded figures vanished as the swamp transformed into a lush, rich forest of autumn-stained trees. A feingrot slunk into view, identical to the beast that had killed Ames. It tilted its head in taunt.

Dread sluiced through her, thick and heavy. How was that even possible?

"Your brother wouldn't happen to be an Ashen with illusion magic?" she asked.

Mias was more corporeal than Ames's ghostly constitution. Though, she knew from Ames's stories that mixing Ashen and shadow bloodlines could result in variances of appearances and abilities.

Renton didn't answer but unsheathed a serrated knife from his belt.

She bit down on her lip, tasting salt from her perspiration. It stung her eyes and blurred her vision. "The feingrot isn't real, right?"

"I'd like to say no, but anything's possible with Mias. He'll either manipulate creatures nearby to attack or use distractions to sneak in close and carve us up himself. Either way, he's going to take his time."

"Should we be concerned about the Ashen atop the gigantic killing machine?" Vesara cut in.

The other hunter fell in line as well. "Aeyis might be our only ticket out of this mess." He tipped his chin up at Tenah. "How you doing? Name's Gireth. I'm your boyfriend's best friend."

Tenah opened her mouth to protest, but Vesara interrupted. "More like her boyfriend's pet dung beetle."

Tenah considered her options. She could bolt. Leave these dangerous strangers to rip each other apart. There had to be a range to Mias's illusion, but how far did it extend? Ames's range had spanned their entire estate.

Anger burned in her gut. Even if she managed to break free, she wasn't confident she would survive the Boglands alone.

Gireth cupped his hands around his mouth and called out, "What are you waiting for, shit licker?"

The feingrot vanished. Tenah's heart slammed against her ribs as the red leaves of the familiar forest shriveled, emitting tiny wisps of black smoke. Tree trunks cracked in two, twining into grotesque shapes. Roots slithered up from the ground like snakes, weaving together to form mounds that resembled trapped corpses. Rot hung thick in the air, mingled with the coppery tang of Chaos.

"This. This right here is why we hate the Boglands," Tenah mumbled.

She expected a laugh from Renton. Had possibly hoped for it to help calm her fraying nerves. But he hadn't shifted out of death mode, warning her that this was serious.

A mangled cry quickened her pulse.

Fog tumbled in, obscuring most of the enemies that had formed a death ring around them.

"I don't much care for this," Vesara said, retrieving two tiny knives from sheaths along her back and twirling them between agile fingers.

"Imagine a childhood of it," Renton replied darkly.

One of the Corrupt charged, its limbs jutting out at horrible, broken angles. Vesara hurled a knife into its throat, dropping it almost instantly. Brackish, poisonous blood bubbled out. Then enemies were charging them from all directions.

Tenah couldn't move, fear roiling in her stomach as the silver-eyed boy materialized a few paces in front of her.

You will deliver the ruination of this world.

Chapter Thirteen
TENAH

Renton's malicious brother had fished another horror from her mind.

You made a promise to me. You said I would be safe, the silver-eyed boy accused, and Tenah winced as his spine let out a sharp crack. He dropped onto all fours, no longer shadow but a creature mutated by Chaos. Black clouds of toxin streamed behind him as he raced toward her.

Tenah stumbled backward over her boots, her gaze sweeping the road for the others. Of course Renton had vanished. But instead of directing her rage at him, she was furious with herself for her cowardice. When had she ever relied on others to fight her battles? Had death robbed her of courage?

Red flames erupted along her arms. She forced her legs to halt on the road. Whatever this fight took, no matter the amount of magic she had to expend, she *would* live to hunt down the demon that was her father.

She fired two bolts of magic in succession. Her shots missed as the Corrupt hit the ground, its limp body skidding close to her legs. Stunned, she gazed down at its corpse. A serrated knife jutted from its eye.

Renton.

Tenah didn't have a chance to move away before tendrils of black electricity sparked from its body, leaping onto her skin. She jolted upright. Her breaths came in short spurts as the forest darkened around her, sucking her into an inescapable black hole.

She dropped to the ground, curling into the fetal position as she smashed her hands against her pounding temples. The silver-eyed boy she was certain she'd just watched die knelt down beside her. She had the brief thought to run. To fight. Something wasn't right, especially when his harsh smile brought warmth to her chest as he swept her tears away.

Tenah, you're going to have to be stronger. Absorb it. Absorb the darkness, and you will walk free from this.

She bit down hard on her tongue, striving to break whatever spell this was. A memory? Renton's brother fucking with her head? Would she be able to escape it with a bit more of that unholy dark magic pumping through her channels?

Visions of Ames's death resurfaced, only it wasn't feingrot looming over him. It was her father with a blood-drenched blade.

This is your fault, he accused.

She screamed as he buried the blade into Ames's ribs. Again and again. There was nothing she could do to stop him. After all, one strike was all it had taken for her father to kill her too.

Powerless. You are powerless.

The words echoed in her head, bouncing around so fast the ground lurched beneath her.

"Tenah!" Renton's booming voice snapped her back into the forest.

His bright eyes, brimming with concern, met hers over hordes of writhing enemies. Then he was sucked back into battle with three clawing, furious Corrupt. Using spurts of magic to disappear, he made efficient work of cleaving them apart. Gireth wielded his glaive with the same unforgiving, brutal technique. Buried up to his shins in corpses, his grin never wavered. It was as if he'd peered into the depths of the fallen elemental Xith's temples and found the madness there lacking.

She might have stayed ensnared by their undiluted hatred of Corrupt had she not caught the faint glint of a spider web in a beam of sunlight above their heads. Only, this string thrummed like an electric current.

Chaos.

Tenah blasted a spark of red flame into the sky. It sizzled as it collided with an invisible forcefield of magic, and for a moment, an entire web of dark magic rippled into visibility. She could see lines of energy feeding into every monster surrounding them, powering them like some sort of hive mind.

As long as Mias kept them trapped in his illusions, Chaos woman was going to keep sending enemies at them. Tenah needed to get out of Mias's range, then she could better assess how to deal with this situation.

She hoped Mias was distracted enough with the others to let her slip through as she shot off the path, hurtling over gnarled roots and vines. Fog along the forest floor coalesced into growing shapes, propelling her legs faster and faster until...

Tenah halted, fury bubbling in her channels as she found herself right back on the path where she'd started. Mias had run her in a circle.

Absorb it, Chaos tried again, yanking her head down to look at the Corrupt boy's corpse.

Would you give it a rest already? she raged, charging back into the forest with heightened determination. The drumming of limbs pursued this time. Her heart quickened, and her hands crackled with flames.

A Corrupt burst from the fog. Its elongated nails raised up, prepared to slice into her flesh. She devoured the thing in flames. Her eyes snapped wide as it shrieked in agony before exploding into a cloud of black dust that stained the ground.

She stared down at that stain as footsteps pounded closer from all directions. Where was the Chaos caster finding all of them? Could she manifest them somehow? Had they been shadow before that woman had gotten her hands on them?

Tenah needed to move. She knew that. Glowing, orange-slitted eyes materialized in the fog, accompanied by giant black wings and gangly arms with long talons.

Blood hammered in her veins as she crumbled to her fear. She didn't have to verbalize the order—her body was already siphoning the black

Chaos dust into her channels.

There was no other choice. She couldn't be weak. She couldn't be powerless.

Her arms trembled from the immense amount of hot energy she'd absorbed. It lifted her hand and cleaved the air in two.

Climb in, little one.

Tenah held her breath as she stepped into the Void. So many sources of pulsing magic. They expanded beyond what she'd gleaned from astral projecting, an endless sea of possibilities. The birthplace of all magic.

Large antennae bobbed in her peripheral vision, jolting her survival instincts. A long, segmented body scuttled around her in a wide berth.

Corrupt or something more deadly? She didn't care to stick around to find out.

Tenah broke into a sprint, but how far would she need to run before she reached the edge of Mias's range? How did time and space work in the Void?

The thought struck her—she could keep running. Flee so far from the Boglands that Renton would never find her.

Guilt churned in her stomach. Wouldn't that contradict her reason for this second life? She'd bargained in order to save lives, not doom them.

Channels throbbing with dark power, she carelessly burned another hole between worlds and leaped through it. A gnarled tree root hooked her boot, and she tumbled down a small hill, nails scraping moss. She caught herself on a rock just in time to witness a pincer snapping out of the rift. She blew out a hot breath, thankful the creature's body was too large to escape.

"Found her!" a voice yelled.

Whirling around, Tenah came face-to-face with the Chaos caster. Her ruby mouth lifted in a smile. Beside her, Mias's outstretched arms shook with the effort to maintain his illusions as Corrupt flung themselves inside his enormous sphere of warbled magic.

"We need her alive, Svetlana," he said through gritted teeth.

Tenah didn't wait to see what Svetlana had in store for her. Scrambling back up the hill, Tenah tore the rift wide open. The leathery, segmented monster that emerged twisted such horror on Svetlana's face, Tenah didn't know whether to feel elated or disgusted with herself. Unleashing monsters from the Void brought her too close to her father.

The feingrot unfurled its body, stretching up to the treetops. Haunting orange eyes locked on Svetlana, and its mouth unhinged, offering a view of too many sharp teeth.

Svetlana bumped into Mias, jarring him. He cursed as his magic rippled and dissolved.

"Thank Renix," Vesara exclaimed, kicking a Corrupt off her growing mountain of bodies.

"Tolroc!" Gireth hollered, pointing a finger in the direction of the monster Tenah had set loose. He stabbed his glaive into a mutated body and clapped his hands excitedly. "What a treat this is! Wanna take bets on how fast it rips their limbs off?"

As the tolroc rushed Svetlana, Tenah's focus shifted to Renton. Her chest ached at the slash on his cheek. He was panting heavily but intact.

Renton turned to his eldest brother.

"Go ahead and try, filth," Mias uttered, spitting on the ground.

Lightning-tinted flames burst from Tenah's palms. She gathered them into compact spheres she planned to hurl at Mias. Except, the overwhelming metallic scent of a brewing storm lured her attention back to Svetlana.

What was left of the tolroc hit the ground, its tattered body still steaming from the woman's attack. Svetlana had charged herself with so much Chaos, it was impossible for Tenah to ignore. She shuddered. Her body craved the heat and thrum of something more potent.

More powerful.

More sinister.

More.

Growling, Tenah launched her bolts of magic at Svetlana. They were sucked right into her expanding storm of crackling lightning. Chaos exploded from Svetlana's marred hands, forming a crackling net of lightning above them. All heads, including the remaining Corrupt, lifted to witness death given physical form.

Time slowed as Tenah's gaze darted between the storm, Renton, and the others. Renton was shouting for her to run. He seemed to enjoy doing that, telling her what to do as if he knew best. Vesara chanted prayers in old Denesè. And Gireth…

He held out his arms as if to embrace death.

You'd be disappointed.

What Tenah had deduced from Chaos thus far was that it was attracted to power. It wanted to grow. To *expand*. If she could charge herself with enough of it, maybe she could become the sole striking point for the woman's detonation.

Bracing, Tenah invited darkness in. It was a stretch, but the dark magic in her channels seemed to rumble in approval, scorching through her muscles and rattling her bones.

About time, little one, voices cooed. *Let's devour our enemies.*

Only the Corrupt, she commanded, as if Chaos would listen.

Laughter echoed in her head as strands of her own lightning whipped out, leashing Svetlana's magic and tugging it down into every single enemy in sight, including the woman herself.

Tenah expected pain. However, the rush of euphoric power was so much worse. Tingles crawled from her head all the way down to curl her toes in her boots. With this magic, she never had to fear anything again.

Let them suffer.

Burn them. Incinerate their flesh and bones.

Sink our teeth and claws into…

…our vessel. Teach them to bow, little one.

Tenah spilled her magic into the world until the Corrupt and Svetlana were no more.

Panic gripped her around the throat as lightning branched out in search of more enemies. She had no control over it. No way to stop the flow. Dust from the exploded Corrupt spiraled toward her. A tendril of her own lightning twitched up and nicked her eye, leaving a film she couldn't blink away.

You did well. I've got it now.

Her muscles stiffened at the icy words implanted in her mind. Instantly, the flow of Chaos through her channels shut off like a faucet.

An Ashen stood next to her, tall and willowy. Tenah sucked in a breath as he turned his silver eyes on her. There was no other way to describe him but adorable. Though he shared Renton's height, Aeyis's features were boyish enough that she felt the instant need to protect him. He was more spectral than the eldest brother, skin and hair kissed by moonlight, and surrounded by the flecks of the glittering white magic Tenah had become accustomed to from her guardian.

A terrifying thought flashed through her mind. What if Renton had acquired some of that mind magic as well? What if he'd been manipulating her emotions from the start?

Aeyis pushed curls back from his face, and Tenah shivered as a flash of black magic streaked through his temples. Her mouth dried out. Who the hell bred these Murfell boys? Chaos and mind magic wielded in union? Aeyis was an abomination.

No, Aeyis might have answers to harnessing this dark magic.

Please don't tell my brother, Aeyis said. *He doesn't know.*

What? she asked. *That you harbor the same disease he hunts down without sympathy?*

You don't know him.

Aeyis turned on the eldest Murfell. A snarl cut through the humid, coppery air.

"You worthless little twats," Mias bellowed. "I should have drowned both of you in that lake years ago. You disgrace our family. You disgust me!"

Hot magic pricked at Tenah's knuckles, but Aeyis brushed cool fingers against them.

He's mine, Aeyis said.

She caught another surge of black veins beneath his moonlit skin as he struck his brother with such a forceful mental blow Mias started shaking and foaming at the mouth.

Tenah grimaced, her eyes drifting to Renton. Breaths labored and hand still clutching his blade, he looked between his brothers.

"Aeyis," Renton warned, brows kneading.

"One more death on my hands won't taint me," Aeyis replied softly. "No one will even miss him."

Whatever mental words the brothers exchanged finally deflated Aeyis. Freed, the eldest Murfell stumbled off into the trees. Renton started forward as if to pursue, but then the swamps tilted at an angle, and Tenah lurched sideways with it.

Was this another mind game?

Strong, calloused hands steadied her. Over Renton's shoulder, she saw Aeyis discreetly swipe at the drip of black blood from his nose. Renton should be worried for his brother, but here he was, clutching onto her, turning her chin side-to-side with his fingers.

"That was a very foolish thing you did," Renton said. "Are you hurt?"

"I'm fine," she muttered. He was so gentle, so twisted up with concern, she didn't have the heart to swat him away. "Just get us away from this place."

ACT II

THE GIFT OF DESTRUCTION

Chapter Fourteen
TENAH

Night enveloped the crew as the welkin sailed over trees tall enough to reach the stars. Their trunks rivaled the largest buildings Tenah had ever seen. Between pale blue leaves, arched temples carved from marbled wood tediously balanced on their branches.

Like birdhouses, she thought. Nalites—Hathrowyn's warriors—dashed in and out of them, efficient like green hummingbirds, only deadly.

Tenah dropped her head onto her folded arms propped on the middle bar of the welkin's iron platform. It was the only thing keeping her exhausted bones upright when all it wanted to do was shut down. Her legs dangled off the platform edge, heavy and useless.

From her little experience casting Chaos, she'd quickly learned the cost. It was a thrilling rush in the moment but incredibly painful in the hours after.

It's not the power or the high that most shadows become addicted to. It's the relief from the pain Chaos leaves in its wake, Ames had explained to her once.

"Hey. How's it going?" Gireth plopped down next to her, oblivious to the "fuck off" vibes she'd radiated the entire flight.

Tenah sighed and squeezed her eyes shut.

"Have you ever been to Hathrowyn?" he asked, his tone conversational.

She didn't want to be rude, but she was a bit averse to anything born from the Boglands right now, especially hunters that enjoyed wearing tiny skulls and bones.

Gireth chuckled, and her eyes flicked to him. "Not much of a talker, huh? That's okay."

Lit up by moonlight, he appeared close in age to her. His brown hair was so shiny she had the urge to run her fingers through its strands to see if it was actually made of silk. The only flaw in his handsome face was a slight crook to his nose. Broken in a previous fight, she guessed. She didn't miss the way he flexed his biceps as he pulled his hair up into a bun.

"If you don't mind the company, I'm a great distraction. Used to annoy Renton to sleep when we were kids." He wrinkled his nose. "He struggled with that, the sleep thing."

Tenah snorted. "Do demons even sleep?"

"You wouldn't think so, but having relied upon the sleep schedule of demons to survive on Dreaddix, I can confidently say they do." His accompanying smile had the power to convince a shadow to drink poison and enjoy it. His charm was a weapon in itself.

She frowned. "Dreaddix?"

Gireth slung his tan arms over the railing, his expression turning pensive. "I spent three years there."

"Renton too?" Tenah asked, stomach twisting. She denied herself a glance back at the hunter she knew had been watching her with those devastating, electric eyes.

"Nah. Boedworth exiled him from the village when we were kids. Until today, I believed him dead." He smoothed his fingers along the back of his neck as the lump in his throat bobbed.

Tenah's brows furrowed as she rubbed at the dull pain in her chest. The hunter cared deeply for her betrayer. She understood that tight-knit bond. Before the night of terrors in her home, her loyalty to Ames had been fierce. Closer than blood. She blinked away furious tears and dared a glance back at the others, meeting those shocking green-and-yellow eyes, cautious and full of regret. Her gaze dipped to the silvery white line carved into his neck. She knew there were more scars tucked away. Scars on the inside too.

Tenah clenched her teeth. *No, he hunted me. He plotted to imprison me. He stabbed my father. He hates Corrupt.*

She would strangle the part of her brain that wanted to let go of her anger. It was all she had now. There was no space in her wounded heart to build anything with anyone. As soon as the welkin arrived at their destination, she planned on bailing.

Gireth stretched his arms up with a loud groan. Then he rolled flat on his back, tucking his arms behind his head. "I've missed the open world. Time away reminds us what life is truly about, doesn't it?"

"And what's that?" Tenah couldn't help but ask.

He closed his eyes. "Freedom, baby. Sweet, sweet freedom."

With a heavy sigh, she gave in to Gireth. She laid on her back, casting her gaze up at the stars. Not long into his easy chatter about the weather in Mire, she fell asleep.

A spectral figure woke her with a hesitant mental prodding.

I'm not afraid of you, she said, peeling herself off the platform. Her muscles had loosened with rest. How long had she slept? Rubbing crust from her eyes, she bit back a growl of frustration as the film coating her bad eye remained. She didn't want to think about the damage being permanent. Her father had gone years before any signs of Corruption had made themselves apparent.

Aeyis knelt beside her. Pearly white magic hovered over his skin, giving him a dreamlike, monochromatic aura. His presence didn't bother her, even with his lack of expression. Telltale signs of Ashen emotion would come in time as she learned the shift in his magic.

He tugged at a curl of snow white hair. *If only the rest of shadowkind would accept that we're actually quite peaceful. We just enjoy a bit of meddling.*

She rolled her eyes, a smile playing on her lips. Ames had been about as sinister as a gossipy old maid. He enjoyed information gathering over bloodshed. At least, that was what he'd told her.

I do have to apologize, Aeyis said. *I'm not any more versed in Chaos than you are. I know you expected me to be, but I've managed on sheer willpower alone.*

Tenah didn't try to hide her frown. Not when he could pluck the disappointment from her mind. Aeyis hadn't moved from his position, still sifting through her thoughts, no doubt. *And just for reassurance, Renton can't read or alter minds. Mias used to tease him that the magical talent skipped the middle brother.*

Gritting her teeth, Tenah muttered a thanks and rose to her feet. No need to mention that she didn't plan on sticking around long enough to care.

Denoden rose up on the horizon, growing taller among the patchwork quilt of crops as they flew closer. The northern fire kingdom's domes shone like polished gold and jade gemstones. Stone buildings dominated the sky, reaching for the spattering of white clouds, boasting the capital's wealth.

Denoden was the largest city on the Burning Plains. Its surrounding farms provided food for most of the isle, as well as the High Court. More than that, it held the reputation for the liveliest city.

Excitement bloomed in her chest, despite her grim reason for returning to her home isle. She gripped the platform railing, striving to remember her purpose. But now that she was here, the thought of marching south across the border to confront her savage father and his army of feingrot seemed wildly reckless. A fool's errand.

She *could* send word to her warlord uncle…though that might result in more hellfire than what his brother—her father—was most likely spreading through their kingdom.

A day in the city to recoup and strategize would permit her the opportunity to explore the Abyss—the shady underground market of Denoden—where she might find secrets to help grow her power or, better yet, harness her father's darkness. Thank the elementals someone in her family had used that crude ink map of the market as a bookmark in a text on alchemy. She'd spent hours tracing those lines in the manor library, committing them to memory.

The welkin spiraled to the ground, sinking its claws into rich soil. Eager to rid itself of pests, it shook its body, and Tenah's knuckles turned bone white as she clutched the railing.

"Can I help?" Renton asked, extending a hand.

"You don't get to touch me." Her cheeks flushed. Turning away from his aid, she slid down the welkin's stomach. Her palms were scraped raw by the time her boots thudded down on solid ground. It was worth it to see Renton's frown as he dropped down beside her.

Gireth whistled and smacked Renton on the shoulder. "Ren, what have you done to screw things up this time?"

"I think the proper question is what haven't I done?" Renton muttered.

Tenah scrunched her nose in frustration. *Self-deprecating asshole.*

As Tenah stalked toward Denoden's wooden gates, Vesara bumped her with a shoulder. "You should try kicking him in the balls. It's a great stress reliever."

Tenah snorted. "I'm not sure I'd be able to stop with one kick."

A gust of wind rolled through the waist-high cornfields and caught her hair, tossing it into her face. She pivoted, watching in awe as the welkin heaved off the ground with powerful thrusts of its wings.

Her sympathy went out to the beast. Blacksmiths in Firesteep might be able to remove the platform fused to its back, but she didn't think the welkin would trust tools and fire from shadow hands after what it had probably endured in the Boglands.

The impending metal gates of Denoden screeched open, and four soldiers in bronze armor strutted out in unison.

"What nice weapons they have," Gireth said under his breath. "Think they'd trade?" He lifted his worn glaive into the sunlight. It looked like it was held together by strips of worn, dirty cloth.

"You couldn't pay them to take that splinter off your hands," Renton said.

Gireth cracked a grin. "A splinter that has found its way into so many hearts."

"State your business," the lead guard ordered, motioning his squad to a halt a few paces away. His mouth had such a straight cut to it, Tenah wondered if he'd ever learned how to smile or frown.

"I see they sent the welcoming committee," Vesara said, her hands on her hips.

Tenah squirmed at the tension brewing in the hot air. From what she'd read, Denoden didn't have much of a military presence outside of the Embassy, the only legal organization of assassins in operation on the isles. The Embassy was restricted from forming alliances, therefore, Denoden was often overlooked as an ally in anything but throwing extravagant parties and growing corn.

This crew of misfits would rip these guards to shreds.

"If you can't find an answer, we can always escort you in chains," the lead show pony brayed.

"We're in need of temporary shelter. That's all," Renton said.

The guard toyed with the hilt of the sword at his hip. "Is King Izral expecting you?"

Spewing what Tenah could only decipher as inappropriate words in the Denesè language, Vesara took charge, marching straight up to the leader. Though she stood a few heads shorter, her confidence wilted him on the spot.

"You can go tell that worthless pile of cow dung who demands entry," Vesara raged.

The leader's head tilted down to the gold emblem on her leather armor. His brows shot up. When he dipped into a low bow, the three other soldiers followed suit.

"Kala Sut'hik, your presence has been sorely missed throughout Denoden. Please accept our sincere apologies. You've been away so long, I had forgotten your beauty," the leader remarked.

"Feel free to forget everything but my ferocity," she said.

Who the hell have I fallen in with? Two Bogland hunters—one of which had spent time on Dreaddix—a Chaos mind-melting Ashen, and a highly esteemed Embassy assassin? If King Izral was anything but a notorious partier, he would deny them access to his city.

However, if Vesara held some sort of sway here...Surely she could be persuaded to help, right?

The soldiers waved them through the gates. Gireth patted a hand on Vesara's petite shoulder. "Who knew you had connections, Sut'hik? What'd you do to win over the king, threaten to kiss him?"

A swift kick between his legs dropped Gireth to his knees with a grunt.

Vesara crowded his space, a hand balled in his shirt. "Speak of me doing anything with that mongrel again, and I'll sink ten of my dullest knives in you. The rest I'll save for when you're just about healed."

"More than ten, huh?" Gireth huffed, a smile appearing.

Vesara shoved him and stomped through the gates.

"Called it," Aeyis said, giving Gireth's cheek a little slap as he passed him.

Gireth waved a hand at Vesara's back. "Where would she even hide all of them in that suit?"

A laugh bubbled up in Tenah's throat. She didn't fight it. Not when Renton grimaced as though he was caught between arguing siblings.

Unlike Firesteep, where wrought iron gates segregated class, Denoden had no barriers.

The soldiers escorted them through rickety wooden buildings stacked precariously high along dirt roads. Beggars haggled with merchants over ripe fruits displayed in makeshift stalls. Dirt-smudged, barefoot children ran amok, weaving in and out of motorized carts that kicked up dust.

A cough rattled Tenah's lungs as they walked through a cloud of exhaust. Thank the elementals those carts never caught on in Firesteep. Her father had said Sardoth preferred not to put more krotens in enemy pockets for the resources needed to fuel them.

The crew turned a corner at a bustling intersection, entering the wealthy heart of the city. Picturesque marble and stucco monstrosities towered on either side of the stone streets. Architects had carved their legacies into every archway and balcony. Flowering vines draped from open terraces, filling the air with a pleasant scent.

Their escorts disbanded as Vesara pushed open the polished oak doors to a white, six-story villa. Tenah followed the assassin inside, passing two central fountains in an open courtyard. Colorful lizards scuttled along the mosaic floor and up the legs of plush, velvet furnishings where shadows lazed.

Gireth stopped beside a palm bush, reaching out a finger toward an alert little blue salamander. "Whose a little cutie? You are. You are," he cooed. "Hop right up here, little buddy."

Surprisingly, the salamander obeyed, crawling up his arm to perch on his shoulder like a watchdog. Tenah snorted at the shit-eating grin Gireth threw Vesara as he showed off his new friend. Vesara shook her head and quickened her pace through the arched walkways.

When Tenah caught up to her, she asked, "What is this place?"

"My residence," Vesara said coolly.

Tenah cocked a brow, peeking at two young shadows splayed out on the floor, gushing over a book. "Your guests… Are they also…"

"Embassy employed? No. I rent rooms out to anyone in need, no questions asked. Some are here for temple studies. Some seek refuge. Some prefer to sleep by day and enjoy Denoden's festivities by night."

Vesara led the way up a curving, white marble staircase to the second floor. She opened a series of bedroom doors along the way that faced a terrace overlooking the affluent square. There were eclectic tables and chairs on one side and a full bar running beneath a pergola on the other.

"Stay as long as you like." Vesara fluffed the ends of her sleek hair. "You can dine anywhere. Zia will even serve you in your room if you enjoy crumbs in your bed. Security won't be a problem."

Gireth raised his hand, his other snapping over his crotch in protection. His tiny salamander perked up. "Why would anyone in their right mind leave a place like this for the Boglands?"

Vesara glared. "Do you think all of this comes without strings attached?"

"I spent years living out of a metal shed, plunged in six-foot snow drifts. Sign me up for strings," Gireth said. Sensing potential danger, his salamander wriggled off.

Gireth moved onto the terrace and dropped into a pile of silk cushions, giving Vesara a challenging "come and get me" look. Vesara disregarded him, joining three women at the bar conversing over fruity drinks. Gold hoops shone in their ears—symbols of their wealth. Tenah spun one of her own hoops, debating ripping it out.

This normalcy the crew had slipped into was unsettling. Well, with the exception of Renton. He'd propped up against a terrace wall, arms and legs crossed in typical, closed-off fashion. Blood still caked his cheek where he'd been cut.

Urgency to flee tugged at her like a rope around her middle. Chaos dug into the slimy feeling, darkness thickening in her channels. Potent notes of coppery magic burned inside her nostrils. Aching fingers popped in her gloves.

They are a distraction you cannot afford. Seek more power in pursuit of your enemy.

Her eyes flicked around the terrace, fearful Aeyis would pick up on her conversation with Chaos. Would he alert Renton?

Desperate to escape the situation, Tenah stole off in pursuit of her goal.

Chapter Fifteen
RENTON

Two things ensnared Renton's mind.

One, he was pretty sure Gireth had let it slip that he'd spent time on Dreaddix. After all their catching up on the flight over, his friend hadn't mentioned it once. But there was nowhere else on the isles with that much snow. He filed the topic away for later unpacking.

And two, Tenah was up to something.

Renton peeled off the terrace wall when the air shifted, the undercurrent of coppery magic trailing her as she crept off. He was beginning to think she craved trouble. Where would she seek it out now?

Aeyis popped up onto his feet, a furrow between his brows. He hesitated, awkwardly pushing tangles of hair from his face.

They needed to talk, that was for fucking sure. But right now, Renton was more concerned with the safety of the Chaos-wielding, death-defying creature slipping away. More so, he feared for anyone that crossed her path.

She's headed for the Abyss, Aeyis said.

Renton growled. "Of course she is."

Dumbfounded, Gireth looked between the brothers. "All right, boys. There's a secret conversation going on here."

Renton cut for the stairs, his temper flaring.

"She might want some privacy, you know," Vesara shouted from the terrace bar.

"Yeah? In the Abyss?" Renton glared back at the assassin.

Her cocky expression melted. With a quick kiss to the cheek of the Vozarian woman she'd been chatting up, she fell in line behind Gireth and Aeyis on his heels.

Outside the villa, Renton's nostrils flared as he worked to isolate the hint of dark magic that had been woven around Tenah since she'd awakened in the snowy field days ago.

"Do you even know how to get there?" Vesara asked.

"I thought the Abyss was just a rumor." Gireth wiggled his fingers at the word "rumor."

Vesara rolled her eyes. "Does the moon set in the west? Rumors in these parts almost always stem from truth, but I wouldn't expect outsiders to know where the entrances to the Abyss are located."

"Um," Aeyis interrupted quietly, shifting on his feet. "I can just track her. I'm tuned in."

Renton turned to his brother, jaw clenching. "Lead us then."

Aeyis guided them through the impoverished sectors and down into the sewers. Foul stench assaulted their senses. Renton didn't mind so much. It kept the others from opening their mouths. The low-ceilinged tunnel they followed ended at a simple wooden door that must have marked the entrance to the illicit market. Renton homed in on a smear of fresh blood above the handle. He frowned.

Hers, Aeyis acknowledged.

Vesara slid in front of him. "Don't look so horror-stricken. The Abyss's crime lord only keeps magical record of visitors for eternity."

"Can we leave him a love note in blood?" Gireth asked with a smirk.

"You're disturbed," Vesara retorted. She sliced the pad of her thumb and pressed it against the wood. Latches on the other side creaked, and then the door swung inward into darkness.

They stalked the passage like vengeful ghosts, only slowing when low torches came into view, illuminating what appeared to be a dingy slum made up of canvas tents and short, black buildings.

"It's like Cragnore on a bad day," Gireth muttered, rubbing at his nose. "How far does this place go?"

"As far as the capital borders, from what I've been told," Vesara said with a carefree wave of her hand.

Renton lifted a brow. "Does your king know?"

It was hard to believe Izral slept above such an expanse of illegal trade and crime.

"Izral's not concerned," she said, "not with the Embassy in his back pocket."

"I thought the Embassy wasn't permitted alliances," Renton said.

Vesara's pale blue eyes twinkled up at him. "Who's going to stop them?"

They prowled the narrow walkways, catching wary glances from scarred and hooded shadows, until Aeyis stopped before a dimly lit stone building. Dripping beads masked the open doorway.

She's inside, Aeyis said.

Renton's blood pressure spiked in response. *What's she doing?*

Receiving a sermon on the enlightenment found through dark magic in The Tome of Ergh.

Great. Renton tossed aside the beaded curtain and stalked into the shop. Waning candles flickered in alarm, melting in sconces along deep purple velvet walls. He pressed on, entering a circular chamber draped in black-and-purple silk. Skulls dangled from the ceiling by frayed strings, still peppered with chunks of rotting flesh and greasy hair.

He clenched his teeth in disgust then met Gireth with a nod. The shopkeeper was Corrupt. Though the shard's pulse in his heart was weak, the metallic tang lurked beneath potent layers of incense.

The shopkeeper's head lurched up at her intruders. Soulless, black eyes glinted as they took in the bones on Renton's armor.

That's right. Eyes on me, he thought. *What game do you want to play, beast?*

His rush of anger flagged as Tenah's eyes moved to him. Her feigned hatred didn't bother him. Not when the subtle release of tension in her shoulders proved her relief at having aid close by.

Tenah had known exactly what she'd walked into. So why had she come?

"More customers? What will they haggle me about?" the Corrupt croaked, waving a tattered, yellow piece of parchment that reeked of copper. More than likely part of the tome she had been discussing with Tenah.

"Cut the shit. What did you plan to take from her in payment?" Renton demanded.

The shopkeeper grinned with black-stained teeth. Setting the parchment down on the barrel she and Tenah had crowded around, the shopkeeper motioned to the various body parts dangling behind her. A macabre display, one Renton was unfortunately familiar with in his line of work but would never acclimate to.

"Ew," Gireth whispered, punching Renton's shoulder. "I'll knock her out cold while you all run."

The Corrupt's eyes snapped to Gireth as sludge dribbled from her mouth. She was deteriorating fast. Before the shopkeeper lashed out with claws, Renton buried his sword in her neck. Brackish blood splattered against Tenah's neck and cheek. Her eyes shot wide open, and Renton's chest tightened.

Shit. Maybe he should have been more refined with his approach.

Only when the creature had ceased movement did he kick it off his sword. He lifted his head to Tenah once more, prepared to start in on her, but she was gone and so was the page from the cursed tome.

Chapter Sixteen
TENAH

Tenah tucked the worn parchment into her pocket as she retraced her steps through the Abyss. The others would be on her trail in seconds. Still, it felt right to run. To snap up those barriers against everything that threatened her purpose.

What would Ames think of her descent into crime? First, a bargain with an entity of death, and now, chasing down instructions on dark magic.

Chaos had guided her to that shop with the intent to absorb the Corrupt's power—and she'd allowed it. Justified it even. Anything to gain an edge on her father. She'd alleviate the world of one more monster while dulling the gnawing addiction in her bones.

Tenah quickened her pace. She refused to feel shame, no matter how it roiled in her stomach.

Unfortunately, Renton caught up to her first.

"Can we talk please?" His tone was sharp like his blades.

Her sights set on the tunnel that led back into the sewers, she pressed on. She couldn't do this with him. This new life wasn't meant to become complicated. Renton would very much complicate things. Not to mention the possibility that he could still try to arrest her or kill her for the choices she was determined to make.

She didn't want anything he had to offer her. Not when Chaos would give her the means to topple her father's armies on her own, consequences be damned.

"Let me be a lone wolf," Tenah muttered, avoiding his gaze.

His arm shot out in her path, stopping her in her tracks. He backed her against the wall of a brick shop. Half-pinned by his lethal body, Tenah summoned the hottest fire in the pit of her core and used it as fuel to meet his frigid stare.

"And let you tear yourself apart?" He grimaced. "I think not."

"Unless you have another contract on my head that I don't know about, you can forget about me."

He growled. "*No*, Tenah. I can't. And that has nothing to do with the fact that right now our goal of stopping Kherathi aligns."

She squirmed under his direct attention.

"Listen, I'm sorry for hurting you. Let me help. Let's find a better method than that." He pointed at the hidden parchment in her pocket.

"No."

"You can't expect to hold a grudge forever."

"I don't have any expectations when it comes to you."

"No?" He pressed in closer.

Blood rushed low as his eyes dipped to her mouth. Her breath caught when his thumb softly traced the line of her jaw.

She hated the part of her that wanted to experience his arms around her, even if it was just once. Thinking about all the horrendous damage he would do to her heart made her instincts rage like a feral cat.

Renton took her chin between his fingers and tilted her head up, exposing her neck. Her heart thudded out a frantic rhythm. She closed her eyes, hating her body for wanting to melt into him. To give up all control.

A soft tug at her pocket had her jerking away. With a sly grin, Renton waved the parchment in show. Scowling, Tenah lurched for it. He raised it above his head, too high for her to jump.

"Asshole!" She latched onto his arm, prepared to climb him to retrieve what was hers when she became aware of their audience. What had been a private conversation she hoped to forget had transformed into a group discussion.

"Why don't you two handle this like we did in camp?" Gireth asked, sipping from a wooden mug he'd purchased somewhere in the Abyss. "Fight it out of your system on the battlefield."

Aeyis held a mug too but stared down at the foam clinging to the rim with a look of concern. Her hand twitched, wanting to reach out to keep him from drinking it. Who knew what it was laced with.

Everyone else's gaze fell on Tenah.

Honestly, the idea of a fight—an all out release of her magic—was tempting. But could she afford the delay? Lives were at stake. Although, when it came time to fight her father, she didn't want to be rusty. She couldn't protect anyone if she was dead again. And if she only managed to land one solid hit on a Bogland hunter, it would be worth the effort.

When Renton didn't immediately turn down the suggestion, her competitive nature reared its ugly head. What, did he think he was so superior in skill?

He wanted her to pursue a different method. She'd start by pummeling him into the ground.

"If I win, you give me back my page," Tenah said.

His head tilted slightly. "And if I win, your eyes will never skim these poisonous words."

Tenah frowned. "Fine, but my magic's going to need space."

"We have seven training fields in Denoden," Vesara said, covering a yawn. "I'll take you to the one least used since I'm guessing both of you have some frustrations to work out."

With a sassy, hip-swinging walk, the assassin led them back through the sewers and onto the streets. Renton matched Tenah's pace, while the others placed bets on the victor of their fight. Irritatingly enough, Vesara was the only tally in Tenah's favor.

Gireth threw her a sheepish grin. "Sorry. Gotta give it to Ren. We didn't call him Nazrata in camp for nothing."

"Nazrata?" Tenah raised a brow, glancing up at Renton.

Renton dipped his head and sighed. "Means demon-possessed in the old language."

"Are you trying to intimidate me again?"

He glanced over, mischief in his eyes. "Is it working?"

"Not in the least."

His fingers brushed against the back of her hand. "Quit acting like you dislike me."

"It's not an act."

He stopped mid-walk. Reflexively, she stopped too, worried he'd changed his mind about the fight she so desperately craved.

Suddenly, he was invading her space. Solid, armor-clad muscle pressed up against her. His hand slid around the back of her neck, rough fingers tangling in her fine hair. Gently, he tugged her head up, then he brought his mouth nearly to her parted lips.

Tenah's eyelids fluttered. Her pulse thundered so loud she swore he could hear it.

Renton hummed in satisfaction. "Just as I thought."

He dropped his hand and carried on after the others, leaving her heated in more ways than one.

Chapter Seventeen
RENTON

Ruby eyes seared Renton from the inside out.

He squared up a dozen paces from Tenah inside the decrepit remains of a colosseum, his cherished blade in hand. He much preferred her newfound rage over the vacant shell she'd been during their journey to the Boglands. There was nothing worse than recognizing that lack of hope in another soul's eyes.

Vesara waved a hand as she strolled by. "Do your worst. The monarchy abandoned this heap after the formation of the isles broke it beyond repair."

When the crew had gathered on the opposite end of the dirt field, Renton cracked his neck and assessed Tenah's stance. *So many corrections needed.* Though it was hard to concentrate on her technique when a warm breeze tossed her dark locks around her exquisite face. He could still feel the soft touch of it between his fingers.

Renton didn't mask his admiration now. Hell, if he was being honest with himself, he'd been a goner the first time he'd laid eyes on her.

Gireth cupped his hands around his mouth and shouted out. "Remember cheap shots, Tenah. Cheaters always come out on top!"

Vesara slung a knife into the wooden target propped up beside Gireth.

"Giving away your strategies already?"

Insults spewed as the others lined up for a game of knife throwing. Renton couldn't help but notice their natural chemistry. The excited smiles they fought to hide. He'd witnessed the failure of too many clans in training camps due to incompatibilities. Vesara and Gireth both had strong personalities, but Aeyis softened them out magnificently.

Tenah slid her boot over the dirt, drawing his attention back to her. "Your move, Nazrata."

He flashed a wicked smile. Then he vanished into an illusion.

Gods, he'd needed this too. A fight to take the edge off everything. As long as he kept his instincts in check.

Tenah's crimson flames blasted out like dueling snakes. Gireth yelped like a frightened child mid-throw. His knife clanged against the stones of the colosseum wall behind the target.

"Why snakes?" he bellowed. "Their lack of limbs displeases me. I demand more limbs."

Renton shook his head with a chuckle, almost losing hold on his shield of magic. It wasn't always worth the drain on his energy to utilize magic but against Tenah...

His mouth curved up on one side as he closed in on her. His illusion dropped long enough to steal her breath away. "This is what you face should you choose darkness, Tenah."

But there was no malice behind his words. This close, he became lost in her. The flicker of surprise on her face. The little gasp that escaped her full lips. The hint of lavender on her naturally tan skin.

Corrupt, his instincts reminded him. But fuck if he didn't care right now.

"I'm not breakable, Tenah," he said. "Remember what I do for a profession."

She forced him back with a strike of her flame serpent. Renton feigned sideways to avoid a second attack from her hungry flames. They devoured the target the crew had been using to prove their superiority.

"Come on." Gireth threw up his arms. "Important work happening over here."

Tenah muttered an apology as she snuffed out her flames with a wave of her hand, but the damage was already done, the target no more than blackened, compromised wood. The crew stormed off in search of a less dangerous location for their pissing match.

Renton planned to enjoy every second of alone time with the fiery woman challenging his every belief. Tenah seemed to agree, unleashing her magic in all of its fury. She launched bolt after bolt as his illusion flickered in and out like a dying lightbulb.

Glorious speed had always been on his side. But even with his quick movements, he couldn't escape the heat from her magic. Sweat dampened the hair around his temples and the back of his neck as her flames created brilliant streaks of red in the salmon sky while the sun dipped lower.

Another firebolt slammed into the stone wall where he'd just been. He laughed, his illusion fading. He brushed crumbles of stone from his shoulder.

Tenah locked onto him, her next bolt rolling straight and true. It struck him in the arm before he hoisted himself up into the stands and hurled a small knife at her boot. After patting out the flames striving to eat away at his armor, he looked down to see Tenah staring at the knife. Should he call the match?

Some invisible force constricted his body, ripping him from the wall and back into the pit. The air warped with heat as Tenah cranked her flames up another notch. They had a blue tint to their core.

She smiled darkly as he realized what she'd done. Strands of his own magic had been pulled taut between his channels and her fingers, forming a connection like the one the Chaos woman had used in the Boglands.

Gods, Tenah was so much more powerful than what her file had listed. The only other shadow Renton had met capable of demonstrating such magic was Elder Nithril, one of nine High Court rulers, and he'd sacrificed his ability to cast in order to seal the isle portals during Advanth's war, saving countless lives and hindering the spread of Corruption.

There was no doubt in Renton's mind that her family had raised her to become a weapon. Further proof that he needed to keep her out of the hands of evil like Boedworth.

But then what would he do with her?

Flames coiled down the invisible bond of magic she had created between them. They caught him directly in the chest. He grunted as he slammed back against the wall. Quickly, he popped the lid off his last vial of creeping smoke to douse the flames.

Tenah's eyes widened as the numbing smoke coiled down her magical ropes. She severed them with a swift jerk of her hand. Renton didn't bother avoiding the creeping smoke. Let it render every bit of his magic useless. Sure, he wouldn't be able to use illusions to hide from her anymore, but she couldn't puppeteer him with his magic either.

He took the brunt of two more firebolts before the novelty wore off. Then he unleashed the speed he used to hunt Corrupt, leaping over the ring of fire she crafted as a last resort to keep him at bay.

Panic flashed in her wide eyes. She cringed away. Flooded with guilt, Renton pulled his shot, his blade sinking into the dirt beside her. He'd gotten careless. She was unskilled with close combat. He would have to rectify that. Magic always had a delay, one that put casters at a disadvantage against fast, short-range opponents. Not to mention the issue when their magic ran dry...

Tenah didn't waste his hesitation. Her features shifted into something menacing as she drew a whip of flame from thin air and snapped it down against his side.

"Fuck!" Renton exclaimed.

She yanked the flame whip back for another punishing attack. "My wraith taught me to play into the weaknesses of others."

Renton's brows kneaded as he retrieved his blade from the dirt. "And what exactly is my weakness, Tenah?"

Her cheeks flushed, and her eyes darted away for a second. He thought she might not answer, but then she said softly, "Your heart."

His sword arm went slack. All traces of adrenaline evaporated from his body. He opened and closed his mouth several times before he could form words. "How am I supposed to keep fighting after you say something like that?"

Tenah brought her flame whip around for another swipe.

In a reckless move, Renton dropped his blade and caught her fiery wrist. He tugged her against him. Her flames dissolved, leaving behind a line of smoke in the air. Still, she wasn't done fighting. Using his arm for leverage, she swung her body around his side and popped her boot into the back of his knee.

Renton buckled. He wrapped his arms around her and brought her down into the dirt with him. "You cunning woman."

Tenah didn't try to wriggle away. In fact, she seemed oblivious to where their bodies met as she pushed up to sit fully on his hips. This did nothing to tame the longing low in his gut. His muscles tightened, and his hands curled around the back of her thighs, securing her in place.

He liked her thighs. He liked her weight on him too.

"You lit me on fire," he said.

She frowned down at him. "You're not even out of breath. You let me win."

A drop of sweat trailed down her neck and between her breasts. He wanted to lean up and run his tongue along her glistening skin. He wanted to trace his fingers slowly up her curves and sink them into her hair. He wanted to claim her mouth. He wanted to sink into her and make her scream his name.

He shouldn't want any of those things. Desires were a nuisance. Something he only indulged out of boredom. He *should* be long gone, chasing down his demonic employer to assure he couldn't come back to hurt Aeyis or hunting the Chaos lord.

But the urge to drag Tenah's body along the length of him, unashamed that she had to be feeling what she was doing to him in this position, seemed to be winning out.

"I'm sorry," he murmured. "I didn't mean to upset you."

She flushed but didn't pull away as her gaze drifted to his sword laid out in the dirt. "Why do you carry two of them? Seems cumbersome."

He regretfully withdrew a hand from her thigh to rest over his scarred heart where the shard threaded strings of pain through his body. The last thing he wanted was for Tenah to witness him experiencing a full attack from it, writhing in pain or paralyzed for hours.

"The smaller blade I earned in Mire's training camps. It was given to me by a chieftain when I made my first kill without a weapon." He paused, expecting her to ask what he'd killed or how he'd gone about it because she liked to prod at things like that. Renton didn't much care to recite how he'd popped the creature's eyes and snapped its neck.

"And the one on your back?"

"Belonged to my father. You might think it cumbersome, but it's the only piece of him I have left. The blade is too heavy for me to wield the way I like, but it penetrates tougher beasts like no other."

Tenah slid off of him, her mouth pressed in a firm line. "You must hate when I touch you."

Renton pushed up onto an elbow. "When have I ever said that?"

She lowered her head, tucking a lock of hair behind her ear. "You despise Corrupt. You hunt them."

He winced as her words struck true. He *did* hate them. He'd hated them for as long as he could remember. Camps had drilled it in him to cut off all emotional ties to the shadow harboring the curse of darkness.

And the desert... That day had proved just how dangerous Corrupt could become.

Yet, here he was, fantasizing about kissing one. He should turn her over to the High Court. But something inside of him refused to categorize her in any manner except an innocent woman, defiled by the magic of someone that was supposed to love her. He'd met Tenah before Chaos had taken root, and that was muddling his brain. He was beginning to question if the others he'd hunted had merely been victims too.

"I can't deny that hatred. It's been festering in me since I was too weak to fight back. But believe me when I say that I don't think it's possible for me to ever dislike your touch."

A truth that shouldn't have slipped out.

Tenah fell silent, and Renton couldn't stop himself from fishing out the paper he'd taken from her. "I wish you wouldn't start down this path."

Hesitantly, she accepted it. She smoothed the crinkled paper on her lap, written proof of recorded insight into Chaos. Possibly how to control it if the shopkeeper hadn't been spewing lies. "Because you'd have to kill me?"

"Because I care about your well-being. Nothing can be solved through that darkness."

She squirmed a bit, perched on her legs folded beneath her. "So why do you carry a sliver of it?"

Renton went deathly still. "What?"

Her eyes slid to his hand resting over the scar. "It calls to me. What is it?"

Old habits resurfaced, and he deflected, guard walls snapping up. "You're mistaken. Chaos must have messed with your senses."

It physically hurt him to watch her features scrunch up in anger.

"I can't learn to trust you if you refuse to be open with me," she said.

"That goes both ways, Tenah," he said firmly. "You never explained how you defied death."

After a long stretch of tense silence, she replied, "I have no answer to that."

Renton shut his eyes as he released a sigh. There was no one to blame but himself for her deep-rooted mistrust. He'd caused that wound.

"Look," she said, and Renton studied her once more as her hands kneaded in her lap. "My behavior hasn't exactly been…pleasant. I don't mean to be abrasive, but I'd rather not involve you all in this mess. I appreciate that you came back to save me. I understand why you did what you did. If a contract had meant any of the staff in my home that helped raise me could have walked free that night, I would have made the same decision as you."

A knot loosened in his chest. Renton fought the overwhelming desire to pull her in closer. "It doesn't change what I did. Had you been hurt, or had they transported you to Dreaddix—"

"They didn't. So stop beating yourself up about it, okay?"

He shook his head, feeling defeated. "I was a fool to think Boedworth would keep his end of the deal. Years of his lies and…" He dug his fingers into the ground. "And Aeyis…you saw how well he handles himself. He's no longer a child in need of protection. I'm not really sure how to process that."

"He seems kind," she said softly. "He reminds me of someone I lost."

Renton frowned. "We will fix things, Tenah."

But there was no conviction in his words. Even if they managed to stop Kherathi and slay all of his monsters, that didn't mean he knew how to start mending the tattered relationship with Aeyis. Or what to do with her.

Her scorching eyes locked on him. "You assume I want your help."

"I'm hunting your father too."

She frowned. "Then why do you hold back when you fight me? How is that helping either of us?"

He couldn't help but crack a smile at her determination. "You're right. I accept my punishment in the form of another fight."

Chapter Eighteen
RENTON

Renton's head was a twisted mess by the time he arrived back at the villa with Tenah. Their walk had been in silence, but he was content to simply be at her side. Though he was aware of each breath, each movement she made, he wasn't going to push his luck reaching out to take her hand. She'd forgiven him. That was enough for now.

To his displeasure, Vesara snagged her away as soon as they wandered onto the terrace. The instant drop in temperature from Tenah's absence felt like the loss of the sun.

Sighing, Renton dropped into a low chair near the railing. It offered an unbelievable view of Denoden, including the Embassy—a lofty stone wonder that defied gravity. It was as ostentatious as its assassins, brown marble the shade of milk chocolate and windows lined by gold awnings.

A boy named Fen brought him a cup of chamomile tea then peppered him with questions about his armor and Mire's training camps. Renton laughed when the boy's mother Zia, the head cook, scolded and ushered him back into the kitchens, all the while balancing a giant stack of dishes in one hand.

As the tea soothed the buzzing high from his scrimmages with Tenah, his eyelids drooped closed. Would he capture sleep tonight, or would it slip through his trained hands like everything else lately?

Why, of all shadows, did it have to be a Vozarian Chaos caster that caught his eye? He hadn't permitted much time to indulge in desires, only the occasional, meaningless hook up when he visited a tavern or an inn.

Renton folded his hands behind his head and stretched deeper into his chair under the stars. Venomous thoughts immediately slithered in. How long would it take for Boedworth to find them? Because he *would* take revenge. And if Boedworth didn't send an arsenal of trained hunters after them, there was still the threat of Tenah's father. Worse yet, how long until Adra's rebel king, Cirel, picked up where his dead mother Advanth had left off?

The isles were not safe.

Aeyis plopped down in the chair across from him with a soft laugh. Renton cocked a brow in question.

"Tenah called me a meddler for tuning in to her thoughts." Aeyis pushed unruly locks of white hair away from his forehead. "I'm just acting accordingly. What's wrong, brother?"

"Can't sleep, but that's not new," Renton said, folding over to brace his elbows on his knees. His laugh was strained, the truth feeling like ghostly hands dragging his insides out for examination. "I'm not sure what the next move is. Mire trained me to lead, but I can't even make a decision on how to protect everyone. Back then it was easy. Step between the kid and the monster."

Cold magic touched the edges of Renton's mind.

"You think leaving again will fix this?" Aeyis asked. "That you can take on Boedworth, his hunters, and the Chaos lord Kherathi alone?"

"Boedworth will be hell-bent on finding us. Me, in particular. I could buy you some time to find a place to settle down off the isles. Then I can carry out what I was born to do."

Ashen dust churned into small tornadoes along the railing. *Fidgeter*, their mother had called the youngest Murfell boy. At least that much hadn't changed. Still, Renton couldn't help but feel like his brother was a stranger.

"I never wanted to run," Aeyis said. "I didn't in Mire. I don't now. Hunters can come to us. We're in the domain of the Embassy."

"Izral won't let us hide out here forever. Especially when Bogland hunters come knocking at his gates. We'll be tossed out."

Aeyis's swirl of magic collapsed in a sudden heap on the tiled floor. The silver rings around his white irises shone in the ambient light when he turned them on Renton. "I go where you go. Whether that's after Boedworth or to Aranma or with Tenah to Vozar."

A muscle in Renton's jaw flexed. He peered through the railing at shadows parading through the streets. Some of them carried sticks of sparkling fire, their childish laughter almost infectious.

"If it's any consolation, you should know I was never suffering in Mire," Aeyis said. "A smidge from boredom, I'll admit. But I was free to do as I pleased as long as I remained in the village. Boedworth never actually cared about me, and Mias stopped checking in when I didn't play into his attempts to get under my skin. They just wanted something to lord over you in exile to assure your obedience."

Renton sucked in a long breath. All those years he'd imagined his brother tortured or imprisoned. How many bodies had he hauled back to Cragnore in hopes of one day clearing Aeyis's charges? The reek of their tainted blood would never leave him.

He looked over at his brother and asked, breathless, "Why did you stay?"

Aeyis rubbed at the back of his neck, flushing with pink color. "I thought you'd come back for me. You know, if you really cared."

"Aeyis," Renton said carefully, "I was exiled."

"You didn't care about breaking the laws when it came to her."

The shock of Aeyis's words was just as powerful as if his brother had struck him with a fist. He *should* have gone home sooner. Stolen Aeyis away. Fled the isles. Abandoned his duties.

Why hadn't he?

Renton dug his fingers into his temples. "Shit. Aeyis, I'm sorry. I thought I was doing what was best for both of us for once. Working within the laws to clear whatever bullshit record Boedworth had on you so you could move to Hathrowyn with me."

He'd kept the second bedroom at the top of his tree home empty for when he obtained proper documentation to move his brother there. It had a view of the forest and let in delicious scents from the grill house next door.

Now, Hathrowyn and Mire would never be a home for them.

"I never wanted to live in Hathrowyn," Aeyis admitted.

Renton shook his head. "Then why didn't you write me back?"

His brother dragged a finger through his resting magical dust. "Mias found out about our letters. He threatened anyone who might help me communicate with you. Some time after, he told me he'd found your corpse in the Boglands. He's such a skilled liar and his thoughts are so slippery, I started to wonder if he was telling the truth. Why else wouldn't you come back?"

Renton's chest was rapidly caving in. "I assumed you blamed me for father's death."

"I know your heart, brother. We were all manipulated in our own ways. Mias convinced Gireth that you'd wound up on Dreaddix. The oaf stole away on the next flight."

Shaking his head, Renton muttered, "That idiot." The horrors his friend must have endured. "How did he escape?"

Aeyis smiled. "You should ask him. As usual, it's an entertaining story."

Renton snorted. "Not surprising."

"When Gireth came home and Mias started spouting lies about your death, he wasn't...suited for normal life. Dreaddix changed him, no matter how much he clings to his humor. He took up a post in the prisons, and I figured I'd stay a bit longer in case you showed up or Gireth decided he deserved better than the path he'd accepted. I guess we were all just biding time, waiting for the perfect piece to shift into place."

Instead, Renton had allowed Boedworth to break him. Exile him. Torture him. Shattered bone after bone. Carve scar after scar. He'd been worse than defeated. And all those years of suffering abuse within the High Court, Aeyis had been sitting at home waiting for him. Gireth had needed him.

Exhaustion and self-loathing wormed into Renton's bones. "I should speak with Elder Nithril. Explain what happened in the Boglands. He might be able to pull weight. Make sure we're not condemned by Boedworth."

"You and I both know speaking with Nithril won't be enough," Aeyis said. "Boedworth has avoided conviction for his sins thus far. In no way does this end in the system."

Renton glanced over at his brother, worry prodding in his gut. "What are you suggesting?"

The silver rings around his irises gleamed. "We draw Boedworth out. Tenah would let us use her as bait. When I'm done with him, he won't remember his own name, let alone ours."

"Tread carefully, brother. The cost of tampering with the wrong mind—"

"Our mother was careless with her gift. I'm methodical with mine."

"Yeah? Is that what you call being laid out on the streets because the mental chatter is too much?"

Aeyis didn't so much as flinch. "I've changed."

Face scrunching up in conjunction with the sadness creeping through his body, Renton couldn't help his eyes flicking to his brother's neck. Aeyis turned his head to the side and lifted up his hair, revealing a thin, white line behind his ear. The kind left behind from a magic-restricting implant.

"Mias tried to leash me," Aeyis said in explanation.

Renton's heart plummeted into his stomach. There was still so much controversy over the implant. He'd never agreed with the decree to make them mandatory. To force Ashens to undergo a knife because others feared them as a collective? That very law had driven Advanth to start the war at Roan's Wake. But having witnessed the unraveling of his own mother's mind, he understood some Ashen's desire for them. A chance to hear their own thoughts for once and not a hundred others. Years ago, he'd thought to suggest it to Aeyis, but it had seemed so out of line.

Aeyis let his hair fall over the scar. "The implant failed."

"What?"

"I altered the minds of the institute employees. I'm documented as a successful recipient. I played docile for years. Honed my gift. Prepared myself for you to return so we could wipe out Mias and Boedworth together."

"Boedworth won't risk getting close to you after your demonstration in Mire. Using Tenah won't be enough."

More like, he didn't want her involved.

Renton dug into the secrets he'd gathered on his employer. Crimes he'd tried to bring to light in court. "Topaz might do it. He's recently become addicted to the Adran drug. Meets with dealers in the safehouses just outside of Cragnore. Word of product always arrives by coded letter."

"There were dealers in the Abyss," Aeyis noted, his magical dust twirling. "I can crack that code."

Renton gave a low laugh and shook his head. "I don't think I'll ever forget the image of Boedworth crawling on the ground. I'm surprised he didn't shit himself when you took hold of his mind."

Aeyis grinned. "All I needed was another few minutes with him. Mias ruined my fun."

"Typical Mias."

"Typical Mias," Aeyis agreed.

They fell into silence for a beat, enjoying the warm evening breeze and the light banter of street folk.

"How often?" Aeyis asked quietly.

Renton focused on grinding the heel of his boot on the tiled floor. "How often did he order our so-called brethren to harm me? I lost track over the years."

Shattered fingers and toes to start. Broken ribs and collarbones. Then cuts and punctures in areas mostly covered by his armor. No one ever questioned the injuries. In his line of work, who wasn't damaged in some form?

And Renton had believed he'd deserved them all for letting their family fall apart.

"What you deserve is to find happiness," Aeyis said. "Look inward, brother, and seek your truth. If the shard could be removed—"

"Drop it," Renton said, iron coating his words.

Surely Aeyis had ruminated on the memory of their father's death countless times since their reunion. Speaking about it would only give life to it once more.

Pushing down his anger, Renton looped an arm around his brother's head and rubbed a fist into his scalp. "What's up with this hair? Either grow it out or cut it. You look feral."

Frigid magic yanked his hands up into the air, hard enough to earn a grunt from him.

"Point made." Renton chuckled. "The implant really failed?"

Aeyis's smile touched his eyes.

"Cocky. You might be trouble, brother," Renton teased.

"Of course I am. I share your blood."

CHAPTER NINETEEN

TENAH

Tenah thought she had known luxury. Then Vesara escorted her into what she was forcefully told would be her bedroom. Mouth gaping, her eyes roved from the polished cream floors inlaid with specks of gold to the antique bed, desk, and tall armoire to the view of the lush garden through the back wall of arched, open windows. Night cloaked the vegetation, but even so, she could still make out lovely blossoms.

"Don't be upset with me," Vesara said, moving over to the armoire. "Moody hunter boy mentioned your house burned down. I did a bit of shopping on the way back from decimating those two hooligans in target practice."

"A bit? That's quite the understatement," Tenah said as the assassin opened the wardrobe, revealing beautifully stitched clothing with tiny, intricate beadwork.

"Yes, they all belong to you. I owe you a debt for saving my life twice over in the Boglands."

Tenah's brows shot up to her hairline. "The items must have cost a fortune."

"Don't deny me my fun," Vesara stated, hands snapping to her hips. "I'd say I can't return any of it, but I can with a threat or two."

Tenah swallowed down her rising emotions. "Thank you."

"Are you going to tell me what you were doing in the Abyss now?"

Frowning, Tenah fished the crumpled parchment out of her pocket. She'd forgotten about it while training with Renton. Further reason to keep her distance. Time was precious, and she lost track of it when she was with him.

Her mind flashed back to his hands lingering on her body as he corrected her form. Heat rushed through her. One thing was clear—Renton might try to hide his nature under a brusque, scrutinizing exterior, but she'd glimpsed his kindness. That was something she would not allow herself to destroy.

"I was following a hunch, really," Tenah lied.

She spread the parchment flat on the desk. The assassin skipped over. Together, they studied the crude drawings on the wrinkled, yellowing page. There were dozens of them, and only a few resembled anything recognizable like trees, moons, or birds all wrapped up in a snarl of ink.

"What are they?" Vesara asked.

"No idea. Possibly a cipher? In which case..." Tenah sighed. "This page is useless without the rest of *The Tome of Ergh*. That old hag must have known it too."

"And this tome is..." Vesara met her eyes, and Tenah almost smirked at the tiny decorative knives dangling from her pierced ears.

"A potential key to stopping Corruption," Tenah said. Or magnifying her power, but that wasn't something she needed to share with anyone.

"Do you need a lecture from me on why any item spoken of in the Abyss is asking for a bad time?"

"I do not, thanks."

"Not to discourage you, but I've traveled broadly in my profession. Not once have I met a shadow with answers to reversing the disease that plagues these isles. Don't risk your safety chasing hopeless leads in the Abyss. Especially ones that will get you killed."

Staring down at her gloved hands as if she could glimpse the blackened nails and knuckles beneath the supple leather, Tenah slumped down into the desk chair. "If what you say is true, then I do have a favor to ask you."

Vesara's light eyes shone like glass. "I'm all yours."

"My father mentioned how the Embassy often works in conjunction with isle leaders in times of crisis. If your king decreed—"

"Stop right there. It's not in Izral's nature to aid with foreign matters."

Heat licked down Tenah's magical channels. "But it's not a foreign matter. My father's a threat to the entire isle, not just my kingdom."

All life drained from the assassin's eyes. "Then let the High Court deal with him."

"Will they though?"

Vesara headed for the door, signaling the end of their conversation. "I can't speak for the High Court's lack of motivation as of late, but I can say that you would be wasting your time trying to pursue help in Denoden. Sorry to disappoint, fire girl."

With that, the assassin shut the door.

What. The. Hell. After witnessing how the assassin had been received by Denoden's guards, how could Vesara not hold some sort of authority here? Denoden should be fortifying their borders, at the very least.

Frustrated and itching from the blood, dirt, and sweat caked to her skin, Tenah entered the bathing room. She was instantly won over. Carved from pale gray stone and glass, the large room echoed like a cave. Clusters of lightbulbs hung from the ceiling. Heaps of untouched blue candles lined a vanity and a piece of cherry wood fitted over a stone basin.

While the basin looked inviting, she didn't fancy swimming in her own filth, so she cranked on the spout in the glass enclosure. Steam billowed out, and Tenah grinned in anticipation of the sweet relief the hot water would bring.

Sweaty clothes peeled off, she stepped under the punishing stream of water and groaned. It hit knots along her back she couldn't reach to knead out with her fingers. She rested her forehead against the warm stone wall. Dark blood and dirt slithered down its stony ridges and circled the drain.

How had her entire world crumbled in mere days? One moment, she'd been daydreaming about traveling outside the manor, and the next, she'd been forced into freedom at the cost of Vozarian lives.

At the cost of Ames's life.

She focused on the burn of the water on her skin. Lifting a hand, she watched droplets of water trail down her ruined fingertips. No, she wasn't truly free. This life came with shackles. Using Chaos had felt too good. Her hunger for it kept her mind cycling back to the idea of indulging fully in its raw, vicious power.

Your lack of commitment disgusts us, Chaos growled in her mind. *Without our help, you will be destroyed again.*

Again with the fucking voices. Was the death king behind this, or was this the will of the sentient magic alone?

She licked water from her salty lips. *What do you want?*

For you to explore the Void. You will find a path to your father. You will find what you desire, infinite magic prime for the harvest.

She squeezed her eyes shut, visualizing the beast that had crawled out of her rift in the Boglands. Diving into the Void was a risk she wasn't prepared to take right now.

She let a ribbon of Chaos chirp between her fingers, just to get a feel. Her body shivered with euphoric heat. Her vision blurred, and her knee hit the hard floor. Cold, dark, thick air pressed in around her as she was sucked into a memory of the Void.

Silver eyes stared back at her, shining with fear. *Help me.*

She was maybe ten years old, still developing her magic and confidence. Though she reached out a small arm, she quickly snapped it back as Chaos swirled up the older boy's robes, little crackles of lighting striking out in warning.

Tenah, please.

She didn't move for him again, and his face crumpled as he came to understand his fate. Then a fury unlike anything she'd witnessed before took over his sharp features.

I knew you were on his side, the boy said. *You wanted me dead all along. Murderer!*

Chaos speared into his mouth and eyes, muffling his blood-curdling screams. The golden, leafy crown atop his auburn locks transformed into a band of crackling lightning. One eye bled into a terrifying shade of monstrous orange.

No! she yelled, lightning snapping from her fingers and slicing through the memory.

She was back on her knees in the bathing room, panting. Glancing up at the stone wall of the shower, she groaned at the spiderweb of black lines painted there with her magic. Damaging Vesara's house would definitely not convince her to provide military support.

This was all just madness conjured up by Chaos. She'd never met the death king before the gathering in her home. Never even physically stepped into the Void before her fight in the Boglands.

Tenah slammed off the water and clambered out of the shower. Searching for the least revealing outfit she could find in the armoire, she dressed in a flowing red skirt and a matching beaded crop top.

Then she scribbled out a note to her uncle. Gadreel had eyes on most of the isle's unclaimed lands. The desert. The Blackrock Cliffs. All territory otherwise unfit to cultivate. Establishing a line of communication with him might serve her well in locating her father. An alliance would be ideal, but she wouldn't count on it.

Tenah had met her uncle for the first time shortly after her mother had left them. Almost as if Avora's presence had kept him at bay. Gadreel had burst into the manor without invitation, disregarding Tenah entirely. Because her father had been a kind man at one time, he'd invited Gadreel to stay for dinner.

Gadreel had drank too much. Wretched names had been hurled back and forth, birthed from old familial wounds she didn't understand. Supposedly, her father was a traitor to Ruzgorn. Next thing she knew, her uncle had set their parlor couch on fire in what could only be described as an infamous Delemor tantrum before storming out.

Late that night over tea in the attic study, her father had shared insight into their barbaric culture. How killing was revered by Ruzgorn. About the power they gained from it, acquiring the strength and magic of the shadow slain.

Her father had made it clear at the time that he found this repulsive. "Nothing is stronger than the experience derived from patience and drive."

Now, Tenah questioned everything her father had ever told her. Could he have secretly revered that culture? Had Gadreel won him over somehow and they were both working in secret to topple the isles?

Either way, she would find out.

Refreshingly cold magic trickled through her weary mind. *Care to join me on a midnight stroll to the archives?*

Tenah froze. She gripped the letter to her uncle tighter. *Aeyis?*

Sorry, I assumed the mind talk didn't bother you, considering it was your main source of communication with your guardian.

Unbelievable. You've already probed me.

Can't help it. Your mind is like a puzzle with scattered pieces. After a pause, he added, *That sounded bad, didn't it?*

Tenah pursed her lips. *What's in the archives?*

Why don't you come and find out?

She rolled her eyes. *As long as we can make a stop first.*

Booming laughter resounded through the hall as Tenah crept from her bedroom.

Gireth leaned back in a chair on the terrace, engaged in a rowdy game of dice with strangers. His toned, bronze arms were bared in a sleeveless shirt, and he'd switched out his leathers for sweatpants. Stacks of krotens and half a dozen empty pint glasses littered the table.

He tipped his chin up at her in invitation. A few of his partners in crime peeked over at her. Her gaze snagged on the phoenix crest stitched into their fine clothes.

Vozarians, here in Denoden?

Her pulse quickened. Were they visiting or seeking refuge? How much territory had her father crossed with his feingrot army? How much destruction had he spread?

Tenah debated joining only to interrogate them.

They are here for some big celebration, Aeyis informed her.

Gireth picked up on her hesitation and threw up his arms, cracking a wide smile that showed off unnaturally sharp canines as if he'd been cut from the wild. "Come on, live a little."

She *was* curious how a rudimentary game of dice could bring such joy to a table of strangers.

Don't let him tempt you with his vices, Aeyis cut in. *He's lost way more than he's ever won.*

Considering she had neither the time nor the fortune to play, she shook her head at Gireth and broke for the stairs.

Aeyis haunted the street just outside the villa, a looming specter under the evening streetlights. He'd changed into plain, slouchy clothing that matched the bedraggled state of his hair.

Tenah mimicked his long strides. It was hard not to become distracted by the ethereal glare of his magical dust in her foggy eye. She couldn't make out street names or solid forms on her left side. Rapidly, her declining vision was becoming another weakness.

Noting the shift in their surroundings to rickety wooden buildings and broken windows, she asked, "Care to tell me what we're after?"

According to that shopkeeper, the tome is hidden in the archives.

She cursed. "And she only offered me a page of it."

"Yours for the low price of a finger. Strangely enough, the tome was at the forefront of Boedworth's mind too when I latched onto it in Mire. Which makes me interested."

You think it could be a game changer.

I do. As long as we get our hands on it first.

Aeyis cut between two ramshackle houses that looked as though they would collapse with one strong gust of wind. The sight made the holes in her ears itch as if infected. She rubbed at the hardened spots where she'd removed her earrings.

Witnessing how children in tattered, stained clothing pointed at Aeyis and whispered, it was evident Ashens were an anomaly here. Most had sided with Advanth and thus remained on the eastern isles. Tenah fought the urge to shoo the children inside their homes. What if they didn't have homes?

Why else would they be wandering the streets at this late hour?

She peeked up at Aeyis, but he kept his gaze forward, undisturbed by his audience. They stopped when they reached a crooked shack on the corner of a dead intersection. Etched into the wooden sign dangling above the door was the silhouette of a bird in flight.

"Still want to send word to Ruzgorn?" Aeyis asked.

Tenah's cheeks burned as she withdrew the letter from her pocket. "I need to know where my father is. My uncle could help." *Possibly. Or he could make matters worse.*

"I'm not judging," Aeyis said with a shrug. "Do what you have to do."

After entrusting her message with a beast master who promised his bird would recognize the arachnid flag of the Ruzgorn, Tenah followed Aeyis through more impoverished streets until they reached a gem of dominating brown marble.

The Embassy had been visible from the villa, its fancy, gold E a symbol of safety or warning, depending on the audience. Gold awnings hung over the windows. Large potted bushes lined the glass front, allowing a full view of the decadent lobby in shades of gold and brown, warmly lit by sconces.

Aeyis turned down the alley beside the Embassy and examined the steel back door under one lone bulb.

Tenah's brows furrowed. "Wait. The archives aren't in the Embassy, are they?"

"I thought you enjoyed challenges." His smile was a bit more animal than Ashen.

"A challenge is one thing. This is a crime. We could be arrested just for stepping foot in there."

Aeyis rested his lanky frame against the building, nudging away a piece of trash with his foot. "Not if the employees can't see us."

A large figure with charged green eyes peeled from the darkness.

"What the hell are you doing?" Renton demanded, glare locked on his brother.

Another shadow materialized behind him, this one nearly half his size and dressed in a tight, black leather suit. Beneath Vesara's navy cloak, Tenah glimpsed a bandolier of small knives.

Okay, now she was curious too about the number of pointy things this woman carried.

"How you play with fire, wraith," Vesara said in a singsong voice, tossing a knife into the air and catching it between her fingers.

Aeyis tapped light fingers against the building, oblivious to the heat he was being dished up. His mouth twitched when Gireth skidded into the alley. Krotens jangled in both of his stretched pockets.

Gireth braced his hands on his knees as he gulped in stinky air. "Why didn't you…summon me…when you called for Tenah…back at the villa?"

"Punishment for gambling." Aeyis shrugged.

Gireth groaned. "All right. Burned off that entire chocolate pie. What did I miss?"

"If we're about to do what Ghost Boy wants us to do, you are *not* strutting in there with that," Vesara said, eyeing his pants.

Gireth looked aghast, placing a hand over his chest. "Can't blame me for the gift of well-endowment."

"Disgusting. I meant the ruckus in your pockets."

"Ruckus?" He made a show of looking up and down the alley. "What ruckus?"

"You didn't hear yourself running?" Vesara whirled on Renton. "Did they not teach stealth in your hunter camps?"

Renton folded his arms over his black T-shirt-clad chest and cut a glare to his friend. "We never finished camp, did we?"

Vesara muttered something in Denesè.

Touching his pockets, Gireth pouted. "I'm never going to win another haul like that."

"You find a new home for your cheat coin, or you don't go inside," Vesara replied.

Muttering obscenities, Gireth scooped handfuls of krotens out of his pockets and arranged them in a phallic shape on the street.

Vesara tucked her knife away. "How very charitable of you."

"Don't you dare ask me for rent now. This was all I had to my name.

Unless you want to take payment from my body."

Flames ricocheted off the street as Tenah unleashed a bit of rage. "Someone please tell me what is going on here."

"Damn it!" Gireth scooped up one of his krotens and flicked it at Aeyis, who pocketed it smoothly. "I was sure Renton would be the first to lose his cool. Sorry, Tenah. We're going to help you borrow the tome."

Tenah squeezed her eyes shut against the whirlwind of confusion, needing to ground herself. That surge of wicked anger was quickly overtaken by a surprising flood of warmth in the center of her chest. She hadn't felt that sensation since before she'd lost Ames.

But why were they all so willing to make sacrifices to aid her? What did they have to gain? Worse, why was she struggling to come up with a reason to resist them?

"You all need to learn to ask before you intervene, you know that?" Tenah muttered, letting out a heavy breath twinged with smoke—residue from her internal fire magic.

"Is that a yes to us intervening?" Gireth asked, a smile curling on his mouth."

"I need that tome," Tenah replied firmly. She looked to Renton, catching his downturned mouth. *Whatever.* He could judge all he liked.

"You do know the archives are restricted even to me, Ghost Boy," Vesara commented.

"Ren can get us in," Aeyis said.

Renton dragged a hand down his stubbled jaw. "We'd likely make it as far as the lobby when my illusion dissolves."

"Then work on it. Anyone who thinks they glimpse something out of the norm won't remember it," Aeyis said.

"Confident little boy, aren't you? Most of us are immune to the likes of you." Vesara tapped a painted nail against her temple. "We finish our training here."

Gireth clapped a hand down on Renton's shoulder and grinned. "More pressure on Ren to carry through then."

"Fools," Vesara muttered.

Renton sighed. "Not my fault if we get caught. I gave fair warning."

"All we need to do is get through the lobby and into the basement lift unseen. The archives is usually only occupied by historians," Vesara said. "If we *are* spotted, claim that you got lost on the way to speak to me about a contract. Act haughty and rich. They like that."

Vesara walked over to a square cut-out in the building next to the door handle and inserted her hand into the dark space. Tenah stepped closer to catch a better view of the ominous box. "What is that?"

"An identifier lock. If it doesn't recognize my fingerprints, my hand doesn't come back out. When the Embassy lets an employee go, they cut off your fingerprints to assure you no longer have access to their secrets."

A lump formed in Tenah's throat, trying to recall if her father's fingers had been smooth. It stung that she couldn't remember. She hadn't held his hand in ages.

The door clicked, and the crew filed in silently. Tenah held in a gasp as bittersweet magic spilled into the air, forming a translucent bubble that hid them from view. She picked up the tick in Renton's jaw as his fingers curled, veins popping along the back of his hands.

Gireth started down the hall, and Vesara jabbed a finger into his ribs.

I lead, shithead, she mouthed.

Aeyis muffled a snort, and a head turned from the lobby. The assassin adjusted his black-framed glasses then returned to reading his paper. Other Embassy-employed sat in neat, square arrangements of chairs or worked behind long waterfall counters broken up by small chunks of privacy glass, as if requesting a hit on a life was no more unusual than making a deposit at a bank.

Sneaking behind Vesara toward a line of golden doors with buttons, Tenah marveled at the soaring height of the Embassy. Each level above the lobby had an interior balcony draped in greenery and lit by half-moon sconces.

She made sure not to fall out of Renton's illusion, keeping close to his side. When her boot squeaked on the polished floor, he glared down at her as if he might swing her up onto his back. His skin had taken on a sickly sheen. She had the urge to touch him but kept her hand planted firmly at her side.

At the first set of gold doors, Vesara pressed the letter A. The doors pulled apart to reveal a metal box. Tenah stepped in last, forced to press her body against Renton's front. He released a long breath that fanned against her neck as the doors closed.

"I knew you could do it," Aeyis said.

"What is this box of death, Sut'hik?" Renton demanded in a low voice.

Vesara let out an airy laugh. "Have you never been in a lift before? Goes up and down on cables?"

"Hathrowyn has stairs," Renton said. "Thousands of them. Keeps us in shape."

Vesara rolled her eyes. "That's why the High Court are all such recluses."

The metal box lurched into motion, and Tenah held back a bubble of laughter as Gireth's hands smacked against the walls.

"Really? Both of you?" Vesara clapped in excitement. "Oh, I like this game."

The lift shuddered to a halt. Tenah's stomach dropped, reality hitting at the gravity of the crimes she'd committed since arriving, now deep in the belly of an assassin organization.

Stale, musty air struck her as the doors opened. It was twinged with a metallic tang that had hot blood thickening in her veins. *Screw this chemical reaction to dark magic.*

Renton's fingers brushed against her hip. "Hurry, please."

She slowly exited the lift, and the sheer size of the archives tripped up her brain's ability to function. How could such a large structure exist under the city? High ceilings were painted with elaborate murals, much like the ones her father had commissioned in their library. Inspiration much? He *had* worked here in his youth.

Tenah floated down the carpeted stairs into endless rows of bookshelves and desks for studying. Her eyes strained in the darkness, but when she summoned flame, it sputtered out in her palm, leaving her cradling a wisp of disappointing smoke.

The archives do not permit the use of fire magic, Aeyis informed her.

How do we know what to look for? Tenah asked. Her gaze switched between the two dark, towering hallways on either side of the sunken library. Hairs raised along her arms. She tried to rub warmth back into them.

I was hoping it would summon you, Aeyis said.

A menacing growl reverberated through the large, domed room, followed by a commanding "You!"

Tenah startled into the edge of a table. She winced, running a hand over the spot that would surely bruise. When she looked toward the source of the noise, her breath caught.

A cloaked shadow had Vesara pinned against a bookshelf by her throat.

Again, Tenah called for her flames, but they continued their slumber induced by whatever spell had been cast over this place. Renton stretched out an arm to tuck her behind him, half shielding her.

For a moment, no one else moved. No one seemed to know how to navigate the situation. Was this some sort of Embassy guard? Or worse, one of their assassins?

Then Gireth stepped out to play, completely at ease. Pretending to twist a long, invisible mustache, he spoke in a loud, nasally voice. "Aha! My good sir! Finally, the little traitor has been caught. The High Court has been tracking this one for a fortnight."

The assaulter looked at Gireth with dead eyes the shade of driftwood. Beneath his hood, spikes of dark blue hair jutted out like barbed wire in all directions. "Who are you?"

"Who do you want me to be?" Gireth waggled his brows. "I'm quite good at impressions."

Eyes narrowing, the assaulter muttered, "The fuck kind of joker are you?"

Gireth showed a crooked grin, his glaive in his hands in a flash. "The murderous kind."

Before bloodshed ensued, Vesara delivered a swift kick to her assaulter's groin, freeing herself.

The assaulter dropped to a knee, his features twisted up in pain as he threw back his hood. "I should have known it was you stealing from the archives. Slinking off to the Boglands without so much as a notice. Not two weeks later, stuff starts disappearing from these halls."

Vesara patted his spiky head. "Good to see you too, Hass. I see you've finally accepted your calling. Lurking in the archives like the undead."

He jerked away from her touch and shoved up onto his feet. "In your time running around engaging in criminal activity, you seem to have forgotten that guarding the archives is an honor."

"Is it an honor if you suck at it?" Vesara smirked.

Hass spun two small daggers out from under his cloak, revealing the gleam of a golden E pinned on his chest. "Shall we put that to the test?"

Ignoring the threat, Vesara examined her nails. "It's really unfair how you're treating me. You know I would never steal anything for the Boglands."

"Enlighten me then, Sut'hik." He pushed the words through clenched teeth. "What are you doing down here?"

"I don't know. I'm not in charge. I'm just here to provide them with access to all of our secrets."

Hass's face turned tomato red. "You brought them down here, and you don't even know why?"

Aeyis cleared his throat, drawing Hass's furious gaze to him. "We're looking for *The Tome of Ergh*. Its pages may hold the answers to stopping another catastrophic magical war."

Hass took in the rest of the crew. His eyes lingered on Tenah the longest, dipping to her blackened fingertips as he frowned. Tenah expected him to mention her Corruption. Instead, he turned back to Vesara, blades lowering. "So, what, you're working with a team now?"

"Is that so hard to believe?" Vesara asked.

Hass snorted. "Considering you left me for dead when we were partners, yes."

"What can I say? The Boglands have a way of transforming even the vilest of monsters." She gave him a solemn smile then quickly hid it and cleared her throat. "Love to chat more, but we're kind of in a hurry."

With a heavy sigh, Hass sheathed his blades. "I shouldn't be telling you this. *The Tome of Ergh* was stolen three weeks ago. Strange enough, another old employee came in search of it. That's when we noticed it was missing. Shortly after, all hell broke loose in Vozar."

Tenah perked up. "An old employee?"

"I didn't know him personally, but the employee assigned to the archives that night said he had two mismatched daggers and black pits for eyes."

Tenah's heart plummeted. Her knees weakened under her sagging weight. Three weeks ago, Ames had claimed that her father had fallen ill. She'd assumed he'd remained locked up in his attic as he usually did until his wave of insanity passed. Instead, it sounded like he'd been busy traveling.

"Who was sent to retrieve it?" Vesara asked, an edge to her tone.

Hass blinked at her. "No one. The order never came."

"How very curious," Gireth joined in, stroking his chin. "This smells of foul play. An inside job, for sure."

Vesara shot Gireth a furious look. "Can you be normal for one minute?"

"Normal is overrated, baby," he replied with a wink and a sly grin.

Hass straightened. "It would be best for you all to leave before I notify someone of your intrusion. You have five minutes, Sut'hik. No wandering. I swear I have no more mercy when it comes to you."

Vesara blew him a kiss, then the crew piled into the lift. Tucked into the back corner, Tenah closed her eyes. She envisioned her father's war table, warmed by pillars of sunlight through the small attic windows, each little wooden pawn hand-carved with purpose.

Her head was swimming with questions. Everything her father did was calculated. So what kind of sick game was he playing now? What even remained of the shadow mind when Chaos took control? Was her father's trip to the archives purely fueled by Chaos's desire to wield a weapon such as the tome? Or was it a strategic move made by an intelligent, passionate, self-sacrificing lord determined to find a cure for his affliction before it ate him alive?

Chapter Twenty

TENAH

Stress bubbles appeared on Tenah's sweaty palms as she trekked back to the villa with the crew. That made two strikeouts for answers on controlling dark magic. She wasn't foolish enough to make it three and waste more time tunneling down endless wormholes.

Her father's grave was already dug. She *had* to accept that. But one against a horde of feingrot and their puppet master assassin didn't bode well for her, especially when she'd lost against her father before.

She needed an army.

She needed power. If she wasn't going to get her hands on the tome, then maybe it was time to start putting some pressure on the assassin with seemingly endless authority in Denoden while she waited on word from her uncle.

Rushing ahead, she tried to catch Vesara, but the assassin cut into a maze of scarlet tents in the affluent square outside the villa.

Tenah hesitated at the first row of tents, her blood chilling at the crowd gathering in the streets, about to engage in what looked to be one of Denoden's notorious parties. The last thing she wanted to do was attend another social event, especially with the overwhelming influx of shadows—

natives and Vozarians—in the wealthy part of the city.

Pivoting, she hurried toward the villa. Putting faith in others had never panned out anyway. Vesara would turn away another request for help, and Renton would try to talk her out of any immoral acts, unaware that she'd already committed the darkest one by bargaining with death.

It was about time to see what kind of destructive power the Void could offer. Hopefully, Aeyis would keep her dark thoughts secret.

Anxiety brewing in her gut, Tenah took a detour into the kitchens. She needed something to sate her irritating, gnawing hunger. She pushed the door to the kitchen open. A young boy spun around from the sink and tossed his soapy hands up. "Yes! You're a friend of Kala Sut'hik and Ren, aren't you?"

"Fennigan Reys! So help me, if I see bubbles on my ceiling again..."

Shocked that the crew had already made the rounds with the staff, Tenah could only watch with an open mouth as a bronze woman in a crisp, white jacket emerged from a back storage room. She had crystal blue eyes and cobalt hair matching her son's, though she'd pulled hers up into an expert bun.

"Can I help you?" the woman asked, her tone polite enough to make up for her flat expression.

"Sorry, Vesara mentioned I could request a meal."

The cook wiped her nimble fingers over her pockets. "What sounds good, love?"

Tenah licked her lips nervously. The kitchen wasn't as big as the one in the manor, nor as fancy, but its caramel brown walls and wooden accents elicited a warmth that made her feel at home. Though she'd never accomplished cooking anything that wasn't completely charred—her love of fire was too strong—Tenah had spent much of her childhood in the kitchens. The staff had enjoyed feeding her, and she'd delighted in their attention as she'd watched their meticulous work.

Now they were nothing more than ash.

Shoving down that nagging grief, Tenah pointed at the basket of steaming biscuits on a central butcher block table. "Can you spare one of those and some tea?"

Dazzling blue eyes never straying from Tenah, the head cook waved her son away from the sink. "Fen, fetch the woman some tea. And some blackberry jam."

"I appreciate it." Tenah rubbed her thumbs over the tips of her blackened fingers.

The cook nodded. "I'm Zia. Anything you need, you come to me. I'll take care of you."

Cheeks heating, Tenah struggled to hold Zia's firm gaze. How much had Vesara told her? Zia didn't seem too much older, but she exuded a no-nonsense, motherly vibe.

Tenah reluctantly accepted the entire basket of biscuits, stuffed with a jar of fresh jam and peppered jerky, and a mug of citrus tea. Selfishly, she allowed herself to indulge in their company while she ate, grinning as Fen gushed about his new invention while Zia finished prepping late night meals.

Only when she'd left them did her nervous system send waves of unease through her once more. She wouldn't be staying in Denoden any longer. She'd made her choice. No matter how much Renton claimed he wanted to help, she refused to involve him or the crew in her plans. She didn't need her methods questioned. One death on her conscience would have been bad enough, but she carried hundreds branded into her skin.

With the rest of her meal and a few pieces of clothing packed, Tenah strode through the front gate. She wandered far enough from the capital to believe she wouldn't pose a threat to its safety before nestling down in a field of swaying wheat, her heart chugging with staccato beats at what she had planned.

You know what to do, she called out to darkness. *Take me into the Void.*

Chaos chirped from her trembling fingers, cleaving the air in two. It was impossible to deny the longing the dark magic nudged awake within her. As it filled up the holes clawed out by sadness and pain and fear and half a dozen other emotions she didn't want to give space for, she craved more.

Soon, a rift glittered before her like a faint scar revealed in the sunlight.

Elementals, was she making a horrible mistake? How long would this rift linger? Could something dangerous slip out? Would Chaos let her slash another rift to escape?

Shadows had a set number of casts. Most learned their limitations through training, but Ames had never allowed her to exhaust herself enough to learn her number.

Almost as if he'd been afraid of it.

Shaking the negative thoughts, Tenah crawled inside the Void. Chilled air instantly kissed her skin. It was hard not to feel like she'd leaped into the treacherous sea with no safety net and an ecosystem of murderous beasts all around her.

She held still for several breaths. Nothing stirred in the dark pockets of the Void, but that didn't squash her concern. Chaos vibrated her channels in satisfaction.

It wanted her here.

With her damaged eye, she caught a shimmer of faint, gold light. She snagged the feathery strand of energy, sucking at her teeth when it filled her with the comforting warmth of a summer breeze.

Why do you feel so familiar?

She kept a hand running along the string as she followed it, now and then glancing back at her rift to make sure it hadn't shut. Delicately, she tiptoed around writhing sources of magic like they were graves, wary of touching anything teeming with ancient fury.

Her body seized up, halting her before a Corrupted source. Tiny, imprisoned storms of black lightning crackled within its veins of silver light.

This was why she'd come. To seek this power. To pump herself with so much darkness that she'd blot out anything that threatened innocent lives again.

Bring this world's pain to an end, guttural voices chanted.

Tenah shivered, disturbed by the foreign entities speaking temptations into her mind. The strand of mysterious energy burned hotter in her palm, almost as if warning her away from Chaos.

Her head turned toward it. *Where do you lead?*

Never one to restrain her curiosity, she followed the strand deeper into the Void.

A lone, red temple rose up in the distance. Her steps faltered when she noticed her little strand cutting right through its pitch-black entrance. What was a temple doing here in the Void, where supposedly few shadows trekked and none survived for long? This was a space for magic, not worship.

As she moved closer, the voices of Chaos began to chant once more. Tenah wasn't sure if they resided in her mind or if they echoed from somewhere in the depths of the temple. All she knew was the weird energy urging her onward held a peculiar hint of vanilla that quickened her pulse.

She glanced back once more, panic jabbing at her chest when she no longer saw her rift. Her palms slicked over with sweat. She exhaled a hot breath. Whatever dangers threatened her, they didn't matter. Her life didn't matter. She shouldn't even *exist*. The most she could do now was ensure that no one else had to suffer. There would be no more deaths by her father's hand.

When Tenah ascended the temple stairs, an orb of blue light burst to life. Blood drained down into her boots as dread replaced it.

The orb expanded, revealing the death king waiting for her.

"You weren't supposed to be so broken." His frigid tone and smoldering eyes siphoned the residual warmth from her body. "I give you life, and this is how you return the debt? By cowering in fear and avoiding the truth? You haven't changed at all. You're still that pathetic, cowardly child."

Tenah stumbled back a step. The orb light bobbed at his side like some sort of sentient pet as he glided closer. She needed to leave this place, yet Chaos wouldn't heed her demands to open a rift home.

"This was a mistake," she uttered. "I can't be here."

The death king flashed his teeth so fast Tenah almost missed how they'd all sharpened to monstrous points. "You're not dead, but you will be again if you don't incite *change*."

"Change? What change? You don't know anything about me."

Long fingers shot out from his robes and grasped her jaw. His mouth brushed against her ear, drawing her breaths short. "I know everything about you. Every horrible thing you've done."

She knocked his hand away and bolted for the entrance.

"Not so fast," the death king called out. "I have use for you."

Smoky hands of magic latched onto her arms and dragged her back into the center of the temple right as the orb light flickered out.

Chapter Twenty-One
RENTON

Renton strolled Denoden's boisterous streets as if he could outrun his troubles.

The consuming defeat on Tenah's face, combined with Aeyis's claim that the missing Chaos tome was not the stuff of nightmares but a potential tool for overcoming darkness, had ignited a fire within him.

If Kherathi hadn't swiped it, Renton had a hunch on where it had ended up. It was exactly the kind of artifact Boedworth would go to great lengths to obtain. Another invaluable piece to add to his collection.

Renton had left a note in the Embassy lobby for the employee named Hass offering intel on the theft of the tome. Should Hass take the bait and travel with him to retrieve it, the assassin would prove a more credible witness to testify against Boedworth in court. It was a start to dethroning Boedworth and keeping him from Tenah.

What Renton needed now was an efficient method of travel, should Hass decline his invitation.

Cutting upstream through hordes of bustling merchant booths, Renton had to admire Denoden's enthusiasm over whatever celebration was about to unfold. He just wasn't in the mood for it. He browsed a small market jammed between two white stone buildings. Strips of faded cloth draped over the stalls, blocking the harsh rays of the sun. Smoke billowed from the vendors frying up seasoned meat and dough powdered with too much sugar and cinnamon for his tastes. His nose wrinkled at the sticky sweet smell clinging to the air, but in a moment of weakness, he dished out a few krotens for a bag of the treats.

Maybe Tenah would like them.

Venders haggled with shadows over jewels and scraps of rare metal and spices in a manner that confused him, often resorting to name-calling each other's mothers before settling a deal with a handshake and a grin.

A table of assorted small glass orbs snagged his attention. He slipped through two bickering shadows to better examine the cracked, murky orbs.

Damn. Not a single glimmer of life when he picked them up to spin them in his palm.

Sniffing out a potential deal, the haggardly vendor appeared, his gold teeth shining. "Fine artifacts, those transportation orbs. Rare relics once used for the most advanced and rapid travel."

Renton frowned. "Got any that work?"

The vendor's grin dropped. "Sold the last of those to the Embassy, oh I'd say about seven years ago. Haven't gotten my hands on any more shipments."

"Of course," Renton grumbled. Had one been within his reach in the archives? "Thanks anyway."

He turned and nearly flattened a petite shadow.

"I can't say I'm surprised to find you here." Vesara propped her hands on her small hips. She'd swapped out leathers for breathable silks. For as much grief as she'd given on the flight to Denoden, she'd melted right back into her culture. "Still looking for the tome?"

"None of your business," Renton said, brushing past.

To his irritation, she stalked after him like a Bogland insect, deadly and annoying.

Renton tossed her a cruel look. "You don't owe us anything, if that's why you're hanging around."

"Do you generally hate most shadows?"

He pushed on through the crowds. "I'm wary of those my intuition warns me against."

Vesara kept pace, and he didn't miss the way shadow eyes trailed her in admiration.

"Look, it's nothing personal," he clarified. "I just have a thing against your profession."

Everything the Embassy stood for went against Mire's codes. They operated like Boedworth, accepting contracts often formed out of spite or greed, not for the protection of shadowkind. And yeah, he realized their contracts went through a lengthy approval process, but it still didn't sit well with him that the High Court would allow such an establishment to exist. Any time Renton had complained to Elder Nithril about something that seemed unjust, Nithril had explained that balance was essential in their world. In other words, the High Court believed some evil necessary, and they were happy to let the Embassy carry out that evil to keep their own hands clean from sin.

"I quit three years ago. Couldn't complete a contract. So there's that. Proof I have a heart and a conscience," Vesara admitted, rubbing a hand up and down her arm in discomfort. "The only reason I can access the Embassy is because Izral makes special exceptions for me."

Renton processed her words in silence. All right, so his initial impression of the assassin was wrong. She wasn't a mindless killer.

"Not enough for you to open up to me?" Vesara asked.

He pinched the bridge of his nose, fighting the urge to pick her up and set her somewhere else. In a crate beside the vendor's tables. In an alleyway. In a locked vault. He figured none of this would hinder her from returning to pester him.

"I need a transportation orb," he said.

"You won't find one here. The Embassy confiscated them."

Renton sighed. "Yes, I've just been told that."

She pursed her lips. "Grumpy after dinner, aren't you?"

"Probably grumpy because I haven't had dinner."

"I can get you an orb."

Renton paused to meet her flat gaze.

"On two conditions." Vesara held up two fingers, her nails painted a deep blue.

"Please make this good."

"You tell me why you need it, and…" She drew out the word, jabbing a thumb over her shoulder at the central square packed with luxurious red tents. "You attend that tonight."

Renton scowled as he took in the exuberant party decor. Bird and moon paper lanterns strung between tents. Rustic wooden tables and metal fire pits. Tasseled and beaded throw pillows heaped on elaborate woven rugs. And enough barrels of booze to drown the capital.

"Izral's throwing me a party for my return," she said, "but I have no true friends. Hass was it, and as you witnessed, he wasn't pleased to see me."

"That's a bit pathetic, Sut'hik."

She threw out her arms. "Will you just come?"

"All right," he agreed. "As for what I'm doing, I believe the tome is in Cragnore. I plan to retrieve it."

Her eyes glittered with excitement. "I'm coming with you."

"I don't have krotens to pay you."

"Is it this hard to make friends?"

"Usually, you start by being polite," he said. "I'll attend your thing. The orb will be in my hands immediately after. You will stay here to watch over my brother and Tenah in case Boedworth is using this as a way to separate me from them."

Vesara clapped and gave her knuckles a solid pop. "Won't be hard to do. She's quite nice to look at, isn't she?"

Renton's brows lifted. He had a thought to warn the assassin off Tenah, but she'd already slunk off like a nefarious street cat after a mouse.

En route back to the villa to demand Aeyis and Gireth attend the party with him, a breeze from the open gates caught him wrong, tensing up his muscles and awakening the shard in his chest with a jolt.

What the fuck is that?

He diverted, trailing the path of Chaos. Soldiers lazed atop the walls, and Renton frowned up at them. Though, he supposed they didn't see much action with the Embassy looming at their backs.

At least a mile out from Denoden, tucked in a field of swishing wheat, he discovered a body. He'd recognize that smoky hair anywhere. He broke into a sprint, his blood pressure rising.

Renton dropped beside Tenah, ignoring the strange buzzing of a waning rift nearby. His nostrils flared at the scent of storms clinging to her scalding flesh. Without hesitation, he pulled her against his chest, his fingers stroking down the markings along her wrists, more elaborate than they'd been the last time he'd seen them.

Rage flooded in, overwhelmingly thick.

He'd left her to her own devices last night, and look what had happened.

By some unnatural force, Tenah lurched upright and sucked in a lungful of air. The shard launched an attack on his nerve endings, curling his torso over her as he grunted. It had almost become a sign of her proximity, this pain in his heart.

"Renton?" her voice was small. Weak. Unsure.

She extracted herself from his arms but remained on the ground. Her eyes landed on the sliver of the rift, and a shudder rolled through her. "Tell me you brought me here."

Confusion marred his features. "No. I tracked the scent of Chaos and found you and that thing. Tenah, did you open another rift?" His question went unanswered, and unease settled in his chest. Forcefully, he asked, "Did you see anyone around you? What is the last thing you remember?"

"I was..." Her brows furrowed. "I went for a walk. And then nothing. I don't remember a thing."

Renton ground his teeth, sensing the lie twisted around her words.

"Another walk?" His tone was accusing. Clinging to his anger felt better than the helplessness threatening to take over. He wanted to save her, but he didn't know how. "No one crossed your path?"

His mind split in all directions, running through potential attackers. Boedworth's hunters. Her own father.

She shook her head then lowered her chin.

Renton released a breath. "Are you okay, Tenah?"

Her gaze darted around the field, quiet except for the calm breeze. Again, his question went unanswered. Biting back the urge to lay into her for such carelessness, Renton helped her onto her feet and escorted her back into Denoden. Alarm bells were ringing in the logical part of his brain. Something wasn't right.

"Talk about it later?" He turned to face her at the door to the villa, his firm stare conveying he wouldn't let the matter of her safety go.

Tenah nodded but continued avoiding direct eye contact. Whatever had occurred out in that field, she was rattled beyond reason. He wanted to wrap his arms around her. Hold her. Assure her that he would protect her.

But he wasn't sure of anything right now, especially how to comfort someone when they had iron walls in place. The irony wasn't lost on him. He'd kept everyone at a distance for so long, he wasn't sure he was in any shape to form relationships, half-convinced he'd find a way to fuck things up again.

Vesara burst from the villa doors in dramatic fashion and pounced on Tenah. "I need you."

Instantly, Renton slid between them, crowding the assassin's space. "Now is not the time for your selfish demands."

A light hand touched the back of his ribs, spreading heat and prickles of electricity through him.

"It's okay," Tenah whispered.

Renton closed his eyes, physically unable to watch her vanish through the villa doors, tugged along like someone's plaything. Pressing his fingers to his temples, he groaned as he realized he'd left Tenah's desserts out in the field. He turned around. Soldiers should be notified about the rift anyway in case something slipped out.

Then he needed a drink, a strong one at that.

Chapter Twenty-Two

TENAH

The death king had forced her to tear open that rift. There was no other explanation. And from the sheer horror painted on Renton's face, he'd sensed something very wrong about that magic too.

To be so unaware of what was happening to her body—it was a violation. Was she even alive if someone or *something* else was controlling her?

Flashes of a war-torn isle were branded behind her closed eyes, the land decaying under a film of dark smog. The air electric, singeing the inside of her nose.

She swallowed, her hands shaking as she reached up to her tender scalp where the death king had gripped her and forced her down on her knees. That was real, wasn't it? And so were the ruthless waves of darkness he'd pumped into her aching channels until she was numb. Until she was nothing.

Then she'd lost consciousness.

Tenah slid her thumbs over her palms, unnerved by the force with which Chaos had demanded she tear into Renton's chest and uncover what was hidden there when she'd regained consciousness. Whatever force had sunk its teeth in her was tempted by that pulse of something foreign buried inside of him. Her mind flicked to the death king, but what could he possibly want from shadowkind that he couldn't obtain with his own power?

By the grace of Vesara's neediness, she'd pulled Tenah away from his side. Now she just had to keep away from Renton. She'd overstayed her welcome in Denoden anyway. However, the idea of marching south after what she'd just experienced had her stomach churning and her hands trembling at her sides.

She just needed a few moments to collect herself.

Drawing herself back into the present, Tenah asked, "What is this about?"

The assassin's short bob swayed at her furious pace through the villa halls. She wore a long, blue gown with cut-outs along her midriff. Chiffon flowed from her waist to the floor, sewn with so many gems, she shone like a galaxy. Tiny charms jingled on her ankles.

"You're attending a party with me. Not dressed like that, of course." Vesara looked back at her, gaze sweeping up and down her attire with disdain.

Tenah would have argued, but her outfit was filthy. Some of the beading had come undone in her fight with death incarnate. "I'm really not in the mood."

Vesara spun on her, tiny hands clasping her forearms. "And I'm not above begging. I need as much moral support as I can get tonight."

Deflating at the hint of desperation in the assassin's voice, Tenah nodded. "Okay."

Since when did she care about anyone outside of her family? Since a night of drinking might be the perfect distraction from holing up in her bedroom and obsessing over whatever horrible thing had just happened while she'd blacked out.

Up another flight of stairs, Vesara practically carried her through two red, meticulously carved wooden doors. Tenah ran her fingertips over the flame cradled in the hand of the Great Elemental Renix. He'd fought against Xith centuries ago, only to meet his demise.

What a discouraging turn her thoughts had taken.

The doors shut, trapping her inside the assassin's bedroom. Tenah's jaw dropped. Three walls of the room were carved into giant, arched windows overlooking the capital. A massive four-poster bed took up the center of the room, dipped in red-and-purple silks. There was a small crystal pool along the balcony, lined by plush lounge chairs like soldiers on watch.

And the artwork…landscapes crafted so perfectly, they looked like windows to the outside world, begging to be explored.

Vesara vanished into a closet longer than a hallway. Colorful attire flew out at an incredible rate, piling up on the floor.

"Does this have anything to do with the tents outside?" Tenah asked, anxiety blooming in her chest.

Vesara popped her head out. Her arm followed, clutching an expensive-looking ruby, two-piece ensemble with delicate navy-and-cream stitchwork. "I knew I had something to match your eyes."

Face twisting up, Tenah replied, "I'm not wearing that."

"Why not?" Vesara met her challenge with all the wrath of a powerful woman used to getting her way.

Tenah waved a hand up and down at it. "There's nothing to it."

"Do you see how Denesè dress?" Nimble hands somehow forced the outfit into Tenah's fists. From the determined sparkle in the assassin's glacial eyes, there was no resisting. She hastily dressed, the rich material gliding over her skin.

At least it wasn't another blasted gown or skirt. That much, she could appreciate. And while the shorts could have been a hand longer, they *did* breath nice in the hot evening air.

It was better than anything the staff had purchased for her.

Her stomach knotted with guilt. Quickly, she shoved all troubling emotions down and slid the leather gloves Renton had given her back on. Now was not the time to process grief.

With a skilled flick of a knife, Vesara cut the tie in Tenah's hair. Smoky locks tumbled to her elbows in unruly waves. Then she was maneuvered to a gilded, floor-length mirror.

"Modesty's frowned upon in this kingdom," Tenah grumbled, taking in her frazzled reflection. She looked strung out on adrenaline, a strange combination with the outfit that revealed all of her toned midriff, more cleavage than she realized she had, and most of her long legs.

Accent rolling thick and smooth, Vesara said, "There's nothing wrong with showing off. You won't have this body forever."

Tenah's chest heaved with a painful breath. No, she wouldn't have this body much longer because it didn't even belong to her.

Vesara circuited the room, extinguishing candles with her fingers. She regarded Tenah with a troubled, far-off look. "That day in the prison cart, it wasn't the first time I've been arrested. I was twelve when I was thrown into a cell in Corran."

Tenah frowned, picturing the grim condition of that prison. Corran was a small, eastern Vozarian town inhabited mostly by shadows kicked out of the capital, unsuited to civility. She'd ventured there once with her father and immediately decided she never needed to return.

Vesara wandered over to her desk and picked up a pair of large, gold hoops, jabbing them into each ear. "I started out as a pickpocket. Growing up on a farm outside of Denoden, I saw how hard my parents worked for next to nothing, and I vowed never to have that life. So I took to Denoden's slums, swiping from the rich right under their noses. It wasn't long, and I was mastered in the art of cracking vaults."

At the age of twelve, Tenah had been poring over histories of the world in the library, gorging on chocolates, and riling up Ames just for sheer enjoyment.

Crinkling her nose as if she'd caught a whiff of something rotten, Vesara continued. "My family works the crop fields all hours of the sun. Their harvests are meager. Had they sold their land to the king, they might have made enough to settle down in a nice home within the city. But no." She drew out her last word with an eye roll. "Sut'hiks are farmers by blood."

Tenah had yet to force her mouth closed. There was so much grandeur behind the esteemed Embassy employees. It was hard to believe they hadn't all risen from wealth and power.

"There was this homeless girl named Pri. She was a year younger than me. She hadn't eaten in three days, and you couldn't even call what she was wearing clothes. A moth-eaten blanket was more like it. I let her break into a lord's house with me in Corran, intending to split the coin we stole. But Pri was handsy. She touched everything. Broke a vase and startled the lord awake in his bed chambers. I got caught letting her slip away."

Elementals, did Vesara even realize how lucky she was that it hadn't been *her* manor she'd tried to steal from? If Ames hadn't dissolved her mind, her father would have turned her into dust.

"How long were you sentenced?" Tenah couldn't help but ask.

"All of three hours before the Embassy appeared on orders from Izral—prince at the time." Her features shriveled up. "Had he not caught me snatching jewels from the neck of his cousin during a theater show weeks earlier, he might never have tracked me down. I would have remained a farm girl locked in prison for petty theft."

"But you don't like working for the Embassy." Tenah's brows furrowed.

"Oh, I liked it just fine until the royals became too involved in our work. I quit. Went solo for a while. Got myself tangled up in a mess in the Boglands, but that's another story. After I got busted out, I ran into Pri on Denoden's streets. She'd come out on top with the haul she'd run off with. I threw cruel words at her, swearing I would never forgive her. All over three measly hours I sat in a cell. Pri vanished after that. I haven't the heart to track her down. The things I said were disgraceful. I have to live with that every day."

Tenah lowered her head, visualizing Renton's infuriating face and startling eyes. She'd given him hell. Now she was avoiding him entirely.

"When I became successful at the Embassy, the other employees only tolerated me. I was good at my job, but I was also self-absorbed and greedy. You wouldn't think I came from a humble background." Vesara gave an airy sigh. "Living in the Boglands without the fame and piss-poor reputation wasn't bad for me. I learned this puny little heart could love."

Tenah understood. She'd dreamed of giving up her title and wealth to travel the world.

"The point of my rambling is that forgiveness is a gift. You never know when someone is going to rob us of something we cherish too soon. That insufferable sack of knives and bad decisions cares for you. His eyes trail you everywhere."

"Who?"

Vesara groaned, giving Tenah's cheeks an affectionate pat. "The hunter. You look so pale. Go easy on the Vristarian wine tonight."

Face heating, Tenah swallowed and tugged at the hem of her shorts.

"The night is young, and we just escaped prison. That's deserving of celebration, don't you think?"

Shadows poured into the affluent square, dressed in breezy chiffon and silk. Their scandalous attire thankfully allowed Tenah to blend in as she followed Vesara through the maze of tents. Her eyes lingered on shadows in envy, watching them twirl and parade around a giant fire pit to a seductive drum beat.

And the food.

Tenah stopped to absorb all the smells, her mouth watering. Endless spreads of ripe fruits, smoked meats, and hearty pastries that spoke the language of her grumbling stomach. She stole a flaky creation with shredded meat baked into the center, nearly inhaling it. Then devoured two more, blaming the assassin for luring her down here just to sneak away, leaping into the ring of wild dancers.

When Tenah was done gorging, she perused the tents, anxiously searching for a familiar face. She found the boys lounging under their own tent like well-fed street cats. Gireth was sprawled in a mountain of pillows like a throne. Aeyis was hypnotized by the dancers, and Tenah wondered if he was tuned in to their carnal thoughts.

Her eyes sought Renton last, her stomach lurching. He leaned against a support pole with a mug in his hand, his face a blank mask. He wore black pants, fitted around his thighs, and a navy tunic that clung to his chest, the sleeves rolled up to his elbows to reveal veiny arms.

Drawing in short breaths, she turned to Gireth—the safest option.

"The girl parties! She looks good in red too," Gireth noted, giving her a wink and holding out a glass of bubbly wine, which she gladly accepted.

"Probably not the best idea," a low voice warned.

She dragged her gaze back to Renton. His eyes bored through her, the same uncanny shade as the Boglands that had molded him. Hot blood shot through her body, leftover embarrassment from the incident in the field and now the outfit she wore.

Curse you, Vesara!

Pretending she hadn't heard Renton, she forced her gaze out over the dancers, sipping from her glass.

"Lighten up, Nazrata," Gireth playfully scolded.

Renton shook his head. "You've just volunteered to take care of her when she can't handle Denesè spirits."

This only encouraged Gireth's amusement. "Oh no, how terrible, stuck taking care of a beautiful woman."

He reached for the pitcher of wine to refill his empty glass then raised it in cheers to Tenah with a broad smile. She giggled. The warmth from the wine in combination with the heat radiating off the fire lulled her into a relaxed, dreamy state. Soon, it became a game. Every time she felt the urge to peek over at Renton or think about the field or Chaos or the death king or even Vesara's story, she took another drink.

It was hard not to let the lively energy of the festivities wash over her. She debated joining in the parade around the square's fountain when a small hand wrapped around her arm in a death grip.

"Hey," Tenah protested.

"Hush, I just need to borrow you for moral support. If I give you the signal, light his ass on fire, okay?" Vesara said, tugging her through the crowd.

Tenah opened her mouth to protest—she didn't even know what the signal was—when Vesara stopped before a palanquin on which sat a young male held up by armored soldiers. He had a well-trimmed beard, cropped dark hair, and half a dozen gold rings down each ear.

Her body went rigid. Only royalty arrived in such a manner. She considered dropping into a bow, except Vesara's hand kept her upright.

Horror-stricken, Tenah could only stand by as the assassin began laying into the royal.

"You nit-witted dung heap!" Vesara said. "I warned you not to show your smug face here."

The royal smiled deviously as he turned his hand in the air, examining it in boredom. "Your warning seemed more like a suggestion at the time."

"Everything is merely a suggestion to you. I never wanted this stupid party to be about me. Now all of Denoden thinks I'm home for good. And they're calling me Kala. Explain that to me."

As if he hadn't just been the victim of the assassin's fiery rage, the royal stole a look at Tenah, sizing her up with a lazy grin. A shiver walked down her spine, despite the fact that his stare wasn't unkind. An anomaly for someone in such a position of power.

"Who's your plaything, Sut'hik?" he asked, running his hand back and forth over the velvet material beneath him.

Blinking at Tenah like she'd forgotten her presence at her side, Vesara yanked Tenah behind her. "She's no one."

Was blinking the signal? Because Tenah didn't think igniting a royal on fire was a smart idea.

The royal tsked. "Unfortunate. Here I'd believed your little soul-searching adventure had helped you change your ways. Girl, what is your name?"

"Don't answer him." A firm order.

Tenah licked her lips, eyes darting between the high-ranking Embassy assassin and the mysterious royal. Which was more dangerous to cross? After the field incident and too many drinks, Tenah didn't care to aggravate the one with more power to throw her out of the city tonight.

"Tenah Delemor," she said.

The royal sat up, pivoting his body toward her. "How very curious. Your father reached out to me a few weeks ago. Shame about his health."

Shock lifted her brows. Then her hands curled into fists. "What reason would my father have for speaking with Denoden?"

The royal ran his fingers over his lips, mimicking a zipper. "I was sworn to secrecy."

Rage unfurled kernels of fire through her channels. Her father had discredited the northern kingdom in all of his war machinations. Why had he been in communication with their royals?

The royal dangled a slippered foot off the palanquin. "I might be persuaded to part with my secrets if you paid me a visit at the palace sometime. Vesara only shows up to yell and demand things from me." He threw her an accusatory look. "It gets so lonely."

"I suppose if that's a command, I can't refuse," Tenah replied.

His unrefined laughter filled the air, startling her. "Can we keep her, Ves?"

Vesara bristled. "She isn't a possession."

"No?" He feigned shock.

"But something that *is* my possession was supposed to be returned to me this evening."

"Calm down. Don't make a scene." The royal motioned at one of his guards. A silk bag was produced and handed over to Vesara. Before Tenah could ask, the assassin hauled her back under the cover of the tents, stars and flames blurring in her vision along the way.

"Tonight's the night. I think I'll kill him," Vesara muttered.

"Who was that?" Tenah asked, her voice sounding wrong in her ears.

"Izral."

Tenah stopped in her tracks. "That was the King of Vristar you just insulted?"

"Yeah, he's a lech. He thinks everyone is his to play with as he pleases. When he's intrigued by something, he feels entitled to it."

Tenah's brows furrowed. She'd just met the king and disclosed her family name, and he hadn't immediately thrown her in prison. What the hell was going on? Did her father have some sort of secret connection with Izral, and if so, would Izral have insight into his whereabouts?

Vesara grabbed her by the shoulders. "You are never allowed to visit him. He won't give you what you want. He won't spare resources to help you."

The assassin left Tenah slightly irritated and sashayed over to the feast. Emboldened by the wine, Tenah returned to where Gireth was draped over his mountain of pillows. She took his drink and set it down on the barrel serving as a table. His cheeks were flushed, and his smile worn-in as she struggled to hoist him onto his feet.

"You're going to fall asleep if you sit here any longer." She huffed.

His toothy grin was contagious. "Didn't peg you for the wild type."

"What, the prison cart and flames didn't scream danger and excitement to you?" She wiggled her fingers between them as if that were how magic was casted.

It wasn't so much of a dance they partook in but a sloppy, drunken gallop around the square with other shadows. The thundering drums almost felt primal, beating in rhythm with her pulse. It was like shedding a stifling skin. The constricting pressure of everything building within her—she could drown it all in wine and starlight tonight.

On one of their rotations, Gireth dared an invitation for Vesara to join. Clutching a heaping plate of food like a savage beast, Vesara aggressively shot him down.

"I think she likes me." He chuckled, twirling them past Renton, who'd been watching them like a hawk, which only made her want to rebel more.

"You know," Gireth started hesitantly, "Ren's one of the good ones. The best I've ever known actually."

Her hand clenched his tighter.

"I'll admit, it takes some work to get under that thick skin. I suppose I had an advantage, meeting him before Boedworth. Those were his hell-raising days. But as soon as it came time for us to start camp, Renton always took on the hardest missions. He worked tirelessly to improve his skills, picking up slack for the others in our group, including me. He never let anything touch us out in the Boglands when we ran trial hunts, and he took responsibility when we failed. I envied him. I thought maybe if I stayed close to him, I'd learn to fight like him too. Then Boedworth messed up everything." He withdrew a hand to brush a stray lock of his dark hair back. "Here I am, talking up another male when I could be putting in a good word for myself."

Tenah gave his shoulder an endearing pat. "Should we take a break?"

The party had provided an excellent distraction from the thoughts that plagued her, but their romps had churned the wine in her stomach. Wiping perspiration from her temple on the back of her hand, she walked back to the tent they'd claimed. She was determined to steal Gireth's comfy throne of pillows.

Her attention snagged on a curvy woman striding up to Renton, her dark curls swishing over bare shoulders. Tenah stopped to watch as something dark stirred in her chest.

Renton didn't give the woman so much as a look. However, that didn't stop her from resting a hand on his chest. Slowly, she traced a finger down the collar of his shirt, hand slipping under the fabric…

One blink, Tenah was standing beside the tent, and the next she was positioned behind the woman, furious magic tumbling through her channels.

"Back off," she growled, loud enough to alert other shadows of potential danger.

The woman scowled, appearing pained to have to drag her eyes away from Renton. "Excuse me?"

Tenah knew she should let it go. It didn't matter who the hunter decided to waste his time with. But didn't she have a right to ruin his fun after he attempted to stop her from having a good night?

There was a flicker of amusement in his vibrant eyes.

Eager to win back his attention, the woman hooked a finger through his belt as she batted her disgustingly long lashes up at him. "Do you know this girl?"

He considered this with a tilt of his head, unbound hair spilling over his shoulder. "I might, if she'd let me."

Strings of black lightning snapped around Tenah's knuckles, aching to crawl under the woman's flesh and burn up everything inside.

In the span of a breath, Renton transported the woman a safe distance away.

Horror constricted around Tenah as she turned to flee. The world lurched sideways. She stumbled over the uneven street, catching herself on a tent support as visions of dark silhouettes flashed in her blurred vision.

Feingrot, here in the city?

Her heart pounded too hard. It took her a moment of heavy breathing to realize that the feingrot weren't real. That her father wasn't here to orchestrate more death.

Renton's arms ensnared her waist, gently pulling her back against his solid form to ground her when Chaos strived to feed her more fear and despair.

"That's twice tonight you've tried to bail on me." He nuzzled his head into her neck. "I'm not letting you go until you calm that magic."

Her pulse throbbed under her skin, and she wriggled in his hold. "Too close."

"Relax." His mouth skimmed up the shell of her ear. "I won't do anything reckless."

"Oh, but you'll do reckless things with another woman," she retorted, though her body had already molded into him, her muscles slack and magic tamed.

How did he manage to mess up everything and still affect her like this?

Electricity zinged from her head to her toes when his mouth brushed along her neck. Goosebumps rose on her heated skin. Surely, he would feel the spike in her body temperature.

"Is this not what you wanted all along?" he murmured.

Tenah sucked in a breath, struggling to keep her composure as his warm mouth pressed against the hollow behind her ear.

"How is what I did any different from you parading around with my friend?" he asked.

"Parading," she exclaimed, fighting to break free. His arms tightened around her. "I was only having a bit of fun. Renix knows I need it."

His hands dropped to her hips, and her heart fluttered. His thumbs slowly traced over her bare skin. "I wish you'd just admit it."

It was getting hard to think. Between his touch and the mind-melting effects of his prickling magic, the alcohol and the heat.

"Admit what?" she asked breathlessly.

"That you were jealous." His teeth pressed lightly into the spot between her neck and shoulder. "That there's something undeniable between us."

Invisible flames consumed her. She was hyperaware of every place their bodies touched. Every little shift in his body.

"That's...well..."

Words dissolved on her tongue as Renton pressed himself fully against her backside. Her body took over thought processing, fighting between delivering an elbow into his ribs or rolling her hips into him.

"I didn't think you the womanizing type, but clearly, you've had practice at this," she whispered, closing her eyes and resting the back of her head against his chest.

He flattened a calloused palm along the side of her stomach in a claiming way then slowly ran it down her curves to slide around her inner thigh, tugging her closer. "Mmm, I would ruin you, angel."

Desire shot between her legs. She tilted her hips slightly. Just to test.

Renton's low growl rolled through her. He spun her around, his wild eyes alight with lust. Freed from his hold, a sickening feeling overcame her as she caught flashes of scaled Corrupt with horns and leathery wings slinking between dark tents. Worse, she glimpsed markings creeping out of her gloves like overgrown vines. More conjurings of her sick, drunk mind or Renton toying with illusions?

She stumbled back. "Quit messing with me."

She took off for the villa, wine sloshing in her stomach with vengeance. *Stupid.* She'd been so stupid to think that drinking would solve her problems. Stupid for getting tangled up with the hunter.

Tenah made it as far as the villa's front steps when acid burned up her throat.

"I warned you," Renton said, catching her braced against the building.

"Apparently, once is never enough for me." She groaned. "Please leave me alone."

"So you can vomit and pass out in an alleyway? I think not."

She keeled over, and he was at her side in an instant, guiding her down the steps to a large, potted bush. She emptied the contents of her stomach there as he swept back her hair and ran soothing circles along her lower back.

"Don't worry. Vesara can buy a new bush." He chuckled darkly.

After her embarrassing, body-wracking heaves ceased, Renton handed her a piece of folded cloth to wipe her mouth. He took her under an arm and escorted her into the villa.

"You can't pass up an opportunity to see me at my worst, can you?" she muttered.

His mouth pulled down at the corners. "It's not like that."

Tenah let him wallow in silence for a bit before her head found its place against his shoulder. His scent was like a fresh stream or a fall breeze, cool and crisp.

"The drinking had nothing to do with celebrating, did it?" Renton asked softly.

Leaden pressure expanded her lungs. "What does it matter to you?"

They'd reached her bedroom door. He eased back enough to analyze her expression. "Because I care, Tenah. I thought that was obvious by now."

He walked her inside, helping her climb into bed and drawing the sheet up to her neck.

"Why do you have to be so insufferable?" she asked.

His laugh was low, stirring up that traitorous want low in her belly. "I've heard that a time or two before."

She groaned. "Tell me this doesn't last long. My head is swimming."

"Denoden enjoys strong spirits, but they don't like the effect to linger. You'll feel better after some rest."

He moved to leave, and Tenah's hand latched onto his corded arm.

"Please. Don't go." She'd already lost the remains of her dignity letting him watch her barf.

Renton frowned down at her, and she was certain he would brush her off. What reason had she given him to stay?

Pushing out a defeated breath, he grabbed a chair from the corner of her room and dragged it over to her bedside. He flipped it around, plopping down on it backward and resting his arms over the top. "I'm not going anywhere, angel."

What a miserable, leech-like creature she'd become, thinking he was hers to order around after striving to push him away mere hours ago.

"You called me that before. Why?" she asked quietly, worming deeper under the sheet. How could she be referred to anything that close to the gods?

His frown deepened, as if he hadn't been aware of what he'd done. He caught her hand when she lifted it to rub at her foggy eye. "You've been doing that since the Boglands. What's wrong with it?"

Panic bubbling up, she snapped back, "Nothing."

But her anger didn't deter him. Methodically, he worked the leather glove off her hand. His fingers brushed the inside of her forearm in a soothing pattern. Was her skin supposed to be that sensitive?

"Shall I keep a tally on your lies?" he asked. "I'm learning to read you, Tenah."

She swallowed and dropped her gaze to his hand tracing patterns on her skin because she couldn't hold his fervent eyes.

It wasn't her fault. Shutting down questions came as second nature. Ames had constantly nagged her. Was she studying? Had she meditated enough? Why hadn't she progressed with her magic? What did she think was holding her back?

And when her father spiraled into one of his moods, she mastered the art of avoiding conversation altogether.

Renton lifted his hand to stroke a thumb beneath her lower lip. "I'm here when you need to talk. Or when you don't. Now sleep."

Chapter Twenty-Three
RENTON

Renton snuck out of Tenah's room before dawn. Last night confirmed it—this was more than just a natural desire to protect. When she was near, his eyes were drawn to her alone.

He walked the quiet villa halls with purpose, gritting his teeth when he discovered Vesara's suite locked up. He'd expected to retrieve the transportation orb. Now he was empty-handed moments before he'd requested Hass show up. Boedworth would soon receive word from sources Renton paid in the Abyss, enticing him with an offer of topaz at a safehouse outside of Cragnore, a diversion to lure him and a handful of his elite hunters out of their den while he retrieved the missing tome for Tenah.

Brother, Aeyis spoke into his mind. *Care to explain why that archives assassin is arguing with Vesara outside the villa at this hour?*

Renton let slip a low snarl. *Handling it.*

You were going to the Boglands without me. I thought we had an agreement.

My plan was to keep you here. Safe.

When Renton made it out onto the street, three heads snapped to him. Aeyis stood nonchalantly behind Vesara. Her hands were raised, teeth bared at Hass in some territorial animalistic dance.

"Why does Hass get to go with you and not the one who retrieved the orb?" Vesara laid into him. "Do you know what I had to promise in order to get this stupid thing back?"

Hass straightened, his nostrils flared. "What, did you agree to finally carry out your duty to this kingdom? It's so hard for you, isn't it, thinking about anything but yourself?"

Vesara's fingers splayed as if she might claw him to death.

Renton eased between them, fully prepared to catch a fist or a knife. "You're not coming with, Sut'hik. Stay here and make sure no one lays a hand on Tenah."

She held his firm stare. Then she slapped the pouch with the transportation orb into his outstretched hand. "I suppose Hass gets to turn that into the Embassy when you're done with it." She sneered. "The orb won't take you directly into Cragnore. There's too many wards in place. Same with returning home. It'll drop you in the fields outside Denoden's gates, so have fun with that."

Renton slid the orb into his palm and spun it carefully in the early morning sunlight, seeking the image of Brinedale's gloomy rows of neat townhomes in its depths. Boedworth had dragged him there once to carry out an execution. Renton's hesitation had earned him a blade to the stomach.

Bright green light pulsed from the orb, trapping Renton and Hass in a sphere of magic. His brother snuck into the bubble of magic right before it crackled.

"You're a horrible listener," Renton muttered.

Stretched and tugged, they were spat out onto a rain-slick street lined with uniform dark two-story homes. No sunlight pierced the blanket of soupy clouds above Brinedale, making it hard to determine a time of day.

Renton tossed his brother the orb. "Any sign of trouble, and you teleport out of here, understood?"

No one will know I'm here, Aeyis said. *I'll keep a mental sweep of the surroundings for Boedworth and his hunters while you pillage his den.*

Dread wriggled into Renton's chest. This wouldn't go wrong. He'd met his quota for misfortune in this life already. They would finally shake free of Boedworth. They would bring his crimes to light before the High Court. Everything would be fine.

Rain fell in cold sheets. It plastered Renton's hair to his skull and drenched the protective clothes beneath his armor as he wove Hass deeper into the swamps.

There were countless entrances into Cragnore. Natives had burrowed out in all directions much like anthill. Pinpointing them hidden under illusions during a storm however…

Renton tuned in to the shard buried in his heart. He let it guide him past the stone ruins of an abandoned cathedral dedicated to the worship of Sakkren. There the shard dropped him at the bank of a sludge pool. He dipped a finger in and withdrew it, completely dry.

"The hell you doing?" Hass asked gruffly, coming to a halt beside him.

The shard jabbed at his heart, signaling the presence of dark magic. Funny, the very thing that made him cursed was what made him excel at his profession.

"Finding us a shortcut," Renton answered, leaping into the fake sludge pool.

His boots struck the compacted dirt floor of a tunnel. Hass followed suit without coaxing, landing soundlessly beside him.

Renton drenched them in magic, obscuring them from sight as they approached the end of the tunnel. Two hunters in heavy armor blocked the sloping path into the cavernous, stinking pit that was Cragnore. Murky, green orb lights hung from the ceiling like globs of slime, and mottled roots and vines ensnared sleek, granite buildings along a spiderweb of roads.

Hass didn't wait for an order. He struck with precise jabs of his knives. Renton felt a prick of guilt as he stepped over the hunter's bodies. He supposed Hass too had been raised on the idea that everything spawned in the Boglands was evil.

Sweating from the effort of casting magic, Renton allowed his illusion to drop like a curtain. Tossed into the busy flow of traffic through the city,

Hass peeked over the edge of a bridge.

"There's a pervading odor here," Hass muttered, wrinkling his nose.

Renton knew what resided at the bottom of the pit. Stagnant water, intermingled with corpses dropped in by the monsters that hid in the gnarled roots of the alleyways and dead-end tunnels.

"We can't all live in skyscrapers and palaces," Renton said sarcastically. Hass tossed him a questioning look, but Renton simply nodded at two more hunters lurking outside the mahogany doors of Boedworth's domain. "No blades this time. Have some respect for life."

Tucked behind a merchant stall, Hass gave him a nod. Renton had the brief inclination to question what Vesara had done to lose his trust, only because he'd left Tenah in her care. But they didn't have the luxury of time.

Renton kicked the leg out from the stall.

Produce tumbled into the road, causing a motorized cart to slam into a horse-drawn wagon and then into another line of stalls. Shadows and Ashens erupted into a mad dash, eager to avoid the explosion of fruits, vegetables, and splintered wood.

Hass on his heels, Renton charged across the road and dipped into his employer's vile lair. Inside, Renton braced against the wall of the low-lit, smoky space. His breaths came in labored spurts, his stomach churning sickly. He sensed the eyes of gamblers and hunters on him.

"You good?" Hass asked, eyeing him warily.

Renton smashed his fist against his heart. He'd overdone it with the magic. At this rate, Hass might have to carry him out of here.

"Good," he replied, shoving off the wall.

Shadows turned back to their vices, thick puffs of topaz curling in the air.

Hass's mood soured as they moved through thick curtains into the second room of the den where shelves upon shelves of stolen artifacts were locked away behind glass doors.

"Renix above." Hass ran a hand along the glass. "Why would he require such a collection?"

Renton took in the artifacts, eyes lingering on the enchanted mirrors

Boedworth had contracted him to steal from a woman near the edge of Duskhallow, the isle of Ashens. "Power. If he holds all desirable things, he becomes the most powerful."

"Izral won't stand for it." Hass made a fist on the glass as if to break it.

Renton nodded, unwilling to give in to hope that Izral would achieve justice. "What does this tome look like?"

Hass moved through the shelves, occasionally stopping to rant about items that had been stolen from the archives. He paused at the shelf next to Boedworth's desk. "There." He pointed to a leather-bound book sealed with a lock. "That's what you seek."

Renton knelt down to get a better look, disturbed by the thrum of old, acrid magic from its pages.

"Ready for this?" Renton asked, popping a tiny lockpick from within the bracer he'd borrowed from Fen—the boy's latest invention.

"Where do I get one of those?" Hass asked, watching as Renton swiftly opened the glass enclosure.

Renton cracked a half grin. "Speak to the kid in Sut'hik's kitchens. You'll be pleasantly horrified by the weaponry he's designed."

"Huh. Hey, be careful with that thing. The tome is rumored to be cursed."

Renton grabbed the book and dropped it into a sack. "So am I."

A shadow man parted the curtains in the doorway. "What are you doing in here?"

One glance at Hass and they were both racing for the front door, knocking the shadow aside with an elbow to the chin. It was a mad dash once they spilled out of the den.

"Stop!" one of the hunters shouted.

But the streets had yet to be cleared of splintered wood, smashed fruit, and a too-curious audience. Renton and Hass snuck into a dark tunnel formed of tree roots that coiled them back up the streets.

Twice he'd stolen from Boedworth. First Tenah and now a tome Boedworth must have prized if he'd risked stealing it from the Embassy. Such crimes would be severely punished if Boedworth ever got his hands on him or Aeyis.

Back at the hidden entrance to the tunnel, Renton knelt to give Hass a shoulder to step on. Once Hass had climbed out, he reached down to heave Renton up by the forearm.

Pausing a beat to catch his breath, Hass said in a quiet tone, "That seemed far too easy."

Renton swallowed, nodding in agreement. The shard chomped down on his heart with razor teeth, and he practically threw the sack with the tome at Hass. "You should probably hold that."

Hass didn't question him, and soon they raced through the swamps, Renton directing Hass around pools of sludge and traps laid by clever Bogland beasts.

Near the perimeter to Brinedale, Renton called out for his brother, scanning the doorways for a spectral figure. The clouds had sunk lower in the sky, clinging to the glistening townhouses.

His brother never appeared. Panic threaded along his nerves.

"Stay here," Renton said, and the assassin obliged, sinking back into a curtain of vines.

Renton walked the cobblestone streets, boots splashing through cold puddles. Still no response from Aeyis. He stepped up to the door of the first house. A lock clicked, and the shadow that opened it smiled with too-white teeth.

"Hello, little brother."

Mias's fist cracked against Renton's jaw with all the strength of their stocky father, knocking him off the porch. When Renton caught his balance and looked up, Boedworth had exited the house, stalked by two of Mire's hunters.

"Well, well," Boedworth said. "I knew you'd come crawling back to me begging for forgiveness."

Mias jumped down from the porch. Rain and mud sprayed up as he stalked toward Renton.

Brother, I'm almost through Boedworth's mental shields. I just need a bit more time to scramble him.

More time. I can handle that. Flooded with relief that Aeyis was somehow safely hidden, Renton pushed up from the street. His jaw throbbed where he'd been struck, but it was nowhere near the worst injury he'd suffered.

Renton ducked under another rapid snap of Mias's fist and landed a blow to his brother's gut. It felt too good. Years in the making, this fight. Years of Mias's nightmarish illusions and torture. Mias might look like their father, but he was nothing like him in nature.

Other than topaz, there was nothing more intriguing to the councilman than watching punishments. It would be the last one Boedworth ever saw before his mind was forever altered.

Mias delivered a lung-crushing blow to Renton's ribs, curling his spine. Renton returned the favor, and Mias grunted, his mouth pinched tight as if he'd never expected him to land a hit.

"More," Boedworth demanded. "Teach him what it means to cross me. Teach him what he has cost all of us with his foolishness."

Renton turned to spit blood at Boedworth's polished dress shoes and then exchanged another round of blows with his brother. Prickles of icy, bitter magic lashed against his fortified mind, eager to crack it open like an egg. When Renton didn't break, Mias slid pointed iron knuckles onto each hand. Malice flashed through his cruel eyes.

"I have worked tirelessly to protect the Boglands from Adra," Boedworth said. "I bought our safety from their king with that disgusting Chaos lord and his offspring. Then you go and mess everything up. For once, we wouldn't have had to suffer from the aftershocks of war between these insignificant isles."

Renton stiffened. "You allied with Adra."

He should have suspected that Boedworth would turn, but he'd assumed the councilman enjoyed his position with the High Court too much to do something so drastic.

Mias landed an iron blow to Renton's ribs and dragged him upright by his hair, green eyes seething. Another precise hit to the same spot tugged a grunt of pain from Renton.

"You should be freezing to death on Dreaddix for killing Father," Mias uttered. "Now you've doomed us all."

Bones snapped on Mias's next strike, and Renton struggled to catch his breath as Mias dropped him into a puddle on the street. Between the shard and the agony of broken ribs, he couldn't find the strength to stand back up.

Ren!

Just focus.

I think he's high on topaz. It's messing with my ability to grasp onto his deeper thoughts. If he was sober I could have done it. I know I could have.

Renton's hands tightened into fists. *Keep working. We end this here.*

Not at the cost of losing you. Boedworth doesn't plan on letting you walk away from this.

Boedworth let out a sound like a bark. "What is that filthy wraith brother of yours trying to do? Get him out of my head. Show yourself!"

Aeyis stepped out of the second townhouse. His magic had turned black like ash floating through the air. There was no mistaking the pulse of Chaos in the veins, streaking up into his temples.

Aeyis, no!

You will be free from him, brother.

Renton's heart was breaking and not because of the shard's angry response to his brother's dark magic.

A knife whizzed out of the swamps, thudding into the neck of one of the hunters. Blood spurted, then he crumpled to the ground.

Hass.

Boedworth's eyes bulged in his sallow face as he fumbled for an object in his pockets. But Aeyis's dark magic had wrapped around them all like a cocoon of death. Slowly, Aeyis pulled it in tighter and tighter.

Boedworth spewed curses. A flash of orb light cut through the swirling black dust. When Aeyis let his magic drop, the other hunter and their eldest brother lay dead on the street.

Boedworth was gone.

Aeyis staggered, and Renton tried to shove his body up on shaking arms. Screw this shard. Screw Boedworth.

His brother stumbled over and dropped next to him. Aeyis tugged at his arm with hot, electric hands, but they were both too weak to stand back up. Was this it? Was this where all the Murfells perished?

Hass appeared seconds later, wiping blood from the knife he'd retrieved from the fallen hunter. "Maybe fill me in on the entire plan next time, huh?"

He swung Renton's arm up over one shoulder and Aeyis's arm up over the other. Then he lifted them off the ground.

All Renton could focus on was the aura of dark magic surrounding his brother. "How?"

Aeyis's smile was solemn as he withdrew the transportation orb. *Chaos found me the day Mias took me to an institute. That's how I got out without a restrictor. A gift. It's been a gift for me.*

Renton peeked back at Mias's body, acid rising in his throat.

Anyone who considered Chaos a gift wasn't sound of mind.

Chapter Twenty-Four

TENAH

Tenah spent the day climbing the plateau in the city center—and pretending not to be upset by Renton's disappearance. Thoughts of Renton and the Void were supposed to be banished today. Lingering on either subject would only bring about anxiety.

She wandered back to the villa on lighter feet, her mind more organized than when she'd woken to an empty bed that morning.

At her bedroom door, Tenah heard a raspy cough from down the hall. Pivoting, she took in the ghostly figure dragging a larger shadow along, and her heart plummeted.

Renton.

She ran to him, her wicked mind dredging up the pain from Ames's death. Not again. She couldn't lose anyone else. One hand went to Renton's lower side for support. He winced at her touch, and she snapped her hand back, coated in warm blood.

"What happened?" Her eyes roved over him, seeking wounds. Featherlight, she touched his side again. Her fingers dipped in farther than they should.

His breaths were too quick, as if he couldn't suck in enough air to satisfy his body's needs. "Ribs."

"A healer's been summoned," Aeyis assured her, but he couldn't mask the fear etched into his face or the aura of dark magic clinging to his form.

Her vision blurred, her nostrils flaring as addiction for Chaos itched in her channels.

"You're not well, Aeyis." Her voice sounded weak and far off in her ears.

Renton sagged in his grip, and Tenah rushed to hoist him up by his arm, though her effort was in vain. To witness him unable to stand, unable to breathe…

A trickle of cold horror worked through her body. She couldn't do this again.

"Go sit down before you collapse too," Tenah ordered, pointing Aeyis to a chair on the terrace. In reality, she needed the temptation of dark magic as far away as possible. "I can handle him until the healer arrives."

Aeyis's throat bobbed as his brows knitted together. But he didn't argue, his feet dragging as he moved to the chair and sagged into it. She planned to tear into both of them later for whatever stupid act they had committed to result in these wounds. Right now, her main concern was getting Renton to her room to lay down.

He didn't budge as her muscles strained against gravity.

"Why do you weigh so much?" she complained.

"Don't." He tried to swat her arms away.

"He's been fighting us all the way back from the Boglands," Aeyis said quietly.

"Us?" Tenah's nose scrunched. She hooked fingers into the top of Renton's chest piece and brought her face level to his. Even in pain, his eyes glinted with carnal interest. "What exactly were you doing in the Boglands?"

And how had they traveled there so fast?

Tenah clenched her teeth, loathing the broken pieces of her mind that shaped an ugly thought. What if Renton was still consorting with Boedworth? What if he still planned on turning her in?

She directed a fiery glare at Aeyis, demanding explanation.

We retrieved the stolen tome from Boedworth, Aeyis said. *Hass has it in custody, but he thinks Izral will grant us visitation rights as soon as he returns from a meeting at the High Court.*

Her anger dissolved as Aeyis lowered his head and sank his fingers into his hair. Both boys were a mess, which meant she needed to hold everything together. She needed to hold them together.

She took Renton's chin gingerly, wincing at the swollen, bruised skin there. "Hey, if you get to fuss over us, we get to fuss over you. Now put some effort into getting all of this muscle up off the floor because I can't do it alone."

A smile played at the corner of his mouth, but it morphed into a grimace when he pushed onto his feet and she guided him into her room. She eased him back onto her bed, unable to ignore the lilac sheets drinking in his blood.

When would the healer arrive? Was Aeyis certain he'd sent for one in his disoriented state? Why hadn't she worked harder on healing? If she'd focused more on exploring the Void earlier, she might not have been so useless now.

Tears stung her eyes. Her channels roiled with enough firepower to detonate the entire villa. "Tell me what to do."

His chest heaved with effort. "Just…breathe."

"Where's Boedworth now?"

Renton wrapped a hand around her elbow. "No…manhunts."

She ground her teeth, channeling her aggression into unbuckling his armor, slick with rain and blood. She hurled it across the room.

The healer arrived shortly after Tenah had stripped Renton down to his dark shirt and pants. She refused to move from his side until the healer touched her arm and offered a reassuring smile. "I heal for the Embassy. I'll take care of him."

Reluctantly, Tenah backed up. She watched every twitch of the healer's fingers along Renton's side. Beads of pale blue magic threaded into the wet patches on his dark shirt. His short breaths soon turned into deep, relaxed ones.

Mending bodies never ceased to amaze Tenah. Like a magician, her mother had erased her scrapes and bruises when she was a reckless child. Eager to learn the art, Tenah had obsessively combed through medical books in the library up until the morning her mother had vanished.

"Several punctures, broken ribs, and a collapsed lung," the healer said. "Other than that, some moderate swelling and bruising."

Tenah didn't miss the way the healer's fingers paused over Renton's heart. His bright eyes flashed with panic as he grabbed the healer's wrist and gently eased her hand away.

"Will he be okay?" Tenah asked.

The healer set a vial of clear liquid on the nightstand. "He'll be fine. Give this to him in six hours for the pain. Make sure he gets some sleep."

Tenah nodded in relief. "Thank you. Will you please check the Ashen on the terrace? He was struck by dark magic."

"Sure thing, dear."

Hoping the lie would be enough to protect Aeyis from dangerous accusations, Tenah watched the healer close the door behind her. She looked Renton over, the sickening knot in her chest slowly unraveling as his breathing remained steady.

He sat up with a grunt, and when she lurched toward him, he raised his hands to stop her from forcing him back down on the bed. "I'm okay now. Just sore."

"You have two options," Tenah said firmly. "You either lay back down and sleep, or you march into that bathing room so I can clean you up."

Renton cocked a brow, a flash of challenge in his eyes. Tenah moved between his legs and helped him rise to his towering height. She helped him into the glass shower enclosure and cranked on the spout for hot water.

"Hang on." She propped him against the stone wall as she grabbed a stool from a vanity then positioned him on it just out of range of the water.

Looking down at him, bloodied and damp and grinning on his tiny stool, infuriated her. "What were you thinking going after him without all of our help? Vesara and Gireth didn't go, did they?"

"No, just Hass," Renton said, his body relaxing in the steam. He leaned his head back against the wall and closed his eyes, letting out a hum of satisfaction. "Boedworth allied with Adra's king. The contract to capture you and your father was supposed to earn the Boglands amnesty from his attacks."

Tenah stiffened. "There are plenty of Corrupt on the isles. What would Adra's king want with me and my father?"

A muscle twitched in Renton's jaw. "I would imagine it's not good."

"Adra's king doesn't frighten me."

"He should. Advanth was pure of heart before the isles pissed her off, but Cirel has quite the violent reputation."

Tenah frowned, struggling to tamp down on the white-hot magic brewing in her channels.

"He won't touch you," Renton assured her, his features softening. "I'll make certain of that."

"I can handle myself." Her eyes drifted down the length of him. Seeing him injured cut her worse than it should. "Same for you though. No one gets to hurt you again."

His eyes swirled dangerously green.

"Come here." His hands loosely cuffed her wrists and pulled her between his spread legs. Steam glistened on his skin, plastering his shirt to his solid chest. He pressed a delicate kiss to her palm.

Raw, hot desire rushed through her body, settling low in her stomach.

He's injured. He almost died.

Reining herself back in, she asked, "Do you think my father will try to retrieve the tome now that it's been returned to Denoden?"

Renton's forehead creased. "I'm not sure."

She licked her lips, avoiding his intense stare. "It's just…Izral mentioned at the party that he'd spoken to my father. And my father definitely paid a visit to the archives. No one seems to realize or care that he was insane with Chaos." She shook her head. "I feel like we're dealing with too many enemies. Why can't we just set them all on each other and be done?"

Renton's eyes trailed his fingers as he slowly ran them up and down the inside of her arms, awakening wildfire and cold shivers at the same time. "I think you've figured out the High Court's plan. Step back and let the enemies tear each other apart."

"They're supposed to be peacekeepers."

"Their version of peace allows for a bit of turmoil." He tipped his head to the side. "At least, that's what Nithril used to tell me to shut me up when I drifted down the same line of questioning."

Tenah took him in, curious about his past under the guardianship of an elder. She brushed a thumb over a raised scar along his hard bicep. "You don't agree with them?"

"I don't understand this world, or any of the worlds, like they do. The elders have almost two centuries' worth of wisdom. Beyond that, they can tap into the memories of their ancestors through the roots of their forest." He continued tracing soothing patterns on her skin, allowing her space for a storm of troubling thoughts.

Even if she stopped her father, the King of Adra still wanted war. If Izral decided he wasn't keen on fighting back, who else would?

The rhythmic patter of the water grounded her back on her task. She soaked a sponge in the hot stream of water and turned to him.

"Forgetting something?" A devilish smile curled on his mouth.

Hot blood flooded her cheeks. He was still fully dressed. His hand clutched his side as he shook with restrained laughter.

Feigning confidence, Tenah motioned to all of him. "It has to come off."

He raised a brow. "Trying to take advantage of me?"

"That's just what you want, isn't it?"

Renton gave a full laugh and then groaned at the pain.

"You deserved that," she scolded. "Considering you almost died, I do expect you to sleep here under my watch. You'll need someone to remind you to take that tonic. And you need breakfast in the morning."

Elementals, what fiery goddess had possessed her?

Renton drew her up by her elbows. The heat in his eyes turned her core molten. No one had ever looked at her like that before. He'd seen her at her worst. Consumed by unfettered rage. Doubled over in a fit of drunken illness. Marred by Chaos after a magical detonation.

He hadn't faltered once.

"Let me get you cleaned up," she whispered. "I owe you that much."

"Stubborn westerners and their honor."

Renton pulled at the hem of his shirt, jaw clenching.

"Quit." She smacked his hands away. "You act like you've never been babied before."

He blinked up at her, all his defenses lowered. "I haven't."

Chest tightening, she slid her fingers under his shirt and peeled it off his deadly body. She pushed down the urge to ask him about the gruesome scar over his heart and why it sometimes pulsed as if it had a soul of its own.

His eyes were trained on her the entire process, kickstarting her heart. It only settled when she glimpsed the nasty yellowish bruises peppered along his side and stomach. The gouges that had been the cause for all the blood had thankfully knitted back together, leaving nasty pink spots behind. Her anger nipped once more when he stood and pressed her hand flat against them.

"They don't hurt anymore," he said.

She pulled her hand away. "You need to sit."

"I can't take off my pants sitting down."

"Oh." She was certain her gulp was audible. "Right."

Renton's eyes never left her as he finished undressing, testing whether or not she wanted to bail. She'd never been in the presence of a naked male before, but she wasn't about to let him catch on to just how much of a mess she was internally right now. Her blood grew thick in her veins, throbbing under tight skin. Despite his injuries, her traitorous mind was drifting to considerable parts of his body. There was no question, Renton would undo her, piece by piece.

"Tenah," he said, cutting through her daze.

"It's the steam, okay!" she replied, fanning at her cheeks. "Sit down and let me finish this."

He laughed but obliged, taking pleasure in her embarrassment. She cursed herself for watching water run down the cut planes of his chest and much lower. He'd nearly been beaten to death, and she couldn't keep her lust in check.

Renton's arms wrapped around her, his hands cupping just below her backside. She wanted to push them higher. She wanted him to touch her everywhere. Lick, bite, and breathe warmth into her skin.

"I can't stop thinking about you, do you know that?" His voice was low and sultry.

Tenah's stomach went on a wild, lurching ride. "No," she replied, her voice cracking. "But tell me more."

"Mmm, when I'm healed, I'd like to show you."

She was practically panting, his promise building something hot and consuming at her core. She ached to ask him what exactly he would do to her when that time came. Then again, could she handle him?

Tenah wriggled in his hold. "Didn't I tell you to stop misbehaving?"

He let go only long enough to hook his finger in the collar of her shirt and tug her down closer to his face. "I should have warned you from the start, angel. I'm nothing but trouble."

His mouth pressed against hers. Electricity shot from her head down to her toes, so strong she jerked back, wide-eyed and internally combusting.

She threw the sponge at his chest. "Wash yourself. Kissing me with no pants on," she muttered.

She stomped out of the bathing room to hide her full-body blush as Renton's chuckle echoed behind her. Pressed against the wall between them, she noticed fresh sheets on the bed. Someone had changed them undetected and placed a neat stack of clothes on the table for Renton.

How the hell was she going to spend the entire evening with him?

Methodically, she pulled on a long-sleeved shirt, baggy pants, and thick socks. More layers might be needed to ward off temptation. She froze at the edge of her bed as anxiety crept in. Rubbing her thumbs into the center of her palms did nothing to help. Her mind was too far in the trenches of how foolish she was for thinking she could ever have something casual with the hunter when Chaos whispered for her to cut into his scar.

Tenah burrowed into the cool sheets, pulling them up to her ears in a silly attempt to hide. His bare feet padded on the floor, but she couldn't summon up the courage to roll over and face him, instead pretending to be asleep. All traces of the fire goddess had sizzled out.

"Thank you. For everything," Renton murmured, leaning down to kiss her temple.

She only moved when the bedroom door clicked shut, checking to make sure he'd grabbed the healing tonic. She had no right to make him stay. None of this was fair. To have limited time in this new but cursed life. To have found someone she cared for. The pressure building in her chest from the night of the gathering threatened to crush her lungs. If she wasn't so messed up inside, she might have allowed herself to find comfort in his arms, even just for one night.

But she was the offspring of Ruzgorn. A child of fire and Chaos. A shadow doomed to mutation. Her time was borrowed, and one day, the death king would come calling for payment.

Tenah bit down on her lip, fighting to keep tears from spilling. She would drown in them if she let them fall.

The flapping of wings startled her awake. Her welkin messenger had returned. Heart skipping, she rushed to untie the sealed parchment from its scaled leg and tore into it.

I'm sure you've heard the news by the time this letter reaches you. Kherathi's taken Firesteep. You want an army, come to the Scorchlands and claim it. —Gadreel

The air around Tenah became supercharged as Chaos and fire tumbled through her channels unrestrained. Smoke curled in her mouth. The bedroom became too stuffy to breathe in. She needed an outlet for her magic soon, or she'd have another uncontrollable tantrum like the one in the snowy field.

Shredding the letter, she tossed the pieces in the trash can. She'd been such a fool to let this go on so long. Her father wouldn't stop. Chaos wouldn't stop. Even entertaining the idea that he might have been pursuing the tome to heal himself was irresponsible.

Chaos rumbled in approval. *Call on your armies, little one. Take what is yours. Unify our power with Ruzgorn armies and march forth undefeatable.*

For once, Chaos was right. With her father tucked behind Firesteep's fortified walls and the threat of the eastern isles looming on the horizon, she needed an army. Lives were at stake, and she would protect as many of them as she could if the isle rulers refused.

Tenah stormed down the hall in search of Vesara, trailing a blend of fiery Chaotic magic.

A guard stood on either side of the assassin's bedroom doors. Vesara was arguing with them to return to their posts in the palace, but they acted as if she were nothing more than a child begging for attention.

"I get rid of one of you, and two more appear," the assassin said. "Is this a game of multiples? Are you breeding like rabbits in a storage room?"

The first of the guards to notice the Chaotic flames engulfing Tenah's hands reached for his blade.

Vesara spun on a heel. Her expression morphed into guilt. "You heard then."

"Can you take me into the Scorchlands?" Tenah asked.

"That's a day's ride through the desert. The sun would bake us."

Tenah clenched her hands into fists. "Unless your king or the Embassy would be willing to do their *jobs*, I plan to secure an army to protect us all."

Surprisingly, Vesara recoiled. "The Embassy protects the kingdom of Vristar and the archives. They already sacrificed too many employees in the war at Roan's Wake. They won't go for it."

"And your king?" Tenah knew her anger was misplaced, but she had no more control over it than she did the weather right now.

Vesara's gaze darted away. "Useless and uninterested in the state of Vozar."

"Then I'm heading south. If you don't want to come, that's fine. But I'd prefer a guide, especially a loyal one."

After moments of tense silence, Vesara finally nodded. "Meet me out front at sunset. We brave the desert at night."

Chapter Twenty-Five

TENAH

A choir of voices chanted in Tenah's mind when they reached the Ruzgorn camp at sunrise on horseback.

Canvas tents spotted the cracked, thirsty ground as far as the eye could see in the rippling heatwaves, positioned around an old, stone cathedral, though Tenah couldn't recall her father mentioning what god or elemental these barbarians worshipped.

Probably one devoted to Chaos.

She peeked over at Vesara, slouched atop her horse after a tireless night of riding across barren desert.

Hardening her resolve, Tenah nudged her horse toward the first line of dusty tents and prayed Ruzgorn couldn't smell her fear.

They are but flesh and bone, Chaos murmured. *When they burn, they become nothing more than ash in the wind.*

Shut up.

The screams of dying shadows are harmonious.

She gripped her reins tighter. *Don't even think about it. I'm in control today.*

Laughter echoed in her mind. *Vessel. We shall see how much power you hold over us.*

Two Ruzgorn rode up on proud stallions, Vozarian steel strapped across their muscled backs and secured at their waists. Their features were mostly hidden by strips of red cloth.

"You're in Ruzgorn territory," the one with a scar down his left eye said in a gruff tone.

"My uncle summoned me. Gadreel Delemor."

The Ruzgorn exchanged a look. "Right."

Sparks of Chaos arched from Tenah's fingertips. "Not a joke."

The scarred one rolled a beastly shoulder. "I don't know where you got your information from, but we ride in honor of Warlord Hakkan."

Brows furrowing, Tenah took in their waving banners. A sleek, gray hawk outline where she expected a black scorpion. She knew there was more than one Ruzgorn camp, but why would her uncle lure her here?

Unless Gadreel had never planned on giving up *his* army. She tightened her grip on the reins. How she tired of having her strings pulled by shadows who believed themselves superior. What, did Gadreel think she would do his dirty work for him? Take out a few warlords he believed below him? Or did he expect her to meet her doom here?

"Fine. I'm here to challenge Hakkan to blood rite," she said sharply.

Ruzgorn horses huffed and stamped the ground, unaccustomed to settling in one spot for this long with their riders. Survival in these unclaimed lands required constant movement, pillaging, and hunting.

Vesara drew her horse closer to Tenah as they were motioned into camp. "You never mentioned this blood rite to me," she whispered.

Tenah licked her chapped lips. "It's a sacred fight. The rules are binding. Whoever wins acquires the status and power of the slain. There. Now I mentioned it."

Expression stern, Vesara grabbed her arm. "There can only be one outcome. I will not lose another friend, nor can I allow a Ruzgorn warlord to be infused with your power."

Tenah gave a slight nod. She hadn't considered that fact because she wasn't going to lose. More than her need for an army, she would prove that she had the strength to look a shadow in the eye while she dissolved them with Chaos. Dark magic would be necessary to win, but Chaos would not ultimately control her. She would not bow to it.

Ruzgorn dismounted at the cathedral doors. Tenah followed them inside. Rows of crude, wooden benches were angled toward a central dais. Acrid magic had seeped into the very foundation of this ancient place of worship. She would have loved to pick it apart and discover its secrets.

Instead, she cut through the benches to where a Ruzgorn male dined at a small, wooden table positioned under a stained-glass window. He was much younger than Tenah had expected. Two decades at most, with a lean build and smooth, brown skin. His jet black hair was pulled high atop his head, restrained by a band of gold.

The Ruzgorn warlord's ocher eyes flicked to Vesara, and Tenah's hands curled into fists. All right, so she didn't look like a fighter. Regardless, it was infuriating to be discredited, especially by a male with such a pompous air about him.

"Are you the head of this shitshow?" Vesara asked.

The warlord continued picking apart his leg of roasted meat. The lack of respect propelled Tenah close enough to smell the herbs on his meal and the stale note of his drink.

"I called for blood rite," she said forcefully.

Hakkan took his time wiping each greasy finger on a cloth napkin then leaned back in the chair, satisfied with his meal and his piss-poor attitude.

Anger and nerves clawed at Tenah. She looked at Vesara. Was it not as simple as requesting a fight?

In the span of a breath, the assassin was on the warlord. One boot pinned the back of his fallen chair to the floor as she loomed over him, a dagger resting against his throat.

"Now will you show respect?" Vesara's voice was as smooth as silk, and her blade drew a thin line of blood.

Hakkan nudged her hand away, his features void of emotion. "I've heard tales of you. The Embassy's star child. *Kala Sut'hik.* Who sent you here, your gluttonous king or my backstabbing father?"

Caught off guard by his question, Vesara stepped away and sheathed her knife. Tenah squatted next to Hakkan. He made no move to stand up. Up close, he had a dusting of freckles and in the sunlight, sure enough—a red, fiery glint to his peculiar eyes.

Tenah frowned. "You're Gadreel's child."

"By blood only," he replied with disgust, rolling away from her and up onto his feet in a graceful move. "You are?"

"Regretfully, your cousin."

Hakkan's mouth twitched, and his eyes flashed with murderous intent. Then his puffed up warrior charade deflated. "Seems we have a lot in common. Both of our fathers tried to kill us."

It didn't make a difference if Hakkan was family or not. He was the Ruzgorn that stood in her way of power.

"Well, are you declining my challenge?" Tenah asked.

Vesara's wide eyes cut to her, but Tenah said nothing as Hakkan sized her up. When his scrutinizing gaze came to rest on her ruined hands, he didn't even bother hiding his grimace. Blood rite was an honor to Ruzgorn, and there was much honor to be gained from slaying the Corrupt relative of another barbarian clan.

"A death match it is, cousin."

Chapter Twenty-Six
RENTON

Renton's blade cleaved though the training dummy in one solid thwack. He exhaled as the sack of hay hit the ground.

Visions of Aeyis's toxic storm in Brinedale still haunted him. When he closed his eyes, he saw pulses of black through his brother's temples, eating away at his insides. He saw Mias's lifeless body, face down on the street. He saw the burst of green orb light right as Boedworth escaped consequences, just like he always did.

Unless Izral managed to outsmart him in court. How much sway did Denoden's king actually have with the High Court? Or would this all come back on Renton, adding to his lengthy record of misdeeds?

All of these thoughts had swarmed him the instant Tenah had left him in the shower. Suddenly, he'd struggled to suck in air. How did he explain that to her? That his mind was beyond wounded and sometimes it succeeded in convincing him that he couldn't *breathe*. He'd hurried from her bedroom and sought out Gireth to distract him with his incessant chatter. Then he'd slept for almost an entire day, as if his body had been waiting for a culmination of stressors to attack. Once he'd purged them, he could finally rest.

When he'd stirred, he'd hunted down an abandoned training field atop the central plateau in the city where he proceeded to tear his body down all over again. His lungs ached in protest, but he didn't care. He needed it, the *pain*.

Hours passed under a starry sky, Denoden's golden spires reflecting the lights from another round of wild evening antics. Renton ditched his sword for pushups, beads of sweat dripping down his face and splotching the dirt.

It wasn't that he cared for Mias. That brother had been dead to him for years. It was what that death represented. The state of Aeyis's mind. His little brother needed help. It was another internal clock ticking down, interwoven with about ten others.

As thick, gray clouds threatened to rain him out, Renton grabbed his shirt from the fence bordering the field and tugged it on. He strapped on his blades and started down the steep path cut into the side of the plateau.

Suddenly, the shard jerked him to his knees.

It had been acting up more than normal, and he wasn't ignorant as to why. The stupid thing thrummed with energy whenever Tenah was near. Practically sang for her Chaotic touch.

Fat droplets of rain tumbled from the night sky. Water slithered down his head and under his light T-shirt like cool snakes. Tipping his head up, he closed his eyes and melted into the pattering of rain on his sweaty skin until the shard released its death grip on his body.

Rising, he blinked the rain from his eyes. Concern nagged at him when Tenah didn't appear as expected. He'd planned on admitting why he'd left her without explanation. No part of him *wanted* to reject her.

If she wasn't nearby, why was the shard paining him?

A streak of black, low to the streets, darted into an alleyway. The reek of Chaos scorched Renton's nostrils.

Gritting his teeth, he stalked after it, knowing full-well the risk after the shard had just robbed him of control. It pulsed out of rhythm with his heart, the sensation like that of a second heartbeat, guiding him down a dilapidated, dead-end street. He wasn't certain these buildings were suitable for inhabitants. Their fragile, leaning bones had boarded windows and missing roof tiles.

He caught a nimble, fox-like beast slinking through the busted door of the last house tucked against the city's wall. The shard rumbled in approval as he approached the porch steps. A viscous haze of dark magic filled the interior hall and connected living room.

At least he could be certain it wasn't Boedworth, come to exact revenge. The councilman harbored no magical talent, a fact he strived to hide.

Renton studied the decrepit furnishings and decaying boxes of clutter. Plates of rotting food were piled atop empty crates and a makeshift bed. Candles puddled in chipped bowls on the dusty floorboards. Quiet as Aeyis when he didn't want to get caught snooping, Renton combed the first floor. He kept a hand on the hilt of his blade as he snuck into each room along the way, shutting doors behind him to mark them cleared.

It was impossible to detect the source of the magic when it blanketed the house evenly in a potent, thick layer. He crept up the staircase to the second floor. Streaks of moonlight poured through holes in the ceiling. The only other light came from a closed door at the end of the hall. He nudged the final door open and staggered into the doorframe.

Boedworth lay face down in a puddle of brackish, Chaos-tainted blood.

The councilman wore the same suit from the night in Brinedale, as if he'd never made it back to his den. From the wrinkles and dirt stains, it looked like he'd been dragged all the way here to be dumped.

Pulse thumping, Renton scoured the room and found nothing out of the ordinary, save for black scorch marks fanned out around the councilman's body.

He stared down at his slain employer. His chest knotted with too many emotions to unravel.

Could Tenah have…

No. There had to be another conclusion. Another Chaos caster on the isle. There were probably dozens hidden in this city alone.

But after the incident in the field, and then the determined rage in her eyes the night she'd tended to his wounds, it was hard not to jump to her as a suspect. She had no recollection of how she'd ended up in that field. What if someone had been using her? Controlling her like Kherathi had controlled those feingrot the night of the gathering?

Terror gripped his chest, squeezing tightly.

Avoiding the blood spatter, he nudged the body onto its back. Boedworth's pale, bloated face stared blankly up at the ceiling.

Renton tried to think logically. Regardless of who or what had caused this and why, he needed to notify someone. Hass might be a good start. The assassin had proven to be a reliable go-between with Izral so far.

He turned down the hall and froze when he spied a cracked door. He'd made certain to shut them all.

With silent footsteps, he crept toward the door and nudged it open with a boot. An overwhelming stench of Chaos, leather, and cigars rolled out. The office was dark, the single window boarded up tight, but there was the unmistakable outline of a shadow sitting behind the desk.

Crimson sparks erupted from the man's fingers casting eerie shadows over his features. Lord Kherathi lit a metal lantern on the desk before leaning back in the chair and interlocking his hands behind his head.

"Good evening," he said, his accent thick.

Renton stood paralyzed in the doorway as the shard in his chest throbbed. "*You*. You killed Boedworth."

Kherathi's gaze was far sharper than normal for someone lost to Chaos. "He was one of many High Court members aligned with the enemy."

Brows rising, Renton eyed the twin daggers laid out on the desk. Kherathi's body count probably made Vesara look like a saint. How were there no markings on the lord's skin? No blackened veins? He'd witnessed the cost Tenah and his brother had paid after a single use of dark magic.

"And who exactly is the enemy of a mass-murdering assassin?" Renton questioned, jaw muscles tensing.

Kherathi motioned for him to take a seat. Renton knew he should have drawn his blade and thrust it into the lord's chest, but lately, he'd been feeling less like himself. He crossed the room and sat in the empty chair facing the desk.

"I don't think I need to recite Boedworth's crimes to you," Kherathi said. "If anything, you should be thanking me for saving you the trouble of killing him. I'm sure you're aware of the reason he was targeting casters such as myself."

"All I know is he was under the delusion that he'd bought the Boglands' safety with your head," Renton said, tracing a thumb along the scar on the back of his hand. One of a hundred reminders not to ask questions. Three hunters had held him down while Boedworth had stabbed a hot letter opener clean through his hand.

"Adra's king plans to use Chaos to force open the portals between isles. Cirel wants war on a scale Advanth never dreamed of," Kherathi explained.

"Impossible. Not even the elders can awaken them now."

Nithril had siphoned every last drop of his power into the complex spell that had sealed the portals, a heroic effort to slow Corruption's spread. Renton would never forget how it had impacted his family. How it had lengthened his father's travel time on hunts.

Kherathi hefted his boots onto the desk, littering the surface with clumps of dried mud. "Cirel's been experimenting with dark magic to reopen them. Expanding his network to find Chaos casters and shards of a very rare crystal."

This information unfurled more than one petal of unease in Renton's chest. "What is the purpose of these shards?"

"They are the only inanimate objects capable of storing powerful magic. Healers once used them in their practices. Thanks to Advanth's blood sacrifice, the last crystal formation in Roan's Wake became the key to shifting the tides of war. We used the shards to trap the Chaotic souls of Cirel's war beasts."

Renton clutched at the arms of his chair as the room tilted in his vision.

"It gets more disturbing," Kherathi said, his blackened irises watchful of Renton's reactions. "The shards are not a permanent solution. Quickly, we discovered that they *hungered*. In order to keep the beasts imprisoned, we had to implant them inside living vessels. We gathered a few loyal Ashens to carry them, assuming their mental abilities would permit us insight into when the shards would need to be moved into new vessels before Corruption took root. Only, that didn't always work out as planned."

Fuck. Renton clenched his hands into fists. What the fuck was living inside of him? Suddenly, his chest crawled with what felt like hundreds of insects.

He forced a deep breath. He had to keep it together. He couldn't let Kherathi know his secret.

"That is…jam-packed with things I'd like to unload," Renton muttered with a shake of his head. "Cirel would have been a child at the time of the war, right?"

Kherathi didn't even blink. "I've been playing this game with him for longer than anyone realizes. Even before he sank his teeth into my daughter."

Renton's entire body coiled up. "Explain," he growled.

"Your little contract to hunt me? Cirel blames me for his loss at Roan's Wake. Because of that, Tenah became a target. A way to fuck with me." Kherathi withdrew an ornate glass bottle of amber liquid and two tumblers from an oak cabinet then dropped back into his chair. "Sardoth sent me as a warning to Advanth to squash her little rebellion, thinking I would strike fear in her. Truthfully, I didn't see fault in what she was doing. Ashens were oppressed and mistreated. Advanth fought so their voices would be heard. So they had a choice in the matter of magical limiters."

Popping the whiskey cork, Kherathi poured slivers of the amber liquid in each glass then nudged one of them across the desk. Renton stared down at it with a blank expression, all of his energy channeled to the processing of this troubling information.

"Is that why you saw to it to murder Sardoth and his inner circle?" Renton asked.

Kherathi tossed back the whiskey without so much as a wince. "Sardoth's fate was sealed the day he executed my wife." His tone was laced with enough malice to peel flesh from bone. "After which he shipped me off to murder Advanth which turned into a two-year war, leaving my daughter to be raised alone in that god-awful manor."

Brows kneading, Renton scooped up the tumbler and downed the contents. He focused on the burn in his throat. This visit was not going as expected.

"The isles assumed Advanth had turned Corrupt," Kherathi continued. "That she'd been responsible for gathering masses of feingrot and Chaos creatures. But that wasn't true. Things had spiraled out of Advanth's hands. She'd assembled rebels, yes. However, it was Cirel that had summoned monsters onto the battlefield, all thanks to his successful manipulation of my daughter in the Void."

"That's ludicrous," Renton muttered in disbelief.

"Advanth confirmed my suspicions. She admitted to her child having ties to a bloodline that worshipped an entity of death from another world, right before she flung herself upon those crystals to grant us a chance to end the war Cirel had fueled."

Frowning, Renton's eyes moved to the whiskey bottle. Though he craved another drink to numb the barbed emotions inside him, he also didn't want to hinder his reflexes, should the Chaos lord decide to exchange words for weapons.

"After his loss, Cirel vanished." Kherathi took his time pouring himself another drink. "I'm certain he hid in the Void, waiting to latch onto Tenah again like some sort of parasite."

Unhinged fury coursed through Renton's veins. Did this have anything to do with the rifts she'd carved? Or how she'd cheated death?

Renton would tear Adra's king apart before he let him lay a hand on her again. Maybe he already had. She'd been terrified and unwilling to share what she'd experienced in the field when he'd found her. He clenched the armrests of his chair.

Kherathi's chest rose and fell with a heavy breath. "I never expected to love that child. She was the product of a union to create a caster of unique lineage, one with the ability to tap into a higher power of healing that could wipe away the consequences of dark magic."

"She was born a pawn in your game."

"And quickly became my heart," Kherathi said darkly, a promise of death in his words.

Was the lord that much of a fool? Didn't he know he'd hurt her the most?

Kherathi studied the light reflections in his textured glass as he spun it around. With a solid thud, his tumbler smacked down on the desk. "She was six when she summoned her first feingrot inside of our home. Can you imagine?"

Horror churned Renton's stomach, envisioning the nightmares Tenah must have endured. The isolation.

"When I laid into her about the rift she'd burned open and the dangers within," Kherathi said, "she mentioned his name for the first time."

"Cirel," Renton said, sinking deeper into his chair. His bones felt as if they would dissolve.

Flickers of ocher surfaced in Kherathi's harrowing black eyes. "He persuaded her to open rifts to unleash monsters from the Void. Told her he wanted to end his kingdom's suffering. In reality, he wanted to end our world. She wouldn't have remembered. We did our best to keep watch over her, but the staff lost her for a time. Approved leave from my orders, my Ashen and I found her in the woods. She was in hysterics. I cannot fathom what Cirel did to her in the Void. When she begged us to help her forget, I wouldn't deny her the comfort. But Chaos interfered with the memory alteration. It preys on her too, conscious of her ability to purify it, should she find the right source of magic in the Void."

Renton dragged a hand down his face, calluses scratching at his skin. If there was any truth to the Chaos lord's word, Tenah had the potential to save herself. To save Aeyis too.

He straightened up after a deep inhale. "Would an Ashen be able to recover her memories?"

"At the cost of their own sanity, it would still be a stretch."

A sense of hopelessness dragged over Renton. "You must know she's hunting you. She deserves to know these truths. While she's fixated on you, she's not concerned about her own health."

Kherathi gazed into the drained bottle of whiskey as if it might hold the answers. "I can't. There's no telling what Chaos will force me to do. It fed off my hatred of Sardoth that night. I had to watch those events play out through the eyes of a body that no longer belonged to me."

Renton felt ill. It had been easy to convince himself that Corrupt were all monsters, fueled by the darkness breeding inside of them. Kherathi's admissions proved that some kernel of that shadow lingered behind for a time. That they were conscious, and he'd dragged them into Boedworth's hellhole, dumping them there to whatever fate.

"Enough talk of the past. That's not why I'm here," Kherathi said. "I came to discuss that shard embedded in your heart."

Instinctively, the lie slid off Renton's tongue. "I don't know what you're talking about."

Invisible, electric fingers of dark magic burrowed into Renton's chest and wrapped around his heart. He bit down on a growl as the shard responded, pumping what felt like sludge through his limbs to paralyze him in the chair. A second heartbeat thudded out of rhythm with his own.

Gods, he'd known that something foul lived inside of him but not on the level of evil Kherathi had claimed. In the midst of its worst attacks, he'd been convinced that the darkness would split him in two.

"I can assure you I will rid you of Balhudhal, just as I rid the isles of your wretched councilman."

"The beast has a name?" Renton forced the words through clenched teeth.

"The shard won't be able to contain it forever. Near the end, symptoms grow stronger. Your body deteriorates until Corruption sets in."

Fuck. Was that happening to him?

"Do you know how to remove it?" Renton asked.

"I've successfully removed two of them with plans to destroy three more."

Curses formed on Renton's tongue. "Where are these other shards now?"

"Izral employs the Embassy to guard the hosts until I'm in the right... state to remove them."

"Why is Vristar's king aiding you?"

"He isn't the only one involved. Nithril provided intel on your...situation. But then you went missing. Ironic that you would end up running with my Tenah. Though, it's not entirely surprising." Kherathi's gaze dropped to Renton's heart. "Her magic would be drawn to it."

Renton didn't know whether to feel betrayed by the elder or grateful he'd potentially found a way to be rid of the shard. Could Kherathi be trusted though? Even if he claimed he hadn't been in control of his body the night at the gathering, Chaos could take control again and wield the shards for nefarious purposes.

None of this was settling right in Renton's gut.

"The goal is to destroy the war beasts before Cirel catches wind of their location," Kherathi said. "We had a close call with some petty thefts in the archives. Boedworth's hunters were sniffing around for them. The longer those war beasts are permitted to survive, the greater the risk of having to face them on the battlefield again."

"What is the process to destroy them?"

"Dark magic is used to remove the shard from the body. As soon as it's no longer tethered to flesh and blood, the beast will manifest, and then we can slaughter it. There is the risk that the vessels won't survive," Kherathi admitted flatly. "You've carried a sliver of Balhudhal far longer than the other hosts. I believe you witnessed firsthand what the shards can do when their vessels reach their limits."

Visions of the Corrupt in the desert flooded back to him. Soulless black eyes. Ear-shattering screeches. Long, taloned claws digging and digging into his chest. A sliver of black gleaming in the sunlight before pain blinded him.

"What makes you so certain you can kill this beast?" Renton asked, his lungs struggling for air.

Kherathi met him with a steely gaze. "I wasn't Corrupt the last time I fought Balhudhal. Now I have dark power and an army of disposable feingrot. There will be no innocent casualties this time. No distractions. Vozarians were highly motivated to evacuate Firesteep with the threat of my monsters approaching. Firesteep's walls will provide a fortified cage for the slaughter without the need of my daughter's ability to rip open the Void. And Izral was more than willing to take in Vozarian refugees, eager to reunite the western kingdoms under his reign."

Renton took a moment to absorb his words. These were huge actions being taken by two formidable shadows. Was Kherathi making a good decision aiding Izral in doubling his armies? What would the High Court think about Izral reuniting the Burning Plains? From what Renton had overheard, Izral was mostly discredited. No one ever considered him a threat. Maybe they should have.

Kherathi stretched his arms over his head, releasing a chain of pops and cracks in his joints. Though he had no visible signs of Corruption other than his eyes, Renton imagined the lord was in constant pain. "Nothing like a little Denesè celebration to ease the Vozarians' unrest."

Vesara's party. Gods, everything had been orchestrated so fluidly.

The weight of this conversation was beginning to drain the last of Renton's energy. "Why not let the High Court deal with the shards?"

"The High Court refused to house them. Hathrowyn is a refuge, not a vault for monsters. And the farther from the eastern isles, the better. Though, if Cirel acquires enough power to awaken the portals, it won't matter where we hide the shards. His armies will lay waste to everything in search of them. Then he'll move his war to Aranma."

Renton felt sick. Should he mention to the lord Tenah's recent blackout and the rifts she'd carved? Or should he approach the subject with Tenah first to confirm his suspicion that Cirel might already have control of her again?

"Doesn't sound like I have much of a choice, do I?"

"We all have choices." Kherathi capped the empty whiskey bottle and stood. "You've sufficed to keep that beast in check this long. Who's to say you won't live a full life without ever experiencing anything more than side effects? Though you will always be a target with that thing in your heart. You and everyone you love. Should you choose to be proactive, you know where to find me."

With that, Renton found himself alone, suffocating under the weight of his own thoughts.

CHAPTER TWENTY-SEVEN
RENTON

Sword clutched like a lifeline, Renton braced for a sabotage from Kherathi's feingrot when he emerged from the decaying house. Only, none ever came.

His chest heaved, lungs desperate for air. He scanned the street as rivulets of warm rain dripped down his face like tears.

Was this how he would spend his life? Conditioned to expect the worst from others? What if Kherathi *did* actually want to help. How did he even begin to explain that to Tenah? That her father seemed to be wiping the board of their enemies with resounding efficiency? First the tyrant king of Vozar and now Boedworth. Would he succeed in defeating Cirel and his war beasts?

His shoulders drooped. He wasn't sure he wanted the crew's opinion on the matter of the shard right now. Not until he processed things. Because despite the fact that he hated the shard, it had done well to remind him of the torture he deserved for the death of his father. Hell, there were still broken pieces of himself that wanted to keep the cursed thing firmly in place to suffer for his failures with Aeyis and Gireth and all of the Corrupt he'd slaughtered without a care when shadows like Tenah might have been able to heal them.

Body sluggish after coming down from adrenaline, Renton dragged his feet back to the villa. He needed to report Boedworth's death, lest anyone try to pin him as the murderer.

A wall of icy magic hit him from behind as he reached the doors. He spun around, blade raised to the attacker's chin. His heart lurched.

"Aeyis." He dropped his sword. *Fuck.* He'd been so in his head he hadn't even recognized his brother's magic.

With a sunken expression, Aeyis held up a transportation orb.

Renton's brows furrowed. "What are you doing with that?"

The return from Brinedale was hazy, but he was certain they'd left the orb with Hass, along with the tome.

"Hass stopped in. Rumor has it that Denoden's Kala, or queen, set out with a dark-haired Vozarian woman. Something about a death match with Ruzgorn."

A death match.

Renton's hands clenched into fists. "And the orb?"

"Hass ordered us to bring Vesara back."

A growl escaped him, earning wary glances from shadows lurking in the square. "When did we become hunters for Vristar?"

"I'm sorry," Aeyis said softly, his chin quivering. "I didn't sense them leaving. My mind's been a mess since Brinedale."

Huffing out a breath, Renton curled a hand around his brother's neck and drew his forehead against his chest. "This isn't your fault, so quit with that."

After a few light ruffles of his brother's damp hair, Renton released him. Aeyis held out the orb, which Renton took and spun in his hands. How was it that Tenah had just tended to his wounds with flushed cheeks, and now she was hunting down a warlord? How could she not see there were others who cared about her, who would be ruined by her death?

Now you understand how Gireth and I feel about your reckless actions, Aeyis said. *You should take the Chaos lord up on his offer. Let the shard become someone else's problem.*

Renton ground his teeth. Not once in this lifetime had he experienced such a strong tether to another soul outside of his family as he did with Tenah. If he agreed to work with her father, she might turn her back on him forever.

He didn't want to lose her.

"Do you think you can get word to Hass about Boedworth?" Renton asked.

More than happy to announce his death.

Rowdy voices sounded from the terrace above, drawing Renton's head up. He whistled, and shortly after, Gireth's head popped over the railing.

Gireth's smile crumpled, and his tone came out harsh. "This had better be good, Nazrata. I'm about to win a ride on a war elephant."

All right, so Gireth was still understandably upset about being left out of Brinedale.

Renton had witnessed Gireth's temper only once. During training exercises in camp, a hunter had spoken ill of Renton's Ashen mother. Though his father led one of the strongest and most reputable clans, it didn't exempt their family from the cruelty of others. Before Renton could pummel a fist into the shadow, risking his position, Gireth had stepped in. He'd ordered the boy to apologize. When the boy swung at him instead, Gireth had beaten him into a bloody pulp. Several hunters had to pull him off. Even in the face of authority, Gireth still fought and spat insults, dropping two grown hunters with little effort.

There were two very different sides to his friend. That anger remained dormant beneath layers of humor, but it was constantly building. And when it finally erupted, almost nothing would survive against it. Renton imagined Gireth had lived off that pure rage on Dreaddix. Had pummeled feingrot and Corrupt into bloody heaps in the thick snow drifts.

"The others ran off for a death match," Renton explained, striving to keep his features neutral, though his own temper bubbled to the surface.

Gireth slapped his hand on the railing a couple of times. "That'll do it, boys."

Chairs screeched on the terrace, and soon the front doors to the villa swung open. Gireth emerged, glaive in hand, and immediately moved to Aeyis's side, keeping distance from Renton.

Fine. Renton would apologize later. Honestly, they all needed to have a conversation about what they were doing here, lingering as if they wanted to be something more. Maybe a strong, efficient team. If that was true, they needed to clarify some rules.

Aeyis gave him estimated coordinates, and soon the orb spat them out on cracked ground that oozed heat from the sun's unforgiving rays. It took a few more uses of the orb before the promising scent of electrified storms lured them into a Ruzgorn camp.

Fury propelled him into the crowds surrounding a large clearing among their dusty canvas tents. He shoved barbarians aside until he had sight of the fighters causing a ruckus. His lungs compressed.

Tenah was on the ground. Flames surrounded her, keeping a furious warlord from slicing into her with his curved blade.

Renton pushed the last row of Ruzgorn aside, prepared to leap in front of Tenah, but something latched onto his armor and tugged him back. With an elbow cocked, ready to slam into the culprit, Renton spun around.

Vesara stood before him, a dagger raised to his throat. "Don't you humiliate her."

"You going to kill me, Kala?" Renton leaned into her blade. She'd caught him on the wrong day.

With an eye roll, Vesara sheathed the knife back into her bandolier. "No, but all of them will kill us if we interfere." She motioned to the wall of red-cloaked devils surrounding them. "It only ends when one of them is dead. If she wins, she gains the warlord's rank and magic."

Renton's gaze drifted back to Tenah, his frown deepening. She'd clambered to her feet, her flames rising like a wall behind her. Shallow cuts bled along her arms and sunburnt cheeks.

"You were supposed to watch over her," Renton accused.

Vesara rested her forearms on the rickety fence separating them from the field. "Don't act like you didn't have my narcissistic personality figured out from the start. I wasn't keen on letting her burn through me to carry out her goal." After a pause, she added, "She can't stew on her demons, Ren."

Muscles in his jaw worked. "How long have they been fighting?"

She tipped her head to the side, her short hair parting to reveal a cluster of tiny suns inked into the flesh behind her ear. "You don't want to know."

Renton fastened his arms over his chest to keep from reaching for his blades. "She hits the ground again, and I'm going in."

But the way Tenah was working powerful bolts of flame into her opponent? This clearly wasn't an even match. She wasn't fighting against the warlord. She was fighting to wrap a leash around Chaos. To tame it.

She was risking everything. Every drop of her being, all in pursuit of protecting innocent lives. Not because of an addiction or an obsession with power.

Renton knew she hadn't cared for those shadows at the gathering, but their souls obviously meant something to her. Motivated her enough to never want to witness that kind of horror again.

Seeing Tenah clawing and raging against the darkness inside of her tilted his world on its axis and cast it in a new light.

This was a protector.

Not someone who tracked down diseased shadows to slaughter them without second thought. He'd robbed them of a chance to heal. Robbed their families of a loved one. While he'd felt justified at the time, stretching himself paper thin under the belief that he'd been purging the world of threats, in reality, he'd only made it worse by feeding the bloodshed.

Aeyis was wrong. Renton didn't deserve happiness. But what others deserved from him was someone better. Someone with the skill to fight for them, not against them. His path forward would look a hell of a lot different.

Right after he let Kherathi carve the shard out of his heart.

Chapter Twenty-Eight

TENAH

He's scared of us, Chaos purred into her mind.

Tenah clutched a bloody hand to the long cut down her forearm, willing the hot pain away. She wasn't certain how long they'd been fighting, only that her legs were no longer stable and her lungs couldn't suck in enough fresh air through the smoke of their magic. Mercifully, the smoke mostly hid the circle of enlivened Ruzgorn caging them in, though their shouts had become nothing more than indistinguishable chants, voices blending together.

Chaos unfurled tiny branches of electricity through her channels and chirped from her gathering bolts of flame. *Give them the blood and marrow of their almighty warlord. Take what is yours.*

Biting into her lip until blood pooled in her mouth, she strived to bend it to her will. To understand it. To break it.

But the magic detonated from her palms without command, launching Hakkan into the barbaric crowd. His outline warbled in the heat until Ruzgorn shoved him back into the center of the smoky ring. Wild strands of black hair framed his sweaty face. His sword arm trembled with exhaustion just as her fingers shook uncontrollably.

"Why do you hesitate?" he shouted, rage contorting his features. "Why did you come all this way? Just to toy with me?" Nasty burns marred his cheek and the side of his neck. At least he'd moved quick enough to shield most of his face from her attack.

Still, she couldn't absolve the ball of guilt expanding in her chest.

With a swipe of his hand, Hakkan ignited his curved blade in red flames. When he lunged for another strike—so slow in comparison to Renton—she dipped sideways and slammed another bolt of Chaotic, electric fire into his stomach.

There is no controlling us, Chaos rumbled.

Hakkan's back hit the ground, and a memory struck her hard enough to jerk her awareness from the battlefield. She was in the manor library. A younger version of her cousin watched her from twenty feet away, his jet black hair cut sharp at his chin. There was no muscle clinging to his frail bones. She came to understand this was why her uncle had kept him secret for so long.

Young Hakkan made no move to fight. He kneaded his hands in front of him nervously. He hadn't spoken a word since his arrival.

"Show him what a true Delemor fighter looks like," Gadreel instructed.

She glanced at Ames first. Always seeking permission. When he gave nothing away in his expression, her gaze slid to her father. Her throat tightened as intelligent, red-brown eyes met hers. She found no answer within them.

What do you expect me to do? She wanted to ask.

"Don't pity him, girl. Teach him how to be strong," Gadreel had shouted.

Tenah's focus snapped back to the desert ring. For some reason, the hardened warlord splayed out in the dirt made her feel infinitely sadder than the lanky, silent child she recalled. How many horrors had he faced at the orders of his father? And still, Gadreel sought to deliver him pain through her hands.

Hakkan struggled to rise. Some messed up part of her ached to encourage him. He'd obviously worked hard to reach this position. *Get up and fight. Prove them all wrong.*

A thousand laughs reverberated through her mind. Chaos shot through her limbs and forced her over to her cousin. Slowly, she picked up his blade, turning it in her hand. Then Chaos forced her to drive it into his stomach.

The rising chants of Ruzgorn and Chaos should have brought her relief. The title, the power—it was all within her gasp.

But the flash of raw fear in her cousin's eyes gutted her. It was the same look he'd given her when she'd laid him out that day years ago. Only when her father had lowered his head and strode from the library had she realized her mistake.

She'd had a choice then. She wanted a choice now too.

Hakkan's body went limp beneath her. His warm hand cuffed her wrist, eager to draw the blade deeper. "Do it," he choked out, a bubble of blood at the corner of his lips. "We were never meant to be anything more than their puppets anyway."

"Stop," she pleaded, both to him and Chaos. Hot tears pricked in her eyes as dark magic inched the blade in further.

He's done nothing wrong, she cried.

You called on us for help.

I only wanted your power to wield as I wished.

A wish that will never be granted. You are weak. Weak. Weak.

Hakkan let out a horrible, quiet moan. "Finish the job, cousin."

With a scream, she yanked the blade free and threw it across the ring. Blood oozed from his stomach. Desperate, she placed her hands over the wound while he let his own drop to the dirt.

You wretched shadowling! Chaos roared.

Tentacles of black lightning exploded from her back, crackling up into the sky. It was the Boglands all over again. Dark magic formed an inescapable storm above their heads, reflected in Hakkan's wide eyes.

Tenah had no strength to draw it back into her body. The camp fell silent as her magic tore a massive, black scar into the sky, wide enough to glimpse the Void within.

Elementals, what had she done? She tore her hands away from Hakkan as lightning continued to stream from her every burning atom. Her thoughts became fuzzy, her arms leaden with numbness.

You defy us, Chaos said, *but there is no stopping our destruction. This world is ours to consume.*

"Someone help her," Hakkan struggled to call out.

She wanted to scold him. He was the one bleeding out!

Ruzgorn made no move toward her as the ground cracked like broken glass beneath her. Blizzard-cold magic touched the edges of her mind, and she knew Aeyis was present somewhere in the crowd.

However, she wouldn't let him risk his health to stop her this time. She'd prepared for the worst scenario. Fighting to remove a small knife from her boot, coated in the creeping smoke she'd snatched from her visit to the Abyss, she positioned the blade over her stomach.

"Tenah, no!" Renton's voice boomed over the crowd.

She jabbed the blade into her side. The splitting pain was immediate, the injection of neutralizer directly into her channels greeting her with the force of a boulder. She crumpled to the ground. Never had she experienced the heat of her own flames, but she imagined this was what it felt like to be burned alive.

At least Chaos had fizzled out, unable to manipulate her any longer. Though, the damned rift remained. It buzzed above the ring like a horde of insects drawn to bright light.

An icy hand touched her arm. *We're here*, Aeyis said. *Hang on.*

A blinding flash of green light blotted out the desert.

There had been no victory today.

"First thing's first." Gireth's harsh tone commanded attention. He'd taken up position in the middle of the villa terrace hours after their return from the desert, his posture intimidating and all traces of light-heartedness evaporating from his features.

Tenah sank deeper into the chair Renton had delicately placed her in, grimacing at the restricting tug of bandages along her abdomen. A long, pink scar remained where Hakkan had slashed her forearm.

The villa healer definitely thought them all suicidal by now. But the pain had nothing on the vicious ache in her chest at the battered condition she'd left her cousin in, alive but bleeding profusely.

Renton leaned against the wall at her side. He hadn't left her alone since scooping her up in the desert, though he hadn't spoken more than a few words to her beyond ensuring that she was no longer hurting and that Hakkan would survive.

"You." Gireth jabbed a finger at Renton. "You need to tone down the self-sacrificing, not-giving-a-shit behavior. Brinedale could have been a success had you involved all of us."

A muscle in Renton's arm twitched, his brow rising in challenge. "So sure of yourself?"

Gireth stepped closer. A vein bulged in his neck. "We could take this to the colosseum and find out. Is that what you want? I didn't carve my way through hundreds of beasts on Dreaddix just to be left out. We're a team. We're brothers. At least, we used to be."

Renton turned his head away, feigning interest in the skyscrapers drenched in warm sunlight. They reminded Tenah of the thin wafer cookies her favorite chef used to make.

Sensing Gireth's anger turning on her, she shrank in her chair.

"And you," he called out, dulling his steel tone slightly. "That was badass and all, up until the end. I'm not sure what happened, but you need to accept that you have family too. We're here to help in any way we can."

Tenah wanted to dissolve as three other pairs of expectant eyes settled on her. Her attention dropped to the markings that had spiraled up mid-forearm. Would her gloves even hide them anymore?

Sucking in a gulp of air, she did something excruciating. She spoke honest words for once. "I'm sorry. I do value all of you. So much so that I intended to win that army to protect you. I've been told I was destined to be some sort of savior. I've been afraid of that burden my entire life. Of disappointing others when the truth comes out that I can't help anyone."

"And you think any of us feel differently?" Gireth asked. "I might be more animal than shadow. I cover it up with a joke that usually gets me in trouble. We all have our issues. The way we work past them is with support."

Tenah's throat bobbed. "I get that, but unless any of you know how to pinpoint a source of rare healing in the Void, I'm not sure what else to do."

Gireth came to kneel before her. He placed his hand atop hers, and she caught the way Renton shifted to watch them, as if he was debating launching his friend off the terrace.

"Things didn't go as you planned today, but don't count us out, ok?" Gireth's thumb stroked over her ruined knuckles. "I'll see what information I can dig up on the Void." He pivoted on his heel, casting a glare up at Vesara. "Your contributions to the woman that just tried to earn us an army?"

Vesara scowled. After drumming her fingers against her crossed arms, she replied, "I'll speak with Izral."

"See there. She's not completely useless, is she?" His normal grin returned. He patted Tenah's hand and moved to leave. Vesara lunged at him as he passed, latching an arm around his neck. Unfazed by the assassin dangling from him, Gireth strolled down the hall, laughing madly at her attempts to render him unconscious. "Still salty after our last fight!"

"Renton, I—" Tenah started.

"Save it." He strode for the hall then paused. "You know what? No. I have a right to be mad. What was this, a taste of my own medicine after Brinedale?"

Tenah's chin dipped lower. "It was partially fueled by what I felt when I saw you in that condition."

Renton sighed and pinched the bridge of his nose between his thumb and index finger. "We're made of the same stuff, aren't we? Since we're being honest today, I should tell you. Your father paid a visit to Denoden while you were off destroying Ruzgorn."

Her wide eyes snapped up to search his face. "You saw him?"

"Every move he's made has been to stop Cirel. Judging by the way he was drinking, I'd wager he still cares a great deal about you and is fully aware of the damage he's caused."

Betrayal stung deep in her chest. "It doesn't matter. He accessed dark magic knowing full-well what it would do to him."

"Did you ever ask him why? You of all shadows should know not all Corrupt choose that life. I've come to learn that much, Tenah."

Shame burned her face. When was the last time she'd had an actual conversation with her father?

Renton traced a knuckle along her cheekbone. "You are so determined to stop him on your own that you're becoming Corrupt in the process, and it scares the hell out of me."

Then he was gone, taking a piece of her crumbling heart with him.

Her awareness shifted to Aeyis. He'd been so silent.

Tenah, he said. *If it is okay with you, after you rest, I'd like to take a crack at unraveling what has been done to your mind. Something shifted during that fight. I may have an unorthodox solution.*

Fear constricted her throat at the awful things he might find inside her mind. Rejection sat on her lips. But facing this life without other souls to share in her burdens felt like being tied to a rock and tossed into a lake.

She was tired of drowning.

Chapter Twenty-Nine
TENAH

Soon after Aeyis disappeared from the terrace, Fen bounded out with a coffee. He handed over the decadent creation of whipped cream and chocolate chips. "Ma says you haven't moved in hours. We're worried about you."

Tenah didn't have time to respond as Zia swept in to drop a plate of steaming food in her lap—strips of glazed meat and a pile of fresh, seasoned vegetables.

Fen dipped sideways until his upper body was level with her gaze. "You smell like that bad magic, Tenah."

Her smile was a feeble thing as she sipped at the blended hazelnut and chocolate concoction. "You should sell these, Fen."

"I'm onto bigger and better things. Renton helped me fix one of my inventions. I'm pitching it for additional funding in three days."

"Seriously? That's amazing."

Fen beamed. "Whenever I'm feeling down, Ma takes me to the healing pools. A few minutes in the waters and you'll feel back to normal again."

"This coffee is already recharging my bones." She straightened up and bit into a speared piece of meat. Lifting up her ruined hands, she added, "I don't think it will help with this though."

Fen threw his arms out. "It's still fun to swim."

"You're right. Thanks, Fen." She pinched one of his soft cheeks. "You're a great friend."

Beet red in the face, he waved her off as if he'd been licked by a dog. The chilling yell of his mother from the kitchens below had him scooting away with a yelp.

It wouldn't hurt to soak in healing waters. Tenah had work to do in the Void anyway if she was going to figure out how to seal the desert rift.

After polishing off her drink and scarfing down a few more bites of steak and tender carrots, she headed out into the city with sore limbs. She discovered three large, circular healing pools nestled under a pocket of trees and lustrous stars. Steam beckoned from their surfaces, summoning a wisp of joy in her chest.

She welcomed the silence as she entered the mosaic shop and placed a kroten in the palm of a young attendant. He helped her select a rejuvenating tonic to blend with the curative waters of the first pool, then he cranked a wheel at the rocky edge to hoist a rope of lanterns he'd ignited with a spark of fire magic.

Tucked behind a wooden stall between trees, Tenah peeled off her clothes down to nude underthings stitched with elegant silver lace, the least provocative items she'd found after rifling through the armoire in her bedroom.

She breathed a sigh of relief as the soul-cleansing aroma of peppermint lured her to the awaiting pool. Unwrapping the bandage around her stomach, she sank into the waters up to her chin. Instantly, the ache from the wound dissolved, and her sore muscles melted. Swimming easy laps around the pool, she drank in the world around her. Trees danced serenely, and the evening sky stretched on forever, stars glittering so bright, she thought she might be able to touch one if she reached out her hand. Blissed out, she rested her upper body on the grassy edge of the natural pool. It was impossible not to become addicted to the peace that existed here.

Maybe she could enjoy it for a bit once she dealt with her father.

Her mind dragged her back to reality. Was her father still in the city? If he still cared, if there was still a shred of him inside the shell of Chaos, why hadn't he reached out to her? Would he have knowledge on how to mend the rift?

Tenah hadn't noticed the attendant pouring tonic into an adjacent pool until the guest towered over her.

"Making the most of your stay?" Renton asked, a brow raised.

Startled, she splashed peppermint water into her eyes. She hissed at the weird sensation of burning and cool tingling, not daring to flail too much because, elementals above, she was in her damn underwear.

He drew his shoulders tighter into his body. "I didn't mean to make things so heavy earlier. That's probably the last thing you needed." After a beat of silence, he added, "I get a bit intense when I'm all in."

Her chest tightened. "All in?"

Green eyes seared through her. "I am all in, Tenah. But you're still fighting it."

She struggled to maintain normal body functions. *Breathe. Blink. Swallow.* Had it been obvious then? That wedge she'd driven between them? In the end, it would only hurt worse when she turned Corrupt.

Renton gathered the fabric of his shirt between his shoulder blades and tugged it off in a smooth movement. She hadn't intended to watch, but it had been practically torture replaying the shower scene in her mind and trying to imagine what every inch of him felt like.

Her traitorous eyes did as they pleased, taking in the hard-earned cut of his muscles. Steam clung to him in a tempting sheen. She'd have to ask Vesara to recite Denesè prayers for her later because her thoughts were unrighteous, especially as he stripped off his pants. Dark briefs hugged his thick, corded thighs.

In a spurt of rebellion, Renton leaped off the edge of his pool and crashed into the surface, dousing her in a hot spray of water. When he popped back up, his broad smile was devastating. Stunned, she watched him glide over to the patch of land between their pool and drape his arms there.

"How are you feeling?" he asked softly.

Her nerves were too wrecked at this point to summon up a feisty retort. She mirrored his relaxed posture from her own pool, striving to keep her chill as he stared back at her intently. "I'm okay."

"You're a terrible liar."

She couldn't deny it. Not with rivulets of water snaking down the hard lines of his broad shoulders and cut arms. Her eyes dipped to the awful gash over his heart.

It was obvious that he'd dedicated his life to training, had met enemies head-on, and learned what not to do through experience. Her father had preached that scars were reminders, not just of mistakes but of an unshakable tenacity to survive. To keep moving. To keep *fighting*.

"How do I earn your honesty, Tenah?"

A lump formed in her throat at the dangerous way he was drinking her in, as if carefully memorizing every line. Every glaring fault in her design.

Teeth sinking into her bottom lip, she waited for him to discover what she knew existed beneath. But when the gleam of lust remained in his eyes as they rose to meet hers once more, she knew she was in trouble. There was no way she had the fortitude to resist him. That realization dragged her heart into her stomach.

Breaking their locked gazes, she heaved in a breath and ran her palm over the blades of grass. "I'm sore after splitting the sky in two. And I'm absolutely haunted by memories of a version of myself I don't recognize, and I don't like. I don't *like* myself, Renton. And I don't like this constant dread over what the future holds. Is that what you want to hear?"

She braced for the pity in his gaze.

He simply blinked back at her. "That is exactly what I want to hear, as much as it hurts me to know your truths."

Chest tightening, she ripped out a few stray blades of grass. "Your turn. What did my father want from you?"

"He offered to remove a shard from my heart."

Tenah froze. "Why would he want to do that?"

"It houses the soul of a beast the King of Adra wants to unleash upon us."

Pulse throbbing in her veins, she couldn't stop her eyes from drifting to the scar on his chest. The slithering magic she'd detected inside of him was something much fouler than she imagined.

"And if it doesn't get removed?" she asked.

Renton shrugged. "The shard would destroy me. I suppose, in a twisted way, it's payback for all of my sins. Your father thinks he can remove it without killing me. He claims he's done it before."

"There's more of these things?"

"Unfortunately."

She ducked low in the water, a rush of dread overwhelming her. "Did you accept?"

He ran a hand over his hair. "No."

Little embers of fire magic leaped through her channels. "You shouldn't trust him."

"I think you should try to talk with him. I think his motivation to kill Adra's king stems from his deep love for you."

Tenah shook her head. "You warned me before that his mind is too unpredictable. Even if I broke through to him, how long until madness overtakes him again?"

Needing a distraction from the swirl of pain and self-doubt, she undid her braid. Waves of dark gray hair shook free. She took her time washing her hair. When she met Renton's eyes once more, they had shifted to something primal. Something claiming.

His words repeated in her head. *I'm all in.*

A shock of desire flooded low in her stomach.

"Why are you staring at me like that?" she asked, her voice weak.

"Do you want me to stop?"

Her cheeks heated. "No," she breathed.

"Tell me another truth, angel." His voice was low and husky.

Her heart skipped a beat. "If things were…different, I might follow you anywhere."

"Is that so?" His brows lifted. He eased back into the center of his pool. "Would you follow me here?"

Heart racing, she failed an easy shrug. This night was meant for healing, not for giving in to temptations. But her body wasn't listening to her mind anymore.

Renton gave a little taunt with his hand, flashing a devilish smile.

Damn her pride.

Rising from her pool with as much grace as she could muster, she crossed the boundary first. The momentary shock on his face gave her a surge of confidence. That glint in his darkening eyes confirmed that he would not reject her advances.

"Lavender?" Her voice cracked as she stepped into his pool.

His eyes leisurely slid down her body and back up. Slowly, he waded over to her. "Supposed to aid with sleep. Thought I'd put it to the test."

Sinking in to her waist, she wound a lock of hair around her finger. The action only drew his attention to her hands. His rough fingers entwined with hers as he reeled her closer.

Tenah held her breath, her voice a mere whisper. "What keeps you awake?"

"Tonight?" His eyes dropped to her mouth. "You."

Calloused hands wrapped around the back of her thighs and hoisted her up against his hard body. Drawn tight against him, her poor heart kicked into overdrive as his mouth skimmed up and down the column of her neck, teasingly delicate at first.

"Not enough," she whispered, one hand slipping up his neck to grip his hair.

She shivered when he pressed his mouth fully to her skin. He nipped at her flesh between her neck and collar, hitting a tender spot from her fight with Hakkan. She flinched, and Renton immediately drew back.

"I'm fine. It's fine," she whined, eager to salvage the moment.

"Tenah," he warned, gently kissing her collarbone.

Her body sagged as he placed her feet back on the pebbled ground. He took her wrist and placed her hand on the puckered scar over his racing heart. "Trust me. I have a whole list of things I want to do to you, but first, you need to recover."

Giving in to defeat, she traced the outline of the thick scar. "Who did this to you?"

His eyes closed. "The same Corrupt that killed my father."

"These too?" she asked, unable to stop her fingers from tracing over the other smaller scars down his biceps and forearms.

Renton grew very still. "Hazards of my employment."

"Not just from Corrupt," she guessed, her stomach churning with anger. "Boedworth's wickedness needs to end."

"Your father killed him. He won't ever bother us again. Though, there's a chance hunters will still try to fulfill their contracts until the High Court announces his death."

"I don't know what to make of my father's actions," she admitted, her shoulders curling inward as she tugged hard at the ends of her dark hair.

He eased his arms around her waist. "He mentioned that you can heal."

It was hard to focus when his thumbs began stroking distracting circles along her lower back.

"If I was ever capable, that ability is lost." She met his intense eyes. "Aeyis asked to help, but the cost to him might be too great, especially if I still can't figure out healing after he cracks open my mind. There's no certainty that I'm strong enough to fix Corrupt."

Renton took her face in his calloused hands. "You are stronger than you think."

Slipping behind her fortified walls, she pulled out of his hold. "You're wrong. I'm nothing but a coward."

Shadows found solace placing their faith in her, but they were fools to do so. Ames and her father's expectations had smothered her as far back as she could remember.

Renton sighed. After a shake of his head, he rose out of the water. She expected him to leave without another word. Instead, he knelt down at the edge of the pool. Gently, he took her chin in one hand and tilted her head up to look at him.

"I've *seen* you, Tenah. Yes, you carry fear, but it is fear for the safety of others. That is an admirable trait. So don't think for one second that makes you a coward. Your pure heart makes you strong. Don't ever let anyone or *anything* make you think otherwise."

Speechless, Tenah watched him toss his clothes over a bare shoulder and stride through the gate. Alone with the moonlight, she let her body sink to the depths of the pool.

Chapter Thirty

TENAH

I don't mean to interrupt. Aeyis implanted the words in her mind.

The rock Tenah grasped crumbled away. Her body swung out over a thirty-foot drop, her other hand clamping down harder on the side of the plateau in the city center.

After the much-needed soak in the healing pools last night, Tenah had sought to tear her muscles all over again the very next morning. Now she was regretting it.

Yes, you do, she snapped back, fuming as she scaled down the wall to safety. She'd lost track of time while climbing with the aim of untangling all the mottled thoughts in her head, one rock at a time.

Hass will meet us at the back door of the Embassy in an hour. We've been granted an evening with the tome.

Feet back on solid ground, Tenah brushed her dirt-covered hands along her thighs, dreading her trek back to the villa on weary legs. After rinsing off, she hastily dressed in a black, two-piece ensemble—a beaded crop top matched with a voluminous skirt of silky material that fell mid-thigh. She debated between her dirty leather boots and the fancy slippers that wouldn't thud against the Embassy floors. She stuffed her feet into the boots and laced them up. Then she grabbed the cipher page and tucked it into her skirt pocket.

Aeyis lurked beside the alley door of the Embassy. Dark circles lined his eyes, and his locks of white hair stuck out in all directions. Was this part of his trickery, making her feel an instant need to mother him? She noticed a delicate earring on a long chain hanging from his freshly pierced ear, but before she could ask about it, the back door creaked open.

Hass appeared. With a sharp once-over and a nod, he led them into a back hallway. Tenah kept her eyes on Hass, searching for a hint of manipulation. It was just Aeyis's style.

I'd like it to be known that I'm innocent, Aeyis stated.

I find that hard to believe, she replied, entering a less ornate lift behind Hass. It dropped them into the silent archives.

"Over here," Hass instructed, slinking through narrow rows of bookshelves. They hurried after him, stopping in an alcove with a lone table. There, the book sat open, pages worn and scrawled with indecipherable runes.

"Hope you're good at decryption," Hass said with a frown. "I'm sure as hell not. You have three hours until shift change. Then you disappear."

Anxious to dive into the tome's mysteries, Tenah sank into a musty chair and fished out the cipher. Faster than she'd expected, Aeyis scooted a chair up next to her. All business, he flattened sheets of crinkled parchment on the table.

"I took it upon myself to steal a few of those runes from your mind," he said. "According to Denoden's impressive library, they are part of the first language."

Tenah glanced at him sideways, torn between wanting to smack him for always peeping and wanting to hug him for his efforts. "And can you read this first language?"

He tilted his head. "No, but I can use my other notes here to translate it into the present tongue."

"Now I wish I would have brought us some of Zia's tea."

A half hour of painstaking translation, and they had decoded the first page. Aeyis began to read, "'The Order of Equil shall protect the state of the worlds. We exist to maintain balance between all magics born from the Void. We are the protectors of sacred sources. We are the sentinels against the destructive natures of outside forces. This tome shall be a guiding tool for all known magics. It shall recount the efforts of the Order to ward off evil, should we ever face its destructive touch again.'"

Tenah released a shaky breath. "Okay. The Equil needs to tell us what to do about Chaos."

Aeyis ran bony fingers through his curls, revealing the little fracture lines of dark magic along his temples, shaped much like the branches of a tree in winter.

Her heart skipped a beat. She glanced down at the developing whorls on the back of her hands. They deviated around perfect circles then crossed over each other several times like constricting vines.

She grabbed for the cipher and nearly ripped it in two as she shoved it in his face. "Why do our markings look like these symbols?"

His eyes flicked between her markings and the cipher. "That's quite interesting. There's a pattern to Chaos then."

"A pattern that's probably in here." She patted the tome and flipped through it. She'd skimmed through a good chunk of it when Aeyis jabbed a finger at a matching row of runes in the center of a torn page.

Like a court reporter, he quickly scribbled out a translation. Tenah held stale air in her lungs.

"'Chaos is the strongest documented unidentifiable being in the Void. While we know little about its origin, we do know it cannot survive long without a host. Vessels for Chaos span races and include animals. There are cases of Chaos fusing itself with sources of magic where it preys on casters who draw from the source. We believe this is how Corruption initially spread in Daathmorr.'" Aeyis's hands twitched with excitement as he continued to read. "'The most recorded sources to harbor infection were given the name Rama, or blessed pools of healing. We built temples around them to keep them protected, but Chaos unleashed war first upon its appointed protectors, descendants of Xith. For they were the greatest threat to its existence.'"

Imagining a caster siphoning from their bonded source of magic, only to find they'd channeled something terrible into their bodies, chilled Tenah to the bone. Chaos truly was a parasite. An intelligent predator.

She wrinkled her nose. "Xith's descendants were actually healers. History books got that very backward."

"There's solid evidence that you are one of these descendants, Tenah," Aeyis replied, as if merely commenting on the weather. "It explains why your guardian believed you could reverse darkness and why Chaos targets you so ruthlessly."

Her mouth went dry. "Seems like a big piece of information Ames should have divulged."

"You forget, he had his magic tangled up in your father's toxic mind for a long time. Who knows what effect Chaos had on him."

Her eyes darted up to his face then to the black lines etched into his pale skin. Furious butterflies had a cage match beneath her ribs.

"You and my brother are so determined to protect me," Aeyis said. "I'm perfectly content with my choice to use this life to potentially save hundreds of others. If I can help you figure this out, we stand to do a lot of good."

Silenced by his wisdom and bravery beyond his years, she let him continue reading.

"'As with all magic, Chaos does have one known weakness. The markings it leaves in its wake give tell to the power it holds over its host. Discovering the source of its power can aid in driving out the sentient disease.'"

Blood pumped faster through her veins. They were on the verge of something here.

Aeyis flipped the torn page with a huff of breath. "That's it. The rest is missing."

Tenah uttered a string of colorful language that would have made her guardian blush. "There has to be something more in this stupid tome."

Had Boedworth already scoured its contents and ripped out its secrets? Or had Corrupt stolen that knowledge, forcing the hand of its vessel to damage the tome?

Aeyis was silent for a time. "Tenah, I'd like to try diving into your mind.

I'm curious to see what pieces are missing there too."

"You think Chaos did that to me?"

"I do. But I think more memories exist than you realize. I've glimpsed some before Chaos swells to obscure them from reach."

Tenah bunched the tulle above her thighs in tight fists. Had Ames tried to uncover them?

"I don't know," she whispered.

"I'll do my best to keep the pain at a minimum."

Her eyes bore into him with disbelief. "I'm not afraid of the pain, Aeyis. I'm afraid of what Chaos will do to you."

His smile was soft. "I appreciate that, but I haven't been collecting all of this Chaos for nothing." He tapped a finger against his temple. "Your little trick in the Boglands gave me inspiration. I anticipate Chaos launching an attack on me when I enter your mind, hopefully giving you the opportunity to retrieve what it hides."

She bit down hard on the inside of her cheek, tasting blood. "We can try."

Immediately, glacial ribbons of magic blossomed in her mind. She heard a grunt before she was sucked into a foreign memory. She stood in a grand throne room but not in her own body. Swirls of snowy magic hovering over her skin told her everything she needed to know.

Ames had planted this—his own memory—for her to find.

He took in the clusters of nobles with seething animosity, the strength of which shocked her. Such an odd sensation to experience what *he* was feeling for once. When he turned his gaze on the raised throne where King Sardoth lounged, a crescendo of hatred boiled in his gut.

A half dozen guards in phoenix-crested armor posted on either side of his gilded chair, and another half dozen robed figures kept a semicircle of polished floor open before him. Miniature storms of Ashen magic surrounded them, no matter the king's disgust for their kind. He didn't hesitate to take full advantage of their power.

More guards dragged bound shadows into the room, shoving them to their knees before the king. One by one, Ashens were ordered to melt their minds.

Traitors. The king's voice rang out above the murmuring crowd. *Power-crazed Corrupt.*

No, Ames thought. *Servants of Equil. My friends.*

Beside Ames stood her father, absent of laugh lines and crow's feet. Ames kept a steady pulse on him. Kept his thoughts shielded from the prying magic of the king's inner circle. Currently, her father's mind ran through all the scenarios in which he could kill as many shadows in the throne room as possible, starting with the king.

It was like peeking behind the curtain of what had been plotted that day at the gathering.

Their king kept her mother for last, granted a trial upon Kherathi's insistence. Ames struggled to grasp onto Sardoth's true intentions. Sneaking through a winter storm of six trained Ashens proved difficult even for his skill.

A heaving sickness overtook Tenah's body. Her knees hit the floor of the archives, but her mind was still rooted deep in Ames's recollections.

It was astonishing how little she actually remembered of her mother. The woman pushed to the floor had waves of dark blue hair, skin a beautiful shade of light brown, and the most captivating aura.

She radiated life.

And yet, Avora Delemor had come to terms with her fate. She did not bow or plead as Tenah had in death's grip. Her chin remained notched high, where others had trembled.

Something stronger than admiration spread through Ames.

Tread carefully, old friend, he warned Kherathi, whose popping knuckles had him on edge.

The king leaned forward. *You wound me, Kherathi. I have provided you with a life others can only dream of. A title bearing land and fortune. A reputation as one of the most feared and decorated shadows in the kingdom. Is it wrong of me to expect a timely response to my request for your services in these trying times against the Corrupt Ashen queen?*

Kherathi strode forward, breaking from the wall of spectating nobility.

I meant no offense. However, I did respond. It just wasn't the answer you wanted to hear. Now, you drag my wife into this?

Ames grimaced, though his own magic stirred around his shaking hands.

Flames sparked from the king's mouth as he growled. *Let it be known for all witnesses, you would rather Advanth slaughter our isles than raise your blades against her?*

Kherathi tilted his head. It was the same move he made right before he cleaned the chessboard on the lazy afternoons when he'd actually granted Tenah attention.

Hundreds of eyes fell on him, waiting.

I'm not questioning your orders to stop the rebellion, Kherathi said. *I'm questioning your methods. Is it so wrong for Advanth to fight back for what she believes in? We are forcing our will upon her kingdom. Should we not seek to come to a nonconfrontational solution and avoid more blood spilling? My blades have carried out your bidding for decades. Not once have I denied an order, and in that right, I have gathered much experience in the art of war. This is not one we want to start.*

How Tenah had missed this version of her father. His soft but commanding voice, full of passion. When she'd first learned of his profession, she'd found it nearly impossible to merge the honed killer with this version of him she'd loved so fiercely.

With hawklike intensity, Ames kept his focus on the king and his six Ashen executioners.

Your sole purpose is to serve me, Kherathi, the king said. *Without question. Without delay. I give the command, and you strike. I deem the queen's beheading necessary, and you drag your bloodstained daggers across her throat.*

Thick tension filled through the room, quickly rising as Sardoth eased back on his throne with a wicked smile. *I am angry with you, Kherathi. But I am also a sympathetic king. When I realized that your refusal wasn't due to selfishness or betrayal*—the king's eyes slid to Avora, burning with hatred—*but because you were trapped in the spell of an unholy creature descended from the enemy of our ancestors, I knew what needed to be done.*

Dread propelled Ames forward, but six Ashen guards immediately bound him to the spot. Panicked, he looked to Kherathi, also chained to the spot. Veins bulged in his clenched fists, and his expression had turned into something filled with venom.

I'll chalk this up as your one and only discrepancy for years of loyal service, Sardoth said. *But if I ever have reason to question you again, remember this day.*

Sardoth nodded at his line of murderers.

Tenah wanted to scream out, but this was only a memory and one that didn't even belong to her.

Ames. Her mother's voice rang clear in her mind—Ames's mind. *Fear will be her greatest hurdle.*

I can't do this without you, Ames replied, his words drenched in agony. *I have no right raising your child.*

Her mother's corpse thudded to the floor. The following silence was deafening. Guards collected her by the ankles and dragged her from the room, her blue hair fanning out and leaving brush strokes of blood on the floor.

And then, as if nothing out of the ordinary had happened, spectators to Sardoth's wickedness picked up with their hushed conversations about the weather and whose dinner party was next.

The swell of rage inside of Tenah was unreal.

Ames had always been her rock. A calm, collected figure. But on this day, his thoughts were only murderous toward every soul in that courtroom that had given no value to life.

It was the only answer she would get to what happened at the gathering. Maybe some of her father and Ames's behavior had been induced by dark magic. Maybe it had only fed into the plans they had already made on this day.

How did she even begin to grieve a parent that had been absent for so long? There was no emotion to cling to. She'd clawed them out of her heart ages ago when she'd convinced herself that her mother had abandoned her because she'd never loved her. Numbness existed where she ached to feel pain. And where she'd felt pain for her father's betrayal, she only wanted to feel numb.

Was this what had tipped him over the edge too? He'd been sent off to fight in a war he didn't agree with by a king that had executed his wife. A war he hadn't expected to win.

Chaos rippled to the forefront of her mind, and she latched onto Aeyis's arm. His flesh was too hot. Burning under her touch.

Enough, Aeyis, she demanded.

This time, Aeyis tugged free one of her memories. She was maybe nine years old. The death king dangled off the throne in the Void temple. He perked up when she approached, leaping down to sweep her into his arms. He'd grown taller and filled out a bit since she'd last seen him. Wrapped up in him, she didn't feel so vulnerable or alone.

You came back, he said. *Does that mean you will help me end this shadow war?*

She buried her head into his neck, seeking the comfort she was deprived of at home. Seeking understanding and tenderness and love.

Yes, she replied.

The death king had become so much more than family. He was everything. For him, she would offer the world.

With his guidance, she found herself standing before the giant arms of a portal in the Void.

This one won't hurt you so much to open. Just a little bit more, okay? He stroked a finger along the back of her hand. Then he moved to trace the shard of crystal he'd embedded in the stone arms.

Only when the first taloned paw stepped out of the churning rift she'd cleaved open did she understand the depth of his motivation.

Cold magic retracted from her mind, and Tenah found herself on her hands and knees in the archives, trembling uncontrollably. "Why?" Her voice was a ragged whisper. "Why would I do that? Why would I help him summon monsters?"

Aeyis crouched beside her. *You wouldn't have done anything if you knew it was wrong. You were only a child. You were manipulated by a powerful force in a very painful time.*

His finger, too hot for his normal temperature, ran over the symbol on the back of her hand. *I'm beginning to think Chaos's weapon over you is the past, Tenah.*

"It picked a fine weapon then," she muttered, peeking up at him. His lashes were so pale. They framed his unnatural eyes like snow. Markings had drifted just below his hairline. "No more."

It was a while before he nodded in agreement. *For now.*

Chapter Thirty-One

TENAH

Seeking Renton out was a selfish, reckless move. One that would surely cost her heartbreak in the future. But there she stood, mere hours after Aeyis had torn into her memories, her fist hovering over his door. She wasn't certain how long she'd remained frozen in place when he cracked it open. His room was dark, save for the lone streetlamp illuminating his open balcony doors.

The coldness etched into his features dissolved as he looked her up and down. Tenah pretended not to have a visceral, chemical reaction to his presence.

She leaned sideways. "You have a walkout balcony? Who do I have to talk to around here to get that kind of treatment?"

He didn't laugh. *Damn her strained voice.* And she could only imagine what she looked like, hair disheveled and a sickly tint to her skin.

"Tenah."

Her throat constricted as she ran her hands down the smooth material of her skirt. "I…I can't be alone tonight."

The seconds it took Renton to respond felt like a slow kind of torture.

"Come here," he said, wrapping an arm around her shoulder to pull her into his room.

The door clicked shut behind them, throwing them into darkness. When she started to squirm, he nestled her in tight against his chest, leaning his back against the wall. The heavy weight of his arms helped tamp down her panic.

"You're safe with me," he said.

She could live here, armored in him. Breathing in his crisp, mountain scent. She tangled her fingers into his shirt. "Why didn't I do this sooner?"

His quiet laugh rumbled in his chest. He kissed the top of her head and ran soothing fingers up and down her spine.

She sniffled. "I'm sorry."

"For what?" He nuzzled his head into the crook of her neck. Her eyelids fluttered shut.

"For everything."

Renton eased back, though he kept his hands firm on her arms. Muted anger transformed his features as her eyes adjusted to the darkness. "What is this all about?"

"The fight against my cousin. I needed to know if I was even capable. If I could keep it in check while I…while I killed my father." She rubbed at her tired eyes. "My whole purpose has come down to ending him, but I couldn't even kill a warlord. And I know now that the answers to fixing all of this are in that stupid Void temple, but Chaos keeps flinging things at me that I can't process. Except I have to."

"Whoa." Renton cupped her chin. "Slow down. What are you talking about? A temple in the Void?"

She closed her eyes. "I don't know. I'm just all worked up right now. I think I'm going crazy."

When she looked at him, sorrow glinted in his eyes. They were a deeper, mossy green tonight. "You've been through a tremendous amount without sufficient time to grieve."

Tenah nodded. After a pause, she asked, "Do you have anything to drink?"

His hands dropped away from her, and his absence felt like a hole punched through her chest. She wanted to wrap herself in him again.

Stupid, stupid, stupid, Tenah. She was stupid for coming here.

"The villa staff left me a bottle of wine our first night here. I haven't touched it."

She trailed the sound of his voice, and when Renton tugged back heavy curtains from an open window, faint light from the streetlamp revealed the cozy interior of his bedroom. It was as if the villa had accommodated their individual tastes. Her own room had changed to include a beautiful sun-shaped gilded mirror and paintings of Aranma's sweeping landscape. The cotton sheets had also been swapped out to cool silks in vibrant colors. She sweated in everything else.

Renton's room was carved from natural elements. Two dark wood chairs draped in furs were positioned before a dominating stone fireplace. Atop its chunky mantle, a glass orb swirled with curious insects. They pulsed a soothing blue like water reflecting against cave walls.

"Somehow, they discovered my love for tree lights." Renton nodded at the little dancing lights. He fetched two horn mugs from a cabinet in the small kitchen lining the wall opposite of his massive, low-sitting bed.

"From Hathrowyn?" Tenah asked, accepting the mug he'd filled with wine.

She'd read much about the world. Obsessed over it, really. But visualizing things—giving shape to the words she'd consumed—was tricky when she'd spent much of her childhood locked away behind toxic walls and dense forest.

She knew that Hathrowyn's trees shed some of their leaves each night to give light to its suspended, winding streets. By dawn, the lights unfurled back into leaves.

Her eyes roved over the assortment of junk strewn across a hefty wooden table beside his quaint kitchen. The innards of mechanical devices laid out in the middle of metal and leather scraps, tools, springs, and gears.

"Do I even want to know?" she asked, hiding her smile behind a sip of wine.

Renton perched on the corner of the table and swigged at his own drink.

"I've been helping Fen with inventions. Turns out we've got a lot in common. I used to tinker with stuff back in Hathrowyn during my downtime."

"So you do have skills beyond hunting and killing?"

His smile grew. "I have many hidden talents."

Her pulse leaped under her skin. Was it the wine heating her blood or the shadow male she shared a private space with?

Avoiding truths as she did best, Tenah stepped out onto his balcony and hoisted herself up to sit on the stone railing. She sensed his presence and couldn't help but soak him in as he rested against the railing.

It was easy to appreciate him when he wasn't staring back at her with his mind-melting intensity. His straight profile, the ghost of a roguish smile on his face, the beautiful pale hair half-tied back to reveal his strong jaw, and the cut of his powerful form under a fitted, green shirt as he crossed his arms over his chest.

Renton's guard was low this evening, allowing a rare glimpse of his unfathomably gentle soul. Her stomach flipped when his sharp eyes cut to her.

"What happened in the Ruzgorn camp?" he asked.

She rested her chin on her shoulder, the words stuck in her mouth like tacks.

Slowly, he moved between her dangling legs. His hands coasted up her thighs. It was enough contact to shock her heart and loosen her tongue.

"So much about me is...*wrong*. That rift is going to hurt a lot of shadows." Her chin drooped.

Not to mention the countless others she'd torn open for the death king.

Renton took her face in his hand and lifted it back up to meet his gaze. "Keep talking, Tenah. Please let me in."

She shook her head, breaking his hold. Where did she even begin? How could she explain the extent of her concerns over the memory of her cousin? She'd hurt him before. Probably hurt others. The death king, he'd called her...he'd called her a murderer. Could it be true? How many horrors hid in her mind?

Renton dropped his hands to her waist, his thumbs caressing the bare skin where her cropped shirt ended. "I'm tempted to persuade the words from you in other ways."

She shivered, blood rushing to her cheeks and between her legs. "I can't concentrate on anything when you speak like that."

He didn't budge. *Such patience.* It was almost infuriating. As much as she was curious about his persuasion tactics, she was also afraid of them. Her heart was rapidly learning how to incorporate him, knitting deep into the muscle. And she just couldn't have that.

"What is the temple?" he asked, dipping a thumb below the waistband of her skirt. Goosebumps formed where he touched.

A shiver rolled through her. "I don't know, but I think it might hold answers. That or it's a trap laid by Chaos. Every time I enter, something bad happens."

"The rift in the field. Did you try to enter the temple then?"

"Yes." She kneaded her hands in her lap. "When my father's magic struck me down, I found myself in that same place."

No way would she divulge the bargain she'd struck there.

His brows furrowed. "I've not heard of structures within the Void."

"I don't understand why my guardian didn't share more with me. Fuck, if I wasn't so weak-hearted, I might have found the magic to heal my father long ago and avoided all of this pain and trouble."

Renton's palm flattened against her spine, straightening her up. Even perched on the railing, she had to angle her head to meet his eyes. "There is nothing to be gained from playing the what-if game. Trust me."

"Would you kill your father to save your kingdom?"

He grimaced. "I'm not the right person to ask that question."

"Why is that?"

"Because before I met you, I don't think there was anything I wouldn't do. Unlike Chaos that manipulates you, I had a choice in every one of my actions. Every decision I made. Unlike you, there is nothing redeemable inside me."

Tenah couldn't help but place a hand to his cheek. "Do you really think so little of yourself?"

A muscle in his jaw flexed. When he didn't respond, she placed both of her hands on his chest. The solid thud of his heart was a comfort, but the note of dark magic pulsing there stirred Chaos awake in her channels.

She shoved the dark magic back. *Not a single drop of your vileness touches him.*

You are quick to protect this one.

Panic reared up in her chest. She needed a quick distraction from the taunting voices before they caught on to just how much Renton meant to her.

"What did Boedworth do to you?" The question fell from her lips, stemming from her need to crawl inside his mind and examine his frayed pieces.

"It's not a pleasant story." Renton lifted her hand and pressed a lingering kiss to her palm.

"Not many things in our lives have been."

Through long lashes, his eyes darkened a shade as if veiled by storm clouds. "Boedworth's hatred started with my father's opposition of his rise to power. The older clans recognized his wickedness. My father organized many protests and earned his clan the worst of the hunts, spanning as far as Advanth's territory. He was absent for long stretches of time."

Tenah understood the weight of that absence. The loneliness.

Renton absently stroked fingers along her markings. "It should have been Mias's responsibility to care for my mother. She had horrible episodes, withering under the mass of voices in her mind. It was up to me and Aeyis to get her to drink water. Eat. Bathe. She once explained the range of her Ashen gift, and it still disturbs me."

She grimaced. Much of her earlier years were hazy, but for the most part, she'd had Ames or the staff to tend to her needs. "You worry for Aeyis too."

He gave a brief smile. "I know it's hard to believe, but I became quite overprotective of him. Especially when Mias took a position under Boedworth. Mias saw an out from caring for a mother and the siblings he detested, and Boedworth saw an opportunity to further divide us. He single-handedly dismantled Mire's clans until no one survived to oppose him."

"He killed your father." The words tasted bitter on her tongue, fires awakening in her channels. For a moment, she was grateful Boedworth had faced a demon in the end. She hoped her father had made him suffer.

"My father's clan was ordered to Nightfall. When they didn't return, my camp was dispatched as an initiation." He reached out to trace the beaded hem of her shirt. "I should have never left home. But part of me reveled in the fact that I was good at what I did. I assumed I would make quick work of the hunt."

Renton peered out at the swaying trees in the courtyard gardens. The pounding of drums thundered in the distance as Denoden kicked off its nightly festivities.

"Two Corrupt Ashens had ravaged Nightfall. We found my father's clan skewered on the city's spires. A hole had been burned through my father's chest, so hot the wound had cauterized. He'd been dead for days."

Bile rose up in her throat. She would have pulled her ruined hands from his body, horrified with herself for ever placing them upon him, but he kept them trapped over his slow-beating heart.

"My clan was demolished. *Children*, Tenah. We were all just fucking children pretending to be hunters. It didn't matter how hard I fought. It wasn't enough. Corrupt left me for last. I think they reveled in my pain. And then one of them...tore into its own chest with talons." His features twisted. "One breath, I watched it rip out a sliver of crystal, stained black by its poisonous blood. The next, agony stabbed through me, and my vision went black. I was lost in it for a time."

Tenah let her finger run slowly over the ridge of the scar through his shirt. "This."

He nodded.

"Did it feel like death?"

"It felt like hell. Like my entire body would never be whole again. I was convinced I would die there. I wanted to, but then I thought of everyone else in the path of those monsters. And I couldn't give up on them. My father's body was too heavy to drag back to Mire, so I buried him in the sands as deep as my burnt fingers allowed. I walked for five days, driven by the need to warn the other clans, but no one could believe that a child would survive such an attack when my father's clan had not."

Elementals, the horrors he had faced. Not to mention the blisters he must have endured, roasting under the sun for that long.

"I must have been a sight. Covered in blood and sores and reeking of Chaos. Mias spat in my face and claimed me Corrupt. Boedworth exiled me, believing I would die out in the swamps like some wounded animal."

Tenah couldn't help but grip his shirt and pull him closer to her. She rested her forehead against his chest, striving to keep her emotions in check as her magical awareness homed in on that nefarious pulse of something *else* in his heart.

Renton's hand moved up her neck, his fingers curling into her hair. Trees rustled, and faintly, they caught the murmur of Vesara and Gireth bickering somewhere below.

"Party animals." Renton chuckled.

But Tenah wasn't ready to leave the past alone. "Why would Boedworth toss you out just to hire you?"

"Technically, the High Court employs me. Elder Nithril found me on the bridge between isles, near death. He took me in. Cleaned me up. Ordered healers to work on the shard in my heart. No one could make it budge, so Nithril had their minds wiped clean until he could further research it. When he offered me work, I think he mostly wanted to keep tabs on me."

Tenah eased away to examine his face. Did he carry any love for the elder as she had for the wraith that had raised her?

Renton's expression was blank. "It seemed an ideal situation. Earn the trust of the High Court and bring to light Boedworth's true nature. When Boedworth and I came face-to-face in Hathrowyn's temples, he made sure the court saw me as nothing more than a troubled youth. Part of that was my own doing. I acted foolishly, even fell so low as to commit crimes and cast Boedworth's name out as the culprit. Soon, he was the only one granting me contracts. I botched the first one on purpose, and it cost me my mother."

She squeezed her eyes shut, willing his torment away. "Did Elder Nithril know?"

"We could never prove anything in court. Boedworth was always one step ahead, and Nithril's had his fair share of trouble maintaining order after sacrificing his magic to seal the portals." Renton sucked in a deep breath and met her eyes with an intensity that burned down to the marrow in her bones. "So, I became nothing more than Boedworth's weapon, carving my way through enemies to keep Aeyis and the isles safe. Every misstep earned me another scar and another reminder that Aeyis was under his finger. I was fueled solely by anger for a time. Then I didn't let myself think or feel at all." He stroked his thumb along her cheek, and she melted into his touch. "Until I saw you."

Chest aching, Tenah dared ask, "Do you think the isles have always been this way?"

"Yes, I do," he said without hesitation, tucking a lock of her hair behind her ear. "But I know there is still goodness in this world. I've seen it. No matter your past, Tenah, you always have the power to change."

Her eyes widened. For all his scars and shattered pieces, he still had faith.

She could no longer mask her awe for this shadow. She was certain it seeped from every pore. Nothing had ever felt so right in her life as it did with him right now. The hunter made her want to be more than her revenge.

His eyes dipped to her parted lips, and a fluttering tickled her stomach.

"What is it?" she asked breathlessly.

Renton pressed in closer. His fingers curled into the junction between her thighs and hips. His expression darkened into something unholy. "I'm thinking about how much I want to kiss you."

Hot blood pumped thick through her veins. She tipped her head to the side, cracking a nervous smile. "With pants on this time?"

A slow grin curled on his handsome face. "Entirely up to you, angel."

Tenah had never been a patient creature. She launched herself at him, capturing his mouth.

The kiss started innocently, full of all the words she wanted to share with him. He might not see his worth, but she would prove just how much he deserved love.

Her chest tightened at that thought. Before the negative part of her brain could overanalyze it, Renton took control, grasping her chin with his rough fingers. Where he nipped at her bottom lip, his tongue flicked out to lick away the sharp note of pain. She squeezed her thighs around him, eager to lock him in place.

Renton slid his tongue along the seam of her mouth, and she parted for him. A moan escaped her as he tasted her. She gripped his shirt in both hands, unapologetic about the wrinkles she'd leave behind.

She wanted to leave him a mess. Wreck him internally like he was about to do to her.

He stroked light fingers down her neck, drawing her attention away from his perfect mouth and down to where he skimmed fingers along the side of her breast. Then her ribs, as if he was mapping her body.

Renton captured her waist with rough hands and dragged her hips against his hard body. It was just a taste of what he wanted to offer. A promise of the pleasure he would bring. The delicious friction summoned another moan, followed by an impressive string of curses that made him chuckle against her parted lips.

"Filthy mouth," he murmured. "I love it."

Tenah wanted nothing more than to melt into him. To give and keep giving.

An onslaught of sabotaging warnings fired through her mind again, sobering her from the haze of lust. This wasn't right. She couldn't do this in her condition. Renton was deserving of every ounce of love.

But not from her.

He picked up on her sudden tension and leaned back. His pupils were blown wide, his chest rising and falling with heavy breaths. "Don't do this again, Tenah. Don't drive a wedge between us."

The restraints around her heart tightened. Selfishly, she let her eyes sweep over his face once more. Why had this become something she coveted, these stolen moments with him? Allowing herself to get close to Renton put him in danger when Chaos ached to rip into his flesh.

She released her death grip on his shirt. "I shouldn't have bothered you."

Dropping from the railing, she slipped under his arm and rushed to the bedroom door. Her hesitation was enough for Renton to catch up. He rested his palm against the door, loosely caging her in.

"No more running," he said firmly. "I'm not afraid of this, even if it's fleeting. Even if you decide tomorrow that I was nothing more than a mistake. To me, you are everything."

Tenah squeezed her eyes shut, grasping clumsily for her dissolving willpower.

This will only hurt.

She hadn't wanted much in her short lifetime, but everything she had desired had been torn away from her in an instant. That gutting pain… She couldn't go there again.

Renton slid his hands around her waist. His mouth came to rest at the hollow behind her ear. He kissed her racing pulse.

"Not fair," she whispered, resting the back of her head against his chest.

"Weak point, hmm?" His lips skimmed along her sensitive skin until her body was nearly shaking with need. "I'll fight endlessly for you, Tenah. Against whatever enemy. Against your darkness too."

Heart lurching, she turned in his arms. Her eyes locked on his as he lifted her up and pressed her back against the door. He melded his solid form against her, leaving no more room for hesitation as his mouth locked on hers. His tongue swept against her own, tangling in a heated dance.

Tenah wrapped her arms and legs around him. Nothing had ever felt this good. Not even Chaos. She would indulge in one night with this hunter. *One night.* Then she would walk away.

There was nothing tender about the way Renton devoured her, as if he'd been holding back an addiction or choosing to starve himself of affection. Using his hips to keep her pinned, his hands slid under her skirt, caressing bare skin, then cuffed around her thighs. Rough fingers moved down to grasp her bottom, dragging her along the length of his cock and directing pleasure straight to the bundle of nerves between her legs.

She moaned into his mouth, and he smiled against her lips.

"Yeah?" he murmured. Renton sucked her bottom lip into his mouth and sank his teeth into it gently.

Pulse hammering, she let her hands explore, skimming up under his shirt. His skin felt cool against her abnormally hot temperature. She traced her fingers along the dips between the muscles of his stomach, wondering if there was any part of his body that was actually soft.

Curiosity took hold. She let her hands skim lower. When her fingers swept over the steel tip of his cock, he unleashed a delicious groan. She decided she loved that sound. She curled her entire palm around him and cursed at his size.

He chuckled. "Are you intimidated?"

"Never."

"So many lies from this pouty mouth." He kissed the corner of her lips and worked his way to her neck. His tongue flicked against her burning skin, setting off sparks through her entire body. His hands pursued up to her hips where her skirt sat. "This needs to disappear. *Now.*"

Renton lowered her to her feet then took her chin in his hand. He gazed into her eyes with an expression that could only be called savage. Her breaths came out short and tinged with smoke.

When she realized he was waiting for permission, her head bobbed up and down hard enough to rattle her brain. She had to accept that she wasn't going to leave this bedroom intact. He was going to rearrange everything she thought she knew about the world. Alter the very universe until their stars aligned.

He kissed her deeply before sinking to his knees in worship. He made quick work of her boots, positioning them neatly by the door. Then he pressed his mouth between her ribs where her shirt cut off as his thumbs hooked in the waistband of her skirt and dragged it off.

He tilted his head up to meet her eyes with all the intensity of the sun. "I promised myself I would take my time with you, but you are a vision, Tenah. A temptation I cannot ignore."

Her breath caught. Gently, she trailed her fingers from his temple down to his jaw.

"You scare me," she admitted in a soft voice.

His vicious smile pushed heat low in her stomach.

"Not all fear is bad." His hands dug into the soft flesh of her backside before he pressed his mouth to her center.

Tenah's head kicked back against the door. "Fuck," she gasped.

One hand slid down her ass, a dangerously coy finger playing at the edge of her underwear. Squirming, her hands clutched his shirt in effort to heave him back up. "This isn't fair. You need less clothing."

More of that seductive laughter echoed deep in his chest. He stood, guiding her hands to the hem of his shirt. "Strip me."

Her entire face heated as she peeled the shirt off his defined body. "I'm out of my element here."

"You'll survive." He stroked a thumb across her flushed cheekbone. "That drives me insane, by the way. Might have had me on my knees night one."

She sank her teeth into her bottom lip, which was apparently the wrong thing to do. Renton's muscles coiled like he was out for blood. He had her up in his arms in an instant, his mouth crushed to hers.

His tongue explored in slow, tortuous strokes as he walked them over to his bed.

Anticipation fluttered in her stomach when her back hit the soft sheets. He crawled his massive body over her, a predator on the hunt, grinning down at the prize he was about to devour.

He took her wrist in one hand and aimed it at the fireplace. "Give us more light. I need to see you when I send you over the edge."

Heart slamming against her ribcage, Tenah unleashed a tiny jet of flame. Curious little tree lights floated out of their glass homes to dance in the crackling firelight she created.

Renton cuffed her other wrist in his large hand, pinning both of them above her head. Her eyes shot wide in surprise at his forcefulness, but then he placed such delicate kisses along her neck she almost forgot how to breathe.

His free hand wandered, summoning goosebumps on her bare skin. She squeezed her eyes shut, torn between feeling too exposed and wanting to tear the rest of their clothes off.

Tenah wriggled in his grip, entirely at his mercy. "Let me touch you."

His thumb circled a peaked nipple. He bit the other one through the silk of her shirt. A hiss escaped clenched teeth as she struggled to hold still.

"You"—he nipped the soft flesh beneath her ribs—"would rush this."

She would have growled at him if not for his hand pushing up her top. The warm breeze teased her naked flesh before he took her in his hand, applying pressure to her pearly bud hard enough to arch her off the bed with a jolt of pleasure. She cried out.

He rumbled with a low laugh. When his hot mouth replaced his fingers, she lost all reason for fighting this molten connection between them. Every nerve in her body was alive, vibrating with need. His tongue swirled over her, building a fervid ache between her legs.

"Please," she whispered, nearly panting. "I want you."

"Already begging?" he teased but released her wrists. Dragging his skilled tongue and teeth down her body, he paused to leave a kiss against her sensitive inner thigh.

She trembled, hands tangling in the sheets.

Renton sat up. He tucked his knee near her throbbing core. Flustered, she raised her head to look at him. Another wave of heated blood rushed through her at the way he was leisurely drinking her in, etching her into his very soul.

"You look downright sinful all exposed for me, angel," he murmured. "One night won't be enough. We both already know that."

Tenah swallowed. What he wanted was impossible. She couldn't give him more than tonight. But she could revel in it while it lasted, her eyes sliding down the lethal planes of his chest. Over the brutal scar above his heart and the dozens of other tiny scars peppered around it. Down the unholy, raw strength of his stomach.

Her gaze snagged on his erection. She watched as he palmed it through his pants, her mouth watering. Elementals drain her of all magic, she couldn't lose it before he even pushed that mammoth thing inside of her.

"Take it out," he ordered.

She moved a hand up his solid thigh, unable to hide her shaking as she struggled with the laces of his breeches. She dipped a finger along the waistband, heart skipping as she stroked the head of his cock.

Tenah gritted her teeth. It wasn't fair. How he still managed to cling to control was a damn mystery. She was ready to combust.

Deviously, she pulled him free and wrapped a hand around his length, allowing a bit of heat from her roiling magic to seep into his skin.

He grunted, his body bowing over her slightly before he regained composure.

Victory. She flashed a wicked grin.

Renton's calloused hands grabbed her lace underwear and ripped them off. As if to scold her for impatience, he dropped down onto his elbows without warning and dragged his flat tongue against her slit.

She clawed at the sheets, her head dropping back as her eyes closed. She would have shot off the mattress if not for one of his arms now draped over her stomach, keeping her right where he wanted her.

"Fuck, you were made for me." The words brushed against the most sensitive part of her. Gently, he sucked at her clit.

Heat and pressure gathered where he devoured her. She let her legs drop open, and he speared his tongue inside of her, encouraging more unhinged behavior.

She pushed against his shoulder and whined, "Oh, too much. It's too much, Ren."

He slid his tongue out, only to lap at her from bottom to top, ending in a couple of slow rotations around that fabulously, horrible bundle of nerves that had her mind dissolving into absolute worthlessness.

"Not until you take what you need from me," he said.

Digging her fingers into his hair, she allowed her body to rock against him in a frantic, unashamed rhythm.

"That's it." He circled a finger around her slick entrance, taunting.

"Please," she begged.

Slowly, he eased his finger inside of her and stroked it along her inner wall.

"More," she whimpered.

She was desperate for the weight of him pressed against her. She wanted to feel the contraction of his muscles at work. The stretch of his thick cock.

He pushed another finger inside of her. The sensation of being so full had her sinking deeper into pleasure, hinging on a feeling of erupting at her core.

"I'm right here, angel." He sucked her until she came undone, her muscles convulsing around his fingers as crucial pieces of her shattered. She would never find all of them, and even if she did, they would never fit back together the way they were before him.

She was still quivering from the aftermath of a lengthy orgasm when he withdrew his fingers. In a lewd action, he brought them to his mouth and sucked them clean.

Her laugh came out exhausted. "Who the hell are you?"

Renton only offered a sly smile. She hooked her hands under his arms and strived to heave him up her body. No way in hell was she done with him.

Determined to drive her insane with his patience, he worked his mouth up the center of her stomach. Hot breath fanned against her neck as he claimed her there with kisses too. She didn't miss the way he gripped his cock and gave it a stroke from base to tip before resting his forehead lightly on her own.

He sighed. "What am I going to do with you? I'm usually quite unhinged when I fuck. I don't want to hurt you."

Her heartbeat kicked up, nerves rising to the surface at the thought of how big he was. How hard he would drive into her. How deep he would brand himself inside of her, unwilling to be wiped clean from her brain.

Staring back into his electric eyes, she whispered, "I want you any way I can get you. Fuck me up."

Renton growled, his thick cock rubbing against her in slow, tortuous strokes. Once slick, he notched it at her entrance and gently pushed inside a little at a time. His mouth stayed on hers, distracting her from the ache.

When he was fully seated she lost complete control. She squirmed beneath him and fed him little moans. He swallowed them whole like he was hungry for more.

How could she be this full? She was all sensation as he began to roll his hips. Dull pain where he stretched her quickly gave way to overwhelming pleasure.

She wasn't going to survive this.

Spiraling into a place of raw, savage need, she met his hips as he drove into her. She lived for his hands worshipping her body, gripping her jaw and neck to keep her mouth on his, then running along her curves and brushing over her sensitive breasts.

Renton leaned up and hooked his arms under her thighs to grab her ass. She could feel the restraint in his tense muscles, but he kept their pace slow, building that pressure at her core again.

"You feel so good, angel." His tone was all rasp as he buried himself deep, hitting far too many nerves. Withdrawing to the tip, he slammed back in, earning a shockingly loud moan from her parted lips. "I want to stay right here forever."

Clutching his biceps, Tenah pulled herself up to perch on his massive thighs. "And I want to stay right here," she murmured, her hands moving to cradle his face as she kissed him.

Renton took her waist in his hands and hauled her nearly off his cock. "No—"

He brought their bodies back together with force then maneuvered her hips to give slick, lovely friction to that little bundle of nerves.

"I want you aching, Tenah."

Another thrust of his hips drove her head back, and a cry ripped from her throat. Chaos dug sharp, poisonous hooks into her.

Visions of a younger death king slammed into her, drawing a whimper from her parted lips.

The death king's long arm wrapped around her head, tucking it against his chest in a comforting embrace. *We take care of each other. That's how we survive. It's you and me against this horrible, condemned world.*

He took her finger and broke the skin on the tip of a white fang. Crying out, she tried to jerk away, but his grip was firm. *Punishing.* He directed the bead of her blood over his own punctured finger. Foreign words tumbled from his lips before a flash of blue light from his ring overcame her.

His haunting voice echoed in her ears. *Now I will know if you are ever in danger. You do not have to fear death. Not when you have me to protect you.*

Present in her body once more, Tenah blinked up at Renton's twisted expression. Why did he suddenly look like he was in pain? What the hell hurt him?

Warm liquid dribbled down her arm and splattered onto her chest. Her eyes lowered to where her fingers had burrowed into the damaged skin over Renton's heart.

Her stomach lurched.

Ours, Chaos rumbled.

She ripped her claws free—yes, actual fucking claws—and smashed her back into his headboard, desperate to put space between them. Blood oozed from five small punctures in his flesh.

Renton didn't so much as move. Why did he look so unconcerned?

"I'm so…so sorry."

Mortified, she tugged her shirt down and rushed to the bathing room in search of something to halt his bleeding. Her heart beat too fast against her heaving ribcage. Her disgusting claws had retracted, but her black nails remained split entirely in two.

Chaos had done that, and somehow, she hadn't even felt the pain. She wasn't in control at all.

Tenah dashed back to the bed where Renton now knelt, a furrow in his brow.

"Stop freaking out," he said much too softly.

Ignoring him, she pressed the cloth to his chest with trembling fingers.

He took her face in his hands and forced her to meet his gaze. "Stop. It's okay."

She inhaled a jagged breath as he eased the cloth away from his wounds.

"They're superficial," he said.

"This time. What about next time?" All the nagging worries from the archives threatened to flood back in and drown her. "I can't do this with that…thing calling to me," she admitted weakly. She hated that she'd added to his collection of scars.

"Okay." Renton climbed off the bed.

He withdrew a small vial from a cabinet and drank down the contents. By the time he returned to her side, his wounds had knitted back together. He used the cloth she'd retrieved to swipe away the blood. Then he retrieved her skirt and new clothes for him.

Once they'd both dressed, he extended a hand to her. "Come on. Let me cook you dinner."

Her brows rose, her jaw dropping. "Are you kidding me? My magic just tried to kill you."

"I've experienced worse things." No trace of anger or fear in his face. "Look, I'm not going to let you leave on this note. Because we both know you would never permit yourself to touch me again if I did."

Her shoulders drooped. "That's how it should be."

"There is much risk in love, Tenah, but I won't be frightened away from you," he said, taking her hand and pressing a kiss to the back of it. "Dinner. *Please*."

Submitting to defeat, she glanced around his room and muttered, "What could you possibly cook here? Your kitchen sucks."

"Just you wait. I have connections."

She shook her head. *Insufferable hunter.* "And you're able?"

"To cook?" He cocked a brow. "If you haven't already fallen for me, you will after tonight."

Chapter Thirty-Two

TENAH

Renton took her hand, lacing their fingers together as if it was the most natural thing in the world. He led her to her bedroom where she retrieved new underthings, not very apologetic that he'd shredded the ones she'd worn, before he took her down into the villa kitchen.

Most of the lights had been turned off, but Zia and Fen were still hard at work scrubbing down surfaces. Fen's head popped up the instant the door banged closed behind them. He clutched a soapy sponge in his hand. Bubbles covered his forehead and just under his nose.

"Ren and coffee girl," he exclaimed, throwing down the wet sponge with a plop and rushing to try to land a punch in Renton's side.

Renton caught him by the head and spun him so his fists swung through air, bubbles flinging out to cover the prep counter.

Fen released a long groan, his shoulders dropping. "I'll have to wipe that again."

"What did I tell you about attacking our guests?" Zia scolded, never once turning around from scrubbing pans in the large sink. Her hair was unusually sloppy, piled atop her head in a messy bun. Her white coat sleeves were rolled up to her biceps, revealing the lean cut of her arms.

Eyes in the back of her head, Tenah thought.

Fen tapped a finger against the tip of his nose. "Don't swing first. Wait for my enemy to come to me, then use their momentum against them."

Zia whipped around, a hand snapping to her hip. Tenah couldn't help but snort out a laugh. Zia's mouth quivered, fighting back a smile.

"So you are capable of remembering things but only the things the Bogland hunters tell you, hmm?" Zia shook her head and wiped her brow. "And no, Ren cannot steal you away for more training this evening."

Renton ruffled the boy's hair, smirking when Fen swatted at him and missed. "I was actually hoping to borrow the kitchen. Just for an hour or two. I'll replace the supplies and clean up after."

Tenah expected to be chased out of the kitchen with the crack of a towel or the waving of a knife, but the cook's posture softened as her eyes lowered to her hand clasped in Renton's.

Zia held up a finger in warning. "You finish these dishes, and you get me more of that rare spice from whatever mysterious place you acquired it."

"You got it," Renton said.

Sighing, Zia popped the top button on her coat and tossed a final glance back at the heaping basin. "I didn't want to finish those anyway."

Fen climbed onto a stool at the prep table. "So what are we having to eat?"

He winced as his mother snapped her fingers. "Out with you, child. It's well past your bedtime."

The boy slumped down until his chin rested on the table. He blew at one of the bubbles perched there.

"You leave the ice boxes for Fennigan to clean in the morning," Zia instructed, tugging her son out of the kitchen by an earlobe. They could hear the boy's grumbles all the way down the hall.

"So you're training him in combat too?" Tenah asked, turning to Renton.

But he was already sorting through jars of spices with endearing concentration. Selections made, he disappeared into an ice box and came back with a chunk of meat wrapped in thick, waxy paper.

"He wants to join the Embassy," he replied, lining up his supplies in neat rows. Ground beef, rye bread, cream, eggs, broth, butter, onion, and green beans.

She bit down on her lip, struggling to riddle out his plan as she perched on a stool. "Zia's okay with that?"

"Zia's Vozarian husband fought at Roan's Wake. He had no training beyond cooking, but Sardoth didn't take profession into consideration when he drafted his armies. Zia doesn't want Fen lacking in defensive skills." Renton shrugged. "Anyway, the Embassy doesn't just employ assassins. Fen wants to invent weapon tech for them."

"That's incredible. I wish we would have trained our staff in combat." She rubbed at the markings on her hands.

Renton nodded and continued his methodical work. She wondered if cooking was therapeutic for him, eyes glued to his hands as he minced an onion with efficient swipes of a knife and tossed them into a pan with oil.

Cheeks heating, she dared ask, "Is that how you won over Zia? Teaching her son how to fight?"

His eyes flicked up to her briefly. A smirk played on his lips as he turned away to season the cooking onions with a jar of brown powder. The rich fragrance that filled the kitchen made her mouth water.

"That, and rare spices from the Abyss. No need to look so worried, Tenah. I'm set on you and you alone."

Her chin dropped.

Renton chuckled. "What?"

Shaking off his comment, because she *could not* go there, she motioned a hand at his hulking form. "You're kind of a sweetheart under all that, you know."

"I can honestly say I've never been called that before. Many other things, yes. But not that."

"How often do you let others close enough to see this side of you?"

He tossed a towel over his shoulder. "Fair enough."

Moving back to the prep table, he crumbled up rye bread and soaked it in cream before mixing it with ground beef and the seasoned onions. "Care to help?"

"If you need heat, I'm your woman." A spark of flame crackled between her fingers. "For everything else?" She frowned, her flame turning to soft curls of smoke.

"Lucky for you, I have an open position for someone of your caliber." He grinned, motioning to the waning flame on the stove beneath the pan. "Light me up, angel."

Cheeks flushing, she did as he asked then returned to watching him form perfect meatballs with the same hands she'd witnessed cleaving through monsters. She was beginning to treasure these little glimpses of the personality hidden beneath the mask of the soulless hunter. Renton put care into everything he did.

It wasn't long until he slid a plate in front of her. Meatballs and sautéed green beans drizzled in the most heavenly glaze Tenah had ever tasted.

"So much flavor," she mumbled around a mouthful. "You cook like Mel. She was always my favorite."

"Is this what it takes to win you over?" His bright eyes glinted with mischief.

She nodded. "That's how Mire should train their hunters. Lure the prey in with the scent of a well-cooked meal. Though, I require dessert too."

He considered this. "Can't say I've ever made one. I'll learn for you."

Leaning over the table, he snatched the bite off her fork with his mouth. Heat pooled low in her body at his sudden closeness.

When her plate had been scraped clean, his mood pivoted. "The temple in the Void. What is it? Can you show me?"

Fear slammed into her. "Not with that thing inside of you. If he found out or Chaos detected it—"

Renton stilled. "He? Tenah, I would like for you to explain exactly what happened that night in the manor."

She lowered her head and gripped the edge of her stool. "You would think less of me if I told you."

"Your father mentioned Cirel had some sort of connection to you. Is he speaking with you in the Void?"

Her bones chilled, his words detonating like bolts of magic against her chest. She lowered her cheek to the counter. Could it be? She'd never seen a depiction of Adra's king. It seemed outrageous that he would waste time crossing the Void just to meet with her. Didn't he have a war to plot?

But her father considered Cirel his greatest rival. Would it be so farfetched that Adra's king would try to use her against him, especially with her ability to create rifts?

The room spun, and Tenah shut her eyes.

She needed access to that temple. Everything Chaos was trying to hide from her.

"How can I help you?" Renton asked.

"You can't."

"I'm not afraid of Corruption," he said firmly.

Tenah pressed her lips tightly together. "Fine. I ask for one thing. Take me somewhere far outside the city. When I dive back into the Void, I'm not certain who will come out, me or Chaos. If it's Chaos, end it."

Renton's jaw muscles ticked, his eyes swirling with a flurry of dark emotions. "All right."

Chapter Thirty-Three

RENTON

It was nothing for him to speak the lie.

Renton wouldn't be the one to cut Tenah down, should she emerge from the rift Corrupt. Just the idea had him quivering with rage, so much so that Zia would beg to hire him when she discovered how thoroughly he'd scrubbed the pots and pans tomorrow morning. And to that, he'd politely tell her she couldn't afford him.

By the time the kitchen gleamed, Tenah shuffled out of the storage room with sluggish limbs. She rested the mop against the wall and fought off a yawn that spoke to his soul.

Renton took her into his arms, hoisting her up so her legs could wrap around him. He kissed her softly, enjoying the way her hands knotted in his shirt as if she'd bully him into keeping his mouth on hers forever.

Honestly, he wouldn't mind.

When they parted, her head dropped on his shoulder.

"How did I get roped into cleaning?" she grumbled.

His laugh was low and tired. "I told you to sit in that chair and not touch a thing."

Pressing a longer kiss to her neck, he basked in her warmth and the scent of citrus cleaner and lavender. He didn't care that the shard stirred in his chest or that the dark magic in her channels plotted to kill him.

Soon, the shard would be gone, and he could touch her all she pleased.

"Stay with me tonight. No expectations. I just want you close," he said.

Tenah went rigid in his hold, and he took that as a sign to pull away and give her space. She stared down at her hands as they played with the hem of his T-shirt sleeve.

"Tomorrow, I'll take you outside city limits," he said. "I promise."

He would beg if necessary. But then Tenah nodded, and he carried her out of the kitchen, hands fitted around her ass.

"Is this necessary?" she whispered, unable to contain a smile.

"Absolutely. My hands belong on you at all times."

When they arrived back at his room, he poured her a glass of water and collected a knitted throw blanket if she needed it. Struggling to erase images of her stripped down and begging for him, Renton headed toward the bathing room. "I'm going to rinse off."

With her little nod of approval, he removed himself from her side, planning to take extra time in the shower to relieve himself of the urge to sink into her warm heat again.

Under the spray of hot water, he slowly worked his hard cock in hand, bracing his forehead on the stones. He groaned, chasing his release, though he knew it would be a disappointing one.

"Renton?" A knock sounded on the door before it cracked open.

Fuck. He dropped his hand, turning to catch Tenah standing in the doorway. Shame worked through him, but then her face and neck flushed as her eyes dipped and widened.

"I heard… I thought you might…be in pain." Her throat bobbed.

His jaw worked as he debated how to answer. But then she was slipping out of her clothes and stepping into the shower, her peculiar eyes locked on his.

"What are you doing?" His voice was low and sensual. Too filled with desire he was trying to keep in check.

She wrapped a soft hand around his cock. "Tell me how to take care of you."

He sealed his eyes shut, nearly spasming under her touch. He had a mind to send her back to bed, but then she gripped him harder. "That feels good."

Renton watched her as she kept her eyes on the movement of her hands, sliding up and down his shaft with reverence. Unable to help himself, he pushed her naked body back against the stone wall, trapped between his arms that braced his weight.

His mouth crashed down on hers until she had him seeing stars. His release bent him over until his forehead came to rest on her shoulder.

"You are trouble too, angel," he said between soft pants.

He proceeded to gently wash her, taking his time with her hair, placing kisses wherever he pleased to earn little gasps of pleasure from her. After wrapping her in a towel, he shipped her off to bed.

Before dressing himself, he wiped the steamed mirror with a towel and stared at the ugly slash of ruined skin over his chest, accompanied by the five tiny punctures Tenah had left.

Kherathi had offered him freedom from it. But what was the cost to others? Was it the right decision to hand over a shard of power to a warped Chaos lord?

Aeyis, Renton called out, not expecting an answer. It wasn't as though his brother was always tuned in.

What is it, brother?

The response came too quick, and Renton almost growled at him in disapproval. *Anything in that tome of yours mention shards?*

They are mentioned, yes. Says they serve as vessels for magic, dark or light. Xith used them to power his cities, trains, engines, and such. This is fascinating stuff. Conditions to regrow such crystals can only be produced with the right balance of dissolved minerals in the soil combined with extreme heat. Magma, lightning, Chaos...

Renton halted as he tugged on a long-sleeved shirt to accompany the soft, black pants he'd slid on. Courtesy of the villa workers. They'd learned of his preference for uniform, simple clothes.

What Aeyis had discovered gave a whole new perspective to Roan's Wake. The scarred land, incinerated by fire and Chaos. How the High Court seemed to be so hands-off now as if they were waiting for something. Possibly new crystals to form? It would be the most nonviolent form of combating Cirel's war. Pump them full of healing magic and let them purify the cursed souls roaming the wastes of Adra.

Unless Cirel knew about the crystals too.

Renton would have to sit down with his brother soon and delve into this topic. *Sounds like you've been busy. Does your book mention how to remove them from the shadow body?*

Hold please. Give me the night. Hass hasn't been keen on letting me linger in the archives too long.

Renton breathed in steamy air before strolling out of the bathroom. *Don't work too hard.*

He wandered to the edge of the bed, a smile forming as he took in Tenah's sleeping form. She hadn't bothered crawling under the blankets, choosing to curl up under the throw blanket instead.

Unwilling to disturb her with his movement on the bed, Renton dropped into a chair by the fireplace.

Sometime overnight, he'd navigated to the bed anyway. Soft beams of sunlight woke him. Disoriented from a rare full night's sleep, Renton rubbed at his eyes and found Tenah tucked in next to him.

Her dark lashes fluttered open as she unfurled long arms and lean legs. He brushed a lock of hair from her cheek. His fingers traced along the shell of her ear. In the morning light, her eyes were more of a rich shade of brown. Had they ever been red? In fact, all of her features had softened in the time he'd come to know her. The harsh frown of her mouth. The narrowed, distrusting eyes.

He couldn't resist leaning in to kiss her. It was becoming his favorite game, catching her off guard. Tenah yipped and smacked a pillow down on his head. He didn't try to block it. Throwing the pillow off the bed in defiance, he tackled her, splaying her out on the bed.

Staring down at her in wonder, heart swelling at the way she stared back with open eyes, he couldn't help the smile breaking across his face.

"Get dressed, beautiful. We have plans."

Ever since their arrival in Denoden, Renton itched to visit the western plateaus, curious about the views they had to offer. Would he glimpse a slice of paradise? He wanted nothing more than to share that with her.

After dining on blackberry pancakes and freshly pressed juice, courtesy of Zia, they acquired horses and rode out of the gates.

"Where exactly are we going?" Tenah asked, throwing him a suspicious look.

"No interrogations. Just ride." Renton nudged his horse into a gallop, tearing through the waist-high fields, hot air billowing his shirt and hair.

"No offense, but I'm not partial to the secrets you keep," Tenah yelled.

He tipped his head back with a free laugh as he caught her spewing curses. The rhythmic drumming of hooves on the dry ground picked up, and he peeked back, spotting her leaned down against her mare's neck. It looked like she was whispering insults in its twitching ear. The animal would never catch him. He'd purposely given her the slower horse.

Massive chunks of rock, slashed through with lines of deep red and orange, rose up from the flat landscape. Evidence that the isles had once been part of something much greater.

Renton slowed his horse, enraptured by Tenah's awestruck expression.

"Your riding has improved," he said.

She rolled her eyes. "My riding is exactly the same. The western kingdoms just breed better horses than your wretched isle."

He surveyed the plateau before them, a hand rested on his hip. "Shall we climb?"

Her head lurched to him. "What?"

Renton dismounted. He strode to the rocky wall and gripped the first jutting handholds. "Aeyis mentioned you enjoy climbing. It's a stress reliever, yeah?"

"Aeyis needs to find some other hobbies besides stealing secrets," she retorted.

He was grateful to see her taking up position on the plateau wall.

Tenah rubbed her hands on her pants before finding her first hold. "We're not racing, are we?"

"No race. Just climb."

With no sight of what was at the top, sometimes it was hard to do just that. To keep moving. To force torn, aching muscles to respond.

Renton had buried himself so far down, shredded by Boedworth and hunters he'd once considered family, his father's death and all of his own anger-fueled mistakes, that his climb had taken years. Hell, he still wasn't at the top.

He prayed to higher beings that Tenah would find the inner strength to do what he had never accomplished. He prayed she would come out of the Void whole, or he might find himself back down in that pit, greeting old demons.

Chapter Thirty-Four

TENAH

Tenah's arms were trembling by the time she slapped a hand down on the top of the plateau. Sweat-caked and panting, she yelped as someone grabbed her and hauled her up the rest of the way.

"About time you made it." Gireth beamed. "Took Vesara and me less than ten minutes. Aeyis clung to the wall for what, another forty minutes? It was hilarious."

Tenah glanced over at Vesara poised on the center of the giant, ancient rock, knives all arranged before her, waiting to be sharpened. Then she took in Aeyis, laid out with his eyes closed as if he were begging higher beings to take him into the afterlife.

She snorted, appreciating the fact that he wasn't instantly good at everything.

"Shut up. Heights aren't my thing," Aeyis grumbled.

"Weren't you the one to suggest this idea to the group?" Vesara asked.

"I am my own worst enemy, aren't I?"

Flustered, Tenah rubbed at her temples. "Okay, what's going on here?"

"You asked for me to take you out of city limits," Renton said, heaving his body onto the surface of the giant rock with a grunt.

Panic wormed into her stomach. "Yes, Renton. Away. From. Others."

"And you are." Renton gave her a look, daring her to scale back down after such a rigorous climb.

"I'm offended," Gireth said. "We're not others, Tenah. We're family. Thought we'd made that clear already."

Tenah ground a rock beneath her boot. The last thing she wanted to do was turn Corrupt in front of them, putting them all in danger. "You watched me stab my cousin against my will, right?"

"Our professions literally beg for us to get hurt every day," Vesara replied. "Wait, are we all unemployed right now? Renix above, we are."

Anger jabbed at Tenah's ribs. Was this a joke to them?

A hand touched her elbow and led her away from the crew. Renton released her at the opposite edge of the plateau. He sat down and patted the spot next to him. Her heart gave a wild lurch as she begrudgingly obliged, letting her legs dangle over the edge.

From this height, with the clear skies and the golden sunlight, she could see the coast of Aranma thousands of feet below. All proud mountains brushed with lush foliage, white-sand beaches and glistening turquoise seas so shallow in some areas, coral reefs were visible.

"This is…" Words evaded her.

"Elcana Reefs," Renton said. "Of all the places Boedworth shipped me to, this was by far the most memorable. For the nobleman I had to threaten, memorable for another reason. But I couldn't shake the way the city made me feel."

A buoyant sensation in her chest pushed out her frustration. The world was truly a gem. One shadows had treated poorly over the centuries. Where was talk of that in tomes and temples? Everyone was so caught up in the balance of magic and politics and war.

Sometimes things just needed to be. To exist without complication.

"I've found nature can be healing," Renton said quietly, bright eyes locking on her.

They were silent for a span of time, absorbing the sunlight and fresh air. Tenah had to glance behind them to assure herself that the crew hadn't fallen off the plateau.

Soft snores came from Aeyis's motionless form.

A small laugh burst from her. "I don't think I've ever seen an Ashen sleep."

"I rarely witnessed it myself," Renton said, "but he got wild on Fen's cappuccinos last night doing some research. Now he's crashing and burning."

Tenah couldn't help but grin. It had been hours since she'd had any thoughts of the Void or the rift or her father. And even before the manor massacre, she'd ridden a constant line of plaguing stress.

This peace was foreign to her, but within it, she knew she could mold a version of herself that she preferred. One that enjoyed company. That sought adventure. That wasn't the pillar onto which shadows placed their faith to shift mountains and achieve what had never been done before, not recorded, at least.

From the way Renton was staring out at Elcana, it was evident he pined for a new start too.

His voice was tender when he spoke again. "Move there with me. When this matter with your father is settled. Neither of us have homes to return to."

What a beautiful future.

Misery spread through her body like an illness.

Her gaze dropped to her marked hands and cracked fingernails. "Renton, I'm not..." She frowned, hating that she had to pry the sticky words from her mouth. "That night in the manor, I made a bargain with Cirel to give me a second life. It's possible it won't be a full life. I may never be able to fully heal myself. I may always be bound to him in some form."

"Sounds like another research project," Aeyis interrupted.

Not two seconds after, snores rumbled from him again.

"What is happening right now?" Vesara asked, staring down at Aeyis with wide eyes. "Did he even wake up or is he sleep-talking?"

"He does that sometimes. Scares the crap out of me," Gireth chimed in then leaned over to slap Aeyis in the stomach. Aeyis curled up with a grunt. "Should have joined us for a bit of dice last night, little bro. Vesara still owes me two hundred krotens and dinner."

"Dinner was never part of the agreement," Vesara snapped, flipping one of her knives between her fingers. "And anyway, I don't like to be wined and dined."

"Intel from a Void Walker was, however," Gireth replied, his smile widening.

Tenah's gaze snapped to him. "What the hell kind of dice game were you playing?"

"One with some shady, shady mothers in the Abyss. I'm telling you, the lowest of the low—"

"Get on with it," Vesara cut in.

Gireth's face scrunched up in concentration. "Raging Waters—"

"Raye Witner," Vesara corrected, freshly irked. "A highly esteemed courier for the mainland."

"Right, Rain Whisperer told us there are shadows in the mountains of Aranma that belong to something called the Equil? Anyway, she was going to deliver a message to them about you, though she warned they are pretty selective about taking on newcomers."

Tenah's lungs expanded. If that was true, she wasn't alone in her efforts. There were others that could aid her. Guide her.

"And to answer your question from last night, Ren," Aeyis said, raising a bony arm in the air. "The shard can be removed with either Rama or a greater amount of Chaos. Which is what I'm assuming Tenah's father will do and why he gave fair warning."

Tenah looked between brothers, her hands clenching into fists in frustration at herself. While she'd been tucked in Renton's bed, the others had been working to gather information to aid her.

She settled her racing heart, refocusing on her task. "You *will* keep your promise if I come out different?"

Renton's eyes churned with pent-up anger. "You won't."

Before she could talk herself out of the task at hand, she slashed a hole in the world, just large enough to squeeze in her body. Teeth clenched and muscles braced for danger, she strode into the chilling Void.

Elementals, she hated this place. It was too cold and quiet. Every footstep seemed to echo her presence in enemy territory.

She should have known something was wrong the moment she walked into the temple and only silence greeted her. Hairs stood on edge along her arms. Her confidence withered. What if this was a trap?

Fear swelled in her throat, shortening her breaths.

Shutting down thoughts that this would be her tomb when the utter darkness reminded her too much of death, she forced herself down the temple stairs. At the bottom, she spun and kicked out a boot to ensure her escape.

Tenah found nothing but empty air.

Panic curdling in her stomach, she dropped to her knees, hands frantically reaching out.

The stairs were gone.

Chaos was *definitely* fucking with her.

She sealed her eyes shut. "Is that all you've got?" she called out to Chaos, no matter how much she wished it wouldn't respond.

Chaos rumbled with laughter. *We smell him. We know what he hides in his heart. Your precious hunter.*

The orb light flickered into existence, and with it came the death king.

Chapter Thirty-Five
RENTON

"She's been in there too long," Renton muttered.

As time slipped by with Tenah wandering the Void alone, the entire crew lost their endorphin rush. Other than the incremental tightening of his muscles, Renton hadn't moved. Glaring at the scar of silvery white light gave him some reprieve from his unease as if the act would keep the rift from misbehaving.

How long would this take? How far into the Void did she have to journey? How would they know if she was in trouble? Would Cirel be waiting for her?

His jaw clenched hard enough to ache as he dropped his folded arms. "Screw this. I'm going in."

"Go get our girl." Gireth tossed Renton his glaive.

For the first time in his life, and hopefully the last, Renton entered the Void.

Thick air filled his lungs, pushing at his ribcage. Currents of visible energy buzzed all around him. He could sense creatures lurking in the darkness, but he didn't have time to play into instincts and cut them all down.

Leave them for Gireth to slaughter if he has to come after me.

Tucked under his illusion magic, Renton leaned into the painful tug in his heart to guide him. Ironic, considering he'd cursed the damned shard last night for interrupting much desirable activities.

His illusion flickered and sputtered, so he quickened his pace, never in the same place when monsters with slitted tongues and barbed tails skittered closer. He scanned his surroundings for the peak of a temple. His mind sought to play tricks on him, casting the image of Nightfall's gloomy, blood-soaked temples in the distance.

A prickle of anxiety and his weaning magic had him itching to call out for Tenah, but he didn't dare make a sound as he waded deeper into the chilling expanse of blue.

A lone red building came into view. Perched on a block of smooth stone, it was adorned with curly, gold flourishes. Silver chimes jangled from its roofline, even with the absence of a breeze.

Renton stepped up to the entrance. The doorway was encapsulated in darkness. His nostrils flared, picking up on the sharp, acidic scent of dark magic from within.

Gods, this place felt wrong. It *seethed* with animosity.

Was this what Tenah had faced alone? How many Void Walkers actually stayed sane after roaming this fucked-up world?

Gritting his teeth, Renton stretched his magical ability as far as it would go as he marched inside. Outside of a fight, he was able to concentrate more on maintaining it, but he knew he was rapidly approaching his limit.

The interior was empty, save for a throne, and directly behind it, there was a staircase leading down into darkness.

Shit, this was going to hurt. Weaving his illusion tighter and ignoring his limits, Renton descended into the unknown. The shard throbbed, giving intense fits that had him bracing on Gireth's glaive every few stairs. Its pulse vibrated through every sensitive nerve in his body. He rarely experienced such a reaction from the shard, only when faced with a highly Corrupt enemy.

This pain...

Something else lurked here. Something far more wicked than any creature he'd carved through before. If this kept up, he might not be the one walking out of the Void today.

A faint, blue glow signaled him below. Renton quickened his pace. The last stair dropped him into a dimly lit, seemingly endless hall. Ahead, he made out the shape of a tall figure. Tenah kneeled before the shadow, crushed by waves of darkness pouring out of his cobalt robes.

The shard clamped down, and Renton slammed a hand against the wall for support. Two different colored eyes snapped to him. It was then he came to understand what the Chaos lord had meant. The King of Adra wasn't of this world, his fierce gaze branding him with centuries-worth of hatred.

"Your illusions won't work on me, beguiler," Cirel said in a cool tone. With a wave of a ringed hand, he crushed Renton's last scrap of magic.

Tenah's head whipped to him. "Renton, no!"

He didn't miss the dejected glance Cirel tossed her way. It twisted up his insides.

With a smooth movement, Renton freed a small dagger from his boot and hurled it at the king. The blade nicked Cirel's arm. The line of blood that beaded along the cut was pure black.

Metallic, dark magic slammed into Renton, throwing him onto his back.

"You are the one she wants to protect? That's rich." Cirel sneered.

"What do you want with her?" Renton demanded.

The King of Adra regarded him with a slow, cruel smile. "You would love to know, wouldn't you? For now, I'll be satisfied with the return of my war beast."

Tenah shot a hand out, grabbing Cirel's robes and igniting them with red flames.

The king stumbled back, losing grip on his magic. Before Renton could get his feet under him, Tenah's scorching hands were on him, pulling him upright.

"Keep moving," she said. "This is not your fight."

Renton didn't budge. He wanted to watch the king burn, even if it was only for a few seconds. Cirel quickly suffocated the flames with a burst of dark magic.

Summoning a wall of Chaotic flames at their backs, Tenah dug her fingernails into Renton's arm. "Don't make this your fight, Renton. You will lose."

He would have disobeyed, but the shard was threatening to cripple him right here. If he ended up temporarily paralyzed because of it, Tenah would linger behind. It would put her in more danger. He wouldn't have that.

Renton forced his legs to carry him up the stairs. This fight would have to wait. Oh, but he would have it one day soon.

"It's no use, Tenah," Cirel bellowed from the temple depths. "I own you. No matter what, I will have my war."

Renton paused at the landing of the stairs. Through his teeth, he pushed out the words. "Let me kill him. Please let me kill him."

"Keep moving," she ordered, eyes wide and swirling with emotion. Shame. Desperation. Sadness.

Renton peered down into the stairwell. A true hunter would have thrown themself back in, set on victory or death. The protective asshole in him wanted to prove to the king that Tenah did not belong to him, bond or no bond.

Instead, he took her hand in his and let her guide him out of the Void.

Chapter Thirty-Six

TENAH

Tenah couldn't shed her panic as they raced back to Denoden.

The climb down the plateau had been excruciating, assuming any moment Cirel would appear from the rift and tear out Renton's heart.

Then again, wouldn't he just force her to do it? She'd been so close the other night. Was there a limit or a range to his power? It seemed improbable judging from the potency of it. The only hindrance to his spreading destruction thus far was his lack of efficient travel across the isles.

But with her under his control…

She was his power move. His queen piece.

Cirel could use that mammoth rift in the Ruzgorn camp to march his armies here and spill poison into her homelands. Tenah needed to return to and seal the rift. Then she would ensure her father removed the shard from Renton's heart.

Everything would be fine.

At Denoden's gates, Aeyis's cool press of magic gave her warning. *Your cousin is here.*

Tenah's growl reverberated through the air. "Now is not the time."

Still, she couldn't help the urgency to assure her cousin was in one piece. Dropping from her horse, she allowed Aeyis to guide her through the villa into a small, breezy meeting room.

Entirely dressed down, Hakkan stood beside one of many golden chairs arranged around a polished wooden table. He wore a white T-shirt, cut off at the sleeves to reveal the bindings around his midsection. Three of his cronies stood behind him, tall enough to knock heads with the hanging potted plants.

Tenah stormed up to her cousin. She barely rose to his chin, but the searing glare she bored into him shaved the edge off what seemed to be his permanent scowl. "I'm done fighting you."

Hakkan raised his hands in surrender. "I'm not here for that."

"What other reason would you have for coming then?"

"Oh, I don't know, maybe the giant hole in the sky that's spitting out Corrupt?" His features twisted. "It was just a handful at first. Now they're falling out in clusters. While my warriors appreciate the practice, I'm not keen on losing the one spot we've found in weeks with clean drinking water."

Tenah's shoulders drooped. "I was headed there to deal with it before your interruption."

"Then we're on the same page," Hakkan said, tossing a look at his barbarians. Somehow, they'd been allowed inside the villa with giant battle axes strapped to their backs. It was no wonder Boedworth had managed to steal the Chaos tome. Did the guards posted at the gates do anything at all?

Hakkan leaned closer, his voice dropping low. "Tell me—was that hellhole all part of your plan to kill us off?"

She winced. "It was an accident. As was the…stabbing. You should get that looked at while you're here."

When he drew back, his dark brows were pushed together, creating a wrinkle at the bridge of his straight nose. "Can you close it?"

Suddenly, all eyes were on her. She squirmed, wishing she had the confidence to say that she could fix everything. "I'm going to try."

Because Renton's life depended on it. The safety of her friends and Denoden and all the shadows on her isle depended on it. For once, she needed to take responsibility for her power and for her mistakes.

"And your plans after?" Hakkan pressed.

Chin high, she replied, "I'll head to Firesteep to handle my father."

Hakkan mulled this over, his expression unreadable. "You handle that rift, and you have the strength of my army, cousin. It's time we forge a new path for our family."

Shock twisted her face. "You're…you're offering to help me?"

"I was born to a common Firesteep woman. It's as much my home as any other Vozarian, even if they see me as nothing more than a barbarian."

The pride in his voice had Tenah softening. However, she wasn't so foolish as to jump into a bargain without a care anymore.

"What will Gadreel think about our alliance?" she asked. "I don't claim ties to any Ruzgorn banners."

Hakkan scoffed. "My father wanted you to kill me. You know he believes me a stain on this world. Yet he was the one that sidestepped your father on his warpath to Firesteep. Gadreel could have at least tried to stop him."

Tenah picked apart his words for deception. Hakkan didn't seem the type to play games. "You would desert your culture?"

"I'm not deserting. I'm making much-needed changes for *my* army."

"But the blood rite—"

"I don't give a shit about the blood rite. Neither of us feel any sort of magical pressure to finish the job, right? Here we are, face-to-face, and I haven't felt the urge to cut you down."

He had a point.

"Is it real or just a motivator to kill?" she asked.

"The blood rite does grant the victor a boost in power. That's not a lie," Hakkan said, eyes flashing with remorse. If her cousin had been power hungry at one time, he'd purged himself of the addiction. Hakkan glanced over at Vesara. "In exchange for our aid, we want land. Access to resources within the kingdoms just like all the other natives on this isle. No more barren desert foraging. I tire of it."

Vesara scoffed, but Tenah put her back in line with a firm look.

"You said you owe me a debt twice over, right?" Tenah asked. "Or were those hollow words?"

The assassin went rigid. Tenah was aware she waded murky waters, but surely they could mend their kingdoms with a bit of civil discussion. After all, war hadn't worked for anyone over the last several centuries.

"Could some sort of deal be made with Izral if the Ruzgorn prove their loyalty at Firesteep?" Tenah asked.

Vesara rolled her eyes in dramatic fashion. "This day! You're asking me to get a party boy king to agree to a peace treaty with pillagers? The land they demand is soaked with blood they've spilled."

Hakkan took a step toward her, his tone sharp as a whip. "Tell your king my clan has spilled no blood in Vristar."

Vesara waved a hand as if to shush him. Smoky tendrils coiled around his body as his temperature spiked.

Tenah rested a calming hand on his arm. "I will speak with Izral."

"No," Vesara snapped, tugging at her hair as if she might rip it out. "I'll manage the king on my own."

With that final agreement, Tenah surveyed the room, awaiting opposition. A sliver of unease worked its way under her skin. No one else had spoken up, seemingly content with the direction of their conversation.

Renton gave her an approving nod, his bright eyes sparking with admiration that had her cheeks flushing. "Then we all head south."

As the others funneled out of the meeting room, Hakkan kept his eyes on Tenah. He offered a hand. Feeling a renewed sense of hope, she clasped it. She might have lost her family, but she was working to reforge a new one.

"You should consider a profession in negotiations when all this is said and done," Hakkan said. "You're much better at it than committing murder."

Chapter Thirty-Seven

TENAH

"Where are you, Tenah?" Renton's soothing voice lured her from a daze.

The stifling heat of the desert came back to her as she blinked atop her horse, her stomach immediately tying into knots.

Fading streaks from the sunset painted the crew and Ruzgorn trudging ahead of them in bloody light. At best, this trip would cost them wicked sunburns, the stupid transportation orb having burnt out on them at the worst possible time. Vesara was convinced Izral had something to do with its sudden lack of magic, but Renton had assured her it was a common thing for orbs to wear down with use.

"You could stay behind," Renton said. "Heal the rift when you're ready. Hakkan and I can handle whatever spills out."

Her head jerked to him. "Did you forget that I caused all of this? Because I certainly didn't. I opened the rift. I need to close it."

"You didn't do anything. Chaos did that. That lowlife King of Adra did that," Renton replied, his words laced with fury.

She gripped the reins tighter. "I *chose* to bargain with him."

The muscles in Renton's jaw worked as he scrounged for more

justifications to her inexcusable actions. She snorted. *Good luck.*

Tenah nodded at the crew. "They should have stayed in Denoden. They have no part in this."

"Go ahead and try to send them back."

Imagining how poorly that conversation would go over, she shifted in her saddle. *Hey, thanks for all your sacrifices to help me sort out my shit, but this is where I draw the line.*

Vesara was busy picking her dark nails with a small knife. Aeyis was deep in thoughts, most likely not his own. And Gireth… Well, he was engrossed in a demonstration of the flop of a strange, green, solid food Zia had packed for him. Hakkan didn't know what to make of the jiggly concoction or its goofy, rugged holder.

Renton's laugh was raspy. "Zia would kill him for making fun of her food."

A weak smile crept onto Tenah's face. "Gireth carries on to camp with me then. He'll fare better against Adra's enemies than the all-consuming rage of a Vristarian cook."

Renton's barked laugh earned questioning looks from the others.

"Oy, you on something?" Gireth called out, the green food still jiggling in his palm.

"Tenah elected for you to handle the rift alone. She favors you the least," Renton replied.

"Wait, am I being voted off the isle?"

Tenah jabbed at Renton's side. Her knuckles hit armor, drawing out a curse. This only fueled his entertainment.

"You and Gireth are a match made by the gods." Renton smirked.

She straightened up. Sure, it was just a joke. But her stupid heart couldn't help but pine for her preferred match. Her eyes flicked over to study Renton, her heart lurching.

Tenah urged her horse faster.

The ripple of silvery light was just as prominent as when she'd first slashed it into the sky. Ruzgorn hadn't moved their tents away from it. Instead, they'd formed a tighter ring around it.

"If you sense anything wrong, you let Aeyis know, and he'll communicate with all of us," Renton instructed the crew when they reached the first line of canvas tents.

Tenah dismounted. A hand slid around her waist. Pulling her back against his chest, Renton leaned in to press a kiss to her cheek. "Please be careful."

Head tucked to hide her burning cheeks, she moved toward the rift.

Is he here, Aeyis? she asked. She'd scrawled a letter to her father right before leaving Denoden in hopes that he would aid her with the rift in exchange for the shard in Renton's heart. Hakkan had let her borrow his hawk to deliver the message.

I don't sense his presence. Sorry, Tenah.

Her father's absence stung, but she shouldn't have been surprised. While Renton believed there were still scraps of him left, he didn't know him like she did.

Tenah circled the rift in unison with Aeyis. Vibrations from the energy tickled her skin, setting her nerves on edge.

Chaos purred with satisfaction. *This. This is where we need to be.*

Had she not injured herself to sever her ties with Chaos during the blood rite, she hated to think how big the rift would have grown.

Tenah stopped her pacing, spotting a stain of black ichor in the dirt. Blood from Corrupt. Whatever had been slaughtered here had been dragged off, thank Renix. She couldn't stomach having to look at what she'd unleashed.

Take higher ground in case anything breaks through, Aeyis instructed, lifting a hand to touch the bottom of the rift. A dozen tendrils of black lightning sprang to meet his palm, sinking tiny hooks into his skin like leeches. *You'll need your concentration to seal it. We'll handle the rest.*

She rushed for the cathedral doors, eyeing the bell tower from which she could overlook the entire camp and sound off alerts to Aeyis and the crew if needed. There was no room for her errors today. She would keep them all safe.

Gireth made it to the cathedral door first and held it open for her. "Did I ever tell you about the time I detonated a sludge monster in training camp?"

Tenah shook her head, darting for the stuffy interior staircase off the entrance.

"Poisoned two dozen hunters," Gireth continued, "including our chieftain. They were cleaning the goop out of their sinuses for weeks."

A smile twitched on her lips. "Renton included?"

"Oh, he took the worst of it. Puked all over the battlegrounds. No one told me you had to cut off the beast's head to keep its poison from spilling. I was more concerned about the eight tentacles." He wiggled his arms around for emphasis, beaming under her attention.

"Is this some lame attempt to make me feel better about putting my entire isle in danger by choosing dark magic and opening a doorway for otherworldly enemies to pour in?"

Gireth shrugged. "Nah, just trying to make you laugh. Nothing's funnier than making Renton uncomfortable."

At the top of the bell tower, Tenah wiped the sweat from her forehead and leaned over the wooden railing. She picked out Renton standing next to her cousin, two seasoned fighters deep in strategic conversation.

"I don't have a lick of magical talent, or I'd help." Gireth sighed, laying out on the ground as if he might take a nap, a leg propped up and arms draped over his eyes.

Tenah drew in a deep breath, then she latched on to the fibers of the rift. She wasn't exactly sure what to do with them. What did healing magic even feel like? She might as well smack her head against a rock a hundred times and hope for a result other than blood and pain. She tried to mimic her mother's sense of calm, severing ties to distracting emotions and homing in on the thrum of rift magic.

Mend. Heal.

You defy us, little one. Allow us this doorway, and we will devour your enemies, Chaos rumbled.

Lies.

Tenah widened her stance, muscles burning with lactic acid. Too soon, she trembled from the effort of physically tugging the rift fibers back together. Dark magic buzzed through her channels like thousands of angry insects. Beads of sweat rolled down her neck, slipping beneath her damp shirt. Little curls of hair stuck to her slick temples.

The rift shivered in protest as it fought against her hold. Then Aeyis was applying Chaos to the sky's wound too. She hated that she needed him. Always demanding more from others. *Take. Take. Take.*

Something's coming through, Aeyis warned.

Tenah's heart thumped harder. *Not this soon.*

She pulled harder on the rift threads. A tremor rolled down the length of it right before it split clean open where she'd been applying pressure. Corrupt tumbled out in a mottled heap of furious limbs, honed claws, and a haze of toxic magic.

Her fragile confidence shriveled as Vesara launched into the pack. The assassin buried knives into the eyes of two Corrupt before Renton and Hakkan joined her, their swords quickly coated in a black, oily sheen of tainted blood.

Gireth jerked to his feet, glaive spinning and hazel eyes ablaze with startling rage.

"Nothing escapes this camp," Hakkan bellowed, flames jetting from his palm to eat away at the putrid bodies flooding out of the rift.

It was wrong to kill them. But what other choice did they have? It wasn't like she had the skill to heal them. Even if she could, she was one shadow among an ocean of threats.

Weak. Worthless. Pathetic.

Cool magic trickled through her mind, silencing the chants of Chaos and the clang of weapons and the snarl of creatures that had once had dreams just like her.

Tenah didn't have time to thank Aeyis for the quietude because something whooshed through the bell tower. Turning her head, she caught Gireth shouting and aggressively waving her to the stairs. Then he was gone, ripped from the tower in a flurry of black wings and gnashing teeth.

Her stomach dropped out of her body as she ran to the splintered railing. *No.* That couldn't be Gireth hurtling to the ground, tangled up in a feingrot.

Its talons were latched around his shoulder plates as it drove him into the ground with a sickening crunch.

She tore for the stairs, vital things inside of her twisting and snapping. Breaking from the cathedral doors, she paid no mind to the Corrupt and feingrot tearing apart the camp. Ruzgorn blades were efficiently hacking them apart.

Tenah shoved the now-dead feingrot off Gireth's body, leaving his glaive in its torso. Her shaking fingers pressed against his neck first.

A pulse thumped back, and she allowed herself to breathe again.

"Don't you ever scare me like that again," she scolded, hot tears streaming down her face.

When she clasped his hand to help him up, Gireth brushed her off. "Tenah, I...I don't think I can move."

The raw fear in his voice stabbed at her. She reached again for his hand. "You can. You just have to try."

"I *can't.*"

Terror surged through her as her mind hooked on the thought of his spine possibly being broken. Her eyes skimmed the camp frantically. *Healer,* she screamed down the mental link with Aeyis. *We need a healer.*

You are the only healer in camp, Aeyis replied solemnly. *It has to be you.*

Her throat was ragged as she stared down at Gireth. His eyes were vacant as he gazed up at the sky. She wanted to shake him.

He'd survived Dreaddix. He could live through this too. But she knew his spirit had been broken too. She didn't try to move him again.

"Don't cry for me, pretty girl," Gireth said with a faint smile. "You're too good for that."

Arguing with him would only result in Tenah dissolving into a puddle of sorrow. She looked to the rift, desperate for the healing magic she knew it hid. Too far away. Too overburdened with monsters.

She risked another doorway into the Void, large enough for her to crawl inside. With a protective shield of fiery energy pulled tight around her body, she sprinted for the temple. There was no time for second guessing. Not when Gireth might provoke an attack with enemies, despite his condition.

She raced into the dark entrance, grateful to find it blissfully empty. Cirel was most likely preoccupied with orchestrating his doomsday march. Charging down the pitch-black stairs, plummeting into the heart of her nightmares, she prayed Rama would be enough to save her friend and close the rift.

Corrupt shadowling. Chaos boomed all around her, its words repeating like a fragmented memory. *Such unholy acts you have committed. Shameful, unforgivable acts.*

Recognizing the parasite's attempt to stall her advances, she forged on. Insectile legs scuttled over her boots, flowing in a steady stream. Her vicious flames met them before they had a chance to crawl halfway up her legs. She burned and burned and burned at the heaving mass of them, never allowing her heartbeat to stutter.

Chaos shifted gears. The assault of creatures halted abruptly. Silence fell. A lone torch ignited with blue fire, revealing a dozen stone tunnels, all smeared with dark, metallic blood.

She cursed. The hesitation cost her. Liquid pooled under her boots, slithering along the cracks between tiles like miniature snakes. It was too dark to be blood but felt just as thick as she stepped through it. Too soon, it lapped at her shins.

Tenah thrust her horror down. Just how far did this temple fucking span?

Sloshing through the foreign liquid, she headed for the farthest tunnel. It was her best guess. Chaos would assume her too frightened to cross that far. And it *was* impossible to stamp out the sour kernel of fear in her gut. The liquid had risen to her waist now, staining her exposed stomach. She fought back a wave of nausea.

Chaos has no physical hold on me. It cannot win. Not again.

She waded up to her chest. Her breaths came quicker. Her eyes watched for ripples beyond the ones she created with her movement. What lurked beneath the surface?

Fear surrounded her mind like a vice. What if Rama wasn't even here? What if the source had dried up or withered from the concentration of

Chaos here?

Chaos tore into that uncertainty. Dragged it out with sharp claws as the liquid rose to her chin.

Movements frantic now, she threw herself into the final tunnel. Something wrapped around her ankle and pulled her under with a jerk.

Tenah couldn't help but scream. Liquid flooded into her mouth. It filled her nostrils. Coated her eyes until she could no longer blink against the viscous fluid. She kicked her legs as hard as she could. Her hands slapped against narrow stone walls, her broken fingernails digging into them.

She had to keep going, despite the burn in her lungs. Despite the part of her mind telling her this was surely the end. Death was done playing games with her. The time had come for her to rest for good.

Let us in, little one. Let us in.

Tenah ignored Chaos's tempting call through her channels. Clawing and thrashing and cursing, she wriggled her way out the other side of the tunnel. Her boots struck the stone floor, and she burst from the surface, gasping at the air.

Through the blurry haze of her vision, a golden source of magic burned in the center of the small chamber, shrouded by swirling clouds of darkness. Faces of monsters reared at her from within. But she was not afraid of them. Not after having nearly drowned on some disgusting, unidentifiable substance.

Elementals be good to her, this had better be the gift she'd come to retrieve.

She crawled out of the liquid and reached for the mass of Chaos, eager to touch the foreign energy on the other side.

Something wet leashed around her wrist, ripping her away from the warmth of the magical source and hauling her back into the foul pool of liquid.

Chapter Thirty-Eight
RENTON

They had defiled the camp.

Corrupt and feingrot scurrying on too many or too few limbs. Soaring on membranous and black feathered wings. Ashens in black cloaks, drilling their magic into the weaker minded and turning them against their own. Even Adra's armies—Scourge—in their hellish armor, raising shields against a torrent of Ruzgorn arrows cascading from the sky.

Aeyis had been silent for what felt like eternity. Renton tried not to let that distract him from slashing through enemies. He had to believe that his brother was doing the same, wielding his unfathomable magic against their minds.

Still, he couldn't stop his eyes from drifting to the bell tower where Gireth had posted up with Tenah. Fresh panic coursed through him when he spotted the broken railing. The tower was empty.

Tearing his blade free from the gut of a Corrupt, he scanned the camp.

Aeyis. His brother should be able to pinpoint them. *Answer me, damn it!*

With a snarl, he ripped out his dagger and stabbed it into the skull of another Corrupt. How many had he already felled? How many more would pour out of the rift?

Unhinged, he let rage fuel him. He sailed through clashing armies, spinning and dodging and slicing implacably, poisonous clouds left in his wake. A giant, bulbous feingrot caught his attention, tossing aside Ruzgorn on a warpath for Hakkan. The warlord was already overburdened with enemies.

Renton exchanged his sword and dagger for his father's cumbersome blade and charged the beast. His muscles strained as he met it head-on, boots skidding back on the dry ground. The feingrot knocked the blade aside with a swipe of its great claws. Smaller Corrupt tumbled from its back. Renton carved through them, spitting brackish blood onto their desiccated bodies.

Stomping powerful feet, the feingrot slashed out in a frenzy. He dodged the strikes. The beast released an ear-shattering roar. Renton dove under its maw, hidden from its many eyes, and slashed his blade clean through its neck.

He scaled its corpse, eyes sweeping over the camp. His jaw tightened. There were still so many enemies to slay. The strain on Ruzgorn was evident. It didn't seem fair that they had to take the brunt of this attack when they'd done nothing to stir up trouble in the first place.

Fuck it. Renton would regret the depletion of his energy, but he needed to give the Ruzgorn a chance against the waves of enemies crashing against them and Tenah the opportunity to seal the rift.

Leaping onto the back of a feingrot darting by, he rode it into the Void, where he gathered up his magic and pushed it out to weave an illusion of the Boglands around all enemies in his radius.

A smaller radius than he expected. The strain had his channels contracting in warning of his approaching limit. The shard bit down with ferocity, needing to feed on something now that he'd deprived it of his magic.

But gods, it was a glorious sight. His enemies turned on each other, locked in the illusion that they were fighting Boglands monsters. He understood how this kind of power could be addicting.

A streak of white through the masses caught his eye. It was sprinting deeper into the Void, away from the armies. Horror throttled him. *It couldn't be.* Tenah was somewhere around the bell tower, not leashed to the back of a feingrot. Was his own magic playing tricks on him?

He kept his gaze locked on the feingrot. When it breached the edge of his magical area of effect and didn't waver, invisible hands gripped his insides and wrung them out.

Not an illusion then.

He recognized it for what it was. Bait to lure him out. He had an understanding with Cirel. Only one, and it involved her. The claiming way the king had looked at her, as if she was his property, had almost shredded every bit of his self-control in the temple.

Tenah was right. His weakness was his heart. She was in danger, and he would stop at nothing to get her back.

Renton jumped from the feingrot's back only to collapse onto the ground. With a growl, he slammed a fist against his heart, determined to rattle the shard's crushing hold on him. His illusion crumbled. With its absence, all Corrupt and feingrot heads jerked to him.

CHAPTER THIRTY-NINE

TENAH

Slimy vines tethered her firmly to the back of the feingrot as it streaked across the Void. It didn't slow until it broke through another rift, one that resurfaced in her fragmented memories.

Cirel, hovering over her. His brows vicious slashes over cruel eyes. His hand gripping her hair as he funneled thick, potent magic into her mouth and nose, spreading it inside of her like an infection.

She winced, recalling the tears streaming down her cheeks. The tightening of his hold, so full of betrayal.

You are mine to control. Mine.

Freed from the memory, horror settled into her bones. This rift was her work. The afternoon of confusion in the field outside Denoden's gates, she'd provided Cirel and his armies a bridge to her isle through the Void.

Elementals above, how would she ever make up for all the damage she'd caused?

Greenish, stormy skies rolled on for miles as the beast cut toward a city of glistening black quartz, tucked behind dead trees and a thick slab of seamless, dark rock. She fought against her restraints as the feingrot hauled her through the iron gates.

One glimpse of the snake-like hunks of metal zipping along tracks between sleek, dark buildings, and her heart plummeted. *Zafai.* Adra's most advanced city, founded by Xith. It was where Advanth had ruled and now where Cirel extended his lecherous power.

Lanterns of blue fire cast their eerie glow upon slick, black streets. The feingrot dodged hectic, fast-moving traffic—shadows, carriages, motorized carts, and creatures she didn't recognize from this world. She nearly choked on the clouds of sweet amber smoke, exhaust, and toxins.

How had they not all turned Corrupt? Some bore symptoms—physical mutations—but nothing beyond wings or horns or markings like her own. The rumors circulating Firesteep had depicted Adra as a writhing mass of demonic creatures in need of purging.

Her blood heated. She supposed those spun tales gave Sardoth and the High Court greater cause to condemn these beings to death.

The feingrot skidded to a halt before the arched doors of an impressive, black cathedral. Every facet was chiseled with meticulous hands. Golden light poured out from windows along its mammoth front, highlighting winged, stone creatures perched on its ledges like ancient sentinels.

Tenah gagged as her restraints slithered away from her limbs. She didn't hesitate, leaping from its back. Without so much as baring a fang, the feingrot sauntered off, leaving her alone in the night with only the far-off murmurs of street conversations, rumbling vehicles, and whooshing trains to accompany her.

What was the point in running? Cirel had proven his reach spanned all the way to Denoden. Even if she made it back to her isle, he would just ensnare her with his magic again.

But then why had he brought her all this way?

A giant mechanical clock built into the central tower of the castle chimed. The distinct clack of heels penetrated the night. Dressed in a flattering dark velvet and lace suit, a shadow woman appeared, her white locks twirled up into a smooth, tight bun.

Her words lacked emotion when she spoke. "You are at the mercy of Adra's king now."

Tenah scowled. "I don't recognize a king that spreads Corruption and manipulation."

In a flash, the woman's murky brown pupils narrowed to slits. Claws elongated from her fingertips. "You will address King Cirel with respect."

"I will address him however I please. I owe him no such honor."

A strong force collided with her shoulders. Tenah stumbled backward. Warm blood dribbled from where the woman's claws dug into her arms. Magnificent, feathered wings spread behind the woman's back, blotting out the view of the cathedral.

"You owe him your life, you wretched lich!" the woman hissed.

Tenah didn't recognize the word, but her temper bit back anyway. "Had I known who he was, I never would have agreed to a bargain. He misled me."

The woman brought her sharpened teeth closer, snapping them in warning. "You so much as utter one disgraceful word under your breath in his presence, and you will suffer."

Tenah went limp in the woman's clutches. "Whatever. Just take me to your king."

Vicious appearance gone once more, the woman flicked Tenah's blood from her nails and cut for the castle doors. She didn't wait to make sure she was being followed.

They navigated a maze of halls constructed from black stone and lit by ancient candelabras. When Tenah glimpsed the sprawling city through narrow, glass windows, her mouth parted in awe. It was no wonder the other kingdoms had sought to destroy Xith. Between his healers and his expansive kingdom, it was hard not to see him as a threat.

Fools for not seeking his alliance.

Tenah lost track of their route by the time they reached a windowless sitting room. The ceiling soared above—they had to be in one of the four sharp towers. A fire roared in a stone hearth. Other than two wingback chairs facing the gyrating flames, the room was oddly sparse.

"I gave no order for violence, Millicent." A low, melodic voice impacted the room like a detonation of magic. Millicent—the woman who'd dragged

Tenah here—backed away from the open door and dropped to her knees in supplication.

"Apologies, my king," she said, her tone edging on desperation. "She spoke ill—"

Invisible energy crushed down on the room, sending Tenah to her knees too. Her bones creaked from the pressure of Cirel's magic. She gritted her teeth, shame curling in her chest.

To say it was strange to gaze upon Cirel in this world, clad in his fine navy dress clothes, was an understatement. He'd existed solely in the Void all the years she'd known him. Nowhere else. As a child, she'd often wondered if she'd conjured him up, a figment of her wild imagination.

Cirel was very much real.

His mismatched eyes trailed the ribbons of blood down Tenah's arms now splattering on the floor. "That rug is over five hundred years old, Millicent. Clean up your mess."

The woman crawled out, unable to rise under the force of her king's unnatural magic.

Cirel lowered himself before Tenah. "Forgive her. I provide her with work to keep her out of the topaz dens, but she has a tendency to lash out, regardless."

"The girl, I can forgive," Tenah muttered, humiliated at her inability to move.

His lips parted briefly, and she caught sight of sharp, pearl white teeth. Her internal alarms fired. She needed distance from him.

"Just look at you, blighted by Chaos." He reached for her arm.

Tenah writhed against his invisible hold, but the king was fully in control. Light fingers traced the markings on the inside of her arm. Her eyelids fluttered at his electrifying touch. She couldn't hold back a shiver.

"If only you'd cooperated," he said at length.

"Cooperated?" Tenah snapped back. "How can I cooperate when you rob me of consciousness and bend me to your will?"

The king was unfazed by her insolence. This close, she glimpsed the tiny strands of Chaos sizzling in his orange eye. She inhaled the scent of brewing storms and a hint of something smoky.

Strange. He wore no crown in this world.

Cirel's fierce gaze held hers. She envisioned him younger, without the hard edge of his madness, his thin body free of Chaos's leash.

"Stop looking at me like that," he said, his tone severe.

Her chest heaved, seeking enough air to fill her lungs and keep her terror at bay. "Like what?"

He frowned. "Like there's hope. Like I'm fixable."

She bit down on the inside of her lip. She didn't miss the way Cirel's gaze dropped there for a moment, eyes gleaming as if he could smell the blood she drew.

Millicent burst back into the room. She carried a silver tray of medical supplies in one hand and a bucket and cloth in the other. She set both on the end table between the two chairs. When she moved toward Tenah, Cirel raised a hand.

"You will not touch her again unless you wish for death," he said. "Fetch us drinks and then leave us."

Millicent bent in half to show respect, then she was gone once more.

The pressure lifted, no longer grinding Tenah into the rug she'd bloodied. She drew in a full breath.

His voice softened as he examined her wounds. "My magic can be a bit overwhelming."

Then the King of Adra delicately cleaned and bound her wounds with surprising care.

"Why?" she whispered, throat swelling.

"You believe my intentions to be sinister," Cirel said, his thumb drifting along her arm. Softly, it traced her markings.

A weak laugh escaped her. "You made your intentions clear when you sent an army through that rift you forced me to open. You told me once how much you hated war. Yet, here you are, stirring up another one."

His devastating features remained unreadable. "I can explain why it's a necessary evil. Would you care to sit? You look unwell."

"I'm unwell because *you're* near."

Cirel wrapped a hand around her bound arm. Dragging her up his body until her nose was a hair away from his own, his mismatched eyes seared into her with murderous intent.

Venom filled her mouth. "Go ahead. Compel me."

His magic burrowed into her, constricting her throat and crushing her lungs. He held her life in his hands. Held her so tightly she wasn't sure if he would ever let her go.

"I could take whatever I want from you," he murmured, his lips brushing against her own.

Trickles of cold fear rushed through her veins, contradicting the heat spreading low in her gut.

"I've thought about it, you know. Ever since our bond brought you back to me in the Void. Breaking you. Fucking you. Killing you. Nothing seems strong enough to make up for what you did to me."

He tilted her head further, and she shivered as he ran his hot mouth up her neck. She hated the snapping of lightning through her body. Squeezing her eyes shut, she bit back a cry as his teeth pressed lightly into her flesh.

"Nothing except your soul in my hands. Forever mine to torture."

He stepped back, wearing a wicked grin. His magic drove her into one of the chairs. Only then did he release her from his hold. It was like being in a room with her father again. Fleeting glimpses of cherished normalcy, enough to trick her heart, right before a demonstration of shocking brutality.

Except her father had never laid hands on her.

It made her question how much of a splintered mind could be healed. Could Cirel be healed? Would she eventually turn into a monster capable of harming those she loved too?

She clutched the armrests, her chest aching. She'd hurt Renton without realizing.

Combined with her tiring efforts in the Ruzgorn camp, Cirel's magic took a toll on her. The heat from the fire might have lulled her to sleep, had she not been on edge, clinging to adrenaline.

Cirel sat in the opposite chair and crossed his legs. His face was pensive as he poured them both a glass of red wine.

"Drink," he ordered, handing her the glass.

She stared at it until he forced her hand to take it. His eyes watched her without blinking as he maneuvered the glass to her lips. She drained it.

"I had anticipated your father's appearance after you opened the rift in that barbarian camp. It was supposed to be a beacon announcing my return. One I believed he would not ignore."

Tenah's hands shook with the urge to punch the king in his striking face. "Is that what this all boils down to, a feud between you and my father?"

"Your father made it about him when he speared my mother on a crystal and gathered up the bloody slivers, absorbed in his hunger for power."

"A hunger that developed because you summoned war beasts," Tenah practically spat.

"No." Cirel's orange eye seared into her. "*You* summoned them."

Tenah shoved up from her chair and encroached into his space, Chaotic flames snapping from her fingers. "Don't try to lay this at my feet when you have twisted me, manipulated me. You are flawed, so *very* flawed in your reasoning."

Her attempt at intimidation failed miserably as his homicidal expression melted. His eyes swept over her face with the comfort of someone that had known her far too long. He gave a solemn smile.

"What are you scheming?" she demanded, edging backward.

Cirel's tone was smooth, almost decadent. "Your father will have the decency to give back what he stole from me, or I will destroy him. Isn't that what you wanted when you made a bargain with me? Why are you fighting this now?"

She swallowed and pushed off his chair.

Entranced by his thumb sweeping over his full mouth, he smirked. "Were our times together so bad?"

"Our…friendship was never healthy."

"No?" His head tilted to the side. "Wanting to rebuild this world into something better isn't healthy?"

"Not when you trick me into methods I wouldn't normally agree with."

"And yet you sought me out when you were defeated by your father,"

Cirel said, his liquid silver eye shimmering with loathing. "Why do you think you ended up in that Void temple—*our* meeting place? It wasn't a coincidence. It wasn't *my* doing. It was because you wanted my help. It was because you *needed* me. That has always been the case."

Her magic exploded, the detonation shattering a vase on the mantel of the fireplace. Ceramic pieces rained down on the stone floor. "I am tired of your blatant lies!"

Cirel rose in a too-quick movement. "As to be expected from a Vozarian. You are quick to discard truths. What's next, Tenah? You going to murder my followers too? Join in with your mad father and slaughter innocents?"

Her clenched knuckles turned bone white as her entire body quaked with hatred.

The door to the sitting room burst open. A Scourge warrior clad in heavy, black armor entered. "My king. The rift is waning. It won't hold for our armies much longer."

Cirel kept his eyes on her. He spun his winged ring around his index finger. "It will be dealt with. Won't it, Tenah?"

CHAPTER FORTY
TENAH

Tenah walked the barren halls in union with the King of Adra.

When they reached a set of black doors from which she could hear strange music and a murmur of indecipherable voices, Cirel spun around to face her, invading her space. Momentarily shocked by his intensity, she licked her lips. Her eyes flitted around the hall for an escape. A window. Something she could use as a weapon. *Anything.*

Cirel had always been captivating in a way that wasn't normal. He didn't just draw attention—he enslaved it. Even now, she wrestled to avoid the magnetism of his beauty and dull the terror his haunting eyes summoned within her.

She had been caught up in him years ago, that much she could admit. But she no longer wanted to play these warped games with him.

His hand touched her jaw softly, guiding her back to meet his gaze. "We dreamed of a kingdom reborn from ashes. Does that really mean nothing to you?"

His mood swings were giving her whiplash. An effect of his toxins? Or had he always been difficult to predict?

"They were dreams of troubled children. Nothing more," Tenah whispered, sadness welling in her hollowed chest.

Ire flashed over his face. Cirel righted this with a tight smile and drew back. "Dreams. Of course."

He pushed open a door, waving her into a grand, windowless room wallpapered in dark blue with silver whorls like a frothing ocean. Hundreds of shadows and humanoids unfamiliar to her bowed when she entered.

It was unsettling to say the least.

From one kingdom where her reputation was tarnished to another, where they seemed to worship her as if she belonged here. In *their* rebellion. With her marked hands and wild appearance, she did fit in.

She looked back at Cirel. "What have you told them?"

He smiled, dipping his head to a ring of shadows with twisted branches for limbs. "That you are the bringer of a new world order. A goddess."

Tenah bit down on her tongue, eager for the pain to distract her from the desire to lash out at him in public.

Years ago, this might have been her path. Before fear had consumed her. It wasn't so farfetched to imagine she would have sided with her only friend.

But Chaos had driven Cirel too far off the edge of reason. And now, witnessing the reverence in the gazes of the beings surrounding them, winged and horned and taloned alike, she knew there was no killing him. For if he died, his kingdom would avenge him, just as they sought to avenge his perished mother.

Tenah stalked him through the crowds. "You wage wars and host parties simultaneously?"

Cirel ignored the scathing look she bored into him. He was too busy drinking in the respect his subjects offered him. Only when he ushered her through another door into a cramped stairwell did he shed his kingly duties.

She followed him up and up the spiral stairs, high enough that the wind howled like an eidolon through the gaps in the stones. They reached a landing where a giant hole had been punched out, revealing the churning, endless storm that blanketed Adra. A wave of coppery toxins struck her, and Tenah scrunched her nose.

"How do you live among it?" she asked.

Cirel's gaze was measuring, as if the answer should have been obvious. "Where else can we go? The isles labeled us a threat. Aranma cast us out centuries ago. Our only answer was and still is war to carve a place for ourselves in this world."

A giant lump shifted under mounds of hay, sending her lurching back. The winged beast that shook free was terrifyingly beautiful. All sleek angles and smooth, ebony scales. Its red eyes gleamed with understanding, no trace of sinister magic clouding its bright mind.

The welkin tucked its wings in close as Cirel swiftly climbed onto its back. "Are you coming?"

Swallowing, she shook her head. "I don't fare well with flying."

He held out his hand, his expression dark. "You've never flown with me."

Knowing he would force her onto the welkin's back, Tenah took his hand and tucked her body against him, arms locking around his waist. While he wasn't muscled like Renton, his lean torso was still hard like stone. With her cheek pressed against his shoulder, she could smell hints of sandalwood and smoke beneath his constant, invisible swarm of magic.

The welkin shot out of the tower, and a screech ripped from Tenah's throat as they dropped hundreds of feet before leveling out above the city.

Lightning had nothing on the welkin's speed. As branches of it discharged from murky, greenish clouds, the welkin banked with efficient shifts of its wings. Its shriek, like metal shredding, rivaled the tireless thunder.

Tenah buried her face into Cirel's back. She hated the way flying throttled her stomach. There was nothing more she wanted right now than to retreat into the crisp sheets of Renton's bed again, embraced in his safe arms.

Renton. Was he alive? And poor Gireth…

"Open your eyes. Witness what has been done to my kingdom," Cirel demanded.

A river of bones and ruins flowed beneath them. It ran on for endless miles, cutting through the land like a scar, halting only for the mountainous heaps of toppled buildings.

Tenah's breath grew heavy in her lungs. "What is this place?"

"Roan's Wake. My kingdom's grave."

Bile rose up in her throat as she struggled to make sense of the carnage. Any time her father had talked about the war, reenacted it on his tables with wooden pawns, she'd visualized bloodshed. But not on a scale like this. This had been an annihilation. This was what her father had been trying to avoid.

"Hathrowyn struck first," Cirel said. "Did you know that? The peacekeepers of the isles. Vozar followed suit shortly after, wanting to claim victory against my supposedly Corrupt mother first. Like it was some sort of race to bet on."

Tenah rested her head against him once more, unable to hold it up anymore. She was so tired of death.

Her hands pressed tight against his stomach as the welkin flipped almost vertical, banking down to land gracefully on a shadow-made mountain. She was careful not to step on the skulls when she dismounted.

Two giant, arched stone pillars stood proud in the valley between bones. One of the ancient gates she'd traced with curious fingers in her books, built centuries ago by the Greater Elementals to house a portal. They hadn't hummed with magic since the elders had shut them down. Those severed ties had kept Cirel temporarily isolated.

"I won't help you," Tenah said firmly. No way would her name be written in history as the shadow that roused them from deep slumber.

Cirel didn't move a muscle. He could be so still at times that Tenah wasn't sure if he was even breathing. Her mind longed to uncover what she'd once known about him. Her father had claimed he wasn't fully shadow, but she'd never asked and he'd never shared much of himself beyond their secret adventures exploring the Void.

"Your father's right hand did such abhorrent work on your mind," Cirel said. "You didn't recognize me that day in the temple. You honestly believed I was some ethereal being come to save you."

"You did nothing to make me believe otherwise," Tenah accused, rubbing at her arms, chilled by a cold front rolling in with the promise of acidic rain.

Cirel's eyes flashed darker. His head lifted to the sky, his shoulders rising and falling with a long, somber breath.

Tenah's brows furrowed. He was so perplexing—wicked and wrathful and then he had these brief moments of such profound sadness.

"I don't understand you," she whispered.

Cirel turned to face the scarred lands as a crack of lightning split the sky. "I thought if anyone could understand me, it would be you. We swore to change this world for the better. That was before you demonstrated your treachery."

Tenah's nails cut into the soft flesh of her palms.

The king whirled around, his silver eye glinting with smothered emotion. "It's time we end this suffering, starting with the fall of your wretched father. Help me awaken the portals. Let us reconnect our kingdoms. Our goals coincide, Tenah."

Weeks ago, she might have done so willingly in exchange for Cirel's aid in defeating her father. But nothing could make this right. Nothing could make amends for this sea of death. Nor those burned up in her home during the gathering.

Revenge was a hollow ending she no longer had the desire to pursue. She couldn't allow Cirel's plan to succeed. While her kingdom might have fallen, Denoden still remained intact, teeming with lively shadows.

The first splashes of cold, metallic rain struck her forehead and cheekbones.

"The answer is no," she said.

Cirel merely blinked back at her. Rain plastered his dark red hair to his sharp features like dried blood. If he was disappointed, he didn't show it. "I understand."

Air slipped from her lips in a sigh of relief. Her attention was snagged by the crunching of bones under hundreds—no, thousands—of Scourge funneling over the crest of the ruins. They carried black flags, the red outline of a winged beast stitched into the fabric.

Her heart stopped. Cirel had spent a long, long time assembling his masses. She should know—she'd helped him gather them. Horned welkins descended from the storm clouds. Creatures that had to be older than the isles. Their wingspans stretched the length of forty Scourge. Chains dangled from their necks and front legs as if they'd just broken free of eternal imprisonment.

"I understand," Cirel repeated, stepping on the skull of what looked like a child, pulverizing it under his boot. "However, I'm not accepting no for an answer."

Chapter Forty-One

TENAH

Chaos lurched Tenah down the rattling bone mountains against her will.

Acidic rain soaking into her clothes as robed casters peeled from the front lines of Cirel's armies, their faces obscured by hoods but exposed hands stained with markings progressed far beyond hers. Lightning flashed as Tenah was forced to line up beside them at the gate arms, ready to perform a miracle for their king.

How did Cirel control all of them? Sure, some of them had probably pledged loyalty in hopes of a better future. But to sacrifice their bodies like this? *Insanity.*

She clenched her jaw as Cirel mounted his welkin and took off into the soupy, low-hanging clouds. The drumming of water on bones was the only sound that filled the valley. Her eyes raked over the silent armies, picking out the glint of Ashen dust among their ranks.

Damn it. She'd never trained in the art of Ashen blocking. Would the damaged pockets in her Chaos-riddled mind be enough to hide the makings of a plan?

If she could spread the darkness…

Tenah invited Chaos into her channels. Blood pumped hot and thick through her veins, enticed by the sheer volume of dark magic streaming into her. It was enough to fry the nerves in her hands. At least at this rate she wouldn't be able to feel the cold soon.

She slowed her heart with focused breaths. And when the casters unleashed their dark magic upon the gate arms, illuminating runes and slivers of crystals embedded in the ancient stones, Tenah followed suit.

If Cirel wanted a fucking doorway, she would give him one.

Boots splashing through murky water collecting on the stone platform, Tenah marched to the base of the gate and smacked a hand onto its smooth, wet surface. She sucked in a breath as her vision dissolved into blue—her astral body instantly drawn into the Void.

If she'd ever explored this particular space before, it was lost to her. A dozen sets of stone arms surrounded her in a wide ring, all different shapes and heights, some spread so far apart they were but a distant mirage in her bad eye.

There were elegant, detailed gates and crude, black gates woven from dead trees. Tenah recognized the fluttering of blue lights surrounding one wrapped in vibrant moss. *Tree lights.* It was the gate to Hathrowyn.

What foolish entity would grant her this power?

Her mouth parted in awe as she spun around and identified the gate for Firesteep etched with flames and Denoden adorned with rays from a central sun at the peaked top. There was a gate with twisted vines and carved eyes for the Boglands. Spikes like a bear trap for Duskhallow—Ames would *not* have appreciated that nightmarish artwork. Wings joined at a point for the Jagged Rocks, home to the welkins.

And solid black marble for Adra.

The other gates she could not place on the isles. She chose to focus on these, beelining for the farthest one that thrummed with a current of energy she'd never experienced before.

She might not have the means to defeat Cirel, but she did have the ability to remove him from the game temporarily. Concentrating all the dark magic in her channels, she imbued it with her will and siphoned power from the other casters. Then she touched a charged hand to the mysterious portal in the Void.

The tether forming between the two gates might as well have sucked the marrow from her bones. Too much Chaos was blazing its way out of her body. The power coursing through her very molecules arched her backward.

Tenah lurched back into her physical body and watched as black lightning snapped from her hands, zigzagging up the stone arms. Her magic branched out to fill the opening between the pillars. The energy churning there expanded like a living, breathing thing.

Heart racing, she let her gaze drop to her ruined hands. Layers of skin peeled away from her fingers all the way up to her elbows. Scales began forming over her raw flesh, accompanied by tiny, curved spikes that protruded along the backs of her forearms.

Great. Her Corrupt form looked a hell of a lot like a welkin.

She wanted to cry out, but all she could do was allow the gate to absorb what it needed from her to awaken. If it took too much and killed her, that was on Cirel's conscience. Not that he would really care. Her rapidly decaying body sagged. Her breaths escaped in raspy pants. Something slithered under her skin along her shoulder blades, but she didn't have the nerve to reach a hand back and examine what it was.

All she could think about was Gireth lying in the desert, his body shattered. Renton and Hakkan, swallowed up by enemies. Vesara and Aeyis, suffocating in a mound of writhing Corrupt bodies.

This sacrifice was worth it. She knew that. But it wouldn't have been so damn difficult if Renton hadn't shown her another path. A future she now wanted more than anything else. One she could never have.

Her Corruption was worth it.

Tenah dug her split fingernails into the grooves of the stone arm, wincing at the inky blood welling from her extending claws. The gate arms were almost entirely illuminated with dark energy, a heaving mass of black magic swirling between them.

The rain picked up, slamming into her with ancient fury, matting her hair to her head, ears, and neck. She could hardly see when the portal had been opened, only sensed that her job was complete when the surge of magic through her channels came to an abrupt halt.

Her arms dangled at her sides.

She stifled a maniacal laugh, the march of Cirel's armies through the portal a harmonious song to her ears, knowing they wouldn't resurface in Firesteep.

Rain slithered down her face. She tasted briny blood on her lips, but from where? She honestly didn't care to know.

When enough of Cirel's armies had vanished through the portal, she drew in a heavy breath and severed the link between the gates, effectively trapping them inside the Void.

"Fuck all of you," she muttered, dropping to her knees.

It was a small act of redemption in a large scale of damage she'd caused in her lifetime. She just hoped the Ruzgorn could handle the last of the armies that had managed to spill through the desert rift. Hopefully, it would seal itself soon enough.

A fist collided with her jaw, sending her tumbling down into the graveyard of skeletons. Vision swimming, she rolled onto her hands and knees, struggling to crawl away from whatever had struck her.

Icicle hands gathered her up. She stared back into the white eyes of an Ashen with curved horns. Chaos markings covered his face like war paint.

What did you do? he demanded.

Tenah offered him no response. Her head was pulsing in time with her heart.

The Ashen shook her, nearly spitting with anger. She couldn't hold back a scream at the brutal crunch of his magic on her mind. *You might as well admit you tampered with it,* he said. *I've already sent word to Cirel.*

Tenah braced for another violent attack, tears leaking from her blurry eyes. The Ashen dropped her suddenly, his body jerking upright. Crumpled on the ground, she watched as black dust funneled into his ears.

You need to get out of here, Tenah, Aeyis said.

Her entire body went rigid.

No. She scanned the remaining armies in the bone valley. *Where are you?*

Why are you here?

Frigid magic drew her up on unstable legs and propelled her away from the gate. Her fingers rose against her will, tearing a small rift. More skin dissolved from her arms, and she could feel her bones aching to crack.

Aeyis, she cried out. *If you're here in Adra, you are coming with me.*

Your sacrifice won't be for nothing. It's okay. Go. I've survived this long on my own. I can hang on a while longer and buy you time to reach the temple.

Her gaze locked on a hooded figure, white locks curling out from beneath it. When his head lifted to hers, Tenah's body slumped in horror. Aeyis's eyes were stained black as a starless night.

Go! he urged.

Heart sinking, she had no power to deny him and no time to waste as Cirel descended like a furious god from the clouds on his winged mount. Stumbling into the Void, thick, hot tears rolled freely down her cheeks.

I'll come back with help, she said. *I promise you. I won't leave you behind.*

The world would not be robbed of another kind, generous Ashen like him. Shadows might see him as nothing more than a threat—an entire war had been fought because of that misjudgment—but Aeyis deserved his life.

Why did she get to have two?

Chapter Forty-Two
RENTON

Surrounded by enemies, where Renton cut down two, three more appeared, their swords gleaming as they raised them for a killing strike. He pushed out the last scrap of his illusion magic. Pain fired through his body as he had to wriggle his way out of the death march like an insect, hidden by the fabric of his weak magic.

A Scourge warrior trailed him. Renton's adrenaline kicked up another notch. The warrior's face was obscured by the skull helmet of a beast—a trophy from his kill. His black-and-gold armor was streaked through with red war paint. His beady eyes swept around, his gauntlet reaching out as if he could pluck Renton's magic out of the air.

Behind the Scourge, the rift was shrinking.

Thank the gods, Renton thought. Was that Tenah's doing? Was she free from her restraints?

No longer able to heave his weight across the ground, Renton rolled onto his back. If he had to die, he was going to do it glaring up into the face of his killer.

Fuck.

How did it come to this? Why had the High Court allowed Cirel to amass such forces? Why hadn't anyone stepped in to stop him? All of their centuries of accessible knowledge buried in the roots of their trees, and still Cirel would win this war.

"I smell your fear, hunter." The Scourge's boots thunked closer.

Renton could see his cruel smile in anticipation of a fresh gutting. Had the shard not rendered him immobile, Renton would have taken his time destroying this one.

The Scourge grinned down at him and hefted his battle axe. Renton drew in his last breath and waited.

A choking sound bubbled out of the Scourge as the end of a dagger jutted from his neck. The Scourge dropped to his knees, eyes wide. His skull helmet hit the ground hard as he toppled over.

Kherathi planted a boot on the Scourge's back as he walked over him to get to Renton, sheathing his bloody dagger.

"Come to finish the job yourself?" Renton bit out.

"I'm here to keep you from making another mistake. You chase after my daughter, and you hand Cirel a piece of his war beast. I thought I'd made that clear."

"Currently, I'm not chasing after anyone," Renton said, frowning as his dignity slipped away like sand in an hourglass. "Why aren't you saving her?"

Kherathi crouched beside him and scratched his jaw. "No point. She'll be home soon enough."

"Do you know this for a fact?" Renton's words were near a snarl as he examined the Chaos lord's frustratingly calm expression. He still hadn't puzzled out just how mad Kherathi was. Just how ruined his mind had become.

Kherathi didn't respond, his gaze drifting out into the Void.

"Look, the shard is yours," Renton said, a note of anxiety in his tone. "Just let me retrieve her first since you refuse to do the job."

"What's holding you back?"

Laid out on his back, Renton bared his teeth. "Rip it out of me then if that's the only reason you came here!"

"I assure you I will do just that. But unlike Cirel's plans for you, I intend for you to live."

Renton fell silent as Kherathi hefted him up onto the back of a feingrot drenched in his Chaos magic.

"Is that how he controls her? Pumps her full of Chaos?"

Kherathi paused for a moment. "If their bond was as simple as that, I wouldn't feel so inclined to tear Cirel apart. Chaos does allow for manipulation, if you are strong enough. Unfortunately, their connection is not of this world. Chaos knew exactly what it was doing when it forced me to kill her that night. Until I learn how to break that foul magic and free her soul, she will remain at the mercy of Adra's king."

Chapter Forty-Three
TENAH

Stumbling across the Void, Tenah craved the torture the ravenous parasite in her mind would bring, gutted by the fact that not a single flicker of her stupid magic obeyed her command to retrieve Aeyis.

Finish the Corruption, she said. *I'm done fighting you.*

Chaos speared into her, instantly transforming her surroundings into another memory.

She was ten years old, seeking her only friend within the Void, her stomach in knots over the state she would find him in.

Black feathers tumbled from the sky. A gust of wind snagged them, weaving them together to form an endless narrow, dark tunnel around her. Though the feathers held their collective shape, they hadn't stopped their circular motion, as if they were conducting some sort of hypnotic dance meant to confuse her.

The feathers constricted tighter, jabbing into her side. Panic coiled in her chest. She was about to scream out when blue orb light burst to life at the end of the tunnel. Blinking back tears, she made out a tall, lean figure, his wild auburn curls crowned with thin tendrils of black lightning.

Cirel.

He wore the same white dress shirt and black pants as the night Chaos had infected him. The hot tears she'd been fighting to restrain tumbled down her cheeks at the recollection of how she'd abandoned him.

But he was alive. Alive and somehow unmarked by dark magic.

That weak reassurance vanished as a haze of black smoke materialized around his form. When his eyes darted to her, one iris burned a monstrous orange.

Cirel had always held an air of sophistication. Now his movements were too quick. Too sharp, like a predatory animal.

A pulse of invisible magic rolled out from his body and crushed her to her knees.

Bow. His voice was so quiet, yet it rang loud in her ears. Never had he asked her to do such a thing. They'd always been equals in the Void.

Cirel, she cried out.

His eyes narrowed. His magic clamped down, grinding her into the ground. Her bones groaned under the pressure. Fear licked up her spine.

He was going to kill her.

This was not her friend. She needed to get away.

Shooting out a sphere of protective energy to momentarily break his hold, Tenah scrambled over to the feathered barrier. She clawed at the feathers, but there was no give beneath their velvety softness. It was as if the tunnel was made from solid bone.

Cirel's posture righted. He blinked a few times. *Tenah?*

The intense pressure vibrating her protective shield dissipated. She scuttled back against the wall as he rushed toward her.

Cirel flattened his palms against her shield and hissed as it burned him. He examined his wounds in disbelief before his features transformed with anger. The silver eye glinted with a confusing mixture of emotion while the orange glowed brighter. *Why are you acting so frightened? You did this to me. You brought me into the Void. Why continue pretending you care about me?*

Her heart plummeted into her stomach. She withdrew her shield, leaving a ghostly silhouette of smoke behind in the air.

Cirel grinned, so vicious she had the urge to bathe the entire tunnel in flames to escape him. Creatures in her nightmares curdled her blood less than this boy.

You don't look… She trailed off, swallowing her words.

I'm here. I'm alive and stronger than ever. You know me.

Tenah squeezed her eyes shut. She wished she could stop replaying his Corruption behind closed eyes. She wished things could return to how they were before.

A hand touched her chin softly. When she opened her eyes, Cirel crouched before her. *I would never hurt you. I hold you too close to my heart.*

He rested a hand over his chest, and the blue gem in his winged ring flashed. A family heirloom, he'd told her. Not from Advanth though. From his father, who did not rule in this world.

She couldn't help the sigh of relief. He was truly alive. He was here with her. Everything would be the same.

Reaching out, Tenah cuffed his wrists and turned his hands so she could examine the damage she'd done. Droplets of golden healing magic bubbled on her fingertips.

Cirel ripped his hands free as if he'd been bitten by a snake. *Stop that. Don't ever touch me with that horrible magic. Do you understand? It would ruin me.*

She failed to mask the horror on her face, even as his fury waned.

The Void takes care of me now. It listens. It grants me what I need. He brushed a lock of hair from his eyes.

Her brows furrowed. Did the Void listen to her too? There must be some truth to his words, for it had led her to him.

I'm sorry, she whispered pathetically.

He leaned his head closer. *I'm alive because of you. Had you not brought me into the Void, our enemies would have slain me too that night my mother was butchered.*

Cirel interlocked his fingers with hers, and the wave of calm that washed over her was impossible to ignore. It was the same flutter of excitement she felt when soaking in the histories of the world or tracing over ink maps in the library.

There is something you can do to help me, he said.

She nodded eagerly. *What is it?*

You can share in this power. The two of us will be stronger together. We can shift power back and forth when the other is in trouble.

Tenah pressed farther into the wall. The magic that had suffocated him oozed out into the air behind him, coiling up above their heads. Guttural voices sounded from somewhere in the tunnel. Or were they in her head?

You left me, remember? His orange eye shimmered. *You owe me this much.*

Tenah shook her head, her breaths shortening into panicked little gusts. *I'm so sorry.*

It won't hurt.

She knew it was a lie. She'd heard his screams. Had seen the terror in his eyes when he'd been consumed.

Cirel lifted his hand, and Tenah watched in horror as black smoke bled from his wounded palm. It tumbled into the space between them, looming over her as it took the shape of a giant wolf. Smoke billowed from the hollows where its eyes should have been.

You can try to avoid it, he said. *Your family can try to keep you from it. But this is your fate.*

The smoky wolf opened its maw, and she screamed. Agonizing pain ripped down her throat and into her lungs. Filled up her ears and blinded her eyes.

So much darkness. It had no end. Thankfully the pain did. Soon, she found her entire body numb. Numb but slick as she reached out to touch solid, wet ground.

Her eyes adjusted to the forest outside the manor, cloaked in night. Leaves crinkled under her weight as struggled to push her body up. Voices called for her, desperation thick in their tones. Had she been missing? Why did her body thrum as if she'd touched a live wire?

Hands gripped her arms and hauled her out of the leaves. Disoriented, she looked up into the distressed, wide eyes of her father. Ames stood behind him, panting.

It was her father's shaky embrace that shattered her. Why were they looking at her like that?

When she spotted the black stains her tears left on her father's shirt, she knew. A wail tore from her throat. The Void. Cirel. They hadn't been another nightmare then. They were *real*. Cirel had let that bad magic hurt her.

Her body felt wrong, her skin too tight and itchy as if sunburnt.

Make it go away, she begged. *Make me forget him.*

Ames winced and shared a glance with her father.

"Do it. Now," Kherathi ordered.

Ashen magic blasted into her mind. Memories snapped and frayed and twined together in new patterns. And then Chaos poured out of her, streaming into her father's chest.

Completing the transfer of Corruption.

There was no more pretending. Despite Chaos's best efforts to pump her full of self-hatred, Tenah's mind felt lighter than it had in years. Now she knew the truth, and she could finally, finally…

Breathe.

Those little prickles of healing magic she'd once held in her hands gave her the strength needed to push up on her feet. There was no hesitation as she entered the temple. Shadows had bared their hearts to her. Had protected her. Shown her love and compassion and hope.

Forging through the bottomless, pitch-black depths of the temple, black clouds of smoke coalesced around her. The tang of copper filled her nose and mouth. The air thickened as if she was trudging through Bogland swamps. Curls of magic snagged around her wrists and ankles.

Futile efforts to hold her back.

But it was easy to see how shadows became lost in this. How they could give up on ever glimpsing the sunlight again. Give in to the ravings of a thousand maddening voices determined to cut them down and weaponize them.

Chaos plucked at that taut thread of fear.

She forged on, knowing she had to keep moving. *It was me all along. You wanted me from the start, and everyone else has been sucked in because of my fear.*

Radiant, golden light sliced through the darkness. She cringed away from the purity of it until her eyes adjusted. Then she drank in the beautiful sight of Rama within her reach.

She dipped a hand into the slash of raw energy. A blissful warmth greeted her, the texture almost fluid as it ebbed and flowed over her skin. Laughter bubbled up in her throat, but it felt like a dishonor to unleash it. A slap in the face to everyone that had pushed her toward this. It had been so *easy* all along.

Rama coiled up her arm, and she permitted a sad smile.

Yes, you belong to me, she said. *I'm sorry I lost you.*

The spikes and scales along her arms vanished, revealing smooth, glowing skin. Vision returned with sharp clarity in her damaged eye. Warmth kissed her mind, and she was blessed with the loveliest memories. Ames chasing her around the courtyard gardens on summer days, the light scent of flowers and fruit in the air. His awkward grins as if he'd never known happiness before and wasn't worthy of it. How he'd looked at her mother with unwavering love.

Her father before Corruption. How she'd loved napping in his office chairs as he worked on correspondences for the king. How passionate he'd been about life. How he'd told her she was brilliant every day, even when she'd thought her casting lackluster. How he'd made her feel important and loved. How she was his whole world and he would do anything to protect her.

Golden tendrils of magic burst from Tenah's hands, whipping out to eat away at the temple's dark magic. When the stone chamber was purified, the strands settled overhead like a glittering spiderweb holding up hundreds of tiny little dew drops.

Tenah didn't fight her curiosity to touch one. It drew her into a vision of a child—a boy with fiery red hair and tattered clothes—writhing in a cloud of dark magic.

Realization dawned on her. She knew what they were. Rama was showing her troubled souls in need of purification.

And in the center of the spiderweb, there were two large concentrations of pulsing, gold light. She touched the smaller of the two and glimpsed her father. He had worked so hard to keep all of this Corruption to himself after he'd absorbed it from her.

Her smile dropped as another shadow came into view, chained and smeared with blood.

From the crown of her head to her toes curled in her boots, horror trickled through her veins.

Renton.

ACT III

THE GIFT OF FORGIVENESS

Chapter Forty-Four

TENAH

Blistered skin pulled and split as Tenah jerked awake under a Ruzgorn tent. Curses tumbled from her cracked, bloody lips. She lurched upright. Small hands caught her shoulders and steadied her. The nails were painted in what looked like the essence of the galaxy—black with flecks of gold and silver and white.

"Renix above, you're alive," Vesara said. "And don't you look like hell."

"How did I get here?" she demanded. The last thing she recalled was tearing a hole in the Void and racing across scorching desert.

Reaching out to push Vesara away, Tenah's gaze skimmed over the camp in search of Renton. The scenery curdled her blood. Curls of dark smoke climbed the silky, blue sky. Empty tents dotted the thirsty ground. Tattered flags billowed in the dusty wind. What was left of her cousin's armies had moved into the inner ring of tents surrounding the air where Tenah's rift had finally shut.

She couldn't find relief though. Not after glimpsing the pile of burning bodies, both Corrupt and enemy alike, far out from camp, warbled by the heat.

"Cousin." Hakkan knelt in front of her view of the flames. "We found you unconscious and badly burned about a half mile outside of camp."

But she didn't want Hakkan's attention either. She peeled off the bed, wincing as she rose, and shuffled toward Gireth's form on a makeshift bed of sticks and hide. Vesara and Hakkan looped her arms over their shoulders to escort her.

"He's alive. Just heavily medicated," Hakkan clarified. "Passed out the second his head hit something soft."

Tenah took Gireth's rough, bronze hand in her own, willing life into him. "His back…"

"Fractured," Hakkan said, eyes flashing with remorse.

She clenched her jaw until her teeth hurt. She could wallow in all the ways this was her fault. Cirel. The armies she'd helped him acquire. The massacre at the gathering. Gireth's broken body. Aeyis's Corruption. Ames's death.

But that would only allow Chaos to fester. She had to build upon those horrible mistakes instead.

Focusing her mind, she invited Rama into her channels. Strands of holy, comforting magic flowed from her fingers into Gireth. She wasn't certain this would work. Rama had healed wounds inflicted by Chaos, but could it heal natural wounds too? She debated how much magic to give him in one session, knowing she needed to keep some for her father. Gireth hadn't so much as twitched, his breaths heavy with a drugged sleep.

Holding her fear in check, Tenah dared ask, "Renton?"

Vesara and Hakkan exchanged confused looks.

"He wasn't with you in the Void?" Vesara asked.

The vision Rama had shared in the temple was real then. "Fuck!" Tenah said. "Stupid Murfell brothers!"

Vesara stiffened at her side. "What's going on?"

"Aeyis is a self-sacrificing bastard who is trapped in Adra, and my father has Renton—whether that's against his will or not is yet to be uncovered."

Vesara clicked her tongue. "Idiots. The both of them."

A hoarse voice interrupted. "If this is another mirage, I give up. Tell the gods to smite me."

Tenah's head whipped around to Gireth. He had a fist raised in the air, shaking slightly in feigned anger. Her heart swelled as he rolled up and swung his legs around to stand.

"Gireth!" she cried out, throwing her arms around him, ignoring the sharp lance of pain everywhere the sun had burned her. She'd not allowed Rama to touch her blisters. Not when she needed every drop to heal others.

His hands gripped her hips, pulling her flush against him.

"Is this real life?" he murmured against her neck.

"Real life," she replied.

"You did it, Tenah. We all knew you could."

A feminine snarl broke them apart. They turned to Vesara stomping over to a dark brown horse. She mounted it.

"Hey!" Hakkan shouted, lurching toward her. "What do you think you're doing with my horse?"

"Something I should have done ages ago," Vesara said.

"What, steal it?" Hakkan's brows furrowed.

Vesara peeled away from camp, her residual anger enough to warn that, whatever her task was, it wouldn't be pleasant. In a spray of dust, the assassin became a speck on the heat-warbled horizon.

"Yeah, all right. Sure, you can borrow her," Hakkan grumbled, shoulders dropping in defeat as he stalked off. "You wouldn't think I commanded a band of ferocious warriors."

The ride south to Firesteep eroded Tenah's sanity.

Would Aeyis be able to hold on while she saved Renton and healed her father? Was she sacrificing one life for another?

Up ahead, Gireth spread his arms out wide atop his horse. He tipped his head back in the desert breeze, filled with new appreciation for life.

Hakkan rode at her side, clinging to his foul mood since he'd had to borrow a "lesser" steed from his second-in-command. She'd healed his cut too, ignoring his protests about how it enhanced his intimidating appearance. In all honesty, there was little intimidating about her moody cousin. She was proud to claim him. Hakkan was a protector like her. More than that, he was a dreamer, set on creating a better life for those under his wing.

What remained of the Ruzgorn rode at their backs, forming a protective half circle that kicked up a wall of dirt like a tornado behind them. Hakkan had ordered three dozen of his warriors to remain at camp in case the rift split open again.

Their procession slowed at the dominating white stone gates of Firesteep. All was quiet beyond. Merchant stalls abandoned. Store fronts dim and purged of the usual bustle. The silence unsettled Tenah, twisting her stomach into tighter knots.

What had happened here when her father attacked? Without a king and a portion of their elite soldiers, had Firesteep fallen quickly?

She closed her eyes, trying to shut down images of Vozarians screaming, rushing for the gates.

"The capital looks…evacuated," Gireth said with a confused frown.

"Senses sharp," Hakkan reminded his warriors. He took initiative and led the way through the gates.

Tenah's palms slicked over as Chaos called to her from within the city. A heartbeat of darkness, festering inside of her father. The lump forming in her throat felt like a boulder crushing down on her windpipe.

Feingrot slunk from alleys and rooftops. Her father's personal guard, forged from teeth and claws and unfettered hatred. Ruzgorn didn't hesitate. Blades and axes sang through the air. Brackish blood spattered the sandstone buildings and streets. Flames ignited from Tenah's fingers.

"No," Hakkan yelled, embedding his curved sword into the skull of a beast. He pointed a finger down the street. "Your father is your target today."

She nodded, shaking out her magic. Hakkan was right. Her goal was to soothe the afflicted soul pulling the strings here.

Gireth followed her up the winding streets. Two massive feingrot paced at the entrance to the stone temple of the city catacombs.

"Fun time!" Gireth whooped in excitement, dropping from his horse and spinning his glaive with deft hands. Watching him with his weapon was like witnessing living art—powerful yet elegant.

Tenah froze in her saddle under the piercing stare of the closest feingrot.

Maltar. It was the only beast she'd named as a child, one that had often roamed the manor halls when her father and Ames were absent. The first beast she'd set loose upon their world. Maltar had preyed on her for years, taking pleasure in drawing out its hunt as her fear magnified.

Her heart skipped a beat. Had her father kept the beast as a trophy?

Are you ready to accept that you belong to us? Chaos taunted.

"Are you sure you don't have that backward?" she said, snapping gold-hued flames into existence.

The feingrot did something unexpected. It took a step back.

Now the beast was the one afraid. Tenah could get used to this new magic. Flashing a wicked grin, she leaped from her horse and detonated. A sphere of golden energy blasted out to swallow up the entire street.

It was a relief to know she didn't have to worry about her magic harming Gireth. She was no longer a harbor of destruction.

Gireth's arm held still in the air, sharp end of his glaive poised over the other feingrot. His eyes shot wide open as the beast mutated, shrinking to waist height. Fur shifted from black to a pale gray, and the barbs along its tail retracted.

"What the—" he started.

The beast, healed of its infection, jumped at him. Gireth caught it with one arm as it licked from his chin to his hairline. Dark locks matted with slobber and mouth splitting into a wide grin, Gireth lost his edge, dropping his glaive to sink both hands into its lush, thick fur.

"Agh! You're just a good wolf, aren't you? Aren't you?" he gushed. When he deposited the wolf onto the ground with a pat between its twitching ears, he turned on her. "Could have said that's what you were going to do in the first place."

It hadn't occurred to Tenah that feingrot might have been something else, just as Corrupt had once been shadow. She would have laughed at this new discovery and at Gireth's pouting, had she not been focused on her haunter.

Touched by her healing magic, Maltar hadn't changed. What remained was still a creature from nightmares. A true monster at its core, birthed from another world. His black fur ended at its shoulders, the charred bones of its ribs revealed.

Tenah held her breath and waited. The beast blinked at her with clarity, as if seeing her for the first time. Maltar lowered its head then bounded into the catacombs.

"Old friend?" Gireth asked her.

"Something like that."

Gireth approached the catacomb stairs. Metal loops along the stone walls held vases of drooping flowers to honor the dead inside. Thick, potent magic rolled out from the depths, and he whistled as he strode inside.

Tenah shook her head and hurried after him. "You're a bit of a masochist, aren't you?"

"You learn what works when you're dumped on a wasteland isle to die. You can cower, or you can chase down your fears. I figured the outcome was better for me if I did the latter."

She tilted her head at him. "Loan me some of your bravery?"

"I think you mean stupidity. Anytime, Tenah. Anytime."

The air grew stuffy, tinted with acrid magic trapped within the walls of sarcophagi. Tenah's nostrils flared, and her fingers twitched in want of the dark magic lingering here. Would that addiction ever cease?

They drifted around snaking bends and down more stairs. Gireth hooked an arm around her waist and pulled her behind a stone column. Footsteps thudded at the end of the hall. Tenah peeked around the column, heart lurching at the sight of her father.

Lord Kherathi had his head and a hand braced against a sarcophagus. Black blood trickled down his arm from broken fingernails. His breathing was sickly raspy.

Could it…could it be that her mother was buried here?

Swallowing that pain, Tenah moved toward him.

"Stop." Her father forced the words through gritted teeth. He coughed and swiped at the blood on his chin. "Don't come any closer."

She pumped her channels full of healing magic, pushing it outward in hope of cutting through her father's shrouding darkness. The instant her magic touched his skin, his spine cracked backward at an unnatural angle, severing her already fragile heart. A series of pops sounded from his body as he pivoted to face her, black, soulless eyes gleaming.

"A feast it's been, feeding on this shadow's fear," Chaos spoke from her father in a choir of demonic voices. "But it's nothing compared to what you taste like."

Clouds of black magic tumbled from his hands. It spread out to encompass the hall.

Tenah formed a bubble of golden light around her and Gireth.

"Release him," she ordered.

Chaos laughed. "It's far too late, little one. His mind is beyond the reaches of healing, even by a descendant of Xith. How easily a shadow can be devoured from the inside out."

She shoved down every horrible, sharp, gutting feeling that would topple her delicate fortitude and let Chaos take her over.

"Give me the word," Gireth murmured, barely able to restrain the urge to kill.

A tendril of Chaos slashed against her bubble of light, cracking it open as if it were a fragile eggshell. In an instant, a feingrot barreled into her side, tossing her against the catacomb walls with enough force to rattle her teeth. Before she could clamber to her feet, gnashing teeth came at her.

The beast jerked to a halt, held at bay as Gireth latched onto its tail. He dragged it back into his reach, grasping its top and bottom jaws in his bare hands, oblivious to its razor teeth puncturing his skin.

Something absolutely primal glinted in his eyes.

With great effort, Gireth ripped the feingrot's head in two, brackish blood and saliva flinging out into the air. He tossed a piece of its carcass in the direction of her father.

But Kherathi was already gone, a trail of Chaos left in his wake.

Chapter Forty-Five

TENAH

Frustration mounting, Tenah blasted a concentrated pulse of golden magic out to cleanse the catacombs and heal Gireth's fresh wounds. Clouds of dark magic vanquished, and they were able to spot a narrow slit in the sandstone wall.

She cradled a ball of red flame in her palm, grunting as she wriggled inside.

"Worth me shoving my big ass in there?" Gireth asked. Despite his attempt to shift back to humor, there was still a feral edge to him. One Tenah appreciated in this situation but otherwise terrified her out of ever wanting to fight against him.

"It opens up to a network of tunnels in what looks to be the Blackrock Cliffs," she answered.

He shimmied in behind her, grunting at the press of unyielding rock against his body.

"Well, this is fun," he replied sarcastically.

"These must be Embassy tunnels. My father talked about them once, but it seems strange that Sardoth wouldn't have closed them off."

"He may not have known about them. Which puts Izral on my radar as one sneaky motherfucker." Gireth's eyes dropped to her dancing flamelight. "What do you think Vesara's doing right now?"

Tenah pursed her lips, brows kneading. "If I had to guess, possibly using Izral's body as a sheath for all her knives."

"She still owes me two hundred krotens." His voice held a note of sadness.

Tenah had the thought to ask what happened to the dinner he'd claimed Vesara owned him. She reconsidered. It wasn't her business anyway.

The tunnel expanded into a cavernous hall. Her jaw dropped. Thousands of blue and white gemstones shimmered from a city hewn out of black stone. An entire civilization hidden within the cliffs.

"Plan or wing it?" Gireth asked, creeping a few steps toward the ledge that dropped off a hundred feet into a pit.

But Tenah was too far gone into despair as she took in the three shadows chained to the rocky floor, two of which she didn't recognize. But the third…her lungs collapsed, shriveling inside her ribcage. She couldn't suck in enough air to refill them.

"Plan," she forced the word out, eyes honed on Renton's hunched form, shirtless and bound with blood-soaked bandages.

It was too late though. Gireth had already bolted after her father, who was casually descending the outer spiral of stairs down into the pit where Renton was held prisoner.

"Plan!" Tenah screamed after him, her fists dripping golden flames that no longer soothed her.

Her gaze cut back to Renton, fear blooming at his unnatural state of calm, as if he'd accepted death.

She blasted a nimble bolt of flame at her father across the cavern. It arched over the pit like a shooting star. Her father latched onto it with thin, crackling strands of Chaos, redirecting it into Gireth's chest.

A spike of horror jabbed at her sternum as Gireth teetered on the edge of the stairs. Mind racing, she shot her next bolt of holy magic into the pit. It struck the body of a winged beast, purging Chaos in an instant.

Save him, Tenah ordered.

It was a vision of beauty to watch the cleansed welkin rise from the pit, white feathers rippling with purity. Two tails flicked behind it for balance as it leveled out in the air. It caught Gireth on its back right as he tumbled off the edge of the stairs.

Tenah's head snapped back to her father. With each stride she took after him, she delivered another bolt of golden magic. All she needed was one good hit, and maybe it would clear his mind enough to stop this.

In his current state, she couldn't trust that he would value the lives of his prisoners. He'd dedicated his life to destroying Cirel, just as she'd been determined to take down her father for his own crimes. What were three shadows to him in the wake of all those he'd already sacrificed to purge the world of a greater terror?

But those toxic, all-consuming emotions would never lead to salvation. They would never fill the hole in his chest. They would only drive him further into his own personal hell, where Chaos pulled all of the strings.

Kherathi turned and squared up with her, only a flight of stairs between them. Insanity blazed in his black eyes, reflected in the light of the cave crystals. "There is no stopping this."

Arms thrumming with adrenaline, Tenah brought a wave of Rama down on her father. It sloshed and cascaded over the stairs into the pit. Feingrot howled at the touch of her magic, purified of Chaos, only to be slaughtered by those still infected.

Her father remained untouched.

"I can't break them," Gireth roared from the pit. He was hammering at Renton's chains with his glaive. "Blasted Vozarian steel!"

Renton just stood there, head bowed and face hidden by his long hair. His hands remained folded in submission.

Tenah's heart broke.

When she looked at her father again, he was watching Gireth's violent outburst without emotion. Anguish overtook her composure as her father descended the last flight of stairs.

"You wanted me, remember?" she said to Chaos. "Release my father, and you can have me instead."

This mess could have been avoided if she'd accepted Chaos from the beginning.

Dark laughter echoed through the cavern. "Foolish shadowling. We already have you. And now we will have our war beast too."

Chaos lashed out from her father's expanding sphere of lightning, shattering gemstones that rained down like unfinished diamonds. Tenah didn't have time to deflect the blow of magic. Lightning speared into her chest, bleeding an obscene amount of energy into her channels. Her screams sounded wrong in her ears, like they were coming from someone else. Her vision blurred, and her body swelled and swelled, on the brink of erupting.

Rama flared up in response, cascading through her channels to purge them of darkness. It seemed that healing magic had a mind of its own too, and it wasn't prepared to let her fall.

Tenah stayed crouched as a thunderous boom discharged from the pit. She crawled to the edge of the stairs, perturbed by the sight of Gireth surrounded by monsters. The winged beast she'd cleansed leaped from the masses and scooped him out of harm's way.

But that left the prisoners at her father's mercy. The shadows on either side of Renton strained against their chains, hovering three feet above the cavern floor as dark magic poured into them from her father's seemingly infinite well. It cut deep, spilling their tainted blood until a pool formed beneath their feet.

"Please," Tenah cried out. "Please don't do this. I know everything. I know that you sacrificed yourself to take this curse from me. If you're in there, please fight against it. I *need* you."

Her father paused. His casting hand twitched. Bands of Chaos shot out from his sphere wildly as if straining to maintain hold.

"You don't know a thing," he said. "I didn't sacrifice anything. I wanted this power."

Flames coiled around her hands, tinted with gold and black streaks, a heaving mixture of all the emotions and power she could no longer contain.

"I know that you love me," she said.

Her father shuddered, then he turned to look up at her from the pit, agony etched into his face.

"I do love you, Tenah. It was and always has been my greatest fault and my deepest fear." His sphere of darkness expanded, snapping with volatile electricity. "But do not interfere with my plans again."

CHAPTER FORTY-SIX
RENTON

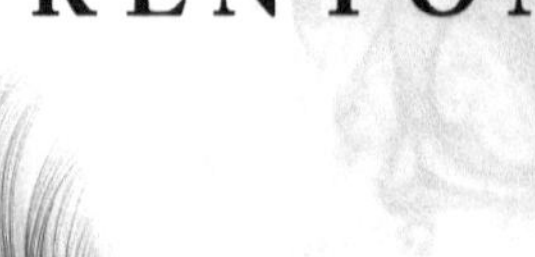

Renton tilted his head up at the cavern ceiling, eyes closed as the other shard hosts burst into clouds of poisonous dust. Gods, what he wouldn't give just to capture another blissful moment with Tenah before he went out. Just one more opportunity to dip his hands in her hair. To press his mouth against hers and steal her breath.

He knew a lifetime with her was too much to ask. If there were gods beyond the Greater Elementals, why would they heed his wishes? He'd done countless horrible deeds in his years on this planet. Burned a sacred temple in Hathrowyn to lay the blame at Boedworth's feet. Cut the throats of countless shadows that had wronged Boedworth, convincing himself that the blood on his hands was justifiable because of their Corruption, even if they hadn't progressed to physical mutations. Dragged Corrupt after Corrupt into Boedworth's den because he'd been conditioned to believe they were nothing more than evil incarnate.

No holy gaze would cast upon him. He was right where he belonged, chained down like a demon.

"Gireth," Renton grunted, faintly registering the presence of a winged beast at his side. His shackles jerked against his wrists as his friend jammed the pointed end of his glaive into the locks. "You need to leave."

"You need to shut the fuck up and quit acting like you know what's best," Gireth raged. "You don't, you hear me? You belong with us, not in a grave."

Kherathi approached, unconcerned about Gireth's presence. The lord had promised Renton that he would live as he'd shackled his wrists. But what were the promises of a madman, especially when he'd just killed the other two hosts?

Gireth whirled around to face the Chaos lord. He quickly found himself launched across the pit by a bolt of ruby flame. Feingrot closed in around him, forming a barrier of predators to cage him.

Kherathi stopped before Renton. "This will be excruciating. I will do my best to draw out the darkness. I don't expect to walk out of Firesteep today. Do you understand?"

His inky black eyes gleamed with purpose, conveying his wishes for the protection of his daughter. Renton nodded, tensing as Kherathi eased a small blade into the puckered skin on his chest. One quick slice and warm blood spilled from the wound, stained black by the toxins of the shard.

His stomach churned. "How could I have been so close to Corruption?"

"The shard was satisfied to feed off your magic for some time," Kherathi said. "It stands as evidence of your power."

Renton had never thought of his magic as a gift, but now he was thankful for it. More than that, if he did survive, he was anxious to test that power. He held back a smile, knowing how infuriated Tenah would be in their next duel.

When Kherathi drew his blade back, tendrils of his searing magic wormed into Renton's scar. Deeper and deeper into tissue, shocking his heart out of rhythm for a few beats. Renton's mouth parted, but no sound came out as waves of pain split him apart. Chaos slithered through his body, seeking out weakness, eager to fester inside his channels. Then his vision went black.

Was this what his father had experienced when Chaos had robbed him of life? Renton had spent so many years striving to be different from his father. To be more obedient. More restrained. Less passionate. His father's morality had been what had gotten him killed after all.

But now, Renton was grateful for the similarities. If he could speak to him one last time, it would be to thank him for teaching him how to love.

Chapter Forty-Seven

TENAH

Tenah snarled at her father, all traces of her inner balance shredded as Renton's body crumpled to the ground. A sliver of black crystal hovered above him, ripped from his heart. A prison for Cirel's war beasts her father had claimed he would destroy. Two other shards accompanied it, floating over the dust of the other prisoners.

No. Renton would live. He had to live.

Gireth howled with palpable fury, hacking a wide berth in the enemies surrounding him.

Something brushed against Tenah's side, startling her. Intelligent eyes stared back at her.

Maltar. Carefully, she slid a hand over its short, mottled fur. The beast lowered its front limbs, inviting her onto its back. She obeyed. Powerful muscle rippled beneath her as Maltar leaped into the pit, finding rocks along the walls to slow their descent.

Maltar took hits left and right from feingrot, but they had nothing on his speed and strength. A pure predator, Tenah was happy to have him on her side as his claws found purchase and his teeth ripped out throats. They charged toward Renton as the cavern quaked from the dark energy now streaming out of the tiny shards.

The shards exploded, sending out black clouds of magic that began to coil into three large, monstrous shapes. Tenah looked to her father and Renton's body, too close to the manifesting war beasts. Her father worked to remove Renton's shackles.

Damn it. They were moving too slow.

She screamed out as the largest of the war beasts solidified directly behind them. Inferno eyes, molten orange, its dark, rocky body pieced together over a magma core.

Her father paid the beast no mind as he siphoned Chaos from the nasty gash in Renton's chest, just as he'd done for her years ago. Skin flaked from his muscle and bone. Blackened scales rippled down his arms, and multiple horns sprouted from his temples, curling back around his ears.

But his efforts would be in vain if she couldn't get to Renton in time to mend his damaged heart.

Feingrot parted for her, turning their sharp teeth upon the conjured war beasts instead. Her father finished with Renton's motionless body and then stepped between him and the nightmarish monster.

Tenah dove off Maltar's back. She grabbed at Renton's shoulders, the only part of him that wasn't yet coated in blood. His skin was on fire, rivaling her own hot-blooded touch. She lifted his head onto her lap and swiped fingers over his cheek. Feingrot closed in around them, forming a protective ring.

"You're going to be fine." She sniffled. "You told me you're all in. If that's true, you're not allowed to die first." Her fingers trailed to his neck, shaking as they waited for a pulse, her heart cracking into more pieces. She funneled strands of Rama into his body, begging the magic to be enough. She wanted to be enough.

Gireth's mount smashed down next to her. Expression dark, he hoisted Renton up by the arm and laid him over his mount. Then he held out an arm for her.

A seismic roar detonated through the cavern, shaking rocks and stalactites loose. Tenah's hands shot up to cover her head and ears. Rocky debris struck her shoulders before Gireth draped himself over her as a shield.

When the cavern stopped quaking from Balhudhal's horrible cries, Gireth peeled away.

"Time to go," he said firmly. She didn't budge, and Gireth took her arms, hoisting her to her feet. His gaze was stern. "This is the wrong time for bravery."

The roars of feingrot accompanied the sonic booms of magical detonations reverberating through the cavern.

"I won't leave things like this," she said. "What if my father fails to kill these things?"

Gireth dropped his hands, his expression stern. "You're walking out of these cliffs today, got it? Nothing touches you. Chaos doesn't get to win."

Her chest filled with warmth. Their crew was a mess. Criminals, runaways, prisoners, Corrupt. All deemed wild and dangerous.

She wouldn't have had them any other way.

With a great thrust of wings, the welkin carried Gireth and Renton out of the cavern. Tenah turned to find her father among the war beasts.

You again, Balhudhal raged, lowering its massive head to Kherathi. *I will rip you apart and feast on your blood for imprisoning me.*

Her father peppered the war beast with a storm of Chaos lightning, pumping it into the cracks of its rocky armor. But it was three ancient creatures against one Corrupt that kept coughing up blood after absorbing Renton's disease.

Balhudhal swiped his body-length talons through the cavern floor. Her father barely moved out of range. *I smell the stench of fear.*

Tenah's gaze darted to the second largest beast, a creature of swirling, gray smoke and charred bones. She whistled for Maltar, grabbing a handful of fur to pull herself onto its back. Wielding healing magic in whip form, she leashed onto the beast's skeleton. Its harrowing cry stabbed at her eardrums, powerful enough to crack the ceiling. Beams of sunlight broke through, luring Balhudhal's head up.

It rumbled in satisfaction. *Freedom. It has been too long since we've roamed this world.*

Tenah practiced deep breaths, striving to maintain her cool. If these beasts escaped, if they climbed out of the cavern and ravaged her isle… Elementals save them all. She'd witnessed firsthand how much damage feingrot had done in her home, and now she watched as they failed to hinder the war beasts in the slightest.

The sound of marching soldiers drew her eyes to the tunnel. Vristarians clad in black and gold emerged, the badge of the Embassy pinned to their leather armor. Leading them, Vesara wore a thin coronet of gold above her jet black brows. Her knives glinted as they hurled through the air, slamming into the third war beast—a fanged harpy with snow white wings.

Reinforcements had come.

Tenah's rigid body went slack, and she found rhythm in her breathing once more. Her healing magic blasted up into the shadow beast's core. It whirled its giant hollows for eyes down to her level. Then it unleashed a shockwave of Chaos unlike anything Tenah had experienced before.

Rama was slow to shield against its attack, and she smashed against the cavern wall. Stars bloomed in her vision. Warm blood dribbled from a cut in her skull. Images flashed before her darkening eyes.

Cirel, consumed by dark magic, screaming for her help.

Maltar prowling the manor.

Her father, more creature than shadow, laying waste to shadows with fire and lightning.

There were visions she'd never experienced too. Endless fires sweeping through forested mountains. Isles tumbling from the sky, sinking deep into the ocean, and summoning treacherous waves that crashed against the coasts of Aranma.

Tenah pressed her back further into the cavern wall. She didn't know what to make of what she was witnessing. Deep in her bones, she wanted to run. No sane shadow would stand before this war beast's darkness and not cower.

But sanity was for the weak.

Snarling, she unleashed a burst of Rama, forcing everything she had into a final, wishful attack. Her magic ate through the beast's smoke. Devoured its bones until nothing remained except for a sliver of white crystal.

A purified shard.

She rushed forward to catch it, just missing as it struck the floor and shattered into a million pieces, too small to hold anything more than a whisper of magic. Her hands slammed down on the rough bits and pieces.

One war beast down and she was nearly drained of healing magic. It waned in her channels, giving way for Chaos to sweep in and breed self-doubt.

Her eyes drifted to her father, who battled to restrain Balhudhal with a net of sizzling dark magic. Balhudhal cleaved its talons through the fault lines in the cavern ceiling. Magma shifted its rock armor around to accommodate the narrow escape in the cliffs, and then it pulled itself free.

Her father wasted no time giving chase. He blasted flames from his hands to launch himself into the air, a fire god out for vengeance against an old enemy. Feingrot scaled the walls, trailing after like a horde of bloodhounds.

Stomach heaving, Tenah watched the harpy ascend from the cliffs next. Vesara briefly locked eyes with her from across the cavern. Then they both launched into motion.

Astride Maltar, Tenah urged the feingrot up the cavern stairs. They raced through the catacombs and burst out onto the streets, only to find the capital already ablaze beneath Balhudhal's wrath. Historic buildings and bell towers, famous armories and shops. Merchant stalls burned like torches, spilling plumes of black smoke in the sky. Vozarian in Denoden could probably see the smoke signaling the destruction of their homes.

Atop the cliffs, Vesara and her assassins fought with a handful of Ruzgorn against the harpy's vicious speed. More of her cousin's warriors leaped over rooftops toward Balhudhal.

She spotted her father standing on the palace roof, launching assaults at the war beast as it unleashed fiery hell in the center of Firesteep. Feingrot failed to find purchase in its rocky exterior as it bled magna to incinerate them.

Tenah scraped her source of healing magic clean. Its slow regeneration was definitely concerning, something that would only improve as she continued to wield it. She would need to be precise with her attacks.

She patted Maltar's neck. "Get me closer."

Maltar launched its powerful form up the jutting stones of the nearest building. Racing across the rooftops, she grimaced as the streets filled with magma, spilling out from the tidal wave Balhudhal was summoning. One that would devastate the capital, Ruzgorn and Embassy assassins with it.

Elementals, she hoped Cirel didn't have any more war beasts.

Tenah gathered Rama into a churning sphere between her palms. Then she took aim, launching it at the largest crack in Balhudhal's armor, right beneath its outstretched arm. Her magic impacted right on target, causing Balhudhal to lose hold on its wave of magma. She breathed for what felt like the first time in minutes when it fizzled out.

Her father seized the opportunity and increased his attacks. Branches of lightning snapped from his form, lashing at the war beast. Balhudhal let out a roar that shook the terracotta tiles beneath Maltar's paws, sending it careening toward the edge of the roof. Heat scorched Tenah's skin as she dangled above the alleyway that rippled with magma. She hissed, clinging tighter to his fur.

Balhudhal turned its wrathful gaze on her.

"Tenah, move," Hakkan shouted from the adjacent rooftop. He launched himself across the narrow alleyway, thrusting a shoulder into Tenah to knock her away from Balhudhal's sweeping arm. She raised her head in time to see Maltar and Hakkan pushed from the roof.

"Hakkan!" she shrieked, scrambling toward the edge. Her cousin clung to the roof tiles with one hand, legs swinging out over the bubbling magma. She clasped a hand around his forearm and heaved.

But Balhudhal hadn't given up on them, despite her father doing his best to lure the beast's attention back to him. Its fist smashed through the building, leveling half of it in one strike.

Tenah was launched into the air. She screamed as her cousin hurtled into the magma. Gone in an instant. Her father roared her name before it swallowed her up too.

She didn't fight against death this time. Somehow, that felt like the right thing to do, even though she doubted Cirel would be able to revive her this time. Her heart only carried sorrow for her cousin who wouldn't even be mourned by his father.

Hakkan.

Why was death taking this long? The magma should have incinerated her flesh and bones by now. She lifted her hands through the molten substance. Her pulse quickened when she glimpsed the aura of golden light surrounding them.

Rama had shielded her.

She didn't have much time to claw her way out, sensing it dwindling in her channels. This wouldn't be a fight she won with healing magic alone, but maybe she wasn't supposed to. The elementals had blessed her with the affinity for more than one type of magic. There had to be a reason for it.

Right now, she needed raw power, and she knew where to get more. She called out to Chaos. *You want me to become a vessel, so be it.*

Dark energy blasted from her palms, shooting her up through the magma and into the sky. Black feathered wings tore from her back. They snapped out wide to catch her weight.

Her lightning crackled down to strike her father but not with the intent to harm. She'd infused the branches of lightning with strings of Rama, hoping it would be enough to keep darkness in check. All she wanted was to siphon the power in her father's channels. *Her* power.

She left him a drained husk braced on his knees.

This curse belonged to her anyway. And with Rama, she should be able to manage it.

You bow to me now, Tenah commanded, launching her Chaotic energy at Balhudhal. *As will your king.*

Something inside of her shifted. Some part of her soul, patched together by Cirel's foreign magic. She wasn't sure what that change meant, if she'd severed their bond or enhanced it. Regardless, the power flowing into her now, wherever it stemmed from, was enough to rupture Balhudhal's core. Rocky armor and magma rained down onto the streets.

Tenah paid no mind to the lingering whirlwind of Chaos hovering toward her, magnetized to her channels. It slammed into her, penetrating her skin. Dark magic burrowed into her very bones. Bled into every crook of her mind.

Vision dissolving, she tumbled from the sky. Her wings fluttered uselessly, bent at awkward angles from her rapid fall.

Something collided into her side. She struck the top of a building and skittered across its roof, breaking delicate bones in her wings. While she hadn't felt pain, her nerves entirely shot, she'd heard the audible cracks.

Her father pulled her up into his arms. Cradling her against his chest, he wept a decade's-worth of tears.

Chapter Forty-Eight
RENTON

The cutting of the shard from Renton's heart had been unfathomable. Worse than any pain that had ever been inflicted upon him, a dull knifepoint slowly piercing every nerve over and over again.

But then her touch was upon him, her hot tears splattering down on his jaw and neck. Staining his very soul with the love that she spilled.

Love. Could it be possible? Was a shadow like him allowed to love a goddess?

He surrendered to her touch, enticing him back to the realm of the living. He thought to force his eyes open, just to take in another look at her, even though he'd memorized her features. The woman that had burned her way into his life so vibrantly he would never recover. He would never see another light again.

Tenah was beautiful and fierce and sensitive. She made him hopeful after a lifetime of suffering. She was the sunset bleeding over the crest of that impossible hill he'd been climbing, tempting him with what sprawled on the other side, should he prove his worth and finally reach the top.

His heart thudded beneath her palms as if she owned it.

It's yours, he wanted to say. *I'm yours.*

He would willingly give himself, over and over again. Whatever she needed, he would provide it. She made him want to be more than the shell of a tormented hunter.

When his eyelids fluttered open, he absorbed smoky sky instead of black rock, and the lack of warmth from her tender hands on his chest was starkly absent.

Something was wrong.

Renton winced as pushed up onto an elbow. The gash in his chest shot wicked pain through his body.

"Easy," Gireth murmured. His friend sat a few feet away, back propped against the wooden support of a Ruzgorn tent.

"Take me back in," Renton ordered.

Gireth folded his arms across his chest, tanned muscles flexing and expression challenging. "Yeah? Why would I do that when I'm responsible for your well-being?"

"My well-being could be a hell of a lot better if Tenah was here with us, not trapped in a cave with monsters."

Gireth's cold stare wavered as it drifted to Firesteep's walls in the distance, his throat bobbing. "I know."

At least the rumbles from within the Blackrock Cliffs had ceased. Renton didn't know what to make of that, only that the vision of the nightmare—blurry glimpses of the monster named Balhudhal—would haunt him for eternity.

"You prove to me you can stand and hold a blade, and I'll take you back in," Gireth said.

Renton urged his body to comply, but it took most of his concentration just to force a breath from his aching lungs. He touched fingers to his scar—covered now by a loose, charcoal tunic—running them over the bumps from the stitches there.

The corner of Gireth's mouth tugged down. "Sorry, the stitches aren't perfect. There wasn't time for Tenah to completely mend it, so I did what I could."

"Thank you, brother. Thank you for everything."

Gireth swiped at his nose with a knuckle and sniffled. "It's nothing."

Rolling back onto a strip of animal hide serving as a cot, Renton asked, "The other hosts?"

"Turned to dust."

Renton groaned, pressing the heel of his palms against his eyes and wincing at the pain from the movement. When he removed them, he spotted two bobbing silhouettes in the sky.

"Gireth," he called out.

The welkins coasted into better view. Renton pushed up from the cot in horror. Only one of the riders was shadow in form, the other two Corrupt. The first rider, Lord Kherathi, clutched Tenah, broken wings and all, tight. The second rider, astride a midnight black welkin built for speed, resembled his brother.

"No need to strain yourself," Gireth said, leaning over to pat his shoulder. "I get it. You owe me big time."

"Not what I was going for," Renton said, growling as he strove to rise on two numb feet.

Gireth's meaty paw held him in place. "Ah, sure it was. Brothers for life—"

"Shut the hell up and look."

Head tilting to the sky, Gireth snapped upright. "Oh, shit. Forget the mushy stuff then."

Renton brushed passed him, unsure at first if his legs would hold his weight. But the sheer will to embrace Aeyis and Tenah powered his muscles along. He registered Gireth shouting out orders behind him, elaborating on how idiotic Renton was. How he would destroy his body and suffer the consequences in old age.

Renton halted as both welkins landed on the desert ground. Immediately, he crushed his brother's mutated body against his chest, ignoring the little tear in his stitches.

Easing back from his brother, he knew better than to ask what Aeyis had been through. His brother's blackened eyes and spiked shoulders, casting a hard edge to a soft soul, told him such nightmares couldn't be put into words right now.

And all because Cirel had wanted to watch the world burn. Wasn't that the root of this mess?

Loosening his grip in time for Gireth to attack Aeyis, Renton dragged his eyes up to Tenah. His heart stuttered at the sight of her cracked, charred arms and mutilated wings.

"What have you done, angel?" Renton murmured.

Kherathi dismounted, though he didn't seem inclined to hand his daughter off. His eyes shone a dark rust color, not the endless wells of black Renton had come to know.

"You don't look so good yourself," Kherathi said, gaze dipping to the blood oozing through Renton's mysteriously acquired shirt.

"You're…" Renton's words faltered.

"Sound of mind. She's done incredible work. She'll need time to heal."

"And Balhudhal?" Renton asked, peering out at Firesteep's gates, shrouded in clouds of smoke.

"Obliterated, along with the other beasts. Though I wouldn't say that's necessarily a good thing."

Renton's jaw and fists hardened. "What's that supposed to mean?"

"Tenah absorbed his Chaos instead of purifying it. Things will be rough for her when she comes to. I think I've proven that the balance of magic requires more than one stubborn old soul."

The Chaos lord's eyes flicked to Aeyis, and Renton couldn't help but shift a bit in front of his brother, as if to cut off their internal conversation, whatever it was about.

"What about you? What will you do now?" Renton asked.

Kherathi tipped his head in contemplation, gears whirling almost audibly. "Considering Izral and the High Court expected me to die today, I'd say I'm no longer welcome on the isles. Which leaves me to entrust her to you." His ocher eyes dropped to Tenah. "*Temporarily.* You break her heart, and I'll flay you alive."

The shock of the warning jerked Renton back to balmy evenings in his family cottage, on the receiving end of one of his father's famous lectures.

"You could come with us. I have a contact that can provide us with a place to lay low until she's back on her feet," Renton offered.

"I doubt my presence will promote healing."

"You don't know that."

"Just until she's back on her feet." Kherathi's welkin dropped down in a bow with a snap of his fingers, a hint of metal tainting the dry air.

Renton threw Kherathi a calculating look.

"Old habits." He gave a sad smile.

A pang of distrust wedged its way into Renton's chest. Had he made the wrong decision in inviting the lord? Years twisted by Chaos maybe wasn't wiped away so easily.

But Tenah would need his advice. His secrets on how to keep Corruption at bay for such an extraordinary amount of time. Renton never wanted to see her in this state again. If that meant keeping her father around, Renton would just make sure to keep a pulse on the situation.

A procession of shadows in black-and-gold leather marched toward them from Firesteep's gates. Renton's brows lifted at the sight of Vesara crowned, no longer shirking her responsibility.

They all waited for her to make the first move.

"I ought to kill you for the stunts you pulled," Vesara shouted at Kherathi, spinning a knife between her fingers. Her gaze dipped to Tenah's broken form, and Renton didn't miss the thin line of blood Vesara's knife cut into the side of her finger. Her face morphed into one of shame.

"For obeying the orders of our king? Or for gaining you a crown and the Embassy?" Kherathi taunted. "*Or* for organizing the death of Cirel's war beasts? Please clarify which stunts you're referring to."

Vesara tsked. "Don't act like you didn't plant all of this in Izral's head to weasel your way back into a reputable position."

"You give Izral too little credit. He willingly suggested my sacrifice to tip the scale of war in our favor against Cirel. Punishment for my unlawful removal of Sardoth from the throne."

Vesara paled. "I suppose you're right. He found a way to imprison me after all."

"Shackled to a crown that gives you power to make change." Kherathi smirked.

Renton fought back a kernel of appreciation for the lord's callousness.

Features turning cold, Vesara tucked her knife away. "It would be best for you to leave now. It would complicate things if my report back to our king proved untrue when he discovers you still alive."

Kherathi bowed his head. "May you rule responsibly."

Her glare was cutting, but she had no sharp response this time.

The Chaos lord slid onto his welkin's back with Tenah in tow, and Renton moved over to Aeyis's winged beast, climbing atop.

Gireth hadn't budged. "If you think I'm riding with my dick pressed up against either one of you…"

Renton tossed him a look of frustration. "Then sprout wings or pray the sea doesn't crush you when you jump."

Gireth remained rooted to the spot, his boots tapping at the ground anxiously. "You know I don't leave a warrior behind," he said slowly.

"She's not a warrior, Gireth," Renton corrected. "She's a queen."

"She's a friend. One that will be in need of some decent company in a palace of snakes."

Vesara didn't cut in with her usual sassiness, and when Renton looked to her in assessment, he recognized the terror in her glacial eyes. She'd faced countless enemies, no doubt, and the thing that struck fear in her was ruling.

Renton gave a nod. "We'll keep in touch."

Then they were sky-bound, dropping off the edge of the Kandar Isles.

Chapter Forty-Nine
TENAH

Tenah jolted upright in an unfamiliar bed. She hissed, crisp white sheets dragging across her raw skin. Her body agonized over the slightest movement as she pulled the sheets all the way back. No more burns or scales or spikes. Only sensitive, angry, pink splotches remained.

Someone had changed her into a pair of sage green cotton shorts and a cream tunic with intricate eyelet detailing.

She laid there motionless, inhaling the peculiar scent of salt on the fresh, warm breeze wafting through two open windows. Golden sunlight poured in, casting the white stucco walls and framed, pastel landscapes in a holy glow. She craved that light, feeling as though she'd been trapped in the dark for years with only the occasional comfort of Rama's touch in her channels as her healing source replenished.

All of Chaos's voices ricocheting in her mind had slowly dulled to a whisper. Tamed for now but a constant reminder of just how much toxic magic she'd devoured in Firesteep when she'd slain Balhudhal.

Tenah wiggled her bare toes, frowning at the plum shade of polish on her nails. Vesara had painted her nails the same color once, and Tenah instantly pined for her friend. For all of her friends.

She swung her legs around to the edge of the bed. A sharp tug at the crook of her elbow alerted her of a needle and tube running from her arm to a skein of some fluid hanging from the wall.

What in the actual hell?

Tenah ripped the needle free and padded over to the nearest window, nerves soothed by the lapping of crystal waves on a white-sand beach before a mountainside city. The little villa she'd woken in was nearly at the top of the city, providing magnificent views of the coral reefs, shipwrecks, and the bustle of colorful, vertical cityscape.

An oasis, she thought, turning around to reassess her room. Tiny, flowering cacti hung from braided ropes, and chunky, knitted blankets rested at the end of the plain bed. Confusion muddled her brain at how she'd come to be in such a place.

She'd fallen from the sky. Heard the distinct crack of her wings when she hit the ground.

Wings.

Tenah reached a hand back and touched the sensitive, bony protrusions jutting from her skin on either side of her spine. She traced them all the way down to their ruined ends.

She rushed into the connected bathing room, eyes shooting wide at the reflection of her mutations. Muscles in her body went slack, dropping her into a crouch. She braced her head in her hands as the world lurched sideways. How long had she been healing, and still she wasn't whole?

The urge to rip the deformities from her flesh was overwhelming. She sucked in a long breath and took another look in the mirror.

Movement in her peripheral had her shifting her body to hide the wings.

"It's okay. I've already seen them." Renton leaned against the doorframe of the small room and folded his arms over his chest. His hair shone like cornsilk, half pulled back. He wore a loose, dark green shirt that suited him. The sleeves were rolled up to his elbows. His black pants hugged his strong legs in a way that sent a shock of heat through her.

He looked surprisingly well, his jaw free of tension, his shoulders relaxed. Tenah closed the distance between them and yanked at the low collar of his shirt. His scar had healed over, faded to a milky white. No pulse of dark magic beckoned from under his skin.

She let her fingers fall away. "How long have I been out?"

His gaze held hers, giving added support to her weak legs and spine. "Two months."

Her hands covered her face as she let out a cry of grief. "Two months. I left him behind. He's… Someone needs to save him."

"Whoa." Renton wrapped his hands around her wrists, pulling them aside so he could level his gaze with hers. "What are you talking about?"

Lip trembling in anticipation of the hatred that would seep onto his face, Tenah uttered, "Your brother. He's in Adra."

Renton chuckled. "You mean the brother that is outside currently shoveling food into his mouth?"

"What?"

"Everyone is safe." He pulled her flush against him, pressing a kiss to her temple. "Still recovering but safe."

No, that wasn't exactly true.

No one else had witnessed Hakkan's death. But the memory would sit heavy in her soul for the rest of her life.

"When you're ready—only when you're ready—Aeyis may need your help healing. He extended himself pretty severely escaping Adra. And I'm certain he has a target on his back after stealing Cirel's mount. Hiding that ferocious thing in the city has been a chore."

A wild laugh escaped her, despite the panic curling in her stomach. "He has some explaining to do. And the others?"

"Waiting impatiently to speak with you. Two months has been like two centuries for us. Aeyis wore a divot in the yard with his pacing. Vesara left a few days ago. She and Izral are planning a meeting with the High Court regarding their next moves against Adra. She keeps trying to pawn Gireth off on us, but he's persistent in his self-imposed duty to remain her guardian."

A smile quivered on Tenah's lips.

It quickly faded as she recalled Vesara's crown. Against her will, the assassin had become the Queen of Vristar. An ache filled Tenah's chest. The crew deserved their freedom after what they'd all sacrificed. They deserved a chance at happiness.

Renton stroked a hand up and down her back, stopping just below her wings. "She's to wed Izral in a month. Apparently, he offered her the Embassy years ago in exchange for her hand. She'd refused him until we pissed her off with our selfless acts."

"Ugh, can I stand up and protest during the ceremony?"

He chuckled, and they eased into a comfortable silence.

"Do I want to know about my father?" she finally asked.

"I caution you not to expect too much," Renton warned. "He's here in Elcana too, but he's been troubled. Frequently, I catch him sneaking out for the night."

Tenah wiped her nose and pulled away from his touch. "He's never been one to settle down. I guarantee he's plotting something."

"Your father may have gone about things wrong, but he was trying."

She nodded, eyes welling up with more tears. Her father's words from the cavern rushed back in. *I do love you, Tenah. It was and always has been my greatest fault and my deepest fear.*

"Hey." Renton smoothed hair back from her face and tipped her chin up. "We're going to be fine. Why don't we take a walk outside?"

Tenah slipped her hand into his. The scrape of his rough skin had become a necessity in her life. They maneuvered out of the bedroom, through a narrow hall with other doors crafted from lovely, fragrant pine, and down two flights of wooden stairs broken up by a landing.

She paused on the bottom step, and Renton gave her hand an encouraging squeeze.

"It belongs to Elder Nithril," Renton explained. "He bought it decades ago after studying abroad. I doubt he even remembers he owns it, and after learning about his disclosure to Izral and your father about the shard in my heart, I don't really give a shit if he tries to take it back. After I stood trial for an inexcusable charge of arson, Nithril brought me here to show me what I could have. What was in my reach for me and my brother if I applied myself."

He squared up with her body, hands coming to rest low on her hips. With the added height of the stair, Tenah was almost level with him. She didn't have time to get lost in the rich greens and yellows in his eyes.

Renton pressed a lingering, claiming kiss to her lips.

"What I want is you, Tenah," he murmured, his tenor eliciting a slow shiver that rolled from the back of her neck down to her toes. "For as long as you'll have me."

Then he stepped back and let her absorb his dream.

The home was lovely. Small but every detail had been chosen meticulously to bring warmth to the soul. The oversized wicker couches in the living room were arranged around a mosaic fireplace reminiscent of western isle design. There was a circular, rustic dining table centered under a gold lantern in one corner, overlooking the sea. And the kitchen was painted an elegant green with gold handles. The absence of upper cabinets allowed for unobstructed views of the glittering, turquoise sea.

She would burst at the seams if this was where she got to stay, especially with Renton.

A thud from outside drew her to a door split in two—the top section had been opened to the elements. Her heart soared as she stepped out onto a lush patch of grass tucked behind a low, stone wall. Beyond, stairs wove down the mountain into the heart of vibrant Elcana.

Tenah had to cling to Renton's arm to stay upright.

Aeyis sat at a delicate, white table, sipping at a steaming cup of tea, despite the warm weather. While she could identify his gangly form anywhere, he hadn't fully recovered from Adra. Two sets of horns curled forward from his skull. Markings darkened the line of his jaw, stark against his long, thin neck.

You are not dreaming, and you are not dead, Aeyis said without glancing up from his untitled book. The press of his magic was frigid and more forceful than she remembered.

Her eyes shot wide at the sliver of white crystal dangling from a thin chain around his neck.

Where did you get that? She'd been pretty sure the shards in the cavern had all been destroyed in the slaying of Cirel's war beasts.

The bone fields of Adra. They're reforming.

Her brows rose, hope cascading through her. *Can they hold more than darkness?*

He gave a slight nod, and her feet carried her over to the table. She reached out to lift the shard between her index finger and thumb, instantly sensing a tug on her internal magic.

Tenah poured Rama into the ravenous thing.

Aeyis's horns retracted. The markings along his jaw slithered back behind his locks of hair.

By the time her work was completed, she was unable to control her grin. She wrapped an arm around his head and tugged him against her. When she released him, his cheeks were flushed, and a low chuckle came from Renton.

Her heart beat for these brothers.

Aeyis removed the chain from his neck and slid it over her head.

Then her gaze drifted to a dark figure perched on the stone wall overlooking the sea. Her father looked frail enough that one strong gust of wind through the mountains at their back might turn him into dust.

Fighting back wave after wave of anxiety, Tenah crossed the yard and climbed up on the wall beside him. She sensed his fervent gaze upon her, but she didn't dare meet it for fear of the tears that would shatter the calm she was clinging to.

"Little one," he started, sending horror slithering through her veins.

"Chaos called me that," she said. Knowing now how many pieces of her past sentient magic had leveraged against her—it was a sickening thought. One that almost pushed her to demand Aeyis wipe all the things she cherished from her mind so dark magic couldn't weaponize them.

But she would never run from it again.

"I can't put into words all the things I need to say," her father said.

"You're not the one that needs to apologize."

He let out a quiet laugh. "Chaos should apologize then?"

"Absolutely."

Tenah fingered the crystal and then went to remove it from her neck.

His hand caught her. "I don't want it. Let me serve my sentence a bit longer."

Her brows furrowed as she took in his features, etched with an undercurrent of pain. If she'd been out for two months, that meant he'd gone that length of time without Chaos in his channels. Tenah knew all too well how bad that addiction could be. The ache it left in the body. And he'd been casting that foul magic much longer than she had.

She let go of the crystal and kicked out her bare feet, her blood pressure rising. "I'm not sure how many rifts I tore for Cirel. He could have more armies and war beasts than we know."

Weeks ago, uttering Cirel's name would have sent her father spiraling down into a foul mood. Now, he just reflected quietly upon her admissions.

"Then we will be prepared," he said after a moment.

"He might use our bond to force me to retrieve the ones I banished."

"You've proven your capability with magic. There is always a loophole. A way out. We'll find a way to sever that bond."

Tenah let herself believe his words. The Kandar Isles had preached for decades the irreversible nature of dabbling in dark magic. Had slaughtered countless tainted souls that might have been salvageable. Yet the Void had given her what she needed, just as Cirel had claimed it would. It had given her the magic to heal Chaos. Surely, the bond between her and Cirel could be reversed too.

But did she have a right to sever their connection after she was responsible for his Corruption?

"I made him. Did you know that?" A warm breeze tossed her hair over a shoulder. "You were gone a lot, and I was alone with magic I didn't understand. I found Cirel. I created a rift to draw him in. I took him from his home in Adra. I Corrupted him when he mentioned wanting to leave. Ames tried to alter that memory to make it seem like I was a victim, but I was always the enemy."

The truth had come out during her healing rest and had resounded through her bones until it became a part of her. One she wasn't afraid of, for she could no longer be weighed down by her childhood mistakes. She had grown since then.

Her father patted her knee. "Chaos is a huge burden. You may think you introduced him to this magic, but from what I witnessed in Adra's throne room, he was already fated for it, born from hate and war. I'm sorry for using you like I did, Tenah. You are much more than a pawn."

Tenah squeezed her hands on the stone wall until they blanched. "I could heal him."

"You could try," her father agreed. "It's not certain that would stop war."

She leaned against his arm, her heart already settling into her decision. Cirel was suffering, and she would be his guide out of the darkness.

Tenah tucked the thought of Adra's king away, soaking in the horizon. She'd traced over the coast of Aranma a million times, but maps hadn't done it justice.

"So…a Bogland hunter, huh?" her father asked.

"Can we not?" She peeled off his shoulder, cheeks flushed bright red.

But she couldn't help a peek back at Renton, assuring herself that he wasn't another fabrication made by Chaos or her mind-meddling friend.

Her family wasn't orthodox, but she wasn't going to let anything take away this future.

Acknowledgements

Goodness, where do I even begin? So many kind souls helped me along this journey and there are not enough words to thank them for the encouragement and advice.

To the readers that gave my book a chance, you mean the absolute world to me. I bow down to you. I have lived my life seeking to entertain you with my stories.

To my husband who has supported my writing goals from day one, yelled at me to get my butt to the coffeeshop, yelled at me for going to bed early when I should be writing, etc. You are a CHAMP. Thanks for juggling the little ones and allowing me to dump all of my world-building mess on you. Your DND knowledge proved most helpful to work out kinks. And thank you for telling me I can't rewrite this book a million times.

To Nicole, (AKA my friend soulmate), for becoming my cheerleader and reading every crappy thing I threw at you and drawing me to the dark side of romance books. Oh, the absolute garbage I dropped on your desk in pre-calculus! Might be the reason I almost failed the class. You have been crucial in my journey. I hope you are able to achieve your goal as an editor! Putting this in print so you ACTUALLY do it!

To Carla for reading nearly every version of this book and still loving all of them. Or at least telling me you loved them, thank you for being a reader and a supporter!

To my writing group, you ladies have helped me grow so much over the years. Without the endless wealth of knowledge you all have shared and the skills you helped me develop, I never would have published this book. Hell, I still wouldn't even know what a plot is! Thanks for always being there!

I have to give it up to the teachers that kickstarted a love for writing by showering me with encouragement. Keep inspiring kiddos to be creative!

To all the coffeeshop employees out there that provided me with caffeine to fuel this dream, you rock! And to everyone I met through writing communities…y'all are unbelievably amazing.

About the Author

Abigail Glenn is a fantasy & romance author. Writing fiction has consumed a large part of her brain since elementary school. She's come a long way from her twenty page tales about mermaids and martial arts babysitters. Now, she prefers darker themes in her books, influenced by her love for video games like Diablo and WoW. Confusingly enough, she also loves romcoms.

Abigail is a financial analyst by day, a mom of two little girls, an avid reader and traveler, a football fan, and a metal music lover. She currently lives with her family in Oklahoma.

Connect with me! One link to rule them all:

https://linktr.ee/abigailglenn